ON EVERY THUG I LOVE

A Romance Collection

MICHELLE ELAINE   SHONTAIYE MOORE
KRYSTAL ARMSTEAD

Cole Hart
SIGNATURE NOVELS

On Every Thug I Love

Mailing List

To stay up to date on new releases, plus get information on contests, sneak peeks, and more,

Go To The Website Below...

www.colehartsignature.com

ON EVERY THUG I LOVE

Atlanta Edition

MICHELLE ELAINE

"Well, Monquez said you gave him an F on his pop quiz because he called you a bald-headed bi—"

"Ms. Perriman... please," Melinda Barrett interrupted the parent in front of her before she repeated the insult her son used earlier in the day. She shook her head and bit the inside of her cheek to stop herself from laughing.

Melinda glanced at the clock on the wall above her whiteboard before looking back at Candice Perriman, who was not only the mother of one of her sixth-grade students, but also a former high school classmate of hers. Their parent-teacher conference for Candice's son, Monquez, was not productive at all. Melinda could have finished with conferences an hour ago but stayed later for Candice, who rushed straight from work. As it was nearing six o'clock in the evening and she needed to pick up her own child, Melinda was regretting the favor she did for her former classmate.

"You don't have to call me Ms. Perriman like you don't know who I am," Candice said, rolling her eyes.

"Well, Candice, whether or not I know you is not the issue here," Melinda said. "What matters is the fact that your belief is untrue. Monquez did not get an F because he was rude and disrespectful. He got an F because he did not complete the reading assignment."

"He was going to get to it."

"I'm sure he had every intention, but the reading was not completed by the assigned date. If it was, he would have passed. To imply that his grade was the result of some sort of personal vendetta is simply untrue."

Candice sighed and folded her arms across her chest. "So, what are you going to do to let him make it up?"

Melinda shrugged her shoulders and pulled a sheet of paper from her folder, sliding it across the desk. "Here is a list of extra credit opportunities that can be completed before the end of the semester. There are no special favors done in my class. If Monquez wants to raise his grade, he can choose any number of items from this list that was already provided to him and his classmates," she said. "It would be in his best interests because the pop quiz wasn't his only recent failing grade."

Candice shouldered her purse and snatched the paper up from the desk. She slid toward the edge of her chair with narrowed eyes while she stared at Melinda. "You know he told me that you give him a harder time than some of the other kids. Whatever issues you and I may have had was years ago," she said, standing up. "If I find out you're taking your personal issues out on my child, I will go to Principal Jenkins about this."

"Candice, I can assure you that is not the case. High school was forever ago, but if you feel the need to take a twelve-year-old's word over mine, then be my guest," Melinda said with a mile-wide, fake smile. "You know where the office is, and I'm sure you have the phone number and email address."

Candice huffed and started toward the door. Mumbling under her breath, she said, "Rude ass. That's why every nigga in the hood dogged your ass out except Jabari. Bougie ass bitch."

As soon as Candice disappeared into the hallway, Melinda shook her head and released the laugh she struggled to hold on to during the conference. *Never again*, she thought to herself as she stood up from her desk. She went out of her way to do a favor for someone who ended up being rude and ungrateful, just like their child. There was no surprise where Monquez learned his unacceptable behavior. Melinda looked up at the clock again and cursed to herself quietly, realizing that she was most likely going to be late to pick up her son. She quickly grabbed her things and paused to trade her heels out for a pair of comfortable flats. She rushed to the door and flipped off the lights before sprinting into the hallway. She was trying to slip into her coat without dropping her bags when one of her coworkers called her name from behind.

"Mel! Hey! Let me help you."

Melinda glanced over her shoulder to see Rashad Patton, another teacher on her grade level. She smiled graciously when he approached her, holding her bags so she could get her arms into her trench coat.

"There you go," he said, sliding the bags back on her shoulder. He started to walk alongside her. "I'm surprised you're still here."

"I'm not supposed to be," she responded truthfully with a sigh. "I stayed to meet Monquez Perriman's mother. Epic waste of my time and energy. Why are you here so late?"

"I had a number of conferences as well and then stayed to finish getting some grades in the system. I didn't want to take it home with me."

Melinda continued the small talk while they made their way toward the exit of the middle school. She had a good working relationship with most of her coworkers, Rashad included. Although her intentions for their relationship were purely platonic, it was obvious to many of their peers that he had a crush on her. He was kind, intelligent, and very attractive. However, Melinda was in a committed relationship. When they stepped outside of the building, she shivered and pulled her coat a little tighter around her body. The late October air was much cooler than she anticipated it would be.

5

"Where are you parked? It's so dark out here with the time change. Let me walk you to your car."

Melinda agreed and motioned in the direction of her vehicle. The pair of coworkers continued to laugh and talk until they reached her Mercedes SUV. Her eyebrows rose when the driver door opened to the Ford F-150 parked next to her. She released a slight sigh as the smile completely fell from her face.

The driver of the truck greeted her. "What's up, Mel?"

"Rashad, thanks," she said, turning toward her coworker. "I'll see you in the morning."

Rashad glanced at the man standing by the pickup truck with narrowed eyes before looking back at Melinda with a look that questioned if she was okay. She nodded and patted his arm reassuringly. "Good night, Melinda. I'll see you in the morning."

After Rashad walked away, she turned toward DeAndre Butler, her son's uncle.

"What's up, Dre?" Melinda asked evenly while she moved to unlock her doors. "Why are you popping up on me at work?"

"Honestly, I was in the area. I tried to call you the other day, but I guess you were busy," he said. He paused for a response that she did not give. After Melinda put her bags in the car, he reached into his pocket to pull out a wad of money. "I've been trying to give you this."

Melinda shook her head, standing inside of her opened car door. "We're good, Dre. I don't need your money."

"Come on, Mel. We go through this all the time. I try to do the right thing and help out with my nephew, and you offend me by turning it down. I know you don't *need* the money. It's quite obvious you and Mr. White Collar are doing just fine," DeAndre commented. Melinda rolled her eyes at his reference toward her boyfriend. "This isn't about you though. It's about Kevin. You and I both know that my brother wants me to help out with his son. Take the money, Mel."

Melinda hesitated before taking the cash and shoving it into her coat pocket. "Okay, fine. Is that all?"

"Actually, it's not. I don't know if you've spoken with my brother lately—"

"I have not."

DeAndre sighed and shook his head. "I figured as much," he mumbled. "Anyway, he—"

"Dre, I don't really have time for this," Melinda said, raising her hands in front of her. "I'm already late picking your nephew up as it is."

She turned and got into her car, but DeAndre spoke again before she could close the door.

"He's getting out soon, Mel."

Melinda paused with her hand on the door handle. "What?"

"Yeah. I don't know all the specifics of it all. He called our mom the other day. You would know if you bothered to keep in better contact with her," he said, "but yeah... Jabari will be home soon. Should be within the next week or so."

Melinda continued to sit there with her hand on the handle and her door wide open. It was already a tiring day. The revelation that her first love and the father of her only child was getting out of prison only exhausted her further. However, she didn't have time to process her own feelings about the situation. She wasn't only running late to the after-school provider to pick up Kevin. With her schedule thrown off, she would be late for her other plans as well.

"I just thought you might want to know," DeAndre said.

Melinda nodded. "Yeah... thanks, Dre. I—I gotta go. Tell your mom I'll call her soon. Thanks for letting me know."

Without waiting for a response, Melinda shut the door to her Benz and started the engine. She watched from her mirrors as DeAndre hesitated but then shook his head and climbed into his truck. She quickly pulled out of the parking lot and headed to her son. Ten minutes later, she sped into the parking lot for Little Angels Learning Academy, where Kevin went after school until she was able to pick him up. It was eight minutes after six, the time when the facility closed for the day.

She grabbed her wallet and hopped out of the truck, jogging to the entrance where Kevin and his after schoolteacher were waiting.

"I know, Ms. Lisa. I know," Melinda said before the retired schoolteacher could even get a word out. She pulled a ten-dollar bill from her wallet to cover the late fee and placed it into the teacher's hand. "I'm so sorry. I had a last-minute conference, and—"

"Ms. Barrett, you know I love Kevin, but the center director is a stickler for punctuality. I can't continue to let you be late for pickup like this," Lisa responded.

"Understood. I'll do better. I promise. Kevin, get in the car," Melinda said, using the remote key fob to unlock the doors. Kevin gave her a quick hug before doing as he was told. "Ms. Lisa, I promise I'll do better. I hate being late, and Kevin being the last kid here."

"I hear you, Ms. Barrett, but actions speak louder than words."

"I understand. Sorry again. I'll see you tomorrow."

Melinda waved goodbye and climbed back into her truck.

"Mommy, what's for dinner?" Kevin asked.

"I don't know, sweetie. Grandma's coming over to take care of dinner," she answered. "You know mommy is going to dinner with Dominic tonight."

Kevin sat quietly in his seat while he stared out of the window, possibly pouting. Melinda sighed heavily. Kevin loved spending time with his grandmother—her mother, Carla. That wasn't the problem. Instead, the issue stemmed from her plans to spend the evening with her boyfriend instead of her son. Throughout the course of her two-year relationship with her boyfriend, Dominic, Kevin had not grown accustomed to sharing his mother's time. Melinda glanced at her son in the rearview mirror and thought about saying something else when her phone rang. She answered, connecting the phone to the speakers of her car.

"Mel, I just got home," Dominic greeted her. "Where are you?"

"Hey, honey. I'm on my way," she said with a smile. "I just picked Kevin up, and—"

"You just picked him up? You were supposed to be home over an hour ago."

"I know, but something came up at work. Conferences ran late. I should be home soon."

Dominic sighed heavily on his end of the call. "We're never going to make it downtown on time. Just forget it."

"Dom, don't do that. My mom already agreed to come over and watch Kevin. Let me just call the restaurant. We might not make the original reservation, but I'm sure we can still get a table."

"I said forget it, Melinda. You couldn't even get your shit together for my birthday?" he asked. Melinda winced at his choice of language while Kevin was in the car. "Tell your mom we don't need her tonight. I'll go get my own damn dinner."

Before she could say anything else, the call ended, leaving Melinda stunned. His mood swings weren't unusual, but Kevin was rarely a witness to their disagreements. She tried to call him back but was met with immediate voicemail. She shook her head and sighed before calling her mother to inform her of the change in plans. Twenty minutes later, she was surprised when she arrived home to an empty garage. She tried to call Dominic again and received voicemail for the second time.

"Come on, Kev. Let's get inside so I can fix you something to eat." Disappointed, Melinda grabbed her bags and led them into the house. "Go put your book bag up and wash your hands. I'll get something together for dinner shortly."

Kevin did as he was told and headed up the stairs. Melinda set her bags down on the kitchen table, including the one that held Dominic's birthday present. After slipping out of her jacket and washing her own hands, she put together a quick meal. Losing her appetite from her earlier conversation, she simply grabbed a glass of wine before joining her son at the kitchen table. Kevin was all smiles while she sat with him, uninterrupted, listening to the events of his day. She didn't attempt to call Dominic again and fought a wave of disappointment at his lack of communication. While sitting with Kevin, she tried to text Dominic a couple of times, but he ignored her messages as well.

"Did you finish your homework with Ms. Lisa?" she asked while clearing the dinner table.

"Yes. Can I get on the game?"

Melinda laughed. "Yes, baby. You can play the game for about thirty minutes before bath time and bed."

Kevin raced up the stairs to his bedroom, leaving her to finish cleaning the kitchen. When she was done, she filled her wine glass again and climbed the stairs to the bedroom she and Dominic shared. She paused in the doorway, looking around the tidy room. There was barely any sign that he came home at all. She doubted he even waited for her after abruptly ending their call. Their relationship was less than perfect, with disappearing acts recently becoming a part of their normal routine. She hoped for a romantic evening, but things quickly went off course again. She hoped he was in a better mood when he got home or at that the very least that Kevin would be sleeping deep enough to not hear their inevitable argument.

An hour later, after Kevin was in the bed, Melinda returned to her bedroom with a third serving of wine. She set the glass on her bedside table and checked her cell phone again. After seeing that there was still no communication from Dominic, she decided to take a bath and slip into something that might ease the tension whenever he arrived home. She took a long, bubble bath and slipped into a burgundy lace negligee that complemented both her curves and her complexion.

Melinda stood in front of her mirror, surveying her appearance. The glasses she wore were more for style than necessity. She removed them, revealing her round, hazel-brown eyes that were accentuated by thick eyebrows that were arched to perfection. She smiled at her reflection, showcasing her deep dimples in each of her full cheeks. She ran her fingers through her dark-brown, silky curls that were cut into a trendy pixie cut that was longer on top and framed her round face perfectly. She smoothed her hands down the front of the lingerie, pausing at her waist, which was defined but thick like the rest of her body. She possessed a shapely physique for most of her life, but she made sure to keep things as tight as she could. The shoulder straps were pulled tight, which had her double D's sitting high, and the high cut of the bottom of the underwear displayed her wide hips and full, toned legs. She embraced the voluptuous curves that often attracted the attention of many men.

After returning to her bedroom, she turned on a few flame-less LED candles to set the intended mood and lay down on her side of the bed. While she waited for Dominic to arrive home, she played R&B music from their Bluetooth speakers and scrolled through social media on her phone. She downed the rest of her wine before dozing off a little before ten o'clock. Two hours later, a few minutes before midnight, she was fast asleep when Dominic finally returned home. She didn't hear when he entered the house or minutes later when he stormed into their bedroom.

"Mel!" he shouted, startling her from her sleep. "What the fuck is this?" Dominic grabbed her arm, snatching her up from the bed.

Confused, her eyes widened when he threw her down on the floor and tossed a handful of money at her. Looking at the crisp, folded twenty-dollar bills falling on her and the ground, she realized he found the money from DeAndre that was in the pocket of her trench coat. Dominic was angrier than she had seen him in a while—his eyes narrowed into dangerous slits while he continued to yell at her.

"Where did you get all this money from?" he demanded.

"Dom, I—"

"Did you wear that shit work? Is that what you're wearing

under your clothes now?" he asked. "Is that why you were late? Huh? You out here acting like a damn ho like usual."

Melinda shook her head at his false accusations while he snatched her up from the ground only to knock her down again.

"Answer me, dammit!"

"Dom, I was trying to tell you," Melinda cried.

Forcefully grabbing her by the arm again, he hastily lifted her up, wrapping a hand around her neck and slamming her against the wall. While he continued to yell at her, he tightened his hand around her throat. She could tell he was intoxicated. She wasn't surprised that he had a few drinks wherever he went that evening. However, the smell of vodka radiated from him. Their relationship was less than perfect, but this was new. He had never choked her before. She was more than alarmed. She was scared.

In the middle of his rant, Dominic slammed her back against the wall again, hitting her head as well. Melinda struggled to free herself from his grasp, digging her nails into his skin when she placed her hand on top of his to try and pry it away. She could feel her face starting to go numb while tears welled in her eyes. When Dominic finally let her go, she bent over, her hand rubbing her neck while she tried to catch her breath. Out of the corner of her eye, she could see him staring at her, the veins in his forehead bulging. She didn't know what to say or do. For fear of making the situation worse, she didn't do anything at all.

"Answer me, Melinda," he said in an eerily calm tone of voice. "Have you been fucking that lame ass dude at your job? Is he paying for the ass now?"

Leaning against the wall, Melinda closed her eyes and shook her head in response. She didn't think the truth would be any better than the lie that Dominic had in his mind. She didn't think anything was wrong with DeAndre offering money to financially support his nephew. However, she knew that Dominic wouldn't see it that way. Still, she knew she had to say something to change the idea he had in his mind. She wasn't surprised that he referred to Rashad as *that lame ass dude* from her job. Dominic was suspicious of him ever since the two met at the school's Christmas party the previous year. The last thing she needed was any more problems at work.

"Dom, no. I'm not messing with anybody else. You know that," she said, looking at him with teary eyes. "I've never been unfaithful to you."

There was a moment of heavy silence in the room. It was true. Since the beginning of their relationship, Melinda had barely looked at another man, let alone stepped out on him. However, Dominic had admitted to a physical encounter with another woman he met at a bar a year earlier. At the time, he called it an unfortunate mistake and swore it only happened one time. Melinda wasn't sure she believed him but didn't dare to question it.

"Then I'm going to ask you one more time, and don't even think about lying to me, Mel," he said firmly. "Where the hell did all that money come from?"

Melinda sighed heavily, closing her eyes while she leaned against the wall again. "I got the money from DeAndre," she said quietly. "He stopped by my job because he hadn't been able to get ahold of me. He just wanted to help out with Kevin. That's all."

"That's all?" Dominic questioned with a laugh. He shook his head and repeated himself. "That's all?"

Because her eyes were still closed, Melinda did not see it coming when he reared back and hit her with a backhand that sent her flying halfway across the floor. Dominic crossed the room, standing over her while the fire returned to his eyes.

"You out here accepting handouts like some fucking beggar?" he shouted.

Melinda shook her head, while raising her hands to try to shield herself from any additional blows. "No! I tried to tell him I didn't need it," she cried. "I told him we were good."

"But then you took it anyway! You run your mouth so much

on the phone with your friends but couldn't tell him no until he left your ass alone!" Dominic shouted at her. Despite her raised hands, he continued to hit her. "All the things I do for you and that boy, and you out here looking like you're needy... in front of him of all people. I bust my ass every day to make sure that you and Kevin have everything that you need. This house... that truck you drive... all the shoes and purses in your closet. Everything I've ever done for you since I found your ass working in that damn club..." Dominic's physical and verbal assaults continued until he tired himself. He mumbled something about staying somewhere else that night and stormed out of the bedroom, leaving her on the floor—crying in the fetal position.

Melinda lay on the ground until she heard the garage door slam and his car speed away. After she was sure he was gone, she slowly pushed herself up and limped toward their bathroom, her leg sore from a kick to her shin. She stood in front of the mirror, staring at her reflection in disbelief of the number he did on her. Some of the marks he left on her face and body were still red imprints on her light complexion, but some were already starting to bruise. After she carefully washed her face, she traded her lingerie for a more comfortable sleep shirt and made her way back into the bedroom. She grabbed her laptop and submitted a time-off request for the rest of the week as well as a request for a substitute teacher. There was no way she could go into work. Not with the way her face looked.

2

J abari shifted in the passenger's seat of the truck and turned to look at DeAndre while he sat behind the wheel focused on the road ahead. "Why didn't Mama ride with y'all to pick me up?"

DeAndre shrugged his shoulders instead of responding. When he noticed Jabari staring at him expectantly, he finally answered. "I don't know. I think she said she had to get some stuff together."

"Get what stuff together?"

DeAndre shrugged again and turned his focus back to the road.

Jabari shook his head and laughed. "Come on, man. For real? You know I don't like surprises. I told her not to make a big deal about this."

Their younger sister, Symone, leaned forward from the back seat and patted Jabari on the shoulder. "You know your mother, bro. You knew she was going to make a big deal about this."

Jabari laughed and shook his head. "Yeah. You're right. I should have known better. Who all did she invite?"

"I don't even know," DeAndre answered. "She didn't tell us much."

"Yeah. She really didn't want us to tell you shit," Symone said with a laugh. "Make sure you act surprised."

"Alright. I can do that." Jabari laughed. "Have either of y'all spoke to Mel?"

The truck fell silent. Symone shook her head, and Jabari looked toward DeAndre for an answer. He shrugged his shoulders again.

"I mean... not really. She ain't really been picking up the phone. I had to pop up on her at her job last week so I could give her some money for Kevin," he said. "I told her you were getting out, and she said she was gon' call Mama. I don't know if that happened. If she did, Mama didn't say anything to me about it."

Jabari shook his head and settled back into his seat, staring out of the window. The rest of the ride was relatively quiet for the Butler siblings while he was lost in his thoughts. He wasn't too shocked that Melinda had not answered the phone for DeAndre, because the two had a love-hate relationship. However, he was surprised to hear that she wasn't keeping up with Symone. The two always had a good relationship. He received most of his updates about Melinda from his sister. Symone and DeAndre didn't have much to say about the situation, but they understood Jabari's frustration. He had not seen Melinda in a couple of years, but everyone knew he still held feelings for her.

Growing up, Jabari and Melinda were elementary school classmates and friends since their homeroom teacher sat them next to each other in the second grade. Having last names that were close alphabetically, they were always around each other, their friendship growing throughout the years. Even though they were seemingly headed in different directions, even at a younger age, they remained close. Melinda was a top student that always excelled, eventually graduating second in their high school class. Jabari was never as invested in academics, but neither were most of the guys Melinda entertained. She was known for dating some of the rougher guys around the neighborhood that her mother referred to as being a part of the "wrong crowd". Many of the guys she was involved with, Jabari associated with. During high school while Melinda buried herself in the books, he started spending more and more time in the streets. Regardless of people questioning Melinda's problematic relationships or why she maintained a friendship with Jabari, she never judged him or looked down on him.

The summer after high school, the pair of friends started to see each other in a different light. After a few months of messing around as friends with benefits, they became an official item. Jabari shared that she was one of the few constants in his life— one of the few things he was sure of. She was one of the few people in life that he felt knew him completely and accepted him anyway. Melinda only started to question his life choices when she became pregnant with Kevin during her sophomore year of college. Up until that point, Jabari was making money any way he saw fit—robbing, stealing, selling drugs. You name it, he did it and showed DeAndre the ropes. However, all of that changed the moment he held his newborn son. He made a promise to Melinda to get his life together, and he tried his best. He stopped hanging with his usual group of friends and started spending less time in the streets. He even got a legitimate job working construction with his older cousin. Everything was good until things completely fell apart two years later.

One night, celebrating a friend's birthday at a house party ended terribly when he and a couple of friends were involved in a fight with another group. A guy died as a result of his injuries, and Jabari ended up with a manslaughter charge and a prison sentence of ten years. Melinda was completely devastated. Even then, she never left his side. They initially remained a couple with intentions to stick it out for however long he was behind bars. Things didn't work out that way. Jabari had not seen Melinda since a year into his sentence. She maintained a smile during their visit, but he was unable to ignore the undeniable sadness in her eyes. He couldn't stand to see the woman he loved struggling to mask her unhappiness—unhappiness that he was responsible for. It killed him to know that there was nothing he could do to fix it.

Jabari ended up doing what he thought was best at the time. He let her go. He ended their relationship in an attempt to allow her to reclaim the happiness he ruined when he separated their young family. In the moment, he thought the move was for the best. Looking back, if he knew how things would end up, he would have made a different choice. After the breakup, they initially remained cordial, but eventually, communication became strained. Jabari asked DeAndre to look out for her and help out with Kevin however he could, but Melinda started to pull away from the Butler family as a whole. She never kept them from Kevin, even allowing them to take him to visit his father. However, she came around the Butlers less and less. Things eventually got to the point that whenever she and Jabari spoke, it was only about their son. He had to hear from his brother how she dated a few neighborhood guys after their breakup, and his sister informed him of her eventual relationship with Dominic when it became serious enough for her and Kevin to move into his home.

Of course, he wanted her to be happy. While he was behind bars, all he cared about was the safety, happiness, and well-being of her and their son. That didn't stop the twinge of jealously he experienced when Symone informed him that Melinda finally stopped messing with the neighborhood goons and moved on to Dominic. Someone who appeared to have his stuff together. Someone who didn't hesitate to step up to the plate and take care of the family he left behind.

DeAndre pulled into their mother's neighborhood with his siblings still unusually quiet. He cut his eyes over at his older brother. "Bruh, don't worry about it. I'll give her a call after you get settled. Might even pop up at her job again if you want me to," DeAndre said with a laugh to try to lighten the mood. Jabari simply nodded in silence without looking at him.

"What in the world?" Symone laughed when DeAndre turned onto their mother's street.

Jabari shook his head and laughed as well. "What the hell is this? Mama don't even like having all these people in her house."

They all laughed, knowing he was absolutely correct. Their mother, Sonya, lived alone in a spacious house but enjoyed her solitude and did not like playing hostess. She never volunteered to hold gatherings for extended family during the holidays, even though their family was quite large. Because of this, they were all surprised to see the cars parked in the driveway, lining the street and causing DeAndre to park a few houses away. He shut off the engine, and they exited his truck.

While DeAndre led the way up the sidewalk, Symone grabbed Jabari's arm, pulling him back. He raised his eyebrows. "What's good, Symone?"

"I know you're thinking about Melinda and Kev right now, but try to put that out your mind for the moment," she said. "Mel ain't never been the petty type, and I know she ain't gon' keep Kevin away from you. I'll give her a call a little later. In the meantime, Mama went through a lot of trouble to get all this together, so try to keep a smile on your face. Okay?"

Jabari nodded and smiled while shoving his hands into the pocket of his jeans. "I got you."

"Good," Symone said, linking her arm with her brother's. "Now let's go get some of this food. I know she threw down!"

Jabari laughed, and the pair started toward the house. While they approached the front door, he was glad his brother and sister brought him decent clothes to wear. All he really wanted to do was eat some good food, get some sleep in a real bed, and figure out when he would be able to see his son. However, he would do his best to do exactly as Symone asked, regardless of whether he was in the mood for all of the people waiting for him or not. As expected, from the several cars outside, Jabari was bombarded with a crowd of family, friends, and acquaintances the moment he stepped through the front door. While he was trying to speak and acknowledge everyone, he heard Sonya yelling over the crowd.

"Move! Move out my way so I can get to my baby!" she said, pushing her way past different people to get to him. She wiped her hands on the dish towel thrown over her shoulder before wrapping her arms around him for a big hug. "Welcome home, baby!"

"Hey, Mama," Jabari said with a genuine smile.

Sonya pulled away from their embrace but held onto his hand and led him through the crowd of people to the kitchen. He smelled the food as soon as he entered the house, but the aroma grew stronger when they stepped into the kitchen—instantly making his mouth water.

"I don't know what they were feeding you down there, but mama's got all your favorites," Sonya said as she started to uncover a few of the dishes. "Go on and wash your hands and sit down."

Jabari quickly did as he was told, and Sonya handed him a plate piled high with fried chicken, macaroni and cheese, collard greens, and potato salad. She grabbed him a glass of lemonade before joining him at the table. Jabari said a quick grace and started to eat. His mother was an exceptional cook, and her food was one of the things he looked forward to the most when he found out he would be released from prison early. Sonya shouted to DeAndre, Symone, and the rest of the group that they could eat now that Jabari had his plate. At twenty-six, Jabari was the oldest with DeAndre one year behind at twenty-five, and Symone being the baby at twenty-three. The siblings were all close, even though they joked that Jabari was secretly Sonya's favorite child.

She released a relieved sigh and patted Jabari's cheek before rubbing his arm. "You look good, baby."

Jabari smiled between bites. "Thank you, Ma. I'm glad to be home."

"And I'm so happy to have you home. Four years was a long time," she said with a somber look. She looked down for a moment but forced a pleasant smile onto her face before looking back up at her oldest. "Now, we just need to keep you out of trouble. You've got a few more years on probation. I want you on the straight and narrow."

"That's the plan."

"Good. Your cousin Alex already has a construction job lined up for you. I know you used to work with his old company before you went away. It's just something to put money in your pocket until you find something else if you want. He's around here somewhere with the details," she said, looking around but not seeing him. Instead, she spotted DeAndre off to the side chatting with some unfamiliar girl that wasn't appropriately dressed for the cool, November weather. She eventually turned back around, rolling her eyes. "I still don't know why you have to stay with your brother. You know you always have a place here."

Jabari nodded, laughing slightly. "I appreciate that, but what grown ass man wants to be under his mama's roof?"

Sonya shrugged. "I'm just saying. You know what Dre is into," she said. "I swear that child is going to be the death of me. Running in these streets and behind all these fast-tailed heifers. It's a miracle I only have one grandbaby."

Jabari laughed louder. "Mama, let that man live. What better way for me to make sure he gets his shit together than staying with him to see to it?" he said. "Besides... it will only be temporary. Whatever company Alex is working for will pay well. You know that man doesn't play about his money."

"You got that right." Sonya laughed.

After he cleaned his plate, Jabari grabbed a cold beer and headed into the family room to catch up with his cousins and a few other family friends. They were laughing and joking for close to an hour before the doorbell rang. Symone excused herself from the group and headed to the door with the assumption that it was one of the few family members that had not yet arrived. Jabari took a sip of his beer and watched Symone while she opened the door. Out of the corner of his eye, he saw the smile fall from her face and be replaced with shock. She said something he couldn't hear over his loudmouthed cousins and then stepped out onto the porch, closing the door behind her. He frowned in confusion but rejoined the conversation. A few moments later, he was surprised when Symone stepped back into the house with his son. He paused for a brief moment before setting his beer down and rushing across the room to him.

He grabbed Kevin up into a big bear hug, holding him close for a few moments before sitting him down on his feet. "It's good to see you, man. How did you get here? Your mom dropped you off?"

Kevin nodded. "Yeah. She said she had something to do and that Aunt Symone is going to take me to my granny's house later."

"Oh yeah? Well, take your coat off real quick and get comfortable. I'll be right back."

Without another word, Jabari quickly rushed out of the front door. He looked up and down the street in both directions before he spotted Melinda walking down the sidewalk back toward her vehicle. Her pace was brisk, and he jogged in her direction to catch up with her. "Hey!" he called to get her attention, but she didn't turn around. Jabari wasn't sure, but she might have even started walking faster. He had to run faster to close the distance between them. "Melinda!"

She froze right as she reached the driver's door of her truck.

Jabari finally reached her, stopping a couple feet away to maintain a comfortable distance. "For real, Mel?"

"For real, Mel, what?" she asked, turning around to face him. He didn't know what to make of her tone. Her eyes were hidden behind dark, oversized sunglasses so he couldn't read her facial expression either.

"You just gon' drop Kevin off and leave?"

Melinda shrugged her shoulders and pulled the belt of her jacket tighter around her waist. "I have some errands to run."

"Come on, Mel. Nobody even knew you were coming. I didn't know if I was going to see Kevin today or not. Symone and Dre said they ain't heard from you lately."

"I've been a little busy lately, but I talk to Symone. As far as your brother is concerned, he always knows how to reach me when he needs to. He just popped up at my job last week," she said. "I'm not running away from anybody or trying to avoid your family if that's what you're trying to imply."

Jabari detected a bit more attitude in her tone than usual when she mentioned his brother. He didn't know what that was about, and he didn't want to question it in that moment either. "Still though... you couldn't have popped in for a quick moment? No 'hey, how you doing?'" he asked. "You ain't never had no problems with the family before."

"Ain't no quick moment with your family, Jabari. I love them, but I don't have that type of time today. Your mother would have made me a plate and forced me to sit down while your cousins talked my ears off."

They both shared a brief laugh, knowing that she was right. Sonya always loved Melinda and definitely would have made her stay longer than she intended. Jabari's smile widened when he noticed the slight smile tugging at Melinda's lips. He wished that he could see her eyes—the hazel-brown eyes he fell in love with years ago.

"Alright then," he said, taking a step back. "I'll let you go so you can run your errands or whatever... but stop by sometime when everybody else isn't here and you have more time. You know my mother would love to see you."

"I'll keep that in mind," she said with a slightly wider smile. She unlocked the truck and paused, turning back toward Jabari. "How are you doing?"

"I'm good... all things considered," he answered. "Definitely glad to be back home."

"Well, you certainly look good," she said. "Welcome home, Jabari."

He smiled and nodded in response. "Thank you."

"Symone is taking Kevin to my mom's house to spend the night," she said. "You should ride with them if you want. I'm sure my mom would love to see you as well."

"Bet. I'll do that," he said. "I'll see you later, Mel."

Jabari took another step back while Melinda climbed into her truck and closed the door. He stuck his hands back into the pockets of his jeans, watching her every move. He stood there long enough to see her turn on the engine and pull away from the curb. After watching her taillights until her truck reached the end of the street and turned the corner, he started back toward his mother's house. He shook his head, regretting his actions three years earlier. His relationship with Melinda was the only one that ever mattered to him. In his mind, there was no denying that she was the love of his life—his soul mate. He was glad to see her, but a quick conversation on the sidewalk outside of his mother's house wasn't nearly enough. He wanted more than that. He wanted her.

❧ 3 ❧

"So what's really been going on with you?" Melinda's best friend, Sasha, asked.

Melinda rolled her eyes as she continued to drive. After dropping Kevin off with Jabari and his family, she ran a number of errands. Now that she was finished, she was on her way home and hopeful that she would beat Dominic there. "Nothing is going on with me. Shit! I don't know why everyone keeps asking me that," she said in an irritated tone. "First my mama, then my coworkers, now you... goodness!"

"Because anybody that knows you can tell that something has been off with you," Sasha responded. "You ain't been acting like yourself. Something's been different for a few months now."

"I'm fine." Melinda's tone was dismissive, but she knew that Sasha was right. Of course, she wasn't acting like herself. How could she act like herself when she hadn't felt like herself for quite some time? It was no surprise that her loved ones were able to see through the façade she unsuccessfully tried to maintain. Sasha's voice broke through her thoughts.

"And where were you last week?"

"What are you talking about?"

"I stopped by your job to bring you lunch and see the kids,

and you weren't there," she answered. "That fine ass Rashad told me you called out a couple of days... unexpectedly too."

Melinda blew a frustrated breath. "I don't know why people keep popping up at my job like it's some hangout spot. DeAndre came through there the other week wanting to talk about Kevin."

"Well, I don't know about your brother-in-law—"

"That's not my brother-in-law," Melinda mumbled.

Sasha ignored her. She never cared for Dominic, and she didn't hesitate to let Melinda know. "You didn't answer your phone all week. I don't know why you're acting like what I did was out of the norm. I stop by to see you on the regular. You know those kids love me."

Melinda rolled her eyes again while she turned into her neighborhood. For the second time, Sasha was right. Melinda's students knew her well, and she stopped by for frequent visits. She sighed heavily.

"So... are you going to tell me what's going on, or do I need to pop up at your house too?" Sasha's voice filled the inside of Melinda's truck.

"No!" Melinda blurted. She paused to calm herself as she approached her house and pressed the garage door opener. "Please don't pop up over here. We'll get together soon. I promise."

Melinda's stomach dropped when the garage opened and she saw Dominic's car parked inside. To start the weekend early, she took a half day from work and picked Kevin up early so she could take him to see his father once he made it home. She spent the rest of the afternoon knocking out the list of errands, mostly for Dominic. She was supposed to beat him home and unfortunately failed to do so. While she sat there with the garage still open and her engine running, panic ran through her when she saw the door open and Dominic step into the garage.

Sasha was still talking—most of which Melinda barely heard.

"Keep acting like you don't know what I'm talking about, Mel. Don't make me call Ms. Carla. You know good and well—"

"Sasha, stop!" Melinda interrupted her. "I gotta go. I'll call you tomorrow on my way to get Kevin." She didn't wait for an answer before ending the call.

Melinda felt her body tense all over when Dominic slowly approached her car. He was still dressed in the button-down and slacks he wore to the office, but he removed his tie and undid the top couple of buttons. When he wasn't violent or angry, it was easy to see how attractive he was. Standing right at six feet tall, he had a smooth caramel-brown complexion and athletic build that showcased all the long hours he spent in the gym. He looked more like a professional running back than a corporate attorney.

They met two years earlier while Melinda was waitressing at a strip club. It was during her first year of teaching, and she was working at the club on weekends to earn extra money. She crossed paths with Dominic when he came into the club with a group of friends for a bachelor party. She was one of their waitresses, and they instantly took an interest in each other. By the end of the night, Dominic left her a five-hundred-dollar tip and his phone number. She called him the next day, and they were together ever since. In the beginning, he was a breath of fresh air. He was different from the drug dealers and street dudes she dated before and after Jabari. Each of those relationships being more of a dead-end than the last, she appreciated what Dominic brought to the table. He was a career-minded individual that enjoyed going on real dates and having stimulating conversation. He got along well with her parents and most of her friends, and he loved Kevin. He was supportive of her desire to obtain her specialist degree and all other goals she had for herself. A full year passed by before she realized that all that glittered wasn't gold.

The first time Dominic hit her was three months after she and Kevin moved into his house, after a year of being together.

He spent the night out with friends and came home intoxicated, much later than he promised. A conversation about honest communication and respect turned into an all-out argument and a slap to the face for Melinda. He was immediately apologetic, promising to never do it again. She believed him and didn't say a word about the situation to her family or friends. For a while, he kept his word. Until a couple of months later when Melinda discovered he cheated on her. Another argument turned violent followed by an empty promise of never putting his hands on her again. The last few weeks there was increasing tension in their home, which culminated in the explosive exchange that left her nursing a healing black eye over a week later. She felt like she was on pins and needles, never knowing what to expect from him and hiding the truth from her family and friends.

When Dominic reached for the handle, Melinda pressed the unlock button, allowing him to open her door.

He smiled at her and removed her sunglasses, tossing the Dior shades onto the passenger's seat. "Why are you sitting here with the engine running?" he asked. "Come inside." He leaned inside the truck, reaching across her body to shut the engine off. He unbuckled her seat belt and took her hand.

Melinda hesitated but then allowed him to help her out of the vehicle. "I have your dry cleaning in the back, and I picked up—"

Dominic silenced her with a kiss. "We'll get it later, baby."

"I tried to get here before seven. I was held up on 285 by an accident," she explained.

"Mel, it's fine," he said with an easy laugh. "Relax. I'm just glad you made it home safely, regardless of how long it took."

"Uh—okay."

Still holding onto her hand, Dominic closed the garage and led the way into the house.

Melinda's eyes widened with surprise when he steered them into the formal dining room, where the table was set for a candlelit meal. "Babe, what is this?"

Dominic shrugged his shoulders and untied the belt on her trench coat. "Dinner. I wanted to surprise you," he said. He took her coat and purse, setting them in an empty chair at the table. "That's why I asked you to take of those things for me... so I could take care of this."

"Wow... I'm definitely surprised," she said. Dominic pulled out a chair for her to sit down. "When did you have time for this?"

Dominic sat to her right, at the head of the table, and shrugged his shoulders. "I make time for what's important—for things that matter to me," he said.

Melinda nodded and looked down at the food before her—a strawberry spinach salad and crab and shrimp alfredo. Two of her favorite dishes, although she was recently trying to limit her carb intake. Whenever he made time to get into the kitchen, he was a surprisingly good cook.

Dominic opened a bottle of wine and filled their glasses. "Before you say anything, I know you've been limiting pasta and other carbs, but I also know you love this dish. You deserve to treat yourself every now and then, so eat up," he said. "Besides... I don't know what you've been stressing about anyway. You look great, Mel... and you know I love your curves." He leaned over to kiss her lips again.

After he blessed the food, the two ate their meal. Melinda enjoyed the dinner and their conversation. Although they were few and far between in recent months, these were the moments she enjoyed. These were the moments that added reason to her justification every time she considered leaving him. These were the moments that made her stay. After dinner, they enjoyed slices of double chocolate cake from one of her favorite local bakeries.

Dominic softly touched the side of Melinda's face, caressing her cheek before his thumb softly brushed under her right eye—the one that was still slightly bruised. The action, although minimal, was the first acknowledgment of her injury since the incident happened. That night, when he left, she had no idea where he went. He returned the following day hungover like nothing happened. "Mel..." he sighed, "baby, I'm sorry."

Melinda bit her bottom lip and looked down instead of maintaining eye contact with him. She noticed that he was wearing the TAG Heuer watch she purchased for his birthday the previous week. He cupped her chin, raising it so she would look into his eyes.

"I'm serious. I didn't mean to come at you like that... I just got beside myself, and I—I... there's really no excuse for what I did," he said. "I know I've said before that it won't happen again, but trust me this time. I don't want to be that guy. I don't want to hurt you. There's been so much stress at work, but I know that's no excuse. I'm going to get the drinking under control and be my best self for you. You deserve someone who is going to keep their word and be the man that you need."

"Dom, I need you to be the best version of yourself for *you*. Not me. Be better because it's important to you to be a respect-ful, decent man. Don't make it dependent upon me," she said. "If you make sure that you're a better, more caring person at your core, then you won't hurt me when a conversation goes left. You'll make sure that your treatment of me won't depend on however you're feeling that day."

Dominic dropped his hand, resting his forearms on the table. He hesitated for a moment but sighed and said, "You're right, baby. You're right." He didn't say anything else, instead picking up his fork again to finish eating his cake.

Melinda wasn't sure what to make of his silence. She hoped he didn't take her words the wrong way. She almost regretted her statement, but it was her truth. She felt it needed to be said, and she hoped he could hear and accept her words without her having to pay for them later. She eventually picked her fork up as well, taking her time to finish her dessert. Dominic waited for her to finish and then gathered their plates. Melinda followed him to the kitchen, pausing near the island while he loaded the dishwasher.

"I didn't mean to offend you with what I said."

"I'm not offended," he responded without looking at her.

"Dom, I just... I hate when things go there," she said. He closed the dishwasher and turned to look at her. For the first time in a long time, she saw regret in his eyes. Genuine remorse was written across his face. Unexpected emotion arose, causing her voice to crack when she continued to speak. "My face... you can't hit me in my face like that. I've tried my hardest to keep our business inside these four walls, but if I'm walking around with black eyes and shit, everybody is going to know."

Dominic walked over to her, wrapping an arm around her waist. He brushed her curly bang away from her eyes and kissed her forehead. "I know, baby. I don't know how many times I need to say it until you believe me, but I'm sorry... I'm so sorry."

Melinda nodded in acknowledgment and didn't resist when he kissed her lips again. She melted into his arms, wrapping hers around his neck while he rubbed her back. He kissed her neck and lips again, moving his hands from her back to untie the wrap dress she wore. Dominic pulled away from her lips long enough to look her body up and down with desire in his eyes.

"Do you forgive me, baby?"

Melinda nodded again and stepped out of her high heels. Dominic pulled her dress off her shoulders, causing it to fall to the floor. When Melinda pressed her lips against his again, she quickly started to unbutton his shirt, eventually taking it off and leaving it on the kitchen floor with her dress. "You want to go upstairs?" she asked softly.

Dominic shook his head, kissing her again and directing her to the family room. He sat her down on the couch, spreading her legs and dropping to his knees in front of her. He paused and kissed the insides of both thighs before taking off the lace underwear she wore. Melinda closed her eyes and exhaled in pleasure when she felt his warm, wet mouth kissing her lower lips. He ran his tongue up and down the folds of her quivering pussy before softly sucking on her clit. She moaned, calling his name and grabbing at the fabric on the seat cushions while he continued to lick her with intensity. Before she knew it, her legs were shaking while her wetness poured onto his face, soaking his mouth and neatly trimmed beard.

Dominic pulled back and quickly moved to unbuckle his slacks. He pushed his pants and underwear down and laid Melinda back while laying on top of her. He spread her legs, lifting one with his right arm while he used his left hand to enter her. He tongue kissed her with passion while stroking her hard and deep. He repeatedly told her how sorry he was while he kissed away the tears that fell from her eyes. Melinda wrapped her legs around his waist and grabbed his body, her long, red nails digging into the flesh of his back. He kissed her neck and then spoke into her ear, telling her that he loved her more than anything. Melinda chose to believe him. Regardless of the insults her hurled her way and the physical pain he inflicted during moments of conflict, she chose to believe that, deep down, he still held the same love for her that was present toward the beginning of their relationship—before she moved into his house. Before the first time he lied, cheated, or laid hands on her.

"Damn, baby," he mumbled, closing his eyes and savoring how good she felt.

"Dom, uh—oh my God!" She held on to him even tighter while she felt a tingle run up her spine.

After they were done, they lay on the couch in each other's arms, laughing and talking until they fell asleep. Melinda was thankful for the evening and the rest of the weekend, which was smooth and without incident. She was appreciative of the peaceful weekend because when she returned to work, it was an entirely different story. Monday there was no peace. Monday completely kicked her ass.

When the final bell rang, Melinda released a heavy sigh of

relief while watching her students exit her class. She was used to kids becoming increasingly unruly the deeper they got into the semester. However, she didn't expect the type of behavior the day brought until after Thanksgiving. *Thanksgiving,* she thought with a sigh. She would be happy to have a break and be even closer to the end of the semester—an even longer break. Once the class was empty, she busied herself with grading papers for a half hour before she started to pack her things. She glanced at her watch, satisfied that she would have plenty of time to pick up Kevin and make dinner before Dominic arrived home from work.

She slipped into her coat and shouldered her bag on the way to the door. With her keys in her hand, she smiled, happy for the day to be over. Before she could reach the hallway, her boss, Principal Jenkins, stepped inside her classroom. Melinda greeted her with a pleasant smile.

"Hey, Ms. Jenkins. I was just on my way out," she said. "What brings you by?"

"Actually... I wanted to catch you before you left," Ms. Jenkins said, closing the door behind her. "Have a seat for me really quick. I know you need to pick up your son, so I'll try to make this quick."

Melinda hesitated before taking her seat. Ms. Jenkins had an open-door policy, and the two maintained a good relationship. However, she was not expecting the impromptu, end-of-the-day meeting. She forced a smile onto her face. "What's going on?"

"I wanted to check with you to see if everything was okay." Ms. Jenkins asked, "Is there anything going on outside of work that I should be aware of?"

Melinda's smile dropped. "No. Why would you ask that?"

"You haven't seemed like yourself lately," Ms. Jenkins answered. Melinda fought the urge to roll her eyes at that comment being made by yet another person in her life. "Whatever the issue is, it appears to be affecting your work performance."

"My work performance?"

Ms. Jenkins nodded. "Yes, Melinda. Your last observation was less than stellar. I know you're aware of that."

Melinda nodded. She and Dominic were up the whole night arguing before her most recent classroom observation. She did not have the energy or the patience for the lesson she planned that day.

"And the front office has also received a couple of complaints from some of your parents."

"If this is about Monquez Perriman—"

"It's not, Melinda. I know he's a handful, but Ms. Perriman wasn't the only parent to complain," Ms. Jenkins explained. "Apparently, the students are saying that you've been short with them, distracted in class... They even brought to my attention a mix-up and confusion over grades."

Melinda didn't respond. Everything her boss said was true, and she didn't like excuses or explanations. She sat with her hands folded in her lap while Ms. Jenkins continued.

"Then you unexpectedly called out week before last leaving your team completely unprepared. According to your grade chair, you didn't set your substitute up for success. They had to assist on your behalf." She paused, sighing heavily. "I know your recent work performance is not suggestive of who you are as an educator. You're an amazing asset to our team, and I'm glad to have you... but we need to get things turned around. Whatever is going on, I need you to fix it. Quickly."

"Understood."

Ms. Jenkins nodded and stood up. "I hope you do, in fact, understand, but I still need to make it plain. If I don't see a turn-around in your performance, we're going to have a different conversation. This one was a warning, but the next will be on paper."

"I hear you, Ms. Jenkins. I understand fully."

Ms. Jenkins nodded again before leaving without another word. Melinda released a heavy sigh, shaking her head in frustration before collecting her things. After a brief hesitation, she left the classroom and headed for the exit. She rolled her eyes heavily when she saw Rashad unlocking and getting into his car, which was parked right next to hers. He looked up, making eye contact with her.

"Have a good evening, Melinda."

"Yeah, okay," she said, rolling her eyes.

Rashad frowned and got out of his car, closing the door and walking around to Melinda while she approached her driver side. "Is there a problem?"

"I don't know, Mr. Grade Chair. You tell me," she said. "The last thing I needed was any more bullshit at work, and you had to complain to Principal Jenkins about my absence the other week."

Rashad sighed and shook his head. "That's what this about?" he asked with a frown. "I didn't run to the principal's office, if that's what you're thinking. She was on our hall and popped in on your substitute to see how it was going. Apparently, it wasn't going well, and she came to me with questions. You didn't necessarily give me a heads-up or leave me with any answers. I didn't know what to say."

"You're a smart man. I'm sure you could have found some way to cover for me."

"So you wanted me to do a favor for you... like we're friends or something?"

Melinda tilted her head to the side and looked at him with arched eyebrows. She was aware of his interest in her but made it clear that she was unavailable when he asked her out on a date a while ago before he knew she was off the market. "Rashad, please don't tell me this has anything to do with me turning down your advances. You know I'm in a relationship. I have been for a while," she said. "But because I won't give you the time of day, you throw me under the bus to our boss? That's real childish. I would have expected more from you." She turned her back on him, opening her door.

Rashad reached across her and closed the door before she could climb in, prompting her to turn around and glare at him with narrowed eyes. He shook his head at her. "See that attitude right there is probably why you have so many parent complaints. I didn't say anything about you turning me down. This doesn't have anything to do with that. I actually thought we were friends... but friends don't lie to each other. Not the way you've been lying to me."

"What is that supposed to mean?"

Rashad smirked and stuck his hands into his coat pocket. "When you called off work, I texted to see if you were okay. You told me you had a stomach bug, but then you showed up to work the following Monday with your eye all jacked up. When I asked about that, you told me you tripped and fell. Classic lie, by the way."

"Excuse you?"

"Which one is it, Melinda? Did you have a stomach virus or fall and hit your face?" he asked, his eyes searching hers for answers. "Or was it something completely different?"

Melinda continued to glare at him without a response.

"Exactly, Mel. Exactly," he said, shaking his head. "Like I said... have a good evening."

Rashad turned away, heading back to his car. Melinda stood there fuming until he pulled out of the parking lot.

❧ 4 ❧

The buzzing of his cell phone woke Jabari up from an unexpected nap on the couch. Without opening his eyes, he grabbed the phone off the seat cushion next to him and answered sleepily. "Hello?"

"Hey, Jabari... did I wake you?"

His eyes opened when he heard Melinda's voice. Sitting up quickly, he cleared his throat and responded, "I dozed off after I got in from work, but I'm up. What's good?"

"I didn't want to bother you. I just—"

"Really. It's no bother. I'm just waiting on Dre to get home so we can grab something for dinner," he answered. "What you got going on?"

Jabari had not seen Melinda since the day he got home. As suggested, they both visited each other's parents but didn't cross paths again. They traded a few text messages about Kevin after Jabari got a phone, but this was their first call. He was happy to hear her voice.

"Honestly... a lot," she said with a slight sigh. "But I was actually calling you about Thanksgiving. I'm sure your family has plans now that you're home."

"Yes and no." He laughed. "Nothing out of the ordinary.

Mama said the day I got out was a one-time deal. We might stop over one of my aunts' houses, but then it'll just be me, my brother, and sister at my mama's spot. She ain't about to have all those people in her house again."

Melinda laughed heartily. A sound he missed hearing over the years. "I feel her on that. You know I'm not a fan of crowds either," she said. "I was wondering if you wanted to spend time with Kevin during the day."

"Of course," he answered quickly. He knew he couldn't make up for lost time, but he would gladly spend as much time with his son as possible. "Just let me know what time works for you."

"Any time really. We don't have plans," Melinda responded. "My parents are going on a cruise."

"What about your boyfriend?"

Melinda hesitated. "He's going out of town to visit his family, but I'll be here. I'll probably use the time to catch up on lesson plans and Lifetime movies."

She laughed, but Jabari didn't find anything funny about her spending the holiday alone. "You're more than welcome to eat with us," he offered.

"What? Oh, I don't know about that. I don't want to impose."

"I'm sure it'll be fine. You know my mom loves you. She was talking my ear off about how happy she was to see you the other day. Trust me... it ain't a problem," he said. "Besides... it will give Kevin the opportunity to spend the day with both of us."

Jabari's suggestion was met with silence, leaving him to wonder if he said something wrong.

"That's very kind of you to offer," she eventually said. "Let me get back to you on that. In the meantime, double check with Ms. Sonya just to be sure."

They both laughed, and Jabari heard the key turn in the lock signaling DeAndre's arrival home.

"I'm sure it's fine, but I'll ask if that makes you feel better," he said, as his brother entered the apartment. "It was good to hear your voice, Mel."

"Yeah... You too. I'll talk to you later."

The call ended, and Jabari looked up to see his brother staring at him with raised eyebrows.

"That was Mel?"

Jabari nodded.

"Oh word?" DeAndre asked, smiling. "What y'all was talking about?"

Jabari laughed at his brother and stood up to stretch his limbs. Ignoring DeAndre's question, he asked, "Where we eating, bro? I'm hungry as hell."

DeAndre rubbed his hands together with a mischievous grin on his face. "I know you love chicken, so we're headed to a place where we can get some breasts and wings."

"Works for me. Let's go."

Fifteen minutes later, DeAndre pulled up to a popular strip club, and Jabari started laughing uncontrollably. "Bruh, for real?"

"Breasts and wings, Brother. Breasts and wings." DeAndre reached into the glove compartment and grabbed a couple of rubber-banded knots of one-dollar bills. "Let's go."

Jabari hopped out of the truck and followed his brother toward the entrance. DeAndre headed straight to the front of the line, paying the bouncer to let them in ahead of the group of people waiting. Once they entered, DeAndre threw around more money for a table and some bottles. Before they could even get settled, another waitress sauntered over with a big smile and an even bigger ass. DeAndre looked up from his text messages, licking his lips and cheesing at the woman.

"What's up, Bree?"

Jabari shook his head and laughed, not surprised that DeAndre knew the woman by name.

"Hey, Dre," she said with an even wider smile. "I saw Tammy came and took care of your drinks. You need anything else?"

"Nah. We're good right now."

Bree cut her eyes at Jabari, smiling in his direction. "Who's your friend?"

"Oh, this my brother, Jabari," DeAndre answered.

"Hey, Jabari," she said in a flirty tone, flashing her smile at him. "Wait! Jabari, Jabari... Mel's Jabari?"

DeAndre shrugged his shoulders while Jabari looked at them both with questioning eyes. "I don't know if I would say all that," DeAndre answered. He changed the subject by asking, "Is Peaches working tonight?" Bree nodded. "Bet. Tell her to come through this way. My brother needs a dance."

"I got you," Bree said with a wink. "Nice to meet you, Jabari."

Jabari nodded and waved in her direction while she walked off. He turned toward his brother. "How she know Mel?"

DeAndre shrugged his shoulders and looked toward the main stage, where one of the strippers was starting her set. "She used to work here for a little bit. As a waitress. She wasn't shaking no ass or nothing like that. I honestly forgot, bro. That shit seems like it was forever ago."

Their bottles arrived, stopping Jabari from asking any other questions. Neither DeAndre nor Symone ever mentioned anything about Melinda working in a strip club. He could only assume that it was to earn extra money to take care of Kevin while he was locked up. Melinda's parents were cool—loving and supportive—but they held her accountable for her life's decisions. They loved their grandson, but they weren't enablers. Melinda had to work for everything she had. He felt a twinge of guilt at what he assumed was her need to work a second job while he was away but quickly shook it off. She handled her business and was doing well from what he could see. Although he had second thoughts about ending their relationship, it appeared to have worked in her favor. She and Kevin appeared to be thriving, so he chose not to dwell on the path it took for them to get there. The end result was what he wanted for her. She was happy.

zzz

A QUICK STOP AT THE STRIP CLUB FOR SOME WINGS TURNED into an all-night hangout. The brothers were joined by their cousins, Tyler and Phil, and a couple of DeAndre's friends—guys Jabari knew were in the streets with him. Jabari looked down at his watch to see that too many drinks and hours had passed. He was just about ready to go.

"Where Candy at... with that fat ass?" DeAndre asked a little too loudly. He bumped into the table when he stood up, knocking over a few cups. Most of the guys at the table laughed at his sloppiness and slurred speech. Jabari just shook his head while he tried to fight a smile. "I'm trying to take her home with me."

"And make your other twelve girlfriends mad?" Jabari asked. Everyone laughed even harder. "Come on, man. Let's go home so you can sleep this shit off."

Jabari stood up as well, signaling that their night was over, and it was time to leave.

"Yeah, we're gon' head out too," one of DeAndre's friends said.

Jabari grabbed his brother's keys, and the group headed for the exit. They made it over to DeAndre's truck, laughing and talking for a few more minutes before one of his friends pointed across the parking lot to another group of guys hanging near another car. Phil, one of their cousin Alex's younger brothers, approached Jabari separate from the ongoing conversation.

"Aye, man, bruh said you working some construction shit right now?" he asked.

Jabari nodded. "Yeah, man. Easy money. You know I was working with him before I went away."

"I know. You left all that shit we into alone."

Jabari shrugged his shoulders. "I was trying to do the family thing. Trying to get my shit together for Mel and Kev." He shook his head at the thought that even while he was attempting to do the right things he still ended up in prison.

"You still on that?" Phil asked.

"Still on what?"

"That family shit. You know Alex was never with the street shit. I know the money he's making may seem like easy money, but trust me... it ain't nothin' like what we got going on. Dre got us out here getting money for real, but who knows what we could do if you were with us too. You're the one that showed him the ropes."

"And I regret that shit every day," Jabari answered truthfully. Phil looked at him with a confused frown. "Look, Phil, I probably ended up losing the family I was trying to be legit for, and none of it was worth it. Whatever y'all got going on now may see cool, but think about how you would feel if you got hit with a couple of charges and a long sentence. Ain't your girl pregnant right now?"

Phil nodded slowly, taking in Jabari's comment. "I hear you, man," he said. "But if you change your mind, I know Dre will put you on without hesitation."

Jabari sighed. He knew that Phil heard him, but he obviously wasn't listening. He didn't have any interests in doing anything that would take him away from his son again. He wasn't trying to work with DeAndre. He wanted to get him out of all the shit he was into. However, he also knew that a late-night conversation in a strip club parking lot was not the place to lecture his cousin. Instead, he nodded and said, "Alright, man."

Phil and Tyler hung around for a few more minutes before leaving. Jabari leaned against the driver's side door, scrolling through social media on his phone while DeAndre continued to joke around with his friends.

"Aye, Dre... ain't that the little crew from the southside we had that problem with over at—"

ON EVERY THUG I LOVE

"Yeah. That's them," DeAndre said. He looked over at Jabari. "Unlock the doors."

"What?" Jabari asked, unsure of what was going on.

"Unlock the doors," DeAndre repeated.

Jabari pressed the key remote to unlock the doors, and DeAndre quickly opened the driver's door. He reached under his seat to grab a gun, worrying Jabari. One of DeAndre's friends pulled a gun from his waistband while the other moved to a nearby vehicle, apparently to grab his own weapon.

"Dre, you're drunk. What the hell are you doing right now?"

"Pull off, man," DeAndre answered without making eye contact with him.

"Bruh, it's a—"

"Pull. Off." DeAndre turned to look directly at him. "It's some business that needs to be handled, and you don't need to be here for it. Mama would kick my ass if I got you in the middle of some shit." Jabari hesitated. "Now, man! Shit!"

Jabari hopped into the truck and cranked the engine. He was starting to back out of the parking spot when he noticed that the group his brother was watching spotted him and his friends. He sighed heavily and put the truck back in park. DeAndre's gun was tucked behind his back when the group of five guys approached DeAndre and his two friends. His brother was outnumbered, and there was no way Jabari was going to leave him hanging like that—whether he was on probation or not. The confrontation between the two groups was escalating, catching the attention of the club's outside security officers. Jabari hopped out of the truck and jogged around the other side to catch one of the guys off guard with a right hook before he could pull the gun from his waist. The group started pushing and throwing punches while Jabari snatched DeAndre away from the group.

"Get your ass in the truck!" Jabari shouted. He opened the passenger's door and pushed DeAndre inside while the others continued to fight. DeAndre tried to get back out, but Jabari knocked him back into his seat. He rushed back around to the driver's side and backed out of the parking spot right as shots were fired.

Jabari sped out of the lot, headed for the nearest highway. He cut his eyes at DeAndre, glaring at him angrily before sailing through a yellow light right before it could turn red. He needed to get the hell away from the strip club as soon as possible.

"What's your problem, bruh?" DeAndre shouted.

Jabari shook his head, nostrils flaring in anger. "I know you not asking me no dumb ass shit like that!" he yelled. "What do you mean? What is my problem? You out here, getting caught up in some dumb ass shit while I'm around. Come on, man. For real?"

"You just left my boys hanging like that! What the fuck?"

Jabari ignored his brother the rest of the way back to the apartment. When he pulled into the lot, he shut off the engine and hopped out, only to be confronted by his brother rushing around the side to shove him in the chest. Jabari shoved DeAndre back, causing him to stumble and almost fall.

"You ain't about that life no more, then cool! But that's why I told your ass to pull off!" DeAndre shouted.

Jabari shook his head at him. "Pull off so Mama could get mad at me for leaving you in the middle of some shit? Nah, I ain't doing that. You think all that bullshit is cool but look what just happened back there! Y'all were outmanned and outgunned. You were about to land your ass in somebody's jail ... or even worse, the morgue," he said. "No, I'm not about that life anymore. Look how well that shit worked out for me. That fast money and street shit ain't worth it, bruh. My bad for ever making you think it was." DeAndre glared angrily turning to look away from Jabari. "It's late as hell, man. Bring your ass inside."

❧ 5 ❧

Melinda placed the phone on the speaker and set it on the counter while she continued to apply her makeup. "How are your parents?" she asked.

"They're good... asking about you of course," Dominic responded without bothering to hide the irritation from his voice. "Everybody's asking about you."

Melinda pulled her eyeliner away from her face, dropping her hands by her side while sighing heavily. "Babe, I told you that I couldn't afford to stay up there the extra day, and Kevin needs to be back in school on Monday," she said softly. The last thing she wanted to do was argue.

Dominic sighed as well without saying anything for a few moments. It was Thanksgiving Day, and he flew to his hometown, Memphis, TN, to spend a few days with his family. An invitation was extended for both Melinda and Kevin. However, she opted to stay in Atlanta for several reasons. She used time during the weeklong holiday break to catch up on overdue graded assignments and lesson planning. However, she also wanted Kevin to spend time with his father for the first holiday in years.

"You could have caught an earlier flight back, but whatever,

Mel. Keep coming up with excuses while I try to explain your absence to my folks."

Melinda rolled her eyes. "Dom, your mother is a retired educator. I'm sure she'll understand that I need to focus on my work. I told you about the conversation I had with my principal, and it's not like your parents aren't going to be here for Christmas."

"Yep. I'll talk to you later." Dominic's tone was short and dismissive.

"Dominic..."

Melinda was met with dial tone, and she shook her head and laughed in disbelief. She quickly finished her makeup and headed down the hallway to Kevin's room. She popped her head in the doorway to see him laying across the bed playing video games. "Put your shoes on and come on downstairs."

Kevin quickly shut off the game and did as he was told, joining Melinda in the garage. She pulled away from their house and started the drive over to Sonya's. Although she wasn't looking forward to the drama when Dominic returned, she was happy she chose to stay in town. Kevin was excited to spend time with his father and the rest of the Butlers, and that thrilled her. He was so young, only two years old, when Jabari went to prison, and Melinda often worried about what type of connection they would have once Jabari was released. She was pleased to see that the bond was strengthening between them, and Jabari had the chance to be the type of father she always knew he could be. The type of father he was showing that he wanted to be.

Melinda pulled up to Sonya's house a short while later and laughed to herself. What Jabari told her was accurate. After the Butlers visited Sonya's sister's home, they returned to her house to eat alone without any extended family. She parked next to DeAndre's truck and was shutting off her engine when the front door opened. She and Kevin climbed out of her truck while Symone walked onto the porch.

"Come on in, y'all. I just pulled the macaroni out of the oven, and Mama's carving the turkey," she said, waving them over.

Melinda walked alongside Kevin, stopping when they reached Symone. "Go on inside, baby. I'll be back to get you a little later."

"Bye, Mom!" Kevin said, taking off inside the house.

Symone tilted her head and gave Melinda a sideways glance, placing her hand on her hip. "Now, Mel... don't start with that shit today."

Melinda laughed. "I already told your brother I wasn't staying for dinner. I have some work to do."

"On Thanksgiving? Girl, please. Get your ass in this house before my mama cusses me out for letting you leave," Symone said, pulling her by the arm. "Even if you don't eat, at least say hey before you run off again."

Melinda didn't protest while Symone dragged her inside. She spotted Jabari a few feet away, hanging Kevin's coat in the closet. She hesitated briefly, admiring his appearance. Growing up as best friends, it took several years before Melinda saw Jabari in the light that allowed her to appreciate just how attractive he was. He was gorgeous—in a rough, masculine type of way. His hair was longer than she was used to, faded on the back and sides and sponge curled on the top, and he allowed his facial hair to grow into a neatly trimmed beard. A couple inches over the six-foot mark, he was noticeably taller than her with a cinnamon brown complexion. He had a smile that she was sure could still make her knees buckle if she stared in his face for too long. The cream-colored, fitted thermal T-shirt he wore highlighted the distinct muscles in his arms and chest—muscles he perfected over the last few years. The outfit was completed with dark jeans and a crisp pair of Timberland boots. While she reminded herself to take in a deep breath, she acknowledged that his rugged good looks literally took her breath away. Just standing in the same room with him stirred feelings in her that she wasn't comfortable with—feelings she knew Dominic would not appreciate his girlfriend feeling for another man.

After closing the closet door, Jabari turned around, laying eyes on Melinda. "Hey," he said as he walked over to her. Without hesitation, he pulled her into a hug, wrapping his big, strong arms around her shoulders. Melinda paused briefly, eventually hugging him back before he pulled away. "I know you said you're not staying, but come say hey to my mom before you head out."

"Uh, oh—okay sure."

While Jabari turned to lead the way to the kitchen, Melinda shook her head at herself for tripping over her words. She spoke to DeAndre when they passed him sitting on the couch, and he waved in her direction without making eye contact or verbally responding. She frowned at his dismissive greeting.

"Never mind him," Jabari said, shaking his head. "His issue is with me, not you."

They continued toward the kitchen, where Sonya was finishing up with the turkey. She set her utensils down and wiped her hands before pulling Melinda into a tight hug.

"I'm so glad you decided to join us," Sonya said. She pulled away and patted Melinda's cheek. "I was so happy when Jabari told me you and Kevin were coming for dinner."

"Oh, I'm not—I just dropped Kevin off for a few hours," Melinda responded. "I've got some work to do. I wasn't planning on staying for dinner."

"Nonsense," Sonya said, turning back toward the turkey. "You're not about to just run up out of here like that. I'll be personally offended if you don't stay and eat. Y'all go wash your hands and come on so we can make our plates."

Melinda turned toward Jabari, her eyes silently pleading for assistance. However, he had a mischievous look on his face that let her know he probably twisted the truth and told his mother she was joining them for dinner.

"Come on, Mel. You heard the lady," he said with a laugh. He motioned for her to lead the way. "I think you remember where the restroom is."

Melinda shook her head and laughed before turning on her heels and walking toward the half bath on the main floor. Soon, they were all seated at the table in the formal dining room enjoying the meal that Sonya and Symone prepared. DeAndre was moody and standoffish, but otherwise, Melinda enjoyed the company. When dinner was followed with sweet potato pie and a few glasses of red wine, she easily lost track of time. While Sonya and Symone retreated to the family room to watch TV, DeAndre took Kevin for a ride to look at houses in the area that already had their Christmas lights on display. Melinda and Jabari were left alone in the dining room. They spent several minutes discussing everything they could think of as far as Kevin was concerned.

"So... how's everything going with you?" she asked before taking another sip of wine and shifting the topic of conversation.

Jabari shrugged his shoulders and smiled. "Everything is good. I've been working with Alex. Making good money and trying to stay out of trouble."

Melinda laughed. "And how's that going for you?"

"Going well, but I ain't gon' lie. It would be real easy to fall back into some of my old habits and associations, especially staying with Dre," he answered, shaking his head when he mentioned his brother. "Luckily, I've got good motivation to keep it together and avoid temptation."

"Oh yeah? What's that?"

"My family," Jabari answered quickly. "Most importantly Kevin. I don't want to do anything to take me away from my family again."

Melinda and Jabari maintained eye contact while she nodded and raised her glass to her lips again. Something about his tone of voice and the look in his eye had her questioning if she was included when he referenced family. She swallowed her wine and broke their eye contact by glancing down at her watch. Before she could say anything else, her phone started to vibrate, indicating an incoming FaceTime call from Dominic. She frantically picked up the phone, eyes darting around for a private place to answer the call.

"Use Symone's old room down the hall," Jabari said, pointing in the direction of his sister's former bedroom. He frowned slightly, noticing the panic in Melinda's eyes when her phone started to ring.

"Thanks."

Melinda quickly pushed away from the table and sprinted toward the bedroom. Right as she closed the door, she missed the call. She sat down on the edge of the bed and called him back. He picked up immediately, and she forced a smile onto her face. Dominic sat behind the wheel of his rental car. "Hey. What are you up to?" she asked.

"About to stop by the liquor store and head over to my uncle's house," he responded evenly. He squinted, looking past Melinda at her surroundings. "Where are you?"

"I told you I was bringing Kevin to his grandmother's house today," she answered.

"Ah, yeah. Your prison ex's mother's house."

"Dominic, don't—"

"You said you were dropping him off and getting some work done. Did you end up staying for dinner?"

"Well... yeah. His mother wouldn't take no for an answer. I stayed to eat."

"Hmmm... gotcha," Dominic said evenly. "Whose bedroom are you in?"

Melinda frowned and shook her head. "I stepped into his sister's room to take your call."

"Any reason why you couldn't answer in front of Jabari?"

"No. I just wanted a little privacy. I didn't know that would be a problem," she answered. "Look, I don't know where you're going with all of this, but—"

"I'm just wondering why you lied to me."

"I didn't lie. Kevin and I will be leaving soon, and I'm still going to get more work done when I get back home. Jabari's mother pretty much insisted that I stay for dinner. That's it. No big deal," she explained. "Just food, conversation, and a couple of glasses of wine."

Dominic smirked. "It doesn't take much more than that to get you out of your clothes."

"Wow, Dom. Really?" Melinda questioned with a frown. "I brought my son to spend time with his family on a holiday, and you're twisting the situation into something that it's not."

"Yeah, okay. Make sure your ass is at home when I call you back," he said.

"Why would you—"

"Melinda, you heard what the fuck I said." Dominic cut her off in a firm tone. "Ain't shit else to talk about. Everything else will be dealt with when I get back."

"What is that supposed to mean?" Melinda asked the question, but she already knew the answer. Another argument. More marks and bruises.

"You heard what I said, Mel. Get your son and go home. If you're not there when I call you back, it's going to be a problem." Dominic ended the call.

Melinda sat on the edge of Symone's old bed with a dumbfounded look on her face. She couldn't catch a break when it came to him. It was one thing for their drama to interfere with her work performance, but she tried to leave Kevin out of their commotion. She didn't want to rush Kevin away from family just because Dominic was in a mood. After agreeing to stay for dinner, she planned to leave on her own time. For a brief moment, she contemplated calling him back but quickly changed her mind. Her thoughts were disturbed by a knock on the door.

"Yeah?" she called out.

The door opened, and Jabari stepped inside the room with a brooding look. He closed the door behind him. Trying to push her conversation with Dominic from her mind, Melinda stood up from the bed and forced another smile onto her face.

"What did he mean by that?" Jabari asked.

Melinda stared at him blankly, blinking her eyes a few times. "What did who mean by what? What are you talking about?"

"Don't play with me, Mel. When buddy said that everything else will be dealt with when he gets back." Jabari asked, "What is that supposed to mean? And why is he trying to rush you back home when he ain't even in town?"

Melinda's smile quickly dropped from her face and was replaced with a frown. "That's none of your business," she responded. "Were you listening to my conversation?"

"Nah. I was on my way back from using the bathroom, and I could hear his voice in the hall—loud as hell," Jabari answered. He paused for a brief moment, looking at Melinda and noticing how uncomfortable she was. "I guess whatever is going on in your relationship is none of my concern, but if there's something going on in that house that could potentially affect my son, then yeah... that is my business."

"Kevin is fine," she snapped. "Are he and DeAndre back yet?"

Jabari sighed and shook his head. "Yeah. Just got back."

"Then we will see you later," Melinda said, stepping around him to head for the door.

Jabari reached for her hand, stopping her. "Mel, I ain't trying to get all in your business, but I didn't like what I heard. I ain't trying to piss you off. I want to keep things cool between us," he said. "You ain't gotta rush out."

Melinda slowly pulled her hand away from his. "Everything is fine. We're cool. I just—I just need to get home," she said. "I didn't plan on staying in the first place. I still have—"

"Work to do?"

"Yeah."

It wasn't entirely a lie. However, her work wasn't the real reason she was leaving, and they both knew it. Jabari was concerned about what he interpreted to be implied threats from

Dominic, but he could tell that Melinda wasn't in a mental space to discuss it any further. As long as his son was good, he decided to let it go instead of pushing the issue. He waited years to get back to her. He didn't want to create any more issues than the ones they already had.

"Alright, Mel. Let me walk y'all out," he said, leaving the room and heading for the coat closet.

6

Jabari pulled up to his cousin's house and shut off the engine. As an early Christmas present to herself, Sonya purchased a new car and gave Jabari her Chevy Impala. He sat behind the wheel for a moment, pulling out his cell phone to dial Melinda's number. The phone rang several times before going to voicemail. Again. He had not been able to speak to her directly since she left his mother's house on Thanksgiving. The entire weekend passed without a word from her. He assumed that she would be out of her feelings once the weekend passed, but it was Monday evening, and he realized he was wrong. He sighed and shook his head, sticking the phone back in his pocket before he exited the car.

His cousin, Tyler, was celebrating his twenty-first birthday. All the cousins and some of their friends were gathered at Alex's house to pregame before they hit the club. Jabari wasn't planning on going out, but he wanted to hang with the guys before they did. He noticed his brother's truck parked on the street. Otherwise, he wouldn't have any clue he was there. Since the fight at the strip club, DeAndre was barely at the apartment. To the best of Jabari's knowledge, he was hopping from one to another chick's house just to avoid further confrontation. DeAndre let it be known that he viewed Jabari as a hypocrite in no position to lecture him about how he should live his life.

When Jabari reached the front door, he wasn't surprised to see that it was unlocked. There were a few people coming back and forth from outside. He let himself in to what looked like a full-blown house party—way more people than he anticipated. What was supposed to be a gathering of the cousins and a few friends was actually a much larger event that Jabari wasn't sure he was in the mood for. Either way, he forced himself to be social while he headed to kitchen. At the kitchen table, DeAndre, Alex, Phil, and Tyler were playing spades. After greeting them all, Jabari grabbed a beer and stood to the side while watching the game play out. When they were done, DeAndre got up to head into another room without ever acknowledging his brother. The others got up to refill their drinks.

"I see Dre still in his feelings," Alex said with a laugh.

Jabari laughed and shook his head. "Nigga called me the feds the other night when I asked him about a bag of money he brought in the house."

Alex and his brothers laughed.

"He'll be alright," Alex said, slapping Jabari's shoulder. "I think he just misses having you by his side. Even though it's only a year between you two, you know he's always looked up to you and sought your approval. He was probably wishing you would be back on that shit with him."

Jabari took a sip of his beer and shook his head. "He of all people should understand why I'm not," he said. "Can't go down that road again, man. Too much at stake."

"I hear you, and I'm proud of you," Alex said. At thirty, he was the oldest of the cousins. "Just make sure you keep your focus on the right things. Show Dre another way of living, and I'm sure he'll come around in time. The sooner he does, the sooner these brothers of mine can get their shit together."

"I don't know about that, big dog," Phil said with a laugh. He filled his cup with liquor and returned to the table. "The streets keep calling me. I'm addicted to the money, man. Ain't no way I can walk away."

Phil said it in a joking manner, but both Alex and Jabari knew he was telling the truth. Alex shook his head and headed into the other room, leaving Jabari alone with the younger guys.

Tyler made his way over to him after grabbing a beer from the fridge. "For real though, man," he said. "Dre's holding shit down and making big money right now. You know how that shit goes though... the more money he gets, the more hatin' ass, jealous niggas lurkin'... just look what happened outside the club the other day."

"Dre didn't go into details about that."

Tyler shook his head and sighed. "The hatin' ass niggas I was talking about. Long story short, they're mad because Dre's getting way more money than them," he said. "Look... I know this might not necessarily be what you want to do anymore. I know you're trying to lay low and stay out of trouble, but can't nobody watch Dre's back like his big bro. Phil and I do what we can, but you were his first protector."

"Yeah, man. I hear you," Jabari answered. He raised the bottle of beer up to his lips instead of saying anything else. He saw no point in continuing the conversation. Tyler and Phil obviously didn't give a shit about him being on probation or his desire to stay out of the streets for the sake of his son. He made a mistake by introducing DeAndre to the life he used to live, sending him down a path he wasn't sure he could pull him back from. He didn't want to do the same thing to Kevin. He had to lead by example.

Jabari and his siblings' father was killed in a carjacking when they were in high school. At the time of his father's death, Jabari just started messing around with drug dealing and other things he knew would never make his parents proud. After Kevin was born, Jabari put the street stuff behind him and was remorseful that this father never got to see the man he had potential to become. When he ended up in prison after the horrible fistfight gone wrong, he once again felt a level of disappointment and defeat at the thought that he let everyone—including his parents —down again. He was determined to do better, if for no other reason than to be around to ensure that Kevin didn't make the same mistakes that he did.

DeAndre came in the room minutes later, stretching his arms before he sat back down at the table. "Alright. Looks like Alex's girl just got here, so he's bailing on the next game." He looked at Jabari. "You trying to get in on this?"

Jabari looked around with sarcastic shock on his face. "You actually talking to me?" he asked with a laugh.

DeAndre rolled his eyes, laughing as well. "Get your lame ass over here so we can beat these fools."

"I might as well," Jabari said, taking the seat that Alex left vacant. "Let's gon' kick they ass real quick so I can head home."

DeAndre shuffled the cards, shaking his head. He looked at Tyler and Phil. "Your big cousin is an old ass man now. Nigga be sleep before I can even make it in the house most nights."

Tyler and Phil laughed.

"Bruh, I gotta be at work by seven."

DeAndre shrugged his shoulders. "I guess," he said with a laugh. "You ain't gon' get you no new bitch acting like an old ass man. Ol' 'I be in the bed my eight' ass nigga."

Tyler and Phil laughed even harder. Jabari shook his head at his brother but laughed as well. DeAndre still appeared to be in his feelings a little by what he perceived to be judgment from Jabari, but at least he was laughing and joking with him instead of giving him the silent treatment. They could never stay mad at each other that long anyway. The two were more than brothers. They were best friends.

"Dre, ain't nobody worried about no women right now," Jabari responded.

"Because you still hung up on Mel?" DeAndre asked while he started to deal the cards. Tyler and Phil both looked at Jabari, anticipating his response.

"No, man." Jabari wasn't even sure he believed his answer, but he didn't want to get into it that night. "Ain't nobody worried about Mel right now. I've barely been home a whole month, bruh. I'm just trying to focus on myself and my son."

"Good, because I was going to tell you to let that shit go with Mel. From what Symone's said, she ain't leaving that lawyer nigga no time soon."

Jabari shrugged his shoulders. "I said I ain't worried about her."

"Cool. Cool... so you open to someone else?" DeAndre asked without looking directly at his brother.

Jabari sighed heavily. DeAndre didn't always associate with the type of women that he would be interested in. No, he wasn't stuck on Melinda, but she had definitely set the bar. Whenever he decided he would be ready for a relationship, he knew it would be hard for anyone to follow behind her. However, he figured whoever occupied his time in the interim didn't have to necessarily check all the boxes on the list of what he thought made his ideal partner. "Someone like who, bruh?" he asked. "I've seen some of the women you've brought around."

"And they've all been tens!" DeAndre said loudly over the laughter of his cousins.

"Tell me anything."

DeAndre waved him off dismissively. "Whatever, man. Anyway... I asked because Bree is around here somewhere. She just asked me about you a moment ago."

"Bree?" Jabari asked.

"From the strip club. You know... the waitress chick."

"With the fat ass," Tyler and Phil said in unison before erupting into more laughter.

Jabari laughed and shook his head at his younger cousins. He looked down at his cards before looking up at DeAndre. Changing the subject back to their card game, he asked, "How many you got?"

An hour later, DeAndre and Jabari beat their cousins in

multiple games of spades, causing them to throw in the towel. Tyler was ready to keep the party going and eager to get to the strip club, Magic City. Jabari was ready to head to the apartment he and DeAndre were sharing downtown. He stood up from the table, covering his mouth while he yawned deeply.

"Alright, y'all. I'm out," he said, dapping up his brother and cousins. "Happy birthday, Ty. Don't go stupid, spending all your money in there."

"I ain't making no promises." Tyler laughed.

Jabari shook his head and started out of the kitchen. He said goodbye to a few other people on his way out of the house. He was unlocking the doors to the Impala when he heard someone calling his name.

"Hey... Jabari!"

He looked over his shoulder to see a short, attractive woman headed in his direction. She had on way more clothes than the first time he saw her. However, he recognized her face and definitely would have been able to notice her figure anywhere although their initial encounter was brief.

"Hey," she said again as she approached him. "I don't know if you remember me. I'm—"

"Bree. Yeah, I remember you," he said. "What's up?"

"Are you getting ready to leave? I know the guys are getting ready to head over to Magic City. Are you coming?"

"Nah. I got work in the morning. I'm headed home."

"Oh," Bree said, pausing to look down at her shoes. She looked back at Jabari before continuing. "I don't know if Dre told you, but he gave me your number."

Jabari shook his head and laughed. "Nah. He ain't tell me that... but that's what's up."

"Yeah?" Bree asked with a wide smile. "So it's cool if I call you or text you sometime?"

"Yeah, Bree. That's cool," Jabari answered. He couldn't ignore how much nicer she looked with minimal makeup and more casual clothes.

"Cool... well... have a good night, Jabari. I'll talk to you later."

"You too."

Bree looked down, smiling a little harder before she turned to walk away. Jabari shook his head and laughed again at DeAndre's actions. He watched Bree's backside until she disappeared into the house before he hopped in his car and pulled off.

❧ 7 ❧

Melinda placed the dishes in the dishwasher before turning back around to face Sasha, who was slipping into her coat.

"Thanks for having me over for dinner," Sasha said.

"You say that like I had a choice," Melinda responded with a playful roll of her eyes.

"You're right. I was definitely about to call Ms. Carla on you," Sasha said while wrapping her scarf around her neck.

"Jokes on you," Melinda said. "My mama and daddy don't get back from their cruise until tomorrow."

Sasha grabbed her purse, sliding it onto her shoulder. "Whatever. I know he's already asleep, but tell my godson I love him," she said. "How is daddy? I mean Kevin's daddy?"

Melinda laughed and shook her head at her best friend. Since she attended high school with them, Sasha was very familiar with Jabari and all the peaks and valleys of their relationship. She sighed heavily before responding. "Jabari is fine," she said evenly.

"Yeah, girl. Fine as hell," Sasha quickly retorted. "I saw a picture that Symone posted from Thanksgiving. I don't know how you walked away from all that deliciousness."

"You know what," Melinda said, laughing. She grabbed

Sasha's arm and started toward the front door. "I think it's time for you to go. Let me walk you out."

Melinda stopped laughing when she heard the sound of the garage opening. Sasha frowned at the look on her best friend's face and how she froze at Dominic's arrival home.

"You good?" Sasha asked with a concerned look.

Melinda nodded and quickly placed a smile on her face. "Yeah, girl. I'm good," she said while she continued walking toward the front door.

When the door opened to the garage, Melinda froze again while Sasha looked back toward Dominic as he entered the house with his luggage from his trip home.

"Hmmm, didn't expect to see you here. Nice to see you Sasha," he said.

"Dominic." Sasha kept her greeting brief and turned back toward Melinda. She gave her a hug. "Thanks for dinner, girl. Don't let it be so long before we link up again, okay?"

Melinda nodded in agreement while they pulled away from their hug. Dominic headed up the stairs without another word. After letting Sasha out, Melinda locked the doors, set the alarm, and climbed the stairs to their bedroom. When she entered, Dominic was standing near their dresser, removing his watch. She crossed the room, wrapping her arms around his waist. "Hey, baby. I'm glad you're home," she said, kissing him on the lips.

Dominic didn't respond or hug her back. He looked down at Melinda with slightly narrowed eyes until she pulled away from him, taking a step back. He put his watch in his watch box without any words.

Melinda sighed. She had hoped that he would get over his attitude from Thanksgiving Day before he arrived home. It was already late into the evening, and she had work in the morning. "What's wrong, Dom?"

He smirked in response and walked away from her, heading for their walk-in closet. Melinda shook her head before following him. She stood in the doorway, leaning against the frame, while she watched him start to undress. He hung up his coat and then started to undo the cufflinks on his button down.

"Are we doing this tonight?" she asked.

"Doing what?"

"This... this back-and-forth... arguing or not arguing... silent treatment for whatever reason."

"You know exactly what the problem is, Mel. I guess I should really be mad at myself for being so stupid. I should have seen this coming a mile away," he said, taking his shirt off and tossing it into a nearby hamper.

"Seen what, Dom?"

"You and your ex. I should have known that he would be a problem for us when he got out," he answered. "I guess I just forgot about your life before me. I thought you would have stepped your game up, but I suppose you still like that street shit... still have a thing for thugs, huh?"

Melinda shook her head and sighed. "Whatever you're thinking is wrong. I just had a holiday meal with my son's family. There was literally nothing more to it than that," she said. "And Jabari... I don't even really talk to him like that, but he's not on that shit anymore. If I thought he was, I—"

Dominic glared at her while he started to take off his belt. Interrupting her he asked, "You defending him to me now?"

Melinda raised her hands defensively. She was already over the conversation they were having. Dominic always knew that Jabari would be released from prison at some point. He should have known her well enough to know that she wasn't going to keep her son from his father. With Kevin only being six, he was depending on his parents to have a cordial relationship. "I'm not defending him, and I don't want to do this tonight," she said, turning to walk away. "I had a long day at work, and—"

Before she could finish her sentence, Dominic whipped his belt, lashing her across her neck and back.

"Ahh!" Melinda shrieked. Touching the stinging spot on her back, she quickly turned around to face him. "What the hell?"

"You not about to walk away from me while I'm talking to you." Dominic took a step toward her, and she subconsciously took a step back. He grabbed her arm and pulled her back to him.

Tension froze her body and fear caused tears to well in her eyes. She didn't bother opening her mouth to try to respond while Dominic tightened his grip on her arm and started another angry rant. She already knew how the night was going to end, and she was beginning to wonder how much more she could take. This wasn't the life she pictured for herself. Something had to give.

zzz

LACK OF SLEEP CAUSED AN UNSHAKEABLE STATE OF GROGGINESS for Melinda the next day. When the final bell rang, she could not contain the exasperated sigh she released. She couldn't even describe how happy she was for the day to be over. Her students surprisingly behaved themselves, and she was luckily able to facilitate her lessons without unnecessary interruption. However, she was exhausted—physically and mentally. The lack of sleep the previous night caused her physical fatigue, but the situation as a whole triggered a mental state that caused a level of discomfort that she could not shake. It was becoming hard to forgive Dominic for something he continued to do—over and over. The more she thought about it, she wasn't sure she wanted to anyway.

Her relationship with Dominic turned into something vile, nothing like it was in the beginning. She would have been better off sticking with one of the guys she dated before him. They were young and still in the streets, nowhere near ready to settle down. However, they never hit her. They never disrespected her and called her out of her name like Dominic did on more than one occasion. With him being five years older than her, Melinda believed Dominic when he said he was ready to settle down and build a future with her. It was what she wanted. However, their relationship was nothing like the example her parents set for her. Reality with him was nothing like the black love fairytale she dreamed of. Dominic's love was distressing and oppressive. It was the polar opposite type of the relationship she wanted to demonstrate for Kevin.

While she sat down at her desk to grade the pop quizzes before she left, she realized that she had to start working on an exit plan. Unfortunately, she knew it wouldn't be that easy to walk away from a man with such violent and unpredictable mood swings, but she had to find a way to do it. She heard the buzzing of her cell phone and reached into her bag to pull it out, seeing that she received a text from Jabari. She sighed and set the phone down without reading his message. She had not spoken to him since she left his mother's house a few days prior. She knew she would need to eventually, if for no other reason than to coordinate Jabari's next visit with Kevin. However, with everything going on with Dominic, Jabari was only clouding her mind. She realized while they were sitting at his mother's dining room table on Thanksgiving that she still had feelings for him. Feelings that surprised her after three years apart. Feelings that could prevent her from evaluating her current relationship clearly.

Instead of responding, she turned back to her papers and spent the next half hour finishing her grades. When she was done, she grabbed her things and headed for the exit. Before she could reach the front door, she could see clearly to the parking lot where her truck was parked near the front entrance. She noticed Dominic's car in the spot next to hers, and her body froze. The last thing she needed was any more drama at work.

"Ms. Barrett!"

Melinda turned to see her principal coming up the hallway with a parent. She turned and waved. "Hey, Ms. Jenkins."

"I'm glad I caught you before you left," she said with a smile. She waved goodbye to the parent who exited the building, leaving the two alone by the front door. "How was your Thanksgiving break?"

Melinda once again found herself forcing a smile onto her face. At least the smile on Ms. Jenkins' face appeared genuine and cheerful, which put her at ease. "It was fine. Can't complain about a few days to rest and catch up on TV," Melinda said evenly. "I was able to get caught up on some work as well."

Ms. Jenkins' smile widened, and she nodded in agreement. "I saw that. You entered all your grades ahead of the deadline. I just wanted to tell you that I noticed, and I appreciate your effort. I thank you for taking our conversation to heart."

"Of course," Melinda said, feeling her phone vibrate again. She tried to pull it out of her pocket and ended up dropping it on the floor. She and Ms. Jenkins bent down at the same time to reach for the phone. Although Melinda grabbed it first, the scarf around her neck slipped to the ground as well, which allowed Ms. Jenkins to see the bruises and welts on her neck from the belt involved altercation with Dominic the night before. Embarrassed, Melinda quickly shoved the phone back into her pocket, grabbed her scarf and placed it around her neck while she stood back up.

"Melinda... I hope I'm not crossing any lines, but are you okay?" Ms. Jenkins asked softly.

"Yes," she answered quickly with another fake and forced smile. "I'm fine. Everything is fine."

"But your neck... what hap—"

"Ms. Jenkins, really... it's fine. I'm fine," she said. "And if that's all, I really need to get going. I need to pick Kevin up from after school."

Ms. Jenkins nodded and motioned toward the door. "Of course. Have a good evening, Melinda."

"You too."

Melinda turned on her heels and left. Securing the scarf

around her neck tightly, she exited the building and crossed the parking lot to her vehicle. Spotting her, Dominic hopped out of his car with a bouquet of flowers. She froze with her hand on her driver's door handle.

"Hey, baby," Dominic said, approaching her quickly.

Melinda's eyes darted around the parking lot before resting on his face. "What are you doing here? I'm picking up Kevin and heading home."

"I know, but I won't be there," he said. Melinda raised her eyebrows, so he explained. "I have to head to the airport for work. I'll actually be headed that way after I leave here. I have to meet with a client in New York. I'll only be gone for a couple of days, but I wanted to catch you before I left."

Melinda looked down at the flowers in his hands, but she didn't reach for them. She was angry and annoyed. He always thought a kind gesture would be enough to make up for his unacceptable vicious behavior. She was over the repetitive cycle. She was tired of him thinking that a nice dinner, expensive gift, or a dozen red roses could serve as atonement for his poor conduct. She opened her mouth to respond but stopped when, out of the corner of her eye, she saw Rashad exiting the building. Without slowing down, he waved in her direction while crossing the parking lot. Melinda nodded and smiled faintly in acknowledgment.

Dominic looked over his shoulders, shaking his head when he spotted Rashad before turning back to face her. "Look, Mel... I don't really know what to say about last night."

"So don't say anything," she said, taking the flowers from his hands. "Thanks. Have a safe flight."

Dominic sighed. "Mel..."

She smiled weakly and kissed him on the cheek. "Call me when you land. I need to get Kev."

Dominic didn't say anything else, and she climbed into her truck. Without even looking in her rearview mirror, she pulled out of the parking spot, leaving him alone.

🜺 8 🜺

Amanda unbuckled the passenger's seat belt and leaned across to kiss DeAndre on the lips. "You sure you don't want to stay over here tonight?" she asked.

DeAndre kissed her back and then shook his head. "Nah, babe. I got some moves to make before I head home. I'm a little tired, and you and I both know that we won't be doing any sleeping if I go upstairs with you."

"You're right," Amanda said, grabbing the door handle. She opened the door and climbed out. "Alright. Call me later."

"I gotcha," he responded before she closed the door. He waited until she disappeared into her apartment building before he put the truck in drive.

DeAndre pulled away from the curb and exited the neighborhood. He checked his phone at a red light before deciding what his next move should be. He was torn between checking on business and going to see Nina—one of the other women he was seeing, but duty called. He hit the nearest highway and continued toward his destination. It was already kind of late, somewhere after midnight, so he decided to handle business and head home. He would get with Nina another day. Fifteen minutes later, he pulled up to the trap. He hopped out of the

68

truck and jogged up the steps to the front door of the house, letting himself inside the unlocked entrance.

"What's up, Dre!"

"Aye yo, Dre! What's good?"

He nodded and acknowledged a few of the guys while heading toward a back room. He tapped his knuckles on the closed door before cracking it open. He peeked inside to see Tyler and Phil before pushing the door all the way and entering the room. He closed the door and sat down on a stool in the corner, pulling a blunt and a lighter from his pocket. "Damn, y'all still in here working?" he asked. "I was sure I would have missed y'all."

Phil shook his head while he ran a stack of bills through a money counter. "Nah, man. Busy ass week. Profitable ass Saturday." He handed another stack to Tyler, who secured it with rubber bands.

DeAndre was always popular and well known throughout the neighborhood. His notoriety only increased as he continued to grow his presence in the streets. Regardless of how many friends or acquaintances he had, he knew there were just as many enemies and snakes hiding in the shadows and pretending to be cool with him. There were very few people he trusted outside of his brother and cousins. With Jabari and Alex choosing to steer clear of his illegal activities, DeAndre relied on Tyler and Phil more than anybody else. They were two of the very few people he would allow to handle the money without him standing over their shoulder. "I can see that," he said, raising the lit blunt to his lips. "Sorry to tie up y'all Saturday evening."

"You know I ain't complaining," Tyler responded. He was as young and money hungry as they came. "Bruh, you ain't never gon' hear me complain about getting to the money."

Phil and DeAndre laughed, but they knew he was telling the truth. If it wasn't about money, women, or his family, it didn't matter to Tyler. It was something the three shared in common.

"We're about finished here though, Dre," Phil announced.

"You ain't gotta stay if you got other moves to make... or women to see."

Laughter filled the room again, almost causing DeAndre to choke on a cloud of smoke. "For real though... I just dropped Amanda off before I came over here. Thought about sliding through to Nina's spot, but I'm a little tired, and she'll drain a nigga." The trio erupted into laughter again. "I'm probably just gon' head home after I finish this blunt."

"Damn, man. Can't even smoke in your own home," Tyler mumbled, shaking his head.

DeAndre shrugged his shoulders. "I can. I'm just trying to keep all this shit away from my brother, man. He ain't with nothin' I got goin' on right now, and you know he can't fail no drug tests. Bruh just got back. My mama gon' kick my ass if I'm the reason he ends up back behind bars." He pulled on the blunt again. "Which is why I'm not even stressin' him 'bout this shit. He don't want to be involved in it, then cool. I prefer it that way. I just want him to let me live."

Phil nodded. "I hear you, man. Alex is on the same shit. I don't know... maybe in a couple of years, I won't want to do this anymore either," he said. "But for now... I'm just trying to get to the bag."

"Indeed," DeAndre said. He asked his cousins a few more questions about the business of the day while he finished his blunt. When he was done, he hopped off the stool, slapped hands with the duo, and headed out to his truck.

He had a couple of missed calls and text messages all from various women. He ignored them all as he pulled away from the trap and started the drive home. As he approached a red light not too far away, the dinging indicator inside his truck reminded him that he needed gas. He figured he could probably make it home but didn't want to take any chances. The last thing he wanted was to be stranded at almost one o'clock in the morning. He sighed heavily and shook his head, changing his direction to head to the nearest gas station. He turned into a well-lit popular chain gas station and pulled up to a pump.

Before he could shut off his engine, a blacked-out sedan with tinted windows navigated its way right in front of him, even though all the other pumps were available. DeAndre wasn't usually paranoid, but he paid close attention to his surroundings. It was necessary given what he did for a living. He sat behind his wheel for a few more moments, discreetly watching the vehicle in front of him. The engine was still running, and there had been no movement from whoever sat inside. Although it didn't appear too out of the ordinary, he still had an uneasy feeling about it. Even though he had a gut feeling to crank the engine and get his gas somewhere else, he didn't. After a few more moments, he made sure his gun was secured in his waist band when he exited the truck. Instead of looking over his shoulder at the idled vehicle, he used the reflective domes that served as mirrors to watch the vehicle on his way inside to pay. Still, no movement.

DeAndre stepped inside of the store, taking his time to browse the aisles of snacks and continue to watch the car sitting in front of his. After grabbing a couple bags of chips and a few White Owls, he made his way to the register to pay. The cashier bagged his items and handed him his change, but he was barely paying attention to anything that was said. His attention was still directed outside. DeAndre shoved the money back into his pocket and headed back to his truck. He tossed his bag onto the passenger's seat and discreetly removed the safety off the pistol in his waistband. He still wasn't sure what was going on with the motionless car, but there was one thing he knew for sure. He had yet to get caught slipping, and he wasn't about to let it happen in that moment either. He moved over to the gas pump and started to fuel his truck. When he was finished, he walked around the back of the truck to reach the driver's door—eager to head home. The moment he grabbed the handle, the front doors on both sides of the sedan opened in front of him.

"Aye yo, Dre..."

DeAndre looked up to see the two guns pointed in his direction and was oddly not surprised. Because his gut was telling him something was off, he was able to pull his piece in time to return fire as the shooting began. Ducking behind the door allowed him to miss a couple of the rounds fired in his direction after he let off a few shots. When he popped back up, he was able to fire at the driver, striking him in the arm, before turning his attention to the passenger. With his peripheral vision, he could see the driver clutching his wounded arm while climbing back into the car. The driver shouted for the passenger to get inside, but he kept firing at DeAndre instead.

Pow! Pow! Pow!

DeAndre continued to squeeze his trigger, sending bullets in the passenger's direction until he struck him in the shoulder and then the neck. The passenger's body instantly dropped to the pavement. DeAndre shook his head at the sound of sirens in the distance and lowered his weapon by his side. He heard the driver shout a four-letter word, followed by the sound of screeching tires while the car peeled out of the parking lot, leaving the wounded accomplice on the ground. He closed and leaned against the door of his truck and set his gun on the hood. Sighing heavily, he waited for the cops to arrive. Luckily, the truck and his gun were clean. Whatever the cause for the shootout was still to be determined. However, he knew that the cashier and the security footage would confirm that his involvement was self-defense. Although he was pretty sure he would avoid arrest, he still knew he had to go to the station for questioning. He silently cursed to himself wishing he would have just gone home.

zzz

ALTHOUGH THE SUN WAS SHINING BLINDINGLY, IT WAS STILL cold outside—much colder than DeAndre expected even though it was early December. He zipped his coat up and looked at the time on his phone—8:12 a.m.—and he had yet to go to sleep. He was sure his tired eyes were bloodshot, but he perked right up when he saw his brother's car pull into the parking lot of the police precinct. Jabari rolled up to the curb and unlocked the doors, allowing him to slide into the passenger's seat.

He closed the door and looked over his shoulder to the back seat where a way-too-energetic Kevin sat, playing on his tablet. "What's up, Kevin?" he greeted him while he fastened his seat belt.

"Hey, Uncle Dre." He looked up at him with a smile before turning his attention back to the electronic device in his lap.

DeAndre settled into his seat while Jabari drove away from the precinct.

"Do I need to take you to your car?"

DeAndre shook his head. "Nah. It got towed. I'll handle that later. I really just want to head home so I can get some sleep." He paused to look at his brother, who barely looked in his direction since he got in the car. "Bruh, I appreciate you coming to pick me up. It was—"

"It's no problem. Seriously."

DeAndre shifted and continued to look at Jabari, whose gaze was focused on the road ahead. He yawned and covered his mouth. "Bro, I—"

Jabari turned to glance at him and shook his head. He nodded toward the back seat where Kevin sat. "Not right now, Dre. We can talk about it later."

DeAndre nodded in acknowledgment, and they continued the ride in relative silence. When they reached the apartment, Jabari led them inside.

"Kev, why don't you go hang out in the room for a little bit while I make breakfast? I'll call you when it's ready."

Kevin nodded and raced toward DeAndre's third bedroom. Jabari didn't know what his single brother needed with a three-bedroom apartment, but he appreciated the space that allowed everyone to have their own room, especially when he had Kevin. After he was sure Kevin was in his room, Jabari sighed heavily and ran his hands over his face. He shook his head and then headed for the pantry and refrigerator, where he started to grab things for a quick, hot breakfast.

"Alright, man. What happened?"

DeAndre slid onto a stool at the breakfast bar and started to relay the events of previous night. By the time Jabari finished toast, eggs, and bacon, DeAndre finished explaining everything. He even added how he didn't recognize the deceased shooter until later, but then realized that he was a part of the crew he and his team had existing issues with. He was one of the guys they fought outside of the strip club. When he was done, he expected a lecture or reprimand from his older brother. However, that wasn't the reaction he received at all.

"That's wild, man," Jabari said shrugging his shoulders. He grabbed a couple of plates. "Hopefully it's all over now. I mean... from what you've said, they don't necessarily seem like the type to let the shooting death of their partner ride, but who knows? Maybe they'll fall back now that they realize what they're running up against."

DeAndre hesitated but then asked, "That's it? That's all you have to say?"

Jabari shrugged his shoulders. "What do you want me to say, man? There's nothing I can tell you that you don't already know. I've told you about this shit already, Dre, but you want to be big man on the block. You should know what comes with the territory. There's no point in me saying the same shit over and over and creating unnecessary tension between us, especially while I'm still living here," he said. "Look, I'm happy last night ended the way it did because things could have gone in an entirely different direction. You already know the alternatives, Dre... and you know where the story ends for most people in your shoes, bruh. Prison or the morgue, man. Prison or the morgue."

He patted DeAndre on the shoulder and went to go grab Kevin, leaving his brother alone with his own thoughts.

9

"You don't have to drive all the way over here if you don't want to," Melinda said. "I can come pick him up. You sound tired."

"I am," Jabari mumbled while he held his phone up to his ear, "but it's not a problem. I might stop by my mom's house."

"You sure?"

"Positive. We'll be over there in the next half hour or so."

After ending the call, Jabari headed to get Kevin ready. He could hear DeAndre snoring on the other side of the apartment and decided against letting him know that he would be out for a while. He led his son down to the car, where they hopped in, and he started the drive to Melinda's house. He inadvertently sighed heavily when he thought about his ex. He stressed to his brother and cousins that he was over her and not trying to win her back. He even entertained Bree—trading texts and calls before meeting up for dinner the other night. However, the more he talked to Bree, the more he discovered that she didn't hold a candle to Melinda. She was cool to talk to, but there was no way she could fill Melinda's shoes. He honestly wasn't interested in anything other than a casual friendship with her.

While he started toward the highway, he slightly cursed to himself for letting Melinda get away so easily, especially with how much they meant to each other at one point. Time and dedication cemented their bond, but nothing made him feel closer to Melinda than when she gave birth to their son.

He was scared out of his mind when Melinda told him she was pregnant and even more so when she went into labor. From his time in the streets, he had seen and done things men twice his age never experienced. Even though he was only twenty years old, there were very few things that could make him nervous or put fear in his heart. But it was something about becoming a father...

Something about knowing that there was innocent life that he created that was dependent on him shook him at his core and changed everything he ever thought he knew. The life that he was living—selling drugs and making fast money—no longer appealed to him. The moment Melinda gave that final push that brought their son into the world, he knew there had to be a better way. A more honorable way. A safer way. A way that would be in the best interest of the two people his heart beat for—his woman and his son. The second he heard Kevin's first cry, he knew that his entire way of living needed to change because he couldn't stand to jeopardize the family unit that they built. He couldn't imagine doing anything that would take him away from the two people he loved the most.

Even when he and Melinda were just friends, he knew he loved her. In the beginning, they shared a platonic bond where everyone knew they were the best of friends. Although they were polar opposites, all of her differences only drew Jabari even closer to her. Over time, Melinda went from the friend that he told his deepest secrets, a friend that knew him even better than his closest homeboys, to a woman he never wanted to live without. He felt like she was his literal other half and that he could not exist without her. The transition in their relationship from friends to lovers surprised them both, even though those around them claimed to see it coming from a mile away. Melinda Lynae Barrett changed his entire world, and he just wanted to spend his life making hers better.

With takeout from her favorite family-owned Italian restaurant in hand, he headed down the hallway of the maternity ward at Northside Hospital. When he reached Melinda's room, he slowly and quietly pushed the door open to see her sitting on the edge of the hospital bed while she rocked their newborn son to sleep. She smiled in his direction when she looked over her shoulder to see him entering the room. She held a finger up to her lips, causing him to move around quietly as he approached them.

"He's almost down," she whispered. A few seconds later, Kevin's eyes opened slowly until he was starting at Melinda with wide eyes, causing her to laugh. "Dang it."

Jabari laughed and set the bag of food on the hospital bed next to her. He sanitized his hands and reached for the baby. "Let's switch."

Melinda smiled and handed the newborn to him. She quickly untied the bag of takeout. "Did you get the—"

"Meat lasagna entrée with a large Caesar salad."

Melinda's eyes lit up. "With an—"

"Extra side of garlic knots. Yeah, baby. I got it."

Jabari stood by Melinda's bedside, rocking his son while he watched her pick up the fork and dig into the lasagna. After placing a large piece into her mouth, she closed her eyes with a look of bliss on her face while she chewed. She swallowed the initial bite and then opened her eyes, looking up at him.

"Thank you, baby. You always take such good care of me."

The right side of his mouth curled up into a half smile while he looked at her with admiration in his eyes. "I'm always gon' take care of you, Mel. Both of you."

A broad smile spread across Melinda's face, highlighting the deep dimples in both cheeks while she looked at Kevin and then back up at Jabari. "I love you."

Jabari bent down and kissed Melinda's lips. His heart was so full. He didn't always feel worthy of Melinda and her selfless, unconditional love, but he wanted to work hard to prove he could be just as good for her as she was for him. "You already know what's up, Mel. I love you too. I'm *gon' always love you. Ain't nothin' ever gon' come between us. It's you and me forever. From this life to the next."*

"And even after that," she added with a heart-warming smile.

Jabari glanced in the rearview mirror at Kevin, whose eyes were glued to his tablet. "Hey, Kev..."

"Yeah, Dad. What's up?"

Jabari sighed. He didn't want to involve Kevin in adult situations, but there was a question in his mind. He felt uneasy about Melinda and Dominic's relationship since he overheard part of their conversation on Thanksgiving. Melinda seemed very tight-lipped during their exchange, and that left him with questions. Questions he didn't necessarily want to ask a six-year-old. However, his main concern was his son and the home environment that he and his mother were in.

"How you like Dominic?" Jabari asked. He glanced back in the rearview mirror to see Kevin shrug his shoulders.

"He's fine. I guess."

"You guess, huh? Is he nice to you?"

"Yeah. Most of the time," Kevin answered. "He got me this iPad."

Jabari nodded. "I see. Does he buy you a lot of stuff?"

"Uh huh. Me and Mommy. He buys her a lot of stuff."

Jabari shook his head and laughed quietly at Kevin relating material possessions to how well Dominic treated them. "So... he's nice to mommy too?"

Kevin hesitated and briefly looked up. "Not all the time."

Jabari's eyebrows knitted into a frown. "What do you mean by that? Sometimes he's mean to mommy?"

Kevin hesitated again, pausing to look out of the window. He shook his head and looked back down at his lap, causing Jabari's frown to deepen.

"Aye, Kev... is Dominic mean to your mom?"

Kevin shrugged his shoulders. "Sometimes, but I don't think I'm supposed to say anything. I don't think I'm supposed to know."

"Why don't you think you're not supposed to know?"

Kevin shrugged his shoulders again. "I don't know. He just... he's only mean to mommy when he thinks I'm sleep or can't hear him."

"What do you hear?"

"I don't know. He just gets mad and yells at her sometimes and says bad words to her."

"Alright, man. I'll talk to mommy about that."

Jabari's nostrils flared while he silently shook his head slowly. He could sense that there was more going on that Kevin either wasn't aware of or was uncomfortable sharing. He saw the way Melinda reacted when Dominic called her on FaceTime out of the blue. He saw how defensive she was when he asked her questions. Although he was relieved to hear that Dominic's issues weren't directed toward his son, he wasn't okay knowing what Melinda was dealing with behind closed doors. She was one of the best women he knew, and she deserved better—whether or not they ever got back together.

Listening to his music and lost in his thoughts, Jabari continued his drive in relative silence. A short while later, he pulled into the suburban neighborhood that housed the large, single family home where Dominic, Melinda, and Kevin resided. He navigated the streets until he was pulling into the driveway. He shut off the engine and hopped out of the car, moving to open the back door. While Kevin hopped out with his tablet, Jabari laughed, shaking his head, and grabbed the overnight bag his son left behind. They were crossing the front lawn when the front door opened, and Melinda came out to greet them.

"Hey," she said with a bright smile.

Jabari locked eyes with her and couldn't deny the feelings he still had. Feelings he wanted to deny and let go when he thought she was in a loving, happy relationship. "Hey."

"Hey, Mommy," Kevin said, hugging her waist.

Melinda hugged him back and then looked back to Jabari.

"Thanks again for bringing him, but I can pick him up next time. You shouldn't have to do all the driving, and I can get to see where you all are staying," she said.

"Yeah, sure. No problem," Jabari responded. After a brief hesitation, he asked, "You got a moment for me to talk to you about something real quick?"

Melinda maintained her smile, but her forehead wrinkled slightly while she looked at him inquisitively. "Yeah," she answered. "Kev, go on in the house for me. I'll be inside soon."

"Bye, Dad!" Kevin gave Jabari a quick hug before disappearing into the house.

Melinda folded her hands in front of her, interlocking her fingers and looking at Jabari expectantly. He noticed a faint bruise on the side of her neck and felt his anger rising. He took a deep breath to temper his emotions. His anger was always one of his worst flaws. His anger led to the fight years ago that cost him his freedom and ultimately his relationship. He wanted to question her about the things Kevin shared with her, but he didn't want to push her any further away by questioning her decision-making. Even though he never could have imagined that Melinda would be the type to put up with a potentially abusive relationship, his intent was to only focus on Kevin's well-being and how he may be affected by Dominic's actions.

"What's going on?"

Melinda's soft voice interrupted the thoughts in his head before he had the opportunity to fully gather them. "Mel, I originally wanted to follow up to our conversation about Dominic," he said.

Melinda shook her head and raised her hands defensively. "Jabari, please let it go. Now is really not a good time to get into that again."

"I'm not trying to upset you, and we don't need to rehash the details of your conversation. We both know the way he spoke to you and the things that he said," he responded. "At the end of the day, you're a grown woman who is fully capable of making her own decisions. I just couldn't get our exchange out of my head, and I kept asking myself why I was so bothered by it." He sighed heavily. "I know I told you that my only concern was Kevin and the environment that he was in, and—"

"I told you that he's fine," Melinda said abruptly.

"Mel, I trust that you wouldn't purposely put him in harm's way, but if I'm being totally honest... I have to admit that Kevin isn't my only concern."

Melinda's eyebrows raised sharply.

"I care about you too, Mel. Having unsettling thoughts about the situation you might be in concerns me as well, because of how I feel about you," he said. "And I know—"

"Jabari..." She sighed.

"Let me finish, Mel. I know that I was the one that ended things between us, and I did that because I wanted you to be happy. Not because I didn't love you anymore. I never stopped loving you. I just wanted you to be happy," he said. "And I thought you were. When Symone told me about Dominic and how serious things were... or are... whatever... When she told me you and Kev moved in with him, I had no intentions to share how I truly felt... how I still feel. I told you once before that I was always gon' love you, and I meant that. You've been the best part of my life for the majority of my life. I still mean everything I said, but I just wanted you to be happy. If you can honestly say that you're happy in your situation, then forget everything I just said, and live your life. You deserve that, but Mel... if there's more to the story and things ain't all they're cracked up to be, I'm here. I'm right here. I know I've only been home for a short while, but I'm focused on keeping my shit together so nothing takes me away again. I know I tried before, and I ended up failing you and Kevin... but I'm not gon' let that happen again, Mel." He paused again. "If you're happy and you want me to drop it, just let me know. I'll leave it alone. I promise I will... but if you're not happy Mel, just say the word. We can figure everything else out together."

Instead of responding right away, Melinda looked down at her hands for a brief moment before looking up at him with watery eyes. "Jabari, I—"

The front door opened again, interrupting them. Jabari looked up in confusion when he saw Dominic headed in their direction with a smile faker than a three-dollar bill.

"I thought he was out of town," Jabari said quiet enough for only Melinda to hear.

"He was supposed to be. Got back this morning unexpectedly," she responded, sniffling while she quickly wiped at her eyes. She dried her tears right as Dominic approached her side and wrapped an arm around her shoulders while he stared directly at Jabari.

"I saw Kevin got home and figured I might be able to catch you out here and have an opportunity to finally meet you," he said in a friendly tone. He extended his hand. "Nice to meet you. I'm Dominic."

Jabari noticed the way Melinda's body instantly tensed up when Dominic approached her. He fought the urge to smirk at Dominic's extended hand. Instead of displaying his contempt, he checked his attitude and shook his hand, even though he really wanted to hit him with a right cross. Especially since he had the feeling that Dominic was responsible for the mark on Melinda's neck. "Jabari. Nice to put a face with a name," he said. He didn't want to lie and say it was nice to meet Dominic when it wasn't.

"Yeah. Likewise," Dominic said with his arm still firmly secured around Melinda's shoulders. "You know... we were just talking about Christmas, and I've got an idea. Why don't you join us?"

Melinda's head whipped in Dominic's direction. "Wh-What? Huh? I don't think... Jabari probably has plans. I don't think he wants to spend the day with us."

"Why don't you let him answer? Besides, he can spend the

day with his son and have some of your home cooking," Dominic said, squeezing her shoulders. "Who could say no to that? It'll give us an opportunity to talk more as well."

Jabari cut his eyes at Melinda and actually did smirk this time before looking back at Dominic. "A day spent with my son and some of Mel's specialties? You're right. Who could say no to that?"

❦ 10 ❦

While sounds of laughter and conversation filled the living area of her home, Melinda busied herself in the kitchen. She pulled a large pan of baked mac and cheese out of the oven and set it on the counter nearby. She set the potholders down and smiled at the bubbling casserole dish with perfectly browned edges. Her grumbling stomach quickly reminded her that she had not eaten all day. Looking down at her watch, she noticed that it was nearing time for everyone to eat. They were only waiting on one person—Jabari. A part of her wondered if he still planned to attend Christmas dinner at her house.

After Dominic interrupted the conversation where Jabari made his feelings clear, Melinda spoke to her ex without ever addressing his comments. The one time he brought it up in a later conversation, she quickly told him that she wasn't ready to discuss it, and he dropped the subject without another word. She pulled her phone from the front pocket of her apron to see if she had any notifications from Jabari and was a little disappointed to discover that there were none. Her concern was that he believed she did not feel the same way she did, but that couldn't have been further from the truth. There was a part of her that was relieved and excited to hear that Jabari still cared for her so deeply even after all their time apart. However, the other part of her, the part that dealt with the reality of her relationship with Dominic, was uneasy about what the future held.

The reason she told Jabari she wasn't ready to discuss their feelings for each other was entirely because she still needed to figure out how to sever her ties to Dominic. There were a number of things to consider. She would have to disrupt Kevin's homelife and find a new place to live. She would need to find a new car. Most importantly, she would have to deal with Dominic's rage when she stated her intent to leave the relationship. Although she feared his reaction, she couldn't share that with Jabari. She needed to find a way out of the situation on her own. In her mind, she knew that he would be back on his way to prison if he ever knew for sure that Dominic was putting his hands on her. That was the last thing she wanted.

Melinda stuck her phone back into her apron pocket and checked on the pot of greens on the stove. Both her mother and Dominic's mother offered to help her cook, but she preferred to prepare the meal by herself so she could be alone with her thoughts. After stirring the greens, she turned the heat down on the stove and took her apron off. Although she was a little disappointed that Jabari had not arrived, she was ready to set dinner out for everyone else. Before she could leave the kitchen, the doorbell rang. Moments later, she heard Kevin greeting his father and released a sigh of relief. She tried to tell herself she was relieved that Jabari showed up for the sake of sparing Kevin from disappointment. However, that wasn't the entire truth. Deep down, she knew she wanted him there as well. When she heard footsteps headed in her direction, she ran her fingers through her hair to fix her appearance before Jabari joined her in the kitchen.

"Hey." His tone was even with a look that was uneasy to read.

"Hey... I was just about to call everyone to the table," she said. "I wasn't sure you were going to make it."

Jabari smirked. "I wasn't sure I was going to make it either. I was actually at my mother's house, and she told me to bring my ass over here or she would drag me here herself," he said, shaking his head and laughing at Sonya's directive. "I figured I needed to honor my word if for no other reason than to spare my son any disappointment. I told him I would be here, so here I am."

Melinda nodded and smiled. "Well, I'm sure he's glad you're here. I am too. I—"

"Yeah. Where do you want these?" Jabari interrupted her while he held up two bottles of wine. "I'm already late. I didn't want to be empty-handed too."

"Oh... I appreciate it. Thank you," she said, taking the bottles from his hands. She placed them in the refrigerator before turning back toward him. "Jabari, I know today is not ideal, but I do want to finish our conversation. Sometime soon."

Jabari shrugged his shoulders. "You're right. It's not an ideal time, and we don't need to get into all of that. You said it's time to eat, right?"

Melinda hesitated but nodded slowly. "Yes. Yes, it is."

"Bet," was all he said before he turned and left the kitchen.

Melinda paused for a moment before asking her and Dominic's mothers to help her finish setting the table and carry the food into the formal dining room. With both sets of parents, as well as Jabari and Kevin in attendance, they filled every chair at the large, cherrywood table. While everyone engaged in genuine, lighthearted conversation, Melinda sat quietly, picking at her plate. She occasionally glanced in Jabari's direction, where he sat at the opposite end of the table laughing and talking with Kevin. He never made eye contact with her. Although she was happy he showed up for their son, his presence at the table made her uncomfortable. There were so many things she wanted to say to him to ease the tension, but it wasn't the right time or place.

While the men at the table engaged in an intense sports debate, Dominic looked down at Melinda's plate to see she had barely eaten any food. He rubbed her thigh under the table and asked, "Are you okay?" Melinda nodded. "You've barely eaten any food."

She smiled weakly and shrugged her shoulders. "I probably did a little too much taste testing in the kitchen," she said with a short laugh. "I'm good."

Dominic looked unconvinced but kissed her on the cheek and turned back to the sports conversation at hand. After everyone finished their meal and dessert, they retreated to the family room to turn on the Christmas Day pro-basketball games and open the last remaining presents of the day. Jabari brought a couple for Kevin, and Melinda had a few for her parents. She sat on the edge of a sofa, watching her loved ones open their gifts. She was completely oblivious to Dominic leaving the room until he returned moments later, standing in the arched opening to the room and clearing his throat. Melinda and most everyone else turned in his direction, while her father grabbed the remote and turned the volume down on the television.

"Christmas is arguably my favorite holiday, and I am so glad that we could all be here together to share a meal and enjoy the day," he said. "I'm grateful to my parents for agreeing to be here today from Memphis as I hope there are more things to celebrate than the actual holiday itself."

Melinda looked on in confusion as he approached her and reached for her hand. He pulled her up to her feet and to the center of the room where all eyes were on them.

Looking directly into her eyes, Dominic continued to speak, "I can't think of a better time to say what I have to say than here on our favorite holiday in front of our family," he said. "Melinda, I love you so much. Words would never be able to do justice..."

Oh no, Melinda thought while she listened to the rest of Dominic's speech. With each word that came out of his mouth, her heart sank further into the pit of her stomach. She looked on in disbelief of his actions. This wasn't anything he discussed in recent months. She could not understand what about the last several months would make him think this was okay. She knew what was happening before he reached into his pants pocket and pulled out the small velvet box. She just had no idea why he would pick that moment to do it.

"Melinda Lynae Barrett, will you make me the happiest man on earth by agreeing to be my wife?"

Her voice was caught in her throat while she stared down at the Tiffany blue box and the breathtaking solitaire engagement ring. The ring was gorgeous, but in that moment, all she could think about was Jabari. Standing with her back toward the couch he sat on, she could not see his face. However, she easily pictured a similar look of shock displayed on his own face. She felt trapped between a rock and a hard place. There was no way she could happily accept his proposal. Not with the way he knocked her around their home the last several months, and especially not in front of Jabari. However, she also did not feel that she could say no. Not when he made a point to ask in a room full of their family members. She knew there would be hell to pay if she embarrassed him in front of his parents.

It was in that moment that she realized Dominic crafted the entire scenario on purpose. He was a master manipulator who flawlessly created the situation knowing that she would feel unjustly pressured to accept his proposal while Jabari was there to witness it. That was the entire reason he extended the invitation for Jabari to join them for Christmas. Not because he was interested in getting along with the father of his potential stepson. No, that wasn't why Dominic invited him at all. He wanted to rub it in his face that he had the woman he left behind, and he intended to keep her. Frustrated tears sprang to Melinda's eyes as the weight of the impossible situation gripped her chest in fear.

Wishing she could disappear, Melinda did the only thing that would prevent another one-sided fistfight. She nodded slowly and said the word "yes" barely above a whisper. She could hear the excitement of their parents while Dominic smiled broadly. He pulled the ring out of the box and slipped it onto her finger.

After standing up, he kissed her on her lips and pulled her into a tight hug, spinning her around. Reluctantly wrapping her arms around his neck, Melinda was staring right into Jabari's face, causing her eyes to water even more. While everyone in the room incorrectly assumed they were tears of joy, she and Jabari knew otherwise. He shook his head slightly before leaning down to whisper something in Kevin's ear. With a smile on his face, Kevin quickly hopped up and rushed toward the stairs, presumably headed to his bedroom. Dominic placed Melinda back on her feet, and their parents approached them with congratulatory well wishes.

A few moments later, Kevin came back down the stairs with his coat on and a football in his hands. While he rushed toward the door, Jabari slipped on his coat and approached Melinda when Dominic retreated to the kitchen to grab a bottle of champagne.

"Congratulations, Mel," he said. "If it's alright with you, I'm going to toss the ball around with Kevin in the front yard before I leave."

Melinda nodded in response. "Yes. Of course, that's fine," she said. She took in a sharp breath and shook her head when she looked down at the ring on her left hand. She looked back up at him. "Jabari, I—"

"Nah... don't," he said, shaking his head. "You ain't gotta explain anything to me. You know I just want you to be happy. If you're really happy, that's all that matters. Best wishes, Mel."

Jabari ended the conversation and met Kevin at the front door. When Dominic returned with the champagne and glasses, she wiped her tears and plastered a smile onto her face. In what should have been one of the happiest moments of her life, she actually felt like she was dying inside. This wasn't any type of way to live at all.

❧ 11 ❧

"Come on, man. Let's go!" DeAndre shouted to his crew while he watched the men work. He sighed heavily and looked at his watch. "I'm trying to get in and out."

Jabari's assumption was correct. The morning he picked DeAndre up from the police station, he told him from what he heard and knew the rival crew would not turn a blind eye to the shooting death of one of their own—whether they were the aggressors or not. Instead of things ending that night with the fatal shooting at the gas station, their conflict continued to escalate over the course of the following weeks. As a result of the ongoing struggle, there were more shootings with bodies dropping on both sides. DeAndre did not like the increased police presence that a street war could bring to the area.

After an incorrect anonymous tip to law enforcement caused a raid on another house in the area, DeAndre knew he needed to move one of his stash houses. If the police returned to the neighborhood with corrected information and the right address, he knew he would be in a bad position. He had no choice but to move accordingly and switch locations. He watched the two men in front of him continue to work as they packed up on-hand product. Leaving them alone, he headed toward the front room. The lights were dimmed while Phil stuffed money into a couple of duffel bags and Tyler stood near a window, peeking through the blinds.

"Aye yo, Dre," Tyler called to get his attention. "I got my eye on something. I could be nothin', but I got a feeling about it."

DeAndre blew a frustrated breath. With the events of the last few weeks, the last thing he wanted was anymore problems, especially in the middle of trying to handle business. "What's going on?" he asked, approaching his younger cousin.

"Look at that car right there... two houses back," Tyler said. "Pulled up a few minutes ago. Ain't made a move. Just sitting and probably watching. Ray hit me about it a moment ago. He's got an eye on it."

Ray was one of the men DeAndre had sitting in a vehicle outside the house, watching the street.

"Can't really see inside, but you know how these fools have been moving," Tyler said. "It could very well be someone else from their crew watching us while we watching them."

DeAndre nodded in acknowledgment. The recent situation was causing him to stay on higher alert than he usually was. He was constantly checking his surroundings and looking at everything suspiciously. It caused things to work out in his favor. "Alright. Bet," he said. "I think they're almost done with the packing, and we're gon' be on the move. Give me just a minute."

He returned to the room further in the back just as the guys finished packing the product. He called them over to inform them of the plan. Luckily, his forward-thinking prepared him for the current situation. Instead of parking in front of the house, DeAndre and Phil's vehicles were parked one street over. They grabbed Tyler and Phil, everyone grabbing at least one bag, and headed out the back of the house without being seen by the car out front. They put the money in drugs into DeAndre and Phil's vehicles. Then the two men who packed the drugs headed back into the house with instructions to enter out the front of the house and hop in the car with Ray, who had another man inside with him. They would pull off, circling the area, before bringing the guys back for their cars several minutes later. That would give enough time to see if the suspicious car parked on the street was anything they should be worried about.

DeAndre cranked his engine. He and Phil waited a few moments to give the men enough time to get back to the empty house. Once he felt confident they were on their way to Ray's car, he pulled his truck around the corner with Phil trailing behind. They rounded the block just in time to see the suspicious vehicle starting their engine. Before the guys could make it to Ray's car, the unidentified car rolled up and opened fire.

Rat-a-tat-tat-tat-tat-tat!

Ray and the men with him immediately returned fire, shooting at each other in the middle of the street. With the amount of money and drugs in his back seat, DeAndre wanted to avoid another trip to the police station—this time in handcuffs. He hung back while Phil pulled around him, approaching the opposition from behind. Tyler leaned out of the passenger's window, busting his gun in their direction and striking at least one of the adversaries. Almost immediately after Tyler's shots rang out, the enemy crew hopped back in the car and sped off. Everyone else hopped back into their own rides and quickly fled the scene.

When DeAndre met back up with his cousins, it was almost midnight. They pulled behind a neighborhood mom-and-pop sandwich shop where DeAndre was a silent partner. He was rarely there, but his partnership provided one of many avenues used to clean his money. Although no one could tell from the outside, the restaurant, which offered dine-in eating, had an office large enough for DeAndre to have a sizeable wall safe. After disabling the alarm, the trio entered the building with their bags in tow and headed straight for DeAndre's office, where he tossed the bags into the safe. He locked it back and shook his head.

"Bruh, you got to find a way to dead that shit," Phil stated.

DeAndre nodded. "You're right."

"For real, man. If that shit went differently back there, we could have been fucked up for real," Phil commented. "What if Ray wasn't on the street? Or if they ran up in the house before we could get the shit out? We would have been down bad."

"I know. I said you're right," DeAndre responded firmly. "Give me a little bit of room to think. Damn! I'll figure the shit out, okay? I don't like the heat any more than y'all do. Why the hell would I want to keep looking over my shoulder every damn day? That shit's bad for business."

"I hear you, Dre. Whatever plan you come up with, I'm down," Tyler said. "Just hope we get this shit handled sooner rather than later."

DeAndre nodded. "You and me both," he said. "Let's get out of here."

They headed back outside and toward their vehicles. Saying their goodbyes, DeAndre instructed Tyler to get rid of the gun he used outside the stash house before they went their separate ways. While he pulled away from the restaurant, he thought about heading to the apartment but decided against it. Since Jabari had work in the morning, he was pretty sure he would already be asleep, but DeAndre didn't even want to run the risk of running into him and answering any questions about the events of the evening. Jabari recently proved that he was beyond lectures. He wasn't stressing DeAndre like that, but everything he warned about was becoming more of a possibility.

DeAndre was nowhere near ready to change his lifestyle, but he would be lying if he said he didn't occasionally question if it was worth it. Without a readily available backup plan, he didn't have any other options but to keep it pushing. He didn't want to think about how his brother was probably right, and he didn't want to spend a sleepless night tossing and turning while he tried to plan his attack to eliminate the pending threat against him. Instead, he headed somewhere he knew he wouldn't have to think about his night or any of the issues he was currently facing. He switched up his route and sent a text to Nina—one of the many women he was entertaining to let her know that he was headed over. Problem-solving efforts would have to wait until the morning.

M elinda sighed as she reached to turn the engine off to her truck. She looked around the visitors' parking area of the deck she sat in, silently questioning her actions and wondering why she showed up unannounced. Her cell phone rang, disturbing the stillness of her vehicle and interrupting her thoughts. She groaned inwardly when she saw Sasha's name on her caller ID. They had not spoken in a few days, and she hoped Sasha had not found out about her engagement before she had an opportunity to tell her. She pressed the button to answer the call. "Hey, girl," she said in a cheerful tone.

"Mel, when were you going to tell me that you were engaged?" Sasha's questioning voice filled the interior of the truck. "And why... why did you say yes?"

Melinda didn't have the energy to try and explain the why to her best friend. That would require her to explain details of her relationship that she hid for several months. No one truly knew the perilous circumstances surrounding her homelife. It would be hard for them to understand why she said yes, knowing that she accepted a marriage proposal she was not thrilled about. She quickly found a way to respond to her best friend without answering her second question. "Girl, it's just been so much going on. I think I've just been caught up in the moment," she responded. "How did you find out?"

"Your boyfriend—excuse me fiancé—just made a post on Facebook and tagged you," she answered. "I guess he grew impatient that you were dragging your feet, so he let the cat out of the bag for you."

"What?" Melinda asked quietly, grabbing her phone and quickly opening the popular social media app. She clicked on her notifications to see what Sasha was talking about. Sure enough, Dominic posted a picture his parents took of them shortly after he proposed and another close-up picture of her ring. "Wow..."

"Yeah, girl. Wow..." Sasha said. "I don't even know what to say. That ring is impressive though. Congrats? I mean... are you even excited?"

"It's just a lot to digest right now. He completely took me by surprise," she answered truthfully. "A Christmas marriage proposal was the furthest thing from my mind. I guess I'm just a little overwhelmed."

Sasha hesitated, but then said, "I see. Well, after you process everything, let me know when you're ready to start wedding planning. You know I'll be with you every step of the way."

"I appreciate that. Look, I'm out doing a little running around, but I'll call you back tomorrow. Okay?"

"Yeah, sure."

Melinda ended the call and rested her head against the headrest while she closed her eyes. She knew her excuse to rush Sasha off the phone didn't make any sense, and she was glad Sasha did not press the issue. It was almost ten o'clock at night. There were no reasonable errands she would have needed to run at that time. She unbuckled her seat belt and unlocked her doors. Sliding her purse onto her shoulder, she hopped out of her truck and crossed the cold and quiet parking deck, her heels clicking against the pavement each step of the way. She reached the glass double doors to enter the building and froze at the call box. She had not thought that part through before driving all the way downtown uninvited. She had barely spoken to Jabari in the days since Christmas, and she had no idea if DeAndre would actually let her into the building. She inhaled a sharp breath and raised her finger to the call box scrolling through until she found DeAndre's name. She waited while she heard the ringing sounds while DeAndre was contacted.

"Yo... who's this?" DeAndre had to shout over the loud noise in the background. She couldn't tell where he was, but she knew he wasn't upstairs in the apartment. She was relieved that Jabari would be alone.

"Hey, Dre. It's Melinda."

"Mel? What you doing over there?"

"Just trying to catch your brother at home. I need to talk to him."

DeAndre hesitated for a moment, and Melinda frowned when it sounded like he pulled the phone away from his ear. A few seconds later, he said, "I'll text him that you're on the way up."

Melinda didn't have a chance to respond before she heard the loud clicking noise to indicate the door was unlocked and the call disconnected. She quickly reached for the door handle, letting herself into the building and heading for the elevator. When she reached the fifth floor, she stepped off of the elevator and headed down the hallway to DeAndre's corner apartment. She barely finished knocking before the door swung open and she was face-to-face with Jabari.

"What are you doing here?" he asked. "Kevin's spending the night at my mom's house."

"I know that," Melinda said softly. "I wanted to talk to you."

Jabari smirked, causing her to shift uneasily in her heels. He could tell how nervous she looked, but he didn't care. He had yet to uncover the full truth, but he knew Dominic was no good for her. Although he caused no harm to Kevin, Jabari knew that, at the very least, he was verbally abusive toward Melinda. He suspected but did not want to assume the presence of physical abuse as well. He was so disappointed in the situation she appeared to be a willing participant in. The situation she had their son in. He could barely stand to look at her after watching her accept Dominic's proposal. He continued to stand in the doorway, leaning against the frame to block her entrance into the apartment. "Your phone's working, right? You should have called."

"You know that I've been trying to talk to you for a few days. You haven't been picking up and only responding to my texts about our son. Really, Jabari?" she asked with visible hurt in her eyes. "You not gon' let me in?"

Jabari hesitated. Part of him wanted to close the door in her face. She had to know that if he really wanted to see her, he would have answered one of her many phone calls. However, after she agreed to be Dominic's wife, he didn't know what else was left for them to say to each other. He knew that he didn't necessarily leave her in the best position when he was locked up, but she was always someone who could make a way when there was none. She was the type of person to keep things together and handle her business. She was a strong, confident woman—or at least that was what he thought. At least that was the version of Melinda Barrett that he used to know. He didn't recognize the woman standing in front of him. The Melinda he knew and loved would have never let a man disrespect her and put his hands on her. He wasn't sure he knew this version of her at all.

But he would be lying if he said he didn't still feel something for her. This was the woman he was supposed to build a life and a family with. The same woman he called his soul mate once upon a time. The one he pictured forever with. Regardless of his frustration and disappointment, he knew he equally frustrated and disappointed her when he ruined the future that they planned years ago.

He stepped to the side and let her into the apartment. While she stood just inside the entrance off to the side, he closed and locked the door before leaving her standing there while he walked back to his bedroom. She sighed heavily and rolled her eyes before following him. While she passed through the kitchen, she noticed the bottle of Crown Royal sitting on the counter. When she reached his room, he was seated on a bench at the foot of the bed staring at the television and holding the controller while he resumed the video game he was playing. Melinda rolled her eyes again, annoyed by his dismissive behavior and the lack of attention he was giving her. For a few moments, she stood inside of the doorway, until he gave her a quick expectant look.

"I know you didn't come over here to watch me play 2K," he said. "What do you want to talk about, Melinda?"

She unzipped her cropped leather jacket and slipped out of it, laying it on his dresser and setting her purse on top. She smoothed down the front of her dress before looking back up at him while he returned his attention to the video game. "I wanted to finish the conversation you were trying to have a couple of weeks ago," she said. "The conversation where you shared your feelings with me. I wanted to talk about us."

Jabari laughed. He raised the cup that sat on the floor by his foot and took a sip. "Ain't no us, Mel. You made this shit clear and obvious when you accepted buddy's proposal," he said without looking at her. "There's just you and me and our son. Kevin's the only thing that matters. He's the only thing you and I have to discuss."

"That's not true, Jabari," she said. He cut his eyes at her. "At least it doesn't have to be."

"How do you figure that?" He leaned backward until his back was resting against the foot of his bed.

"Because you haven't given me the opportunity to respond. Dominic interrupted me that day in the yard, you cut me off at every chance on Christmas, and you haven't answered my calls."

"What's the point? You're getting married. What else could you possibly need to say to me?"

Melinda shook her head. "I'm not marrying him."

Jabari looked back in her direction, examining her hands as they were folded in front of her. She wasn't wearing her ring. "Does he know that?" he asked.

Melinda shook her head again. "No. Not yet."

"Exactly," Jabari said, shaking his head and turning back to face the television. "Seems like you're having the wrong conversation with the wrong man."

Melinda sighed heavily, dropping her hands by her sides. "Jabari..."

He shook his head and sighed but paused the game and sat the controller down. "What, Melinda?" He turned so he was facing her. "You've got my full attention now. What is it that you need to say to me?"

"I—I..."

"Spit it out, Mel. You came over here to get something off your chest. Say it."

"Jabari, I love you," she blurted, shaking her head. "Still... to this day. I never stopped either. Even though I am in a relationship, I don't think I will ever stop loving you."

Jabari looked at her, nodding slowly. He leaned forward, resting his forearms on his legs. He was quiet for a moment, but his facial expression softened. After a moment of silence between them, he shrugged his shoulders. "I was hoping that was the case, but that doesn't change the fact that you just accepted Dominic's proposal a couple of days ago. What am I supposed to do with that?"

"Love me anyway, and don't stop loving me. I told you I'm not marrying him, but I need a little time to get out of that situation."

"I don't understand. Give him his ring back and leave. Is it not that simple?"

Melinda shook her head. "No. It's not that simple. It should be, but unfortunately, it's not. It will probably get a little messy, but—"

"Messy like how?" Jabari's eyebrows wrinkled into a frown.

She shook her head and waved him off. "The details of it all don't really matter," she lied. She couldn't stomach telling him the truth in that moment. "I just need to sort some things out so I can walk away."

Jabari's frown remained on his face. He knew there was something she wasn't telling him. He pushed up from the bench and walked over to her, gently touching the side of her face. "Mel, if there's something going on that I need to know about—"

"There's not," she said quickly. It was another lie, but she felt it was necessary to withhold the ugly truth. She knew in her heart that Jabari would beat Dominic to a pulp or worse if he knew what was really going on inside the four walls of their home. "That day at my house, you told me to just say the word if I wasn't happy, and we would figure everything out together. Well, this is me... saying the word."

"Then, just like I said, we'll figure everything out together."

"Yeah?"

"Yes. I meant everything I said that day."

Jabari's hand moved from the side of her face to her waist. He shook his head again, looking down at her while he licked his bottom lip. The intensity in his stare caused her to back up.

"Why are you looking at me like that?" she asked.

"Like what?"

"Like you've seen me naked... like you're picturing me naked right now..."

Jabari laughed again. "Mel, I know it's been a minute, but I have seen you naked. Plenty of times," he said. "And no, I wouldn't mind doing it again. Right now."

Melinda drew in another sharp breath while he took a few steps in her direction, closing the distance between them and invading her personal space. He placed both hands on her waist. "Jabari..." she exhaled deeply.

He pulled her body against his, kissing her softly on the lips. She closed her eyes briefly, cherishing the feel of his lips against hers. She inhaled another deep breath and released it slowly, allowing the tension to leave her body. When she leaned in to kiss him back, a smile tugged at Jabari's lips while he gripped her waist tightly. They continued to kiss for a few moments before he took a couple steps backward until he was seated on the edge of his bed. Looking up at the only woman he ever loved romantically, he pulled her between his legs and started to untie the belt at the waist of her wrap dress. She didn't protest when he pulled the dress down off her shoulders and tossed it onto the floor. Standing in front of him in only her bra and panties, she silently admitted that she had not been able to resist him since they crossed the line to being more than friends years ago. That fact initially made her nervous when she learned he was being released from prison.

"I regret the day I ever let you go. I was wrong. Wrong as hell. We're supposed to be together. You... me... our son. We belong together as a family," he said, caressing her curves and kissing her neck. He pulled back and started to unhook her bra. "Mel, regardless of what has happened in the past or these last couple of years apart... you and me... our love is forever. From this life to the next."

"And even after that," she added, causing his lips to stretch into an even wider smile.

When Jabari released the clasps on her bra, he removed it, tossing it in the direction of her dress. His large hands cupped her full breasts, massaging them tenderly. He kissed each one before taking one into his mouth. When he licked and sucked her hardened, stiffened nipples, Melinda ran her tongue along her bottom lip before pulling it into her mouth and biting it gently. He moved his lips from her breasts back to her neck, and she pulled her underwear down and kicked them to the side.

Jabari pulled her onto his lap, and she straddled him. She pulled his T-shirt off and dropped it on the pile of her clothes. Wrapping her arms around his neck, her lips found his again. She pushed her tongue into his mouth and simultaneously slipped her hand inside his basketball shorts, feeling around to release him from his underwear. Jabari kissed her neck while she stroked his hardened pole, slowly moving her hand back and forth. He released a low groan and pressed his forehead against hers.

With one arm wrapped around Melinda's waist and his other hand rubbing her round ass, he gave her a quick peck on the lips. "Mel... you sure this what you want?" She nodded. He kissed her again. "I'm just giving you a heads-up. It's been a long time... and I've been drinking Crown all night."

They both laughed.

"Then hell yes... even more so," Melinda mumbled into his ear with another laugh before kissing the side of his neck. She lifted her bottom just enough to allow Jabari to pull his shorts down.

He palmed her ass and lowered her onto his rod, thrusting himself deep inside of her. She moaned softly, placing one hand on the back of his neck and the other on his thigh to balance herself. He stared at her, admiring her beauty while she rolled her hips up and down. During their time apart, he missed everything about her, including the feel of her touch, the taste of her lips, and the way her moans always heightened his desire for her. Melinda continued to ride him, grinding on top of him slowly. Her hands rubbed across his chest, one sweeping over his left pec, where her name was tattooed in bold, cursive letters—right across his heart. Jabari grabbed her waist with both hands to control her movements, forcefully bouncing her up and down onto him.

Melinda's back arched, and she tossed her head back while her eyes shut tightly. "Jabari..." she moaned his name.

"Yeah, baby. This what you wanted?"

Melinda nodded in response, and Jabari lay back, allowing

her to wind her hips and ride him faster and harder. After she came the first time, he switched positions, putting her on her back and holding her legs in the air while he balanced himself on his knees and drilled into her. He closed his eyes and shook his head slowly, knowing there was no way she was getting good dick on a regular basis for her to be as tight as she was. Leaning down, he kissed her on her lips and spread her legs further while he continued to stretch her out. Tears came to her eyes, but the smile on her face displayed her satisfaction. Stroking her intensely, Jabari alternated between kissing her lips and kissing away her tears. Eventually, she was screaming his name and digging her nails into his flesh, clutching his body while her legs shook uncontrollably.

Jabari pulled out momentarily and instructed her to turn over onto her stomach. Melinda's eyes strained open with a questioning look, and he could read the exhaustion all over her face. He laughed slightly. "Mel, I gave you fair warning," he said. "Turn over."

Melinda hesitated but rolled over, her chest flat on the bed while she arched her rear end toward Jabari. He paused for a moment, admiring the view. He loved everything about her, including every inch of her curvy body—from the curls on her head to her pedicured toes. He smacked her ass before sliding into her again. Gripping her neck just right, Jabari pulled her body toward him each time she tried to inch away, pounding into her over and over again until he was also content. When he was finished, they collapsed onto the bed in each other's arms. Melinda was quickly dozing off to sleep, but after looking at the time, Jabari gently shook her awake.

"Hmmm?" She didn't even attempt to open her eyes.

"What time you got to head home?"

Melinda's eyes popped open. "You trying to put me out?"

Jabari laughed and shook his head, tightening the arm he wrapped around her shoulders. "Nah, Mel. I just don't want to cause any more issues with your situation."

"Oh," she said, dropping the frown from her face. "You're fine. I'm fine. He's out of town."

Jabari nodded and kissed Melinda's cheek before she let her eyes close again. Within moments, she was sleeping peacefully. Jabari silently stared at the ceiling, thinking about the near and immediate future until his eyes closed as well.

❧ 13 ❧

"You coming though tonight or what?"

DeAndre sat behind the wheel of his truck at a red light while Amanda's voice came through the speaker of his phone. They hadn't seen each other in over a week, and he wasn't sure he would see her that night either, partially because he had other things to do and partially because she wasn't holding his attention anymore. Nina was getting more of his time, and he recently met another woman he was seeing also. He pulled off when the light turned green, continuing toward his destination. He hesitated before responding. "Uh, I don't know right now. I'll have to see about that, and—"

"Let me know later," Amanda said with an attitude. "Your typical brush-off line. It's cool, Dre. Don't even worry about it."

"Babe, it ain't even like that," he lied. It was exactly like that. He just didn't want her to leave him alone until he was ready to be done with her for good. "For real. I'm about to pick up my nephew. Then I've got a couple other moves to make, but I'll hit you up. I promise."

"Mm-hmm, Dre. Whatever," she said, sounding unconvinced. "Tell me anything. While you running around, playing me in these streets, see don't I find another man. I don't have to deal with this shit."

"Amanda, come on. Don't be like—"

DeAndre was interrupted by the double beep letting him know the call ended. He glanced down at the phone, shaking his head that she hung up on him. He hated for anybody to do that. Ordinarily, he would have called her back, blowing up her phone until she answered. However, he wasn't in the mood for the drama. Instead, he turned up "Ocean Views" by Nipsey Hussle and continued his drive, pulling into the parking lot of the Little Angels Learning Academy minutes later. With Melinda and Jabari both tied up, he was tasked with picking Kevin up from the after-school center. Crossing the parking lot, he entered the building and checked in with the lady at the front desk. A few moments later, Kevin came running up the hall at full speed, hugging his waist when he reached him.

"I didn't know you were picking me up today," he said with a wide smile.

DeAndre laughed. "I didn't either until about an hour ago," he said, leading Kevin toward the exit. "Your mom and dad are busy, so you're going to kick it with me for a little bit."

They reached the truck, both climbing in and buckling their seat belts.

"Where are we going?" Kevin asked.

"That's a good question." DeAndre laughed and looked down at his buzzing cell phone to see a text message from Phil. He looked back up at Kevin. "You hungry?"

"Yeah. Can we get pizza and wings?"

"Oh yeah!" DeAndre answered, responding to Phil's text. "Your cousins Tyler and Phil are going to meet us there. I'll make one of them give you money for the arcade games."

"Cool!"

Kevin pulled his iPad out and buried his nose in the tablet for the remainder of the ride. DeAndre had no idea when Jabari and Melinda would be clear, so he figured pizza would kill two birds with one stone. They could pass the time and fill their stomachs. He enjoyed spending time with his nephew because it was kind of rare. Prior to Jabari coming home, it was sometimes hard for him to connect with Melinda. When Kevin visited family, it was usually Sonya and Symone. After Jabari got home, he wasn't too thrilled about having Kevin around DeAndre after he found out about the ongoing street conflict. However, in the couple of weeks since the shooting outside of the stash house things were quiet for DeAndre's team. So much so that it was concluded that the drama was over. He assumed the opposition took one too many losses and decided to give it up.

With things relatively back to normal, DeAndre assumed Jabari felt more at ease with him and Kevin spending time alone, especially since he and Melinda apparently started back up again. He didn't know all of the details, but Melinda made more than one appearance at their apartment since her unexpectant visit a couple of weeks prior. It was almost like old times again, which surprised him. He wasn't sure if Jabari stood a chance against Melinda's lawyer boyfriend, but he was glad it looked like things were working out in his favor.

DeAndre pulled into the parking lot and spotted Phil's car across the parking lot. Kevin unbuckled before he turned the engine off and quickly hopped out of the truck. With his iPad still in tow, he swiftly crossed the lot with DeAndre trailing behind. "Slow down, man," he playfully chastised while jogging to catch up with his nephew.

Kevin entered the restaurant and spotted Phil and Tyler at a table near the back.

"Big man! What's good?" Tyler greeted Kevin with a fist bump.

They all sat down at the table and chatted while waiting for their pepperoni pizzas and hot wings. It wasn't long before the four finished everything in sight, leaving nothing but clean bones and a few pizza crusts. Kevin made eye contact with DeAndre and nodded toward the rear of the pizzeria, where there were a number of arcade games.

"Oh yeah! Phil, give me a couple of ones," DeAndre said, extending his open hand in his cousin's direction.

"Bruh, what?" Phil asked, laughing. "I paid for the food."

"Bet. You're right," DeAndre said, turning toward Tyler instead. "Ty, pay up."

Tyler shook his head and laughed. "Alright, man. Damn. I should have known Kev was gon' hit my pockets again."

They all laughed. DeAndre took the money from Tyler, counted the bills to a sum of ten dollars, and then handed the money to Kevin. With him being the only child among the cousins, Kevin was extremely spoiled, and everyone knew it. Sonya and Symone were the worst when it came to giving him whatever he wanted. Since he was a well-behaved child, no one minded bending over backward and going out of their way for him. After he took off to the game section, the cousins could speak more openly about the things everyone shielded him from.

"How'd shit go at the spot last night?" DeAndre asked.

Tyler shrugged his shoulders. "Straight. We probably should have moved the stash house sooner," he said. "We're a lot closer to the action now."

DeAndre nodded in acknowledgment. "That could be a good thing or a bad thing. Only time will tell. Sometimes being too close to things is trouble," he said. "Too many eyes watching."

Tyler shrugged again. "Yeah. Maybe. Shit seems to be working for now though. Everything is working just right. Steady profits. Business is booming."

"That's what I like to hear," DeAndre said, raising his beer up to his lips.

The trio talked about business for several more minutes while Kevin played his games. Although he was doing better than he ever had before, he was starting to see things in a different light. The way Jabari viewed things. He wouldn't dare say it out loud to his cousins, but he seriously started to wonder how much longer he would be running in the streets. It was better to bow out at the top before he had the opportunity to end up in one of the two places his brother warned him about—prison or the morgue. He had money—a ton of it actually. He wasn't a starving up-and-comer with something to prove. Everyone knew his worth, and that was just as much of a curse as it was a gift. To the best of his knowledge, the opposition of the most recent months was over. But what would he do the next time someone tried to challenge him so violently? Would he survive? He figured that maybe it was time for him to stop tempting fate.

Several minutes later, Kevin came back empty-handed, and DeAndre figured it was a good time to leave. He stood up from the table, stretching his limbs while he looked at his cousins.

"Alright, y'all. We're about to head out," he announced. "Might take a nap and hit the spot later on, but I'll let you know."

"Bet," Phil responded. "We're probably gon' get going too."

DeAndre slapped hands with his cousins as they all stood up to leave. He held Kevin by the shoulder as they stepped out of the building so he couldn't take off running again. Looking down at his phone to read a text message from Nina, he was distracted. He wasn't paying attention to his surroundings. So he didn't see the suspiciously dark-tinted sedan sitting in the back of the lot near his truck with its engine running. Luckily, Tyler was watching when the doors opened, and three masked gunmen hopped out of the car.

"Dre! Get Kev!" Tyler shouted, pulling his weapon to return fire.

Startled, his confusion caused DeAndre to move slower than he usually would have. When the masked gunmen started firing, he had just enough time to push Kevin behind a nearby SUV. He was trying to pull his gun when the first bullet struck him in the shoulder, causing him to drop his weapon. Tyler and Phil returned fire, shooting multiple rounds in the gunmen's direction. Regardless of how many times they fired, the men only shot at DeAndre. The exchange was brief but damaging. They struck DeAndre multiple times before hopping back in their car and speeding away.

The parking lot was eerily quiet for a few moments before Kevin's cries filled the silence. A few people from inside of the restaurant slowly started to come outside, some on their cell phones, presumably dialing 911. Phil sighed heavily before tossing his weapon and his keys to Tyler. He bent down in front of DeAndre's body, trying to shield him from view. "Ty, get Kev and get out of here," he said. Looking over his shoulder, he glanced down at the guns in his brother's hands. In a low tone, he said, "You know what to do with those."

Tyler nodded in response and did what he was told without a word. Phil kneeled closer to DeAndre's body, telling him that help was on the way while also grabbing his cell phone and turning it off before slipping it in his own pocket. Although the gunmen were masked, the driver was not, and Phil was able to catch a glimpse of his face before they fled the scene. He knew who was behind the shooting. The same crew that was behind the others. The same group they incorrectly assumed left well enough alone. He knew he was going to be questioned by the cops for hours, but once he was released, they were going to pay.

zzz

MELINDA SAT AT HER DESK, ENTERING IN THE LAST FEW grades before she called it a day. She occasionally glanced at her cell phone, waiting for a call from Jabari. They were working on her exit plan—her escape from Dominic. While she was finishing up at work, Jabari went to view a couple of apartments for her before she met up with him to go to a car dealership. It was only a few weeks since they rekindled their relationship, but it almost felt as if no time had passed. Almost as if the last couple of years never existed. Although that was great for her relationship with Jabari, the last few years had in fact happened with Dominic, and she was desperate to find a way to end things in the least messy way possible.

There was a knock on her open classroom door, and she looked up to see Rashad standing in the entryway.

"Hey. Come on in," she said with a smile, waving him inside the classroom. She heard the buzzing of her cell and looked to see an incoming call from Dominic. She ignored it and turned her attention back to Rashad.

"Mind if I have a seat?" he asked.

Melinda shook her head. "Not at all. What's going on?"

Rashad shrugged his shoulders and sat down in the chair beside her desk. "Not much. I know the semester has gotten off to a busy start, but you seem a little more preoccupied than usual. Is everything okay?"

"Actually, it is," she responded with a smile. "Like you said, the semester had gotten off to a very busy start, and I've got a lot going on right now."

"Yeah, I know. I saw the post about your engagement on Facebook. I've been meaning to congratulate you."

Melinda smiled and nodded. She knew he was referencing the post Dominic tagged her in because she never posted anything herself. "Thank you," she said. "Yeah, so as you can imagine, I've got a lot going on right now. Do you think it's starting to show at work again?"

Rashad raised his thumb and index finger to indicate a small amount. "A little bit. Nothing too crazy," he said, "but since I noticed it, I wanted to bring it to your attention before I was accused of being bitter from rejection again." He shook his head and laughed.

Embarrassed by her previous behavior, Melinda covered her face with her hands for a brief moment. She pulled her hands down and looked Rashad directly in the eyes. "I never apologized about that. I am sorry for the way I snapped at you," she said. "I really need to do a better job of not letting my personal life interfere while I'm at work."

"No need for an apology," he said, shrugging his shoulders. "It's cool, Mel. Hopefully your personal life won't have any reason to negatively impact your work anymore."

Melinda hesitated. She hoped he was right, but she wasn't so sure. She was so caught up with the thought of being with Jabari again that she tried to avoid thinking about the complicated reality of things. In all honesty, she had no idea how Dominic was going to react after when he found out she was leaving him. Hindsight illustrated how he treated her as a possession and attempted to buy her love through the course of the relationship. He was sure to flip about losing what he thought belonged to him. She often wondered how she allowed the relationship to play out the way that it did, but regardless, she was determined to bring it to an end.

She smiled at Rashad and said, "I hope so as well, but besides that... tell me what you're seeing and what you think I can improve on in my day to day. I'm really trying to avoid any other coaching conversations with Ms. Jenkins."

"I understand that," Rashad said with a laugh. "She can be just as tough as she is sweet. I didn't know if I was going to make it my first year."

"Really?"

"Really..."

Melinda was in no rush to leave before she heard from Jabari, so she listened to Rashad's stories about his first year working at their school—before Melinda joined the staff as well. They laughed and traded a few horror stories about some of their students' parents and how those situations unnecessarily led to them being called to the principal's office. Before she knew it, another hour passed. She frowned slightly when she looked at her phone. Although Dominic attempted to reach her a few times, she had yet to hear from Jabari. When Rashad looked at the time and decided it was time for him to leave, Melinda agreed as well. They collected their belongings and headed for the front of the building.

As they walked up the hallway, Melinda readjusted her bags on her shoulder. "I really appreciate you popping in to help... and tell me about myself," she said with a laugh. "I know I didn't make it easy for you the first time."

Rashad laughed and nodded. "You're welcome, Mel. I just want you to succeed. The team needs you, and the kids need you too."

"Thank you. It definitely helps to have a friend here," she said.

Rashad smiled and nodded in acknowledgment. They were almost at the exit when they spotted Ms. Jenkins headed to the front office.

"Hey, Rashad, I need to catch up with Ms. Jenkins," she said, "but I'll see you tomorrow. Have a good evening."

"You too."

Melinda quick stepped toward the front office. "Ms. Jenkins!" she called after the principal.

Ms. Jenkins turned around with a warm smile. "Yes, Melinda. How's it going?"

Melinda shrugged with a smile of her own. "It's going," she said. "I know it's getting late into the day, but I wanted to see if I could get some time on your calendar."

"Sure. What's going on?"

"I—I just have a situation. A personal one that I'm trying not to let affect my work performance any more than it already has," she said. "I don't know if it's something I should talk about at the school level or county HR, but I wanted to start with you."

"Of course," Ms. Jenkins said with a smile. "Let's make time tomorrow. I'll check my calendar and send you a meeting invite."

"Thank you."

"Sure. Have a good night."

Melinda nodded and turned to leave. She stepped out of the building and released a heavy sigh. She didn't know exactly how everything was going to play out, but she had a feeling she would end up needing a restraining order against Dominic. She would never let him know where her future apartment would be. However, he knew where she worked. Everybody did and restraining order or not, there were potential concerns about her safety at the building. He wasn't the only one with a history of popping up on her unannounced or waiting in the parking lot.

Shaking her head to herself, she crossed the parking lot and climbed into her truck. She turned on the engine and grabbed her phone to dial Jabari's number. Even if he wasn't going to go to the car lot with her, she still needed to know where to pick up Kevin. The call immediately went to voicemail. Pulling the phone away from her ear, she frowned but seconds later saw Symone calling her. "Hey, girl," she answered quickly. "Do you know where your brother is? I've been trying—"

"Yeah... Mel, his phone is dead, so he asked me to call you," she said slowly and evenly.

"Oh, okay. Where is he? We were supposed to do something tonight, but it's getting a little late. I think I should just get Kev and go home."

"Mel, we're at the hospital. Dre took Kevin to get some pizza after he picked him up, and when they... when they..."

Symone started crying, and Melinda barely heard anything else. After getting Symone to tell her which hospital they were at, she sped out of the parking lot in their direction. She didn't know what was going on, but she knew she needed to get to her guys as fast as she could.

❦ 14 ❧

Jabari hated everything about hospitals. The smell. The claustrophobic feeling from sitting in a crowded waiting room. The beeping and buzzing sounds of various monitors and machines. Most of all, he hated the waiting game. He hated sitting around with his family in the midst of a bunch of strangers while waiting to hear an update about their loved one. It reminded him too much of the night his father died. A night he never wanted to think about. He sat with his head resting in his palms, shaking his head slowly while staring down at the ground. He was replaying his quick conversation with Tyler when he dropped him off at the hospital. The more he thought about the details and events of the day, the more nauseous he became. He knew that divine intervention and his cousin's quick thinking were the only things that kept his son out of harm's way. Although DeAndre was still in surgery, Jabari knew that things could have been even worse—especially if Kevin had sustained any type of injury as well. Thinking about how he was going to explain the situation to Melinda gave him an uneasy feeling. Even though Kevin was physically okay, he was emotionally shaken up, and Jabari felt like he let him and Melinda down again by failing to ensure his safety.

He heard the doors open and the clicking of her stilettos and knew that Melinda arrived. He overheard part of her earlier phone conversation with Symone while one of the doctors was giving an update to him and his mother and knew that she would be there as soon as she could.

"Mommy!" Kevin shouted from the chair beside him.

Jabari looked up to see Melinda rushing toward them. He sat up, leaning back in his seat while he rubbed his hands back and forth across his jeans. Kevin jumped up to wrap his arms around his mom's waist. Melinda hugged him back tightly but made direct eye contact with Jabari. She raised her eyebrows with concern while mouthing, *what happened?* He shrugged his shoulders and shook his head. Melinda shook her head as well before breaking their eye contact. After pulling away from her hug with Kevin, she quickly greeted Sonya and Symone before returning to her guys.

"Hey, Kev, go sit with grandma for a minute," she said while looking directly at Jabari. "I need to speak with your dad."

"Yes, ma'am," Kevin quietly mumbled before doing what he was told.

"Come on," Melinda said to Jabari, motioning for him to follow her outside.

Jabari sighed heavily before slowly pushing himself up from his chair. He stuck his hands deep into the pockets of his jeans, staring at his shoes while he followed Melinda outside. She was an excellent mother. That was one of the many things he loved about her. She was a true mama bear that loved and protected Kevin fiercely. He didn't know exactly what she had to say to him about the day's events, but he was fully prepared for her to bite his head off. He knew she got worked up pretty easily and had the tendency to go from zero to a hundred quickly. When they stepped outside the building and away from the windows, Melinda wrapped her arms around him tightly, catching him off guard. He hugged her back while she planted a kiss on his lips and caressed the side of his face.

"When Symone told me y'all were at the hospital, I feared the worst. She was crying so hard I could barely get any information from her, so I just drove over here as fast as I could," she said. "What happened?"

Jabari shrugged his shoulders but gave her the information that he had—the parts of the story he was able to receive from Tyler. Melinda tried to pull away from him, but he kept his hands on her waist, firmly holding her in place.

"So... Kevin was there? He saw the whole thing?"

Jabari sighed deeply. "Not the whole thing, but he saw enough... too much honestly." He expected to see anger in her eyes, but instead, he saw sadness.

"Yeah... way too much for a six-year-old," she stated somberly. "Any idea how much longer Dre is going to be in surgery?"

"The doc said a few more hours... maybe a little longer. They think he's gon' pull through, but his injuries are extensive. It was pretty touch and go when he first got here," he said, shaking his head.

"I'm so sorry that this happened. Do you want to go home and get some rest? You gotta work in the morning?"

Jabari shook his head. "Nah. I already spoke to Alex. He's got me covered at least for tomorrow, and we'll figure everything else out over the weekend. I think I'm gon' stay here with my mom for a while," he said. He heard Melinda's phone vibrating in her purse, and they both knew it was probably Dominic. He glanced at the time on his watch and said, "You should probably get Kevin and go home."

Melinda hesitated but then nodded slowly. "I'd like to stay a little longer, but yeah... you're probably right." She kissed him again and pulled away from their embrace.

Jabari released a deep breath and followed her back into the waiting room. He stood to the side while she said goodbye to his family and collected Kevin. She turned back to face him, giving his hand a quick squeeze. With them still living in Dominic's house, Melinda thought it was best to wait to tell Kevin about her and Jabari, so affectionate interactions were limited in his presence. "I'll call you later. Probably from Symone's phone if I don't find a charger, but one way or the other, I'll give you a call," he said before letting her hand go. He gave Kevin a big hug. "Alright, man. Go on home with your mom and be good tonight. Love you."

"Love you too."

Jabari watched while Kevin took Melinda's hand and she led him out of the hospital. He spent the next several hours with his mom and sister, eventually dozing off in the busy waiting room. He woke up to Symone tapping his shoulder when a doctor came to give the family another update. He quickly pushed up from the chair and made his way over just in time to hear the tail end of the conversation.

"...he's sedated at the moment. Still critical but stable," the doctor said. "I know you want to see him. However, it will be a bit longer, so why don't you head home. Get some rest. Ms. Butler, I promise someone will call you if there are any changes, but for now, he's stable and in good hands."

Sonya hesitated but eventually agreed. The doctor gave her a friendly pat on the shoulder before walking away.

"Come on, Mom. Let's grab something to eat before we head home," Symone said, wrapping an arm around Sonya while she started toward the exit. After a few steps, she turned around to see Jabari standing in the same spot. "Bro, you coming? I'm gon' stop somewhere for breakfast. You got a taste for something?"

"Nah," Jabari said, shaking his head. "Not hungry. I'm gon' head home and sleep for a little bit before I—I'll get up with y'all later."

Sonya looked at Jabari with suspicious, narrowed eyes. "Before you what?"

"Nothing, Ma."

"Jabari Calvin... if you're thinking about going to see your cousins, don't," she said in a firm tone. "The police have already been by here trying to see if your brother was conscious. I don't know what they have going on, but I don't want you caught up in the middle of it."

Jabari shrugged his shoulders. "I'm going home to get some sleep, Ma. I'll call you later," he said. He kissed her on the cheek, hugged his sister, and headed for his car.

He didn't directly address his mother's concern, because he didn't want to look her in the face and lie. Yes, he was going to get some sleep. But after that, he was absolutely going to see his cousins. They were with DeAndre when everything went down, and he wanted to know the details that Tyler didn't have time to share earlier. Someone tried to kill his brother while his son was present. There were questions that needed answers.

He got into the car and started his drive with his mind deep in thought. He released a heavy, frustrated breath while he sped away from the hospital. This was the type of situation that could easily and very quickly make his old self reappear. The old version of himself that he vowed to put away the day that Kevin was born. Prior to Kevin's birth, Jabari's reckless behavior and involvement with illegal activities was largely in part to the ease at which he made such good money. When Melinda gave him a chance at a real romantic relationship, he questioned whether the risk was worth it. When Kevin was born, he decided that it wasn't. He put forth such an effort to stay disciplined and do things the right way. The one time he messed up cost him four years of his life and his relationship. Even while incarcerated, he promised that he would never put himself in that position again.

But this was personal.

He and his cousins were as close as could be. He knew there was no way Phil and Tyler would let the situation go if they knew who was responsible. If they were going to handle business, so was he—regardless of how his mother may have felt about it. When he got to the apartment, it was a little after eight in the morning. Although it was late for him to finally reach his bed, he knew it was way too early to attempt to reach either of his cousins. Instead, he put his phone on the charger, kicked off his shoes, and climbed in the bed. He was able to get a few hours of sleep before the ringing of his fully charged phone disturbed him.

Without opening his eyes, he fumbled around and snatched his cell off the charger. "Yeah..."

"Hey..."

He instantly recognized Bree's voice on the other end and shifted in the bed, rolling from his side to his back. Although he wasn't interested in her romantically, they remained friendly. However, communication between them was infrequent since the night Melinda unexpectedly showed up at the apartment.

"Did I wake you?" she asked.

"Yeah, but it's cool," he said, looking at the time. "I need to get up soon anyway. What's going on?"

"I was calling because I heard about Dre getting shot."

"Oh yeah? Where did you hear that from?"

Bree hesitated. "One of the dancers at the club is cool with his girl Nina. I guess Nina told my homegirl... and then she told me," she answered. "Is he okay?"

"Yeah. He's hanging in there," Jabari said as he sat up in the bed. "I gotta get up and moving. Let me hit you back later."

Jabari ended the call. After a quick shower, he dressed and shot Tyler a text. When Tyler responded with their location, Jabari let him know he would be there soon. He slipped the phone into his pocket and headed down the hall to DeAndre's bedroom. He pushed the door open and looked around the neatly made room for a brief moment before stepping inside. He opened a couple of DeAndre's dresser drawers and dug around but didn't see what he was looking for. He headed for the walk-in closet, opening a few shoeboxes but still came up empty. After a few moments of thinking, he stepped back into the bedroom and lifted the mattress.

Bingo, he thought to himself when he saw the Glock 40 resting between the mattress and the box spring. It was one of the places Jabari used to hide his guns before he went to prison. He paused, briefly shaking his head at some of the habits his brother picked up from him. He grabbed the gun and tucked it behind his back. He picked up his cell and his keys and left the apartment. On the drive over to Tyler's place, his phone rang again. This time, he looked down to see Melinda's name on his screen. If he couldn't tell his mother the truth about what he was up to, he definitely couldn't share the information with Melinda either. He let the call go to voicemail. Noticing the time, he figured she was on her lunch break, and he made a mental note to call her back by the end of her workday.

He pulled up to Tyler's apartment and noticed Phil's car in the lot when he parked. He quickly jogged up the stairs to his cousin's door and knocked loudly. Phil opened the door a couple of seconds later and held a finger up to his lips, telling Jabari to be quiet when he entered. Across the room, Tyler sat on a stool at the breakfast bar with his phone on speaker.

"Did your brother get arrested last night?"

Jabari heard his aunt Trina's voice and already knew what was up. He sat down on the couch quietly next to Phil. Neither one of them wanted to make their presence known while Tyler spoke to his and Phil's mother, Sonya's sister. The sisters were as close as their sons were, and anything one knew, the other was sure to find out.

"No, Mama. They just took him down there for some questioning," Tyler said in a voice that made him sound like an innocent young child. "He didn't even do nothing."

Phil threw his head back and covered his mouth with his hand so he could laugh quietly. Tyler shot him a look with narrowed eyes, silently telling him to shut up.

"Okay. Tell that fool to call me when you see him."

"Okay, Mama. I will."

Tyler lowered the phone from his ear thinking that the call was wrapping up. However, Trina asked another question.

"Is Jabari over there?"

Tyler looked up at Jabari who shook his head emphatically. He nodded in agreement.

"No, Mama. I ain't seen him either," Tyler lied. "What's going on?"

"Your auntie is heading back up to the hospital soon, and she said she hasn't talked to him since they left this morning," she answered. "When you see him, because I know you will, tell him to give his mother a call."

"Yes, ma'am."

"Alright. Call me later. I'm making that lasagna you like for dinner, so let me know if you're stopping by. Love you."

"Love you too."

Tyler ended the call, and Jabari and Phil busted out laughing.

"Spoiled ass," Jabari said, shaking his head.

"I'll be that," Tyler said, shrugging his shoulders. "I'm sure she'll let me leave with the pan, so y'all are more than welcome to leftovers tomorrow. In the meantime, call your mothers... with y'all rude asses."

Jabari and Phil laughed again. Tyler hopped off the stool and crossed the room, sitting down on the couch opposite his brother and cousin.

"What do y'all know?" Jabari asked.

Tyler and Phil exchanged looks across the room. Tyler looked back at Jabari and asked, "You really want the details?"

"Yeah."

"Alright, but if Aunt Sonya finds out—"

"I'm a grown ass man, bruh. She can't hold you accountable for my decisions," Jabari responded. "Somebody got at my brother while my son was there. I want to know everything you know."

Tyler nodded and then preceded to tell his cousin the whole story. Since Phil was able to get a good look at the driver, they were certain who was behind the attack. Even though everyone thought the original conflict from weeks prior was over, it was the same group after DeAndre again. Tyler and Phil worked with a couple of guys on their team to get the information needed to handle the entire crew including their leader.

Jabari settled back and nodded at the information he was given. "Shit, just let me know what's up. When y'all ride, I'm riding," he said.

Phil and Tyler exchanged looks again. Phil cleared his throat before speaking. "Bruh, I hear you, but you just got home not too long ago. If you get caught up in some shit now, you could—"

"Then let's make sure I don't get caught up in no shit," he said evenly. Phil hesitated, so he continued. "My brother and my son, bruh. I'm at wherever you're at."

"Alright then," Phil said, shrugging his shoulders.

"How long did the cops keep you?" Jabari asked.

Phil shrugged again. "A couple of hours. They ain't really have shit on me," he said. "The cameras at the restaurant weren't working right. The only reason they held me so long is because some bitch ass supposed witness said they thought they saw me shooting. Another one said they thought they could see the driver's face, so the cops assumed I could as well. Of course, that was all true, but I wasn't telling them that."

"What did you tell them?" Jabari asked.

"Shit," Phil responded quickly. "I didn't tell them a damn thing. You know I know better."

"Bet," Jabari said. "My mom said the cops came by the hospital before I got there trying to see if Dre was conscious, so I know they'll be back up there at some point. What did y'all do with the guns?"

"Tossed 'em," Tyler responded. "Ain't nobody finding those."

"Good," Jabari said.

"Oh, bro! I almost forgot. I got Dre's phone," Phil said.

"Oh yeah? Let me see that."

Phil reached into his pocket and handed Jabari the phone. "I tried to get in there, but I don't know the code."

Jabari punched a couple numbers on the screen and the phone immediately unlocked. He shook his head and laughed to himself. "He a lowkey mama's boy," he said. "Code was my mama's birthday." He went to clicked on a couple different things, checking DeAndre's call log and text messages. When he was finished looking through the phone, he looked up at his cousins. "Y'all know this girl Nina that he messes with?"

Tyler shrugged his shoulders. "Yeah. I know who you talking about," he answered. "I've seen her around with him a couple times. She's met us out at the club and shit before. I think she works at the bank or something like that. Why? What's up?"

"Did either of y'all hit her up after the shooting?"

Phil frowned. "Nah. We don't fuck with her like that. I mean, I've seen her around, but your brother keeps a couple in rotation. I don't really know what's what."

"Why you ask?" Tyler questioned.

"Because Bree called me a little bit ago asking how Dre was doing," Jabari answered. "She said Nina told some girl at the club who told her or whatever, and I'm trying to figure out how Nina knew if no one told her. His name wasn't released in the media. How did she know?"

"I don't know, but I'm gon' find out," Phil said. "Hit Bree up and see if she and her friend are working tonight. I'm trying to get some answers."

Jabari pulled out his cell and sent a text. "Already on it."

❧ 15 ❧

The last twenty-four hours had Melinda's head spinning. From DeAndre's shooting to the uncomfortable conversation with her boss about her domestic situation to Jabari's disappearing act, she was tired and irritated. It was Friday night, and she was incredibly thankful for the weekend. She sat at her kitchen with a glass of wine, staring at her cell phone in disbelief for what felt like the hundredth time that day. Jabari's phone went to voicemail again. She was no longer angry. She was worried. Sonya called her earlier, saying that Jabari sent her a text but never came back to the hospital. Something didn't feel right.

Of course, Melinda was worried about his safety. Someone attempted to kill his brother and apparently had been trying to kill his brother for weeks. If Jabari was jumping in the middle of the situation, she was worried what could happen to him. That sparked her other worry. What if he wasn't physically injured on a revenge mission but instead, ended up in more legal trouble? What would that mean for him? What would that mean for *them*? She was so close to leaving Dominic behind. Sure, she should leave the relationship regardless, but part of her knew that the rekindling of her relationship with Jabari was the catalyst that sparked her putting her exit plan into motion. She needed him. Their son needed him. She needed to know that he was okay.

She picked her phone up and called her mother, Carla, who answered on the second ring.

"Hey, Mel. What's going on?"

"Hey, Ma. What are y'all up to tonight?" Melinda was an only child that had not lived at home since she moved out for college. Her parents were empty nesters that seemed to always be on the go.

"Surprisingly nothing," Carla answered. "We're just sitting over here watching TV. I'm not even cooking tonight. Might order some pizza in a little bit. What's going on with you?"

Melinda hesitated. She had yet to tell her mother about the state of things between her and Jabari, largely in part to Dominic. Her mother loved Dominic. In her eyes, he was a stable, responsible man who loved Melinda and Kevin wholeheartedly. He was always on his best behavior in front of her parents, and she never confided in her mother the reality of what she was dealing with. Until recent months, Dominic's unacceptable behavior was infrequent. In the past, Melinda didn't want to ruin his reputation due to situations that were random at best. She was beyond that now. She didn't care anymore about his reputation than he did about keeping his hands to himself.

The picture-perfect image of a relationship that Melinda aspired to was shattered, and she admitted to herself that she was not in love with Dominic—at least not anymore. To be honest, she wasn't sure if she was ever in love with him or if she just loved the idea of what he represented. Not too long after Jabari ended their relationship, she was so determined to stay away from street guys or anyone that closely resembled what she was used to. At the time, Dominic fit the bill. He was kind in the beginning, nice to Kevin, and introduced her to new things—a different type of lifestyle than the other guys she dated before him. She grew comfortable and accustomed to the illusion of safety and security that she incorrectly thought he provided. However, his infidelity and abuse shined a light on all the imperfections of their relationship.

Being cornered into accepting a proposal for fear of an epic ass whooping was the final red flag that she needed. It was the wakeup call that made her realize that when it was all said and done, the heart wanted what the heart wanted. In her case, she wanted Jabari more than anything. She realized that everything she thought she wanted from Dominic, she could get from the only man who ever really had her heart. Before the fatal fight that claimed his freedom, Jabari was providing the safety and security that Melinda wanted for herself and Kevin. Jabari evolved and grew from the person he was in their younger days. He was different from the other guys she dated—the types she wanted to avoid. At least he had been. She feared what his involvement with whatever DeAndre had going on could do for his freedom and their future.

"A lot, Mom, but I'll fill you in on that later," she said. "I know it's pretty last minute, but can I drop Kevin off with you for a few hours?"

"It's already seven o'clock. Why don't you just have him spend the night?"

"That's even better. Thank you."

"You don't have to thank me. I love seeing my grandson. We'll order extra pizza for him. I know that's his favorite."

"See you soon."

Melinda finished her glass and quickly gathered Kevin and the things he would need to spend the night at his grandparents' house. After dropping him off, she started toward Jabari's apartment. Her phone started to ring right as she pulled into the parking deck. She mumbled a curse word when she saw Dominic's name. "Hey," she answered with a fake happy tone.

"Hey, baby. What are you up to?" he asked.

"Just riding around. Kevin's spending the night off at my parents' house. I just dropped him off over there."

"The day ran way longer than I intended, but I'm getting ready to leave the office soon," he said. "You got plans with Sasha or something? Or you heading home?"

"Not sure yet. Probably heading home in a little bit. Not sure if I'll be there before you though."

"Cool. No problem. I'll pick up takeout on the way home and see you when you get there."

"Sounds good."

Melinda ended the call, and she honestly felt terrible. Even though Dominic proved to be a horrible partner and person as a whole, she still felt bad for the things she was doing. She wasn't a liar or a cheater by nature, but that was exactly what the situation turned her into. The sooner she could rid herself from the nightmare her relationship became, the better off she would feel. She dropped her cell phone into her purse and hopped out of her truck. She quickly made her way over to the call box at the door, hoping that Jabari had DeAndre's phone. She scrolled to DeAndre's name and pressed the button to dial the phone. Luckily, the call was answered.

"Hello..."

Melinda rolled her eyes when she heard Jabari's voice. She released a frustrated sigh. There were many things on the tip of her tongue, but she wasn't about to fuss at him through a call box. "Let me up, Jabari."

There was hesitation on his end before he buzzed her into the building. Melinda snatched the door open and took a deep breath, letting it out slowly while she continued to the elevator. By the time she reached the front door, she suppressed her attitude. She knew that she and Jabari could both be hotheads, and she wanted to avoid conflict. She knocked on the door lightly, and it opened seconds later. Jabari held the door open for her while she stepped inside.

"Your mother's worried about you," she said evenly while he closed the door.

"I assume you are too," he responded. "Otherwise, you wouldn't have driven over here out the blue."

Melinda nodded. "I am. Your mother expected to see you at the hospital, and you said you were going to call me."

"I did. My bad," he said, placing his hand on his chest across his heart. "It's been a crazy day, and I got caught up with some other stuff."

"What other stuff?" she asked, shrugging her shoulders. She was met with silence. "I'm not trying to come down on you at all, but your mother's up at the hospital with your brother—your best friend—who is still in critical condition. Calling me or not calling me is irrelevant because I'm here with you now... but what's more important than you being with your mom for your brother?"

Jabari leaned against the front door with his hands in his pockets. "I'll be up there. Probably in the morning," he said, "but Mel, there's something I need to take care of first."

Melinda knew what he was talking about without him getting into all the details. She sighed heavily and shook her head before walking up on him. She wrapped her arms around him for a hug while laying her head against his chest. He wrapped his arms around her, rubbing her back. "Please don't do this right now," she said quietly.

"Don't do what, Mel?"

She looked up into his face. "You know what I'm talking about," she said. "Whatever you're about to get into with your cousins. I know you, and I know them. I have for years. I don't know exactly what's going on, but—"

"What's going on is that some hating ass, bum ass niggas tried to kill my brother and tried to get at him while my son —*our* son was right there," Jabari said. He shook his head while he stared into Melinda's eyes. "I know you're concerned, but you know I can't let that shit ride."

Melinda pulled away from him, covering her face with her hands. "Jabari, please," she said, dropping her hands and looking back at him. "What if something happens? We're so close to getting what we want... being back together. What if something goes wrong out there?"

Jabari pulled her back into his arms. "It won't, Mel. Tyler and Phil know what they're doing, and you know I know how to handle business," he said. "You said it yourself... Dre's one of my best friends. I need to handle this so he doesn't have to look over his shoulder once he's back on his feet."

Melinda looked in his eyes and knew there was no stopping him. No amount of pouting or fussing and cussing would change his mind. All she could do at that point was pray that he was right. Pray that nothing went wrong, and he wasn't taken away from her again.

"You understand, right?" he asked after seeing the worry in her eyes. She nodded. "We're still good?"

"Yes. We are, and I want to keep it that way," she said. "I don't want—I can't—Jabari, it was hard enough being without you the first time, and I—"

"For real, baby. Just let me handle this, and we're good. Everything will be fine," he said, hugging her tighter. He kissed the top of her forehead. "Matter fact, everything should be over with this weekend. We already found you a new place. We'll get your car and get you out of that house within the week, okay?"

Melinda nodded and leaned in to kiss him. With his hands resting on her waist, Jabari kissed her back deeply, pulling away from her lips a few seconds later. He pulled her body closer to his, pressing his hardness against her. He glanced at the time on the refrigerator and then back at her.

"What time you gotta get home?" he asked, kissing her again.

"I got time," she answered breathlessly.

"How much time?" he asked, kissing her neck and unzipping her coat.

Melinda laughed. "Enough," she said while he grabbed her ass with both hands.

Jabari stepped away from the door and took her hand, leading her to his bedroom.

 zzz

PHIL AND TYLER ENDED UP GETTING TO THE STRIP CLUB ahead of Jabari, so they were already seated at a table when he got there. He made his way inside the club and joined them.

"You seen Bree?"

Tyler nodded. "The moment she saw us, she came over asking about you. Thirsty as hell." He laughed. "Does she know y'all are just friends?"

Jabari shrugged his shoulders. "She should, and if she don't, that ain't really my problem. To be honest, we ain't really been in contact like that since Mel came back around."

"I think she missed the memo, bro," Phil said with a laugh. "She's headed over here now though."

Jabari looked up to see Bree moving through the crowd toward their table with a big smile on her face. She greeted everyone and gave Jabari a hug, which he loosely returned with one arm.

"What's going on?" she asked. "Can I get you something to drink?"

Jabari shook his head. "Nah. I'm good. Ain't even gon' be here that long," he answered. "Where's your girl at? Nina's friend."

"Cheyenne? She's around here somewhere," Bree responded with a confused look. "I'm sure I can find her, but... what do you need her for?"

"I just need to talk to her about something. I don't have any way to get in contact with Nina and wanted to give her an update," he lied. "I'd imagine she's pretty concerned about Dre and his condition."

"Oh okay. Yeah... let me go get her."

Tyler narrowed his eyes as he watched Bree disappear back into the crowd. "She acting funny. I don't like that. I bet she knows what's up."

"We're 'bout to find out," Phil said, sitting up straighter when he saw Bree headed toward them with a dancer he recognized.

"Hey, y'all, this is Cheyenne," Bree said. She turned to Cheyenne and said, "They want to give you an update on Dre for Nina. I'll be back."

Cheyenne gave Bree an uneasy look that wasn't lost on the guys at the table. Jabari's forehead wrinkled into a frown as he reached for Bree's hand.

"Why don't you have a seat too?" His tone of voice made it sound more like a command than a suggestion.

Bree hesitated, but when Phil glared at her and pulled a chair out, she sat down. Cheyenne followed suit, sitting down between Bree and Phil.

"What's up?" Cheyenne asked, nervously shifting in her seat. "Bree said Dre's doing alright."

"Yeah. He ain't dead, if that's what you're wondering," Tyler said casually before taking a sip of his drink. Cheyenne frowned at him.

"How well you know his girl?" Jabari asked.

Cheyenne shrugged his shoulders. "Who? Nina? Pretty well I guess. That's my godsister."

"Oh word? So I guess you can tell us where to find her," Phil said.

Cheyenne cut her eyes before giving Bree a questioning look. She turned back toward Phil to respond. "I thought you just needed to give her an update about Dre. I can do that."

"Nah, sweetheart. I said *I* wanted to give her an update," Jabari said. "I need to know how to get in contact with her or where I can find her."

"You say find her like she's lost or something. She's around, but I'm not going to send no niggas I don't know in her direction unannounced," Cheyenne said, pushing away from the table. "If you want to deliver a message, you can send it through me. Otherwise... you can forget it."

Tyler glared at Cheyenne with an angry sneer. "Bitch, I'll—"

Jabari waved a hand in Tyler's direction to cut him off while he glared at Cheyenne. "Nah, let her go. It's cool."

"Y'all on some bullshit, and my time is money. I gotta hit the stage in a minute any way," she said. She looked at Bree, rolling her eyes before walking off.

"Yeah. Alright." Jabari smirked.

With all eyes on Bree after Cheyenne's departure, she shrugged her shoulders and stood up as well. "I don't know what that was about. I guess I should get back to work too, but let me know if y'all need anything else."

Bree started to walk away, but Jabari got up to follow her. Catching up with her through the crowd, he grabbed her arm and pulled her into a back hallway away from the noise from the club.

"Jabari, what the hell?" she asked with a frown, snatching away from him.

"I feel like I should be asking you the same thing," he said, sliding his hands into his pockets. "What was all of that back there?"

Bree shrugged her shoulders. "What was what? That shit with Cheyenne? I said I don't know."

"The looks you two were exchanging and the rolling of the eyes and shit. What was all that energy about?"

"You and your cousins came at her all aggressive trying to get her friend's location. She don't know y'all like that!"

Jabari shook his head. "Come on, Bree. Nina is her godsister, and my cousins are always in this damn club with my brother. Miss me with the bullshit," he said. "She knows them, and she knows whatever is going on that you aren't telling me."

"I don't know what you're talking about. Sorry." She started to walk off again.

Jabari released a frustrated sigh and reached for her arm again, pulling her back toward him. "Bree, look... if you knew me as 'Mel's Jabari', then you knew who I was and what I was about before we met. If there was any doubt, just know that I'm the one that taught DeAndre and those fools at that table everything they know," he said. "We can do this back-and-forth with you playing stupid and shit, but know this... if we find out that you're in the middle of whatever is going on, you're going to have a problem too."

Bree's eyes widened, and Jabari let her arm go.

"You should know well enough to know that you don't want the type of problems that Tyler and Phil can bring."

Bree sighed heavily and looked around to make sure no one was looking. "The problem is that if they find out I told you anything, I'm going to have problems with them too."

"Who is they?" Jabari asked, unconcerned. Bree was cute and all, but whatever she got herself into was her own fault.

"The people who have been gunning for Dre. Carlos and—"

"Carlos and Joey. The ones running that lil' bum ass crew," Jabari said, interrupting her. "Yeah, Bree. We know about them already. What I don't know is how Nina knew Dre was shot. You want to enlighten me?"

A look of defeat crossed Bree's face and she sighed heavenly. "I promise I didn't have anything to do with it."

"Have anything to do with what, Bree?" Jabari questioned with a clenched jaw. She was wasting his time, and he was starting to get frustrated.

She looked down at her feet and shook her head before responding. "Cheyenne is Carlos's sister. She knew her brother and Joey wanted to do business in Dre's area and figured the easiest way to do that was to move him out of the way... permanently," she said. "They thought it would be best if they were able to catch him off guard—while he was drunk leaving the club, while he was stopping for gas by himself late at night, while he was getting pizza with his nephew... shit like that."

Jabari's jaw tightened even further when he heard that the shooters knew DeAndre was with Kevin when they rolled up on him. They knew his son was there and planned the shooting anyway. The anger coursing through his veins was the blinding, illogical rage that he spent the last few years trying to manage. However, he knew there was no use trying to manage the fury he felt in the center of his chest. No, someone else was going to feel it too.

"How did they know when he was by himself or supposedly *off guard?*"

"Nina." Bree sighed heavily again. "Carlos wanted Cheyenne to get in good with him, but she knew he wasn't going to give her the time of day. He ain't never messed with none of the dancers in here, no matter how hard they tried. It was her idea to have Nina come through one night and try to get his attention. It worked, and she's the one that's been letting Carlos and Joey know when and where to find him."

Jabari looked at Bree, shaking his head slowly. He was so pissed he could punch a hole through the wall behind her head. Luckily, Melinda came back around, and he wasn't messing with Bree like that. Still, he wondered about her motives, and why she even pursued him in the first place. Was he just another way to get to his brother?

"How long have you known this?"

"I just found out what they were up to. I swear," I said. "That's why I called to see how he was doing. I felt terrible when I found out what was going on. Dre's always been nice to me."

Jabari's glare was so intense that Bree subconsciously took a step back. He didn't know whether to believe her or not. He chose to test her instead. "Tell your boss you need to go home," he said.

"What? I'm in the middle of my shift. I can't just—"

"You better find a way," he said. "Tell him you're sick or

something. I don't give a fuck. You got five minutes to meet me outside."

"Outside?"

"We're about to go find your friend," he said. "Outside. Five minutes."

Jabari walked away without giving Bree a chance to respond. He didn't need to wait around for an answer, because he knew she wasn't completely stupid. He got Tyler and Phil's attention and signaled for them to follow him to the door. In the parking lot, he filled them in on what he discovered. Three minutes later, Bree came out the front door headed in their direction. It was time for them to go find Nina.

❦ 16 ❦

D ominic sat motionless in the shadows of the parking deck, facing the entrance of the hospital. He circled the deck until spotting the familiar Mercedes-Benz GLC 300—the truck he purchased for Melinda a year prior shortly after she moved into his home. The presence of her vehicle should have been enough for him to confirm her location, but he still wanted to lay eyes on her and make sure. In recent weeks, he grew suspicious. He questioned her words, actions, and where she was when she wasn't with him. Luckily for him, he used her iCloud credentials to extract data from her phone in order to use tracking software to pinpoint her location without her knowing. That was how he found her at the hospital.

Seeing her truck in the parking deck left him with more questions than answers. He felt that something was off when she made it home the previous evening. At the time, she appeared to be in a decent mood. However, she was a little distant, and after only eating a little bit of Chinese takeout, she took a shower and went to bed. Ordinarily, he would have attributed her actions to the result of a long, tiring work week. But Melinda had been distant for weeks. Not drastically, but there were definitely little changes in her behavior that he noticed. For instance, she wasn't the best at keeping secrets from him. As he sat in the hospital parking deck, he had to wonder what in the world as going on. If she or someone close to her was hurt, why didn't she tell him?

As Dominic thought about the change in her demeanor over the last few weeks, he pinpointed the change occurring after their engagement. Sure, he purposely proposed in front of Jabari, knowing that it might draw some sort of reaction. He had to admit that the most recent months of their relationship were not the best. The proposal probably stunned Melinda, but he was not surprised that she said yes. Ultimately, he provided everything he thought she wanted. Being a career professional, his income and lifestyle provided the financial security and stability that most women would dream of. In his eyes, he definitely brought more to the table than Jabari or any of the other guys from her past. Out of all the women in Atlanta, he chose Melinda Barrett, and in his mind, she should be grateful.

He shut off his engine and unbuckled his seat belt. Settling into his seat, he made himself comfortable as he was preparing to wait until Melinda came out of the hospital. He picked his phone up from the cup holder and sent her a text, wondering how she would explain her whereabouts.

zzz

MELINDA SAT QUIETLY, HOLDING JABARI'S HAND, IN THE waiting room for the intensive care unit. The hospital only allowed two visitors into DeAndre's room at a time, so they were waiting for Sonya and Symone to finish visiting with him. Melinda felt the vibration of her cell phone in her purse. Pulling her hand from Jabari's, she retrieved her phone to check her message.

. . .

DOMINIC
5:47 p.m.
Hey baby... just got home from the gym. Where are you? Will you be home for dinner?

MELINDA SIGHED AND CONSIDERED IGNORING THE MESSAGE, but she still had to keep up appearances for the next week or so. Although she was over the charade of a relationship she was maintaining, she couldn't let Dominic know. Not when she still had to lay her head next to his for a few more days. She looked up from her phone, glancing at Jabari, who was deep in thought and staring off into the distance. "Hey... how long you think you'll be here?"

Jabari looked down at his watch and shrugged. "Probably not long. Once my mama and Symone come back out, I just want to go see him for a moment, but then I have somewhere I need to be."

Melinda resisted the urge to release another sigh. Instead, she just asked, "You have more business to take care of?"

Jabari nodded. "Yeah, but tonight should be it. That's the hope anyway."

Melinda nodded in acknowledgment and looked back down at her phone. She briefly considered her words before responding.

MELINDA
5:49 p.m.
Hey! I should be home for dinner. Picking up Kevin shortly. Let me know if you want me to grab some food on the way in.

. . .

SHE PURPOSELY DID NOT SAY WHERE SHE WAS AT THE EXACT moment. She knew there was no way he would be okay with the truth. There was no way he would be okay with her sitting with her ex-boyfriend in a hospital to check on his injured brother. So she did her best to respond without causing unnecessary conflict. A split second later, the phone vibrated again.

DOMINIC
5:49 p.m.
Don't worry about picking anything up. I'll cook. See you when you get here.

MELINDA DROPPED THE PHONE BACK INTO HER PURSE AND looked back at Jabari. "So... you and your cousins didn't take care of everything last night?"

Jabari sighed and took her hand again. "Some things, but not everything. Got some answers though. We'll wrap it up tonight," he said. He raised her hand to his lips, kissing her knuckles. "Don't worry, babe. I told you everything will be fine."

Melinda nodded in acknowledgment, but she couldn't deny the strong feeling of anxiety building in her stomach. Before she could speak again, Sonya and Symone came into the waiting room and headed in their direction.

"He's not awake right now, but you can go in if you want to see him," Sonya said. "He's on a lot of meds for pain and other stuff. I don't know. The doctor explained it, but I couldn't keep up with it all. I can ask the nurse when she comes back around, but—"

Jabari stood up and grabbed his mother's hands. "Ma, calm down. It's fine. Whatever information you missed we'll get another time," he said, interrupting Sonya's rambling. "He's in good hands. The doctors and nurses are taking good care of him. It's fine."

Sonya nodded, taking a deep breath in and releasing it slowly. "Okay. Y'all go on in there and see him."

Jabari turned back toward Melinda, grabbing her hand and helping her up from her chair. She followed him down the hallway and around the corner to the double doors that led them into ICU. Jabari led the way into the room where DeAndre was asleep like Sonya stated. There was only one chair in the room, so he motioned for Melinda to have a seat while he stood by his brother's bedside. He looked at his brother laying in the bed motionless and was angry at the circumstances that caused his current state. He shook his head and touched DeAndre's hand.

"This is fucked up, bruh," he said quietly. "It don't make no sense how all this shit went down, but you ain't even gotta worry about it. We gon' take care of it. Don't worry about that part. We definitely gon' take care of everything. You just focus on resting and getting better. Let me worry about everything else."

Melinda sat with Jabari for another half hour while they visited with DeAndre. Although he was asleep the whole time, the doctors assured them that everything was fine and that his body needed to rest with all the trauma he experienced. When they were ready to go, Melinda followed Jabari back to the waiting room where Sonya and Symone were still seated.

"What y'all about to do?" he asked.

Symone frowned in confusion. "Nothing until Mama's ready to eat dinner, but I'm probably going to just have something delivered," she said. "Are you getting ready to leave?"

"Yeah." Jabari didn't offer any other details about his plans, but he didn't need to. Both his mother and sister had an idea of what wasn't being said.

Sonya looked at him with narrowed eyes. "Jabari..."

"Ma, I came up here because I didn't make it yesterday, but I've got something I need to do."

Sonya shook her head and laughed in disbelief, throwing her hands up in the air. "I don't even have the energy to go back and forth with you," she said. "You're grown, and you're going to make your own decisions. I don't know why in the world you would hop in the middle of this shit and run the risk of ending up like your brother or worse. You just got your girl back. You trying to risk your family again?"

Jabari hugged Sonya and kissed her on the forehead. "Ma, if you knew what I knew and knew that I let that shit slide, you would be equally as upset, if not more. Since we were little boys you always taught me that I was my brother's keeper. I'm gon' handle what I need to handle, and hopefully that's the end of it. Hopefully this is the wakeup call that he needed to leave that shit alone," he said. "Then you won't have to worry about either one of us anymore, but for now, I gotta do what I gotta do. I'll be back up here tomorrow."

Sonya folded her arms across her chest but didn't respond. Jabari gave her another hug and kiss and said goodbye to both her and Symone. Melinda followed him to the elevator. When they stepped inside, he pulled her into his arms.

"I got half a mind to tell you to give that nigga his ring back tonight and just stay with me until your place is ready," he said, kissing her forehead.

"Yeah, but you're not even going to be at your place tonight," she said.

Jabari sighed. "You right," he said when they reached the ground floor. They started out of the building. "I just want you out of that house."

"I want out of that house too, but I have to be smart about it," she said as they exited the building and started toward the parking deck. "We already started this all wrong. No, I don't want to be with him anymore, but I still feel bad about what I'm doing."

"That's 'cause you got a good heart, baby. Me? I don't give a fuck," he said, approaching Melinda's truck. They both laughed.

"I know you don't."

Jabari pulled her into his arms again, hugging her tightly and kissing her lips. "For real though, Mel. I don't give a fuck about

him. It was always supposed to be us. It's always going to be us,"
he said. "I'm not letting anyone or anything else come between
us again, and I won't apologize about that."

"I wouldn't want you to," she said with a smile. She pressed
her lips against his, kissing him deeply.

"Alright. Bet," he said, releasing her from his embrace. "Go
on and get Kev. I'll hit you up later."

"Okay," she agreed. "I love you."

"Love you too."

Jabari stepped back while Melinda unlocked the doors and
hopped into her truck. Watching her taillights, he waited until
she pulled out of view before walking to his own car. Unfortunately, Dominic saw the whole thing.

❧ 17 ❧

Melinda yawned as she climbed the steps heading to her bedroom with a glass of wine in her hand. After finishing the spaghetti dinner Dominic prepared, she cleaned the kitchen while Kevin headed to his room to play video games. As it was nearing ten o'clock, she was relatively tired and planned on drinking her wine, watching a little TV, and going to sleep. When she reached their room, she saw Dominic sitting in silence on the edge of their bed. She paused in the doorway. "Hey... why are you sitting here all quiet?" she asked.

Dominic sat up a little straighter, sighing heavily before he ran his hands over his face. "Come inside and close the door."

Melinda hesitated and frowned. "What?"

Dominic made direct eye contact with her, and his face was void of any emotion. "I need to talk to you about something," he said. "Step inside. Close the door."

Melinda felt uneasy about his request but still did as she was asked. After closing the door, she set her glass of wine down and looked at Dominic with her hands on her hips. "What's going on, Dom? What's the problem now?"

"I don't know. I was hoping you could tell me," he said, sitting up a little straighter and folding his hands in his lap.

"What are you talking about, Dom?"

"I'm talking about... what's been going on with you lately," he said. "Something has been off with you. You've been... a little distant. Unreachable at times and lying about your whereabouts."

Melinda froze. She didn't know where he was going with the conversation, but she knew it was nowhere good. Although she was trying to go along to get along until she could get out of his house, she realized that she must not have done a good job. Something in her actions or behavior was leading to the conversation at hand and putting her in an uncertain situation. She thought about how to respond. However, without knowing how much information he had about the truth, she didn't want to say the wrong thing. Instead, she said nothing.

Dominic got up and walked over to her. Melinda dropped her hands from her waist and looked away. He took her by the chin and turned her face back toward him. "Where were you this afternoon, Melinda?"

"What do you mean? I told you I had some running around to do before I picked Kevin up from my mother's house."

Dominic let go of her chin and laughed skeptically. He shook his head and asked, "Which one of your errands took you by the hospital?"

Panic settled in her chest. "How did you know I was at the hospital?"

Dominic laughed and shook his head again. "It's obviously true. How I know doesn't matter."

"Yes, it does. It absolutely matters, Dom," Melinda said. She stepped around him, moving away from the door. "Have you been following me?"

Dominic forcefully grabbed her arm, pulling her back toward him. "I said it doesn't matter how I know," he said. He continued to hold onto her arm, while his other hand grabbed her left hand, holding it up while he shoved the engagement ring in her face. "What matters is the fact that I put this damn ring on your finger, yet you're running around kissing other niggas in the mouth."

Dominic released her hand but grabbed her chin again, squeezing it tightly. He backed her up until her back was against the wall. She tried to pull away from him, but he held on tighter and slammed her against the wall. She knew she was wrong, and her secrets were uncovered. However, enough was enough. She wasn't about to let him beat her ass again without putting up a fight. While he held her against the wall, her eyes darted around for her cell phone. If she could get to it, she would be able to call for help. Instead, her heart sank to the pit of her stomach when she realized she left it downstairs on the kitchen table when she was cleaning up. She tried to pull away from him again, and he pushed her into the wall again before slapping her across the face.

"How long have you been messing with that damn felon again?" Dominic shouted. Instead of answering, Melinda held onto the side of her face, gingerly touching the stinging red handprint he left on her cheek. Dominic spoke again in a low tone. "I asked how long, bitch?"

In that moment, Melinda blamed herself for allowing the situation to get to that point. She felt to blame for ever trying to see the good in him—for ever accepting his initial apology. She knew she should have left after the first time he hit her and called her out of her name, but she couldn't cry over the past. She had to deal with the here and now. Dominic grabbed her arm again, and she forcefully shoved him in his chest, trying to push him away. She saw the flash of rage in his eyes—the same rage from the night of his birthday when he left her with a black eye. She knew that the situation was about to turn ugly. She quickly turned and tried to make a break for the door. She got close, but before she could reach for the handle, Dominic shoved her in the back, knocking her to the ground. She tried to push herself up, but he grabbed her leg and dragged her away from the door.

Melinda tried so long to protect Kevin and keep him shielded from the things she was dealing with, but without her phone, she couldn't call 911 herself. She had to call her son. "Kevin!" she screamed. "Kev!"

"Shut the hell up!" Dominic yelled, kicking her in the side. "That lil' nigga ain't gon' save you."

He reached for the doorknob, locking it. That gave Melinda just enough time to push to her feet, but Dominic was back in her face in an instant. He grabbed her by her neck, squeezing her throat and trying to cut off her air supply. Melinda's arms flailed around, trying to reach for anything she could grab. Her hand finally rested on her wine. Snatching the glass from the table, she smashed it against his head—breaking the cup and spilling the wine. The red wine dripped down the side of his face and onto the hardwood floors, only angering him further. He removed his hands from around her neck, briefly touching the side of his head. She yelled for Kevin again right before Dominic hit her dead in the face with a punch that sent her flying to the ground.

zzz

JABARI WAS THE LAST ONE TO PULL UP TO THE HOUSE. HE SHUT the engine off and sighed heavily before climbing out of the car. He was ready to get it over with. The night before was a long one. After convincing Bree to leave work early, she led Jabari and his cousins to Nina's house. They sat outside the house for hours until Nina finally showed up in the middle of the night. Once Nina was spotted, Jabari dropped Bree off at her place while Tyler and Phil stayed to get the information they needed. He was confident that his cousins would handle their business, and they did. During their confrontation, Nina eventually confirmed her involvement in having DeAndre set up as well as the information Bree shared with Jabari.

He closed his car door and walked up the driveway to the unassuming suburban home that belonged to Ray, the main enforcer for DeAndre's crew. He knocked on the front door that was quickly opened by Adam, another one of the guys on DeAndre's team.

"Hey, man," Adam greeted him with a fist bump. "They're downstairs."

Jabari nodded in acknowledgment and headed for the door leading to Ray's finished basement. He made his way down the steps where Ray, his cousins, and a few other men were waiting. They all greeted him as he made his way further into the room. Looking around, Jabari noticed there were enough weapons to arm a small militia. He walked up to the pool table in the center of the room where several assault rifles were laying. One of the guys standing by him handed him a blunt, but he shook his head and stuck his hands in his pockets while he overheard a side conversation between Ray and Phil. They were discussing Nina.

"What did you do with the girl?" Ray asked.

Phil smirked. "She set my blood up. The hell you think I did with her?" he asked. "Got rid of her ass. That Cheyenne bitch too. Can't let no shit like that slide. What if Dre didn't make it? Huh? What if the shooters hit Jabari's little boy?"

Ray cut his eyes at Jabari and nodded. "Yeah, I hear you, man. Eliminate the threat and tie up the loose ends."

"Exactly," Phil said, turning his attention to Jabari. "To be honest, I don't know why you spared Bree."

Jabari shrugged his shoulders. "Because she wasn't in on it. She didn't play a role in the setup, and she's the only reason we even found out what happened. She's gon' keep her mouth shut."

"I guess," Phil mumbled, turning his attention back to the gun on the table in front of him.

Ray cleared his throat before he addressed the room. "Alright, man. Listen up..."

Jabari paid attention while Ray laid out the plan for the evening. Apparently, their targets—Carlos and Joey—were at their trap that night. Phil and Tyler were able to retrieve the location from Nina before her demise. Ray already had a couple guys sitting on the location, making sure they didn't lose sight of Carlos or Joey. The plan was to get there, air the spot out, and leave. Ray was still discussing details when Jabari felt his phone vibrate in his pocket. He looked down at the screen to see Melinda's number and let it go to voicemail. She knew he was busy, so he decided to call her back later. But then she called back again and another time after that. Jabari stepped away from the table, to a quiet corner of the room so he could answer her call. Fear gripped his chest as he tapped the screen to answer. Something had to be wrong for her to call him back-to-back.

"Mel, what's wrong?"

"Daddy!" Kevin's voice shouted into the phone.

"Kevin?" Jabari asked with confusion all over his face. "Where's your mom?"

"She's in her room, but the door is locked. I can't get in."

Jabari pressed the phone to his head even closer while covering his other ear. There was some sort of commotion in the background, but he couldn't clearly make out the sounds. "Kev, what's going on?"

"I think Dominic is mad at Mommy. It sounds like they're fighting, and he keeps yelling at her." It sounded like Kevin was crying. "She tried to call for me, but the door is locked. I got her phone to call you."

Jabari's jaw clenched in anger, and he let out a deep, frustrated breath. "Good job, buddy. Look, I need you to stay on the phone with me because I may need you to let me in the house," he said. "I'm on my way."

Spotting him in the corner and the look on his face, Tyler made his way over to him.

"What's wrong?"

"This nigga done put his hands on Mel. I gotta go."

"Say less," Tyler said, slapping hands with his cousin and shaking his head in disbelief. "Let me know if you need me."

Jabari nodded and then quickly left the room. He jogged to his car and sped away from Ray's home. Luckily, Dominic's house wasn't too far away. He was seeing red the entire way, speeding and running lights. He said a silent prayer that he wasn't pulled over before he reached his destination. He was mildly relieved when he pulled up to the house without being stopped by the Dekalb County Police. Parking on the street, he jumped out of the car and crossed the yard at lightning speed, making his way to the front door. He tried the handle, but it was locked.

"Kev, I need you to let me in," he said into the phone. "Do you know where Dominic is?"

"No."

"Do you think you can make it to the front door?" Jabari asked calmly evenly though he felt like he was about to lose his mind. He had half a mind to bust through the door, but he knew there was a chance he was going back to jail that night. He wanted to minimize his potential charges and eliminate breaking and entering from the list.

"Yes, Daddy. I'm coming down now."

During Jabari's short drive, the background noise inside the home quieted. He no longer heard the struggle or either of their voices, and the silence unnerved him. Seconds later, he heard the lock turn before Kevin opened the door. When he laid eyes on his son, he ended their call and placed his phone in his pocket. He pulled Kevin into a big hug before entering the home quietly. Jabari closed the door, pausing in the foyer for a brief moment and looking around. There was no sign of Dominic, Melinda, or the struggle he heard over the phone.

"Have you seen your mom?"

Kevin shook his head. "The door is still locked."

"Come on," Jabari said, heading for the stairs. "Go in your room and close the door. Don't come out until I come get you."

Kevin nodded and did as he was told. Jabari took a deep breath before approaching the closed door he assumed to be the master bedroom. He tried that doorknob as well, but it was locked just like Kevin stated. Jabari raised his foot and kicked the door. The blow he delivered destroyed the lock and forced the door off the hinges. When the door swung open, Jabari was instantly distressed and concerned when he saw Melinda laying on the floor. He rushed over and knelt by her side, observing the cuts and bruises to her face and body. Her lip was busted and bleeding, and her face had too many bruises to count. Both her eyes were blacked, and he wasn't sure that her nose wasn't broken. A few of her nails were broken, also highlighting the struggle that took place. While checking her pulse, he could see the shallow rise and fall of her chest, indicating that she was alive. That gave him momentary relief.

Interrupting the stillness of the room, he heard another door crack open. He looked up to see Dominic standing in the entry way to the bathroom. Although he had a cut on his forehead and a few minor other bruises, Dominic was nowhere near as bad off as Melinda. Jabari was so overcome with rage his jaw was twitching.

Dominic smirked and asked, "You come to collect your bitch?"

Jabari was on his feet before Dominic finished his question. He hit Dominic with a right cross before he could open his mouth to say anything else. Dominic fell on his knees, and when he tried to get back up, Jabari hit him again and again until he was tired. Then he kicked him in the side and stomach until he stopped fighting back. Jabari pulled DeAndre's Glock 40 from his waist and took the safety off. He was aiming the gun at Dominic's head with his finger wrapped around the trigger when he heard Kevin's voice behind him.

"Daddy..."

Jabari blew a heavy frustrated breath. As bad as he wanted to blow Dominic's head off, he couldn't that in front of his son, and

Melinda needed medical attention. Reluctantly, he put the safety back on and tucked the gun back into his waistband. Looking down at an unconscious Dominic, Jabari resisted the urge to kick him again and turned to face a scared Kevin that was staring at a motionless Melinda.

"Hey, man. It's okay," he said, crossing the room to hug Kevin again. "We need to get your mom out of here. We gotta get her some help."

Kevin nodded, and Jabari moved back to Melinda, pulling her up from the ground. Shouldering most of her weight, he ushered out of the house and to the car with Kevin right behind him. He rushed to the hospital, speeding yet again, with Melinda laying across the backseat and Kevin up front. During the ride, he heard Melinda whimper quietly. Although he hated that she was in pain, he was relieved that she was regaining consciousness. Making sure to leave the gun in the car, he managed to get her into the emergency room where she immediately received attention. Instructed to sit in the waiting room until she was admitted and received care, Jabari sat quietly with Kevin. He pulled his phone out and called his sister.

"Hey, Jabari..."

"Hey, Symone, are you still at the hospital?" he asked.

"Yeah. Mom's spending the night with Dre, but I'm about to head home," she answered. "What's up?"

"I'm back up here, but I'm in the emergency room."

"Emergency room? Jabari, what the hell—"

"I'm fine, Symone. It's Mel. I'll tell you the story later, but I need you to take Kevin with you. I'm about to call Ms. Carla."

Symone quickly agreed and came down to get Kevin. Before they left, he took Melinda's phone from Kevin so he could call her mother. Then he continued to wait. More than an hour later, Melinda was triaged and moved to a room. During that time, Carla and Quincy, Melinda's father, made it to the hospital to wait with him. They sat quietly with little to no conversation until a nurse told them they could see Melinda. Jabari entered the room behind Carla, who rushed to Melinda's side with tears in her eyes. He stood near the door.

"Mom, I'm okay," Melinda said through gritted teeth. It was obvious that she was still in pain.

"I'm sorry," Carla said, shaking her head. "I don't mean to get emotional. It's just... I can't believe he would do this. Had he put his hands on you before?"

"Mom, that doesn't really matter right now." Melinda avoided answering the question, but Carla could read between the lines.

"I can't believe you didn't tell me, but like you said, that doesn't really matter right now," Carla responded. "I'm just glad Jabari was there to help you."

Melinda slowly turned her head toward the door, making eye contact with Jabari. She struggled to raise her arm, extending her hand in his direction. He made his way to her side, gingerly holding her hand.

"Thank you," she said with tears in her own eyes.

"You ain't gotta thank me, Mel. You know there's no limit to what I would do for you," he said. He bent down to kiss her bandaged forehead.

"I know... and I'm sorry." Jabari frowned before she continued to speak. "I'm sorry, Jabari. You have to go."

"Go?"

"Dominic is following me or tracking my phone or something. I don't know, and I can't remember how we left the house," she said. "But he probably knows you brought me here, and if he's conscious, he's going to send the cops."

"Even though he—"

"Nothing about the way he acted tonight was logical. You gotta go. The nurse said the cops will be here in a little bit anyway to talk to me about my injuries," she said. "Is Kevin okay?"

"Yeah. He's with my sister for the night."

"Good. Then I need you to go. Go now and let me try to clean this up with the police. Please."

Jabari's frown deepened, but Carla reached across the bed and patted his arm.

"I'll call you later and give you an update," she said.

Jabari sighed and nodded. He hesitantly kissed Melinda on the forehead again and turned to leave the room. He barely stepped out of the room before he saw law enforcement in the hallway. He released a defeated sigh when they headed in his direction.

"Excuse me, sir. Stay right there," one of the officers said, holding his hand up to urge Jabari to stop walking. "Can I see some ID?"

Jabari hesitated but slowly reached for his wallet. He pulled out his driver's license and handed it to the officer that addressed him. The officer looked at the ID closely before handing it to his partner.

"Mr. Butler, can you tell me where you were earlier this evening?" he asked, looking down at the bruised knuckles on Jabari's right hand. "Did you happen to visit 3367 Constellation Lane in the Vista Hill subdivision?"

Jabari sighed heavily and nodded. "Yeah, man."

The officer nodded in acknowledgment. "Okay. Go ahead and turn around for me. Put your hands behind your back," he said.

Jabari did as he was told and listened while the officer hand-cuffed him and read him his Miranda rights. He couldn't believe Dominic had the nerve to call the cops on him after what he did to Melinda. However, he also didn't care. When he told Melinda there was no limit to what he would do for her, he meant every word. If that meant going back to prison, then so be it.

❧ 18 ❧

THREE WEEKS LATER

Melinda shifted in her seat and toyed with the bright pink cast on her left arm while she sat in the visitation center at the jail waiting for Jabari. She sighed and looked around the room at the other inmates that were meeting with their family members and loved ones. Like many others there presumably, she silently wished that her family could be together outside of the jail walls, but luckily, she wouldn't have to wait long. The charges that Dominic alleged against Jabari were ultimately dropped when Dominic ended up facing his own legal issues. However, the arrest was a violation of his probation, and Jabari had to deal with the consequences, which resulted in a ninety-day stay in jail. They were fortunate the judge took into account all the circumstances surrounding his attack on Dominic— including the injuries that Melanie sustained at Dominic's hands.

Melinda ended up with a broken arm, bruised ribs, cuts on her face the required stitches, and black eyes among other minor injuries. Even with the extent of her wounds, Dominic was able to avoid prison altogether. Instead of ending up behind bars, he worked out a plea deal for a charge of aggravated assault and ended up with probation. Although Melinda was still dealing with her own anger in regard to the situation, she couldn't have been more grateful that Jabari showed up for her when she needed him most, regardless of the punishment he ended up facing. The whole situation was a nightmare, but at least it was almost over.

She smiled when Jabari was led out to the visitation center and made his way over to her. Sitting down in front of her, it was hard for him to contain the smile on his face either. Throughout the ordeal that took place over the last few months, Melinda felt lucky. She was lucky that when it was all said and done the two of them were still together, as they both believed it should have always been.

"Hey..." he greeted her.

"Hey..."

He pointed at her arm. "Cute cast."

"Thank you," she said with a laugh. "I let your son pick the color, but I dressed to match so I could be cute today. I know I looked pretty rough the last time you saw me."

Jabari shrugged his shoulders. "You're always beautiful. I'm just glad to see that you're healing." He paused. "How is everything?"

"Good. Getting better," she answered. "Work is good. Kevin is good. He's with my mom today, but I'll bring him next time."

Jabari nodded. "Are y'all staying at your parents' house?"

"No. We're staying with Sasha for a few weeks before my apartment is ready," she answered.

"Were you able to get any of your stuff from your old spot?"

Melinda shook her head. "No. I didn't even want to bother with it now that I have the restraining order," she answered. "I have what I need. My parents and your cousins are looking out."

Jabari shook his head and laughed at the mention of Tyler and Phil. During DeAndre's recovery, he mentioned his intention to legitimize his business dealings and leave the illegal activity to his eager cousins. No one had a clue if or when Tyler and Phil would ever leave the streets alone. When his laughter subsided, he fell quiet, looking deep into Melinda's eyes.

"I'm sorry, Mel."

"For what?" she asked with a deep frown.

"For this," he said, waving his hand around. "For doing the one thing I didn't want to do when I got home and separating myself from you and Kevin again."

"There's no reason for you to apologize. You got me out of a situation I had no business being in. You probably saved my life," she said. "This is temporary. We just have to get through these next couple of months, and everything will be fine. What's a few months when we hopefully have forever?"

The corner of Jabari's mouth pulled up into a half smile. "You're right. Ninety days ain't shit when we're looking at forever."

"From this life to the next," she said with a wide grin.

"And even after that."

Melinda wasn't going to let anything separate her from Jabari again. She messed up when she thought that anyone could ever replace him or that she needed something or someone different. Trying to find something different almost cost her everything, and she wouldn't make that mistake again. Prison. Probation. Ninety days in jail. The circumstances didn't matter. Drug dealer. Thug. Family man. Best friend. Love of her life. Regardless of whatever he was or what he would become, one thing was for certain: he was the only one for her. No matter the situation, she knew that she would always bet on them. She would put that on everything.

ABOUT THE AUTHOR

Michelle Elaine is an author of African American and Urban fiction and romance. Born and raised in Atlanta, GA, she still resides in the metro area with her husband and sons. She has always possessed a passion for storytelling and character creation/development. This passion led to several short stories and development of plots and characters before she completed her first book, *A Good Girl & A Down South Millionaire*. Visit her website and join her mailing list to stay in the know on the latest releases, etc.

Other ways to stay connected:
   Facebook – Author Michelle Elaine
   Instagram – authormichelleelaine
   Website – www.michelleelainebooks.com
   Email – michelleelainebooks@outlook.com

ON EVERY THUG I LOVE

Baltimore Edition

SHONTAIYE MOORE

ITALY

"The fuck you got an attitude for?" my boyfriend Quan asked me with a frown.

"I don't have an attitude." I countered sharply, rolling my eyes. I was putting on my best front, but Quan knew me well. I most definitely had an attitude.

"You mad cuz I'm going out to Victory's?" he questioned. He stood in front of the full-length mirror and brushed off his clothes. A simple navy-blue Nike sweatsuit. His big, bright gold medallion swung as he moved. I glared at him out the corner of my eye. He looked good, but I wasn't going to tell him that. Besides, he had the mirror in front of him, and he could see for himself. Quan was low-key fine as hell with neat shoulder-length dreads that dangled around his brown face. Tall with a little thickness to him, he carried himself with a confidence that was unmatched.

"I said... I don't have an attitude," I repeated, my head buried in my phone. "Do what the fuck you want."

"Bae, why you always gotta act like that every time I go somewhere?" Satisfied with his look, he turned away from the mirror and walked over to where I was stretched out on the bed.

"It ain't nobody but me, Loco, and Raul." He bopped over

and stood to the side of where I was seated on the bed. I didn't bother to look up. After standing there for a few moments and waiting for a response, he reached down and snatched my phone out of my hand.

"Quan, give me my phone," I demanded, looking up at him with an angry glare. I didn't have a thing to hide, but I was still annoyed since he was now deliberately trying to antagonize me.

"Oh, *now* yo' ass can talk? But you didn't hear me talking to you while ago?" He tossed my phone on the bed and waited for me to continue.

"I told you I don't have an attitude. I just hate sittin' in this boring ass house alone while you run around all night with them clowns."

Quan laughed. "You always callin' somebody a clown. They my niggas, and they been around since forever."

"So? What that mean?" I looked up and glared at him. "They're more important than *me*?"

Quan rolled his eyes. "Italy, you already know the answer to that. You talk so dumb sometimes. No, they are not more important than you." He leaned down and pressed his soft lips into my pouting ones.

"So why you never make *real* time for me? You already in and out on business and then when you get back, I gotta sit up in this house on pause while you run around with them. I'm getting tired of that," I admitted.

"Baby, please stop complaining. Everything that I do is for us. This boring ass house—and might I add, *expensive* ass house—is to keep us comfortable and safe."

I glanced up at him, still unmoved by what he had just said.

"Do you want to come?" he asked.

"You know I don't want to go nowhere with them," I grumbled.

"Well then."

"You say it like I'm boring, babe, but you already know the real reason I don't want to be anywhere with those niggas. They always in something. If they ain't on Instagram callin' somebody out, they always shooting at someone or getting shot at. Why would I want to be up in that mix?"

Quan paused and then proceeded to go back to walking around the room, gathering his things so he could leave.

"Right. That's why I prefer you be low-key. Plus, you finer than a motherfucker, and I don't want no niggas up in yo' face." He smiled, but I wasn't even the least bit amused.

"But I hear everything you're saying," he claimed with a defeated sigh.

"Yeah, so if that's the case, then when you gon' step yo' security up? You told me once you step your security up, then we could go out more."

"Soon, babe. I promise. Look, I gotta roll." He looked down at his simple Movado watch. "The show starts at ten. It's 8:45, and I need to meet up with everybody."

"Oh, you doin' a show?" I asked in surprise. I thought he was just going to hang out, but he was actually going to Victory's to get some money for us. "Why you ain't tell me?"

"Because you never asked." He smiled. "I just got back in town after being gone a week. You think I want to be around them niggas when I could be home witcho fine ass?"

He walked over to me and slid his hand into my lace camisole, grabbing my breast playfully. I couldn't help but moan from his touch. Lately, I wasn't feeling it often enough, because he was always on the road. I couldn't complain though. He was doing his thing. Living his dream as an entertainer. An up-and-coming rapper that was spiraling quickly to the top. I was proud of my man. Because of that, I figured I would chill on him. He wasn't on no funny time, and he was good to me. I wasn't gon' press him.

"Hit me and let me know that you made it safely," I told him.

He knew the routine. All he had to do was shoot me a text. That had become our little thing since he started blowing up. Quan swore he wasn't going to be like all the other rappers and let fame get to his head. His goal was to get rich for his family. That was it. He wasn't out there to show off his wealth to the world. It wasn't the reason why he rapped. He rapped because he loved it and he was good at it. For that reason, I wasn't really worried about him getting sucked into that life—the parties, groupies, Instagram hoes, and social media thots. He knew I didn't play that stepping out shit. I didn't do it to him, so he wasn't about to do it to me. I didn't play social media heavy, but if I did, I had no doubt that once a couple people got a look at me, I would soon be posted up on The Shade Room with performers and athletes drooling over me. I doubt he wanted a bunch of niggas that were richer than him hopping in my inbox. I was humble, but I knew I was bad. A timeless beauty with chocolate skin, plump lips, and a soft, ghetto booty. Although I was pretty, I didn't harp on it. I stayed fit and stayed looking good for myself and my man. Quan was all I wanted.

"Of course." He nodded. He leaned down and gave me another kiss. This time, I softened my lips and reciprocated.

"I'll see you later, alright? And I love you." He headed out the door.

"I love you too," I replied softly but loud enough for him to hear.

I smiled but couldn't help but sigh once I heard the front door close. Next to my mama and sister, Quan was my everything. We had been together since I was twenty-two and he was twenty-four. Three years in and we still loved each other like we'd just met. I couldn't lie, loving Quan came with its challenges. Despite those challenges, Quan did everything to make it worthwhile.

Quan and I both grew up on the mean streets of West Baltimore's Harlem Park section. I grew up on Mckean, off W. Lanvale near N. Monroe, while Quan bounced around the neighborhood with his mama. While I stayed out the way, Quan and his team were part of a small but popular crew he'd founded called Big Bank Boys; they were known to the city as Triple B.

Their biggest rival was another local rapper named Leel, who founded the group BGS, or Baltimore Gangsta Squad. Instead of teaming up and making money together, they feuded about who was the hottest, who was the realest, *and* who was the deadliest. Of course, with Quan catapulting quickly to the top and snagging features and shows that helped him live up to the big bank part of his name, jealousy would intensify their beef with both eventually making diss tracks and throwing shots at the other.

I met Quan, Rayquan Jones, through my sister, India, and her best friend, Kayla.

Before Triple B and BGS were rivals, they were friends and frequented the same spots. Truthfully, they were just niggas from the same hood just trying to find a way. Kayla had a baby by Leel's right-hand man, Jahquez, who also happened to be his older brother. Always rocking with her bestie, India would typically roll with Kayla to the shows BGS had throughout the city. I usually never joined them; however, two years back, Kayla happened to be beefing with a young hoe that Jahquez was hittin' on the low. That was the one and only day I tagged along in case some shit popped off. Luckily, I did. If I hadn't, I wouldn't have met Quan.

Quan's presence and charisma were magnetic. I'd never seen or heard of him before, but as soon as my eyes met his, I was drawn to him. Handsome. Neat dreads. Nice body and a whole lot of swag.

"Who's that?" I leaned over and whisper to my sister.

"Who him?" Her eyes followed my gaze. "Oh, he another rapper from the west side," was what she told me. "They all be chillin' at the same spots."

Before I could ask another question, Quan's eyes met mine. I didn't want to seem pressed, so I immediately diverted my gaze, ending all questioning about him. Later that evening, we all wound up at a little after-hours spot in Harlem Park called Jamz for the after-party. Sure enough, the little young hoe that Jahquez was fuckin' came waltzing up in the joint with four or five other bitches like she owned it. Not waiting for the smoke, Kayla, instead, delivered it. As soon as Kayla spotted her, she was on the girl's ass for all the smack she had previously talked on the phone. Of course, her girls were trained to go, and a brawl erupted.

Being the gutta ass Baltimore bitch that I was, I didn't storm into the fight with my hands. I dived in, smackin' hoes with an empty Henny bottle I'd spotted laying around. My sister India knew how I got down, and that was exactly why I was called to roll anytime there was beef. Fists flying, glass shattering, shit got real up in Jamz that night. After bustin' a few heads, Quan was the one to snatch me up and pry the still-intact bottle from my hand.

"Chill, shorty," he told me. "The cops coming. You and yo' folk gon' fuck around and get cased up."

Still in go mode, I glanced around and spotted Jahquez dragging Kayla out, while India had already dipped out and was nowhere in sight. That of course, would be followed by the sound of police sirens out of nowhere that seemed to be getting closer and closer. The staff in Jamz had sure enough called the police on us for tearing up their shit. But I'd be a lie if I said I blamed them.

"Come wit' me. I'm headed out the back before the police roll up in here."

Reluctantly, I agreed. I rolled out the back with and him and left with him, and he dropped me off safely to my home. And hell yeah, I gave him my address so he could drop me right off at the front door. I was exhausted from fighting, and I figured if he was going to do something to me, he would have done it when I got my simple ass in his car. Something told me that he was harmless and I was safe with him. I knew most broads would front and say, you don't know that nigga from a can of paint, but frankly, I was better off leaving with him rather than alone. When the dust finally settled, I learned that after the fight India had left Jamz with Kayla's people, and I was left all by my damn lonesome. I sure would have been in a tough spot if them bitches had seen me alone and tried to roll on me.

Before I got out the car and went inside my house, Quan asked for my number. One date led to two, and two dates led to forever. Quan and I had been together ever since.

While most broads who dealt with rising rappers, dealt with

dog nigga shit—the cheating, disrespect and bitches—I dealt with none of the above. While Quan was a hood nigga to the core, he was raised with respect and integrity. I knew the very moment he took me around his mama that I was in good hands. He treated her like a queen. With the utmost respect. Every dollar he made, she got a portion. *Yes, ma'am, no, ma'am*, all that good shit was part of his everyday vocabulary when he was talking to her. Now I wasn't going to front like he was perfect. He had his moments where he was rough around the edges. He had a little temper and liked to get smart, but all the good in him overshadowed his flaws. He was raised to treat women right. Attention, love, affection, encouragement. Quan quickly became one of the most important people in my life, providing me with everything I needed and then some.

The first big check he got from a show, he immediately moved us from the hood to the suburbs. And by *us*, that was exactly what I meant. Initially, it was just the three of us: me, him, and his mother, Jackie. Although he had a bunch of sisters on his dad's side, Quan was his mother's only child. We all moved into a small but cute luxury condo out in the sticks. As he made more money, he put his mama up in her own townhouse, and the two of us upgraded to a larger one close by so that my mother could move in. I didn't even have to ask. Quan was just like that. He took care of those around him and ensured their safety. The problem for me was, he took our safety more seriously than his own. And lately, that was the biggest reason that we bumped heads. His homies, Raul and Loco, were cool. I couldn't deny that, but they stayed in too much drama. Especially Loco. Quan didn't really need them to be successful. He was dope all by himself. Nevertheless, I always told myself that I would support Quan, no matter what decision he made. I was concerned about his well-being overall. Not just about his rap career. I loved him no matter what. So if he wanted to run the streets with his homies, then that was what it was. Yeah, I was going to bitch about it and do my best to make him see the error in his choices, but I would still support him. That was just what real bitches did.

Despite all that, I loved Quan to pieces. I hadn't gotten a ring yet, but we talked about it all the time, so I knew it would eventually come. He was my forever, and I had no doubt that I was his as well.

INDIA

"Girl, why is you still goin' back and forth with that nigga?" I asked my best friend Kayla. My brother-in-law, Quan, was performing at Victory's in twenty minutes, and she was still arguing on the phone with her baby daddy.

"Nigga, what the fuck that gotta do with anything? I support everything your brother does. That's her *brother-in-law*. How is me going to a show disrespect?"

Kayla paused for a moment. I guess she was giving him his chance to talk and argue some additional nonsense.

"Because my bitch asked me to go so, I'm going," Kayla continued to quarrel with her baby daddy, Jahquez. My eyes slid up and hit the back of my head in irritation. I didn't know why the fuck she wouldn't just hang up on his ass. I couldn't stand him. He was pure drama. Controlling possessive, and to add insult to injury, had the nerve to be broke. He always had his nose up in my direction and kept hoe in his mouth instead of my name when referring to me. Truth was, I wasn't the hoe. I'd admit to being a gold digger, but Kayla deserved the hoe crown more than I.

"I don't give a fuck about that. I'll be in later. Stop blowing me up behind that dumb shit," she snapped before finally hanging up in Jahquez's ear.

"Girl, what's that nigga trippin' 'bout now?" My lip curled as I let out an annoyed groan. While I waited for her response, I continued to drive my Dodge Challenger around the venue's crowded parking lot in search of a space.

"What *ain't* he trippin' about? He still stuck on that dumb, childish ass beef between Triple B and BGS. Leel a grown ass man that's too worried about hatin' instead of perfecting his damn craft. He swears somebody doing something underhanded to stop his bag, but what somebody really need to tell him is that he's falling off because them rhymes he spit is getting wacker by the day. He stoppin' his own bag. He too worried about the shows everybody else bookin' that he ain't bookin' none of his own."

I laughed. She was right. BGS used to be the shit, but now, they had nothing on Triple B. Baltimore always showed love to their local rappers, but lately, BGS hadn't even been getting much airplay in their own city. The problem was, BGS hadn't produced any songs worth actually playing. I remembered the days I was dying to tag along with Kayla in hopes of snagging a baller at one of their shows or events. These days, I was popping up at most, if not all of Quan's shows. Even as far as New York and Philly. If I could drive to it, I was there. Quan kept a bunch of paid niggas around him, and being his sister-in-law, I got first dibs on all of them. Quan had taken off, and although he'd put in a lot of work to get to where he was, it all seemed like it was happening so quick.

"Facts. They beefin' when he should have humbled himself back when Quan first started blowin' up. Could have hopped on a track with him or something."

"Right," Kayla agreed with a nod. "Now he hating because Quan taking off and he sittin' his dusty ass in Baltimore poutin'. Ain't nobody trying to be around that negative shit. They sittin' up making diss tracks about niggas that's getting way more

money than them. But they still throwing them bullshit basement parties and still performing in the same poor ass strip clubs
with a bunch of bald-headed wack bitches. Meanwhile, Quan
selling out big venues in cities all over. I always showed Leel love,
but his music just ain't it no more," Kayla added, keeping it all
the way real. I couldn't help but let out a chuckle as I finally
found a parking spot and eased in.

"Come on." I wasted no time pushing my door open and
hopping out. I had just checked the time on the dash, and it was
five to ten. I was trying to hurry up and get inside. Quan's shows
were usually packed and sold out, and I didn't want to have to
call and beg my sister, Italy's stank ass so we could get in. My
baby sister wasn't really for a bitch constantly calling her nigga's
line directly, so I always had to go through her first whenever I
had trouble getting in the door. Although I was older, Italy was
definitely the spicier one between the two of us. I called her
when it was beef. It wasn't the other way around.

While I waited for Kayla to grab her shit and get out my car,
I brushed off my fire-engine-red dress. I couldn't deny the fact
that I knew I looked good. The dress was screaming on my
milky-brown skin. It stopped right under my ass and showed off
my petite body and smooth, toned thighs. I dug my brush out
my bag and quickly raked through all thirty-six inches of my
Brazilian hair.

"Come on, bitch. Leave that damn phone in the car." Jahquez
was still blowing Kayla's phone up, and frankly, it was getting on
my nerves. I stuffed my brush back in my bag and yanked out my
lip gloss so I could make sure my lips were poppin'.

"Facts. I'm gon' tuck it right under the seat. He definitely not
about to ruin my night."

Kayla tucked her phone, grabbed her bag, and then finally
stepped out of the car in a black romper. With her hair swept up
into a bun, she looked like a fallen angel. A skinny, light-skinned
chick, standing at around five feet five, Kayla's beauty was eye-
catching.

"How I look?" Kayla spun around so I could get a look at her.

"You look good, girl. You always do. Now bring yo' high-yellow ass before we can't get in."

"Bitch, let's go," she said, flashing me an evil grin. I instantly lit up. It was the look of reassurance that I'd been waiting for. She was no longer just Jaden's mommy and Jahquez's girl. For the next couple hours, she was my partner in crime. We were 'bout to have a ball.

❦

After standing in line for twenty minutes, we were finally let into the packed club. I wasn't surprised that it was lit. All of Quan's shows were.

"Let's go to the bar!" I shouted behind me to Kayla, who was trailing close by as we made our way through the club.

"Hold up!" Kayla grabbed my arm and stopped me. "Fuck that bar. Ain't that Loco and Raul?" She pointed. My eyes quickly followed the tip of her finger.

"Hell yeah." Instead of continuing, we made our way over to the two men. They were Quan's right-hand guys. Wherever they were, Quan wasn't too far. We were headed to the VIP section.

"Raul!" I called out over the music so he could hear me. I watched as Raul turned his head from side to side to see who had called his name. I threw my hand up in the air so he would look in my direction. As soon as our eyes made contact, a smile appeared on his face.

"We comin' over there with y'all," I yelled to him. It was a statement rather than a question. Quan never denied me access to the VIP section that he was in, and neither Raul nor Loco didn't mind since they were trying to fuck me. Out of the two, Raul was my favorite. I didn't particularly care for Loco since he was a notorious troublemaker. His reputation, mouth, and delivery kept Triple B immersed in drama. Every other week, he was on Instagram going live and calling someone out. Every other month, he was either shooting or getting shot at. Although Quan was from the streets, he was more laidback and chill. He talked his shit too, but it was his childhood friends that kept him wrapped up in the drama and street beef.

As we proceeded around the ropes to the VIP section, I noticed that the lights on the stage dimmed. I knew what that meant. It was time for Quan to perform.

"Y'all ready to turn the fuck up!" the host bellowed through the microphone.

"Yeah!" the crowd cheered in anticipation of the main act.

"I saidddddddd, is y'all ready to turn the fuck up!" he repeated.

"Yeah!" the crowd chanted. I looked around and smiled at how hype everyone was to see Quan perform.

"Well, coming to the stage for the main event is Baltimore's very own... Quan and Triple B! Give it up for them Big Bank Boysssssssss!"

The crowd erupted as Quan and his crew stormed the stage. Clutching his mic, Quan began performing his number-one hit "Fly Like Us".

You see the watch. You see the chain. You see my bitch!
You see my whip. Can't see my crib. Just know it's lit!
We in our bag. We get that bread. Boy, you ain't tough!
Go get some cheese, you dummies broke. Ain't fly like us!

I swayed and threw my hand up in the air while I vibed to the simple but catchy lyrics aimed at his archenemy Leel. Kayla didn't seem to notice as she dipped, bounced, and swayed to the beat. Jahquez would have had a heart attack if he saw her shaking her ass to a diss track made for his brother. He would have been even madder if he saw Kayla throwing champagne back, blowing blunts of exotic, and dropping it low in front of Quan's homies in the VIP section. To put it simply, Kayla and I were too turnt. While Quan put on a spectacular show, me and my girl partied harder than ever.

After Quan's performance, he immediately strolled down to the VIP section, stopping to greet me first.

"That shit was lit, bro!" I admitted.

"Thanks, India." He gave me a bright smile. I could tell that he was still rushing with adrenaline. He and his crew were always too hype after he performed. It was like they were made for the stage.

"Ewwww. Yo' sweaty ass," I whined as he leaned down and gave me a damp hug, his sweaty dreads brushing against my face. I held my breath just in case his ass was funky too. Although I didn't want his nasty ol' hug, reality was, I loved Quan. He was like the big brother I never had. He always showed loved to me and my girl, and he treated Italy like a princess.

"Fuck you." He laughed. "I ain't finna be here all night anyway. 'Bout to go home, shower, and chill. Yo' folks home whining as usual."

"Yeah, but you gon' carry that ass," I reminded him. Italy had Quan ass on lock, and I couldn't lie, if my sister hadn't snagged him, he would have been on my hit list a long time ago. Since he and my sister had been together over two years now, he was off limits and was basically family. I did some scandalous shit, but I was loyal to my sister. Despite the fact that we lived our lives way differently, she was my best friend, next to Kayla.

"Fo' sho," he admitted. "I'll leave this VIP section to y'all. I'm 'bout to go holla at the promoter and head out."

Quan went to say something else but stopped. I tore my gaze from him and turned to the same direction that his eyes were now fixed in. I froze when I saw Jahquez storming angrily up the steps to where we were posted up at. The VIP section sat above the floor and was roped off.

"How the fuck this broke ass nigga get up here?" Loco laughed. He wasn't talking to anyone in particular, but he intentionally said it loud enough for everyone to hear.

Kayla shook her head and muttered for him to shut up. The way Jahquez was looking, shit was about to get ugly. Jumping over the VIP rope, Jahquez ran up and snatched Kayla by the top of her bun. With a mean grip, he proceeded to try and drag her up out of there.

"Bitch, you hang the phone up on me, see me calling, and don't answer!" he shrieked in fury, making a spectacle of himself.

I looked on in utter shock. This was the fuck shit I didn't like. The nigga must have had a tracker on her or something in order to find her in the giant space. I didn't usually get in the middle of their domestic disputes, but he was all the way out of order.

"Nigga, what the fuck wrong with you!" I screamed, but before I could even get my words out fully, Raul and Loco were up in his face, pushing him. Kayla scurried off the floor and ran back over to where I was standing.

"Fuck is wrong wit' you, nigga? On some hoe shit, grabbing up a broad like that."

I guess the two of them were a little too close for comfort, or maybe Jahquez felt that his actions didn't warrant a shove. Because the next thing I knew, Jahquez had reached down in his pants and snatched out his pistol. I didn't look to see how big it was, what kind it was, *or* what color it was. I snatched Kayla by the back of her romper and took the fuck off.

Pow! Pow!

The sound of gunfire crackling in the air caused everyone to run for safety. The whole entire club instantly turned into a madhouse. If I knew one thing from experience, it was to never head in the direction of the chaos. Spotting a little corner on the side of the couch in VIP, Kayla and I hit the ground and hid on the side of it.

"Jahquez!" a teary-eyed Kayla cried out for her baby daddy.

"Bitch, shut the fuck up before he winds up killing the both of us," I growled. I threw my hand against her mouth to quiet her. I wasn't dying behind her ass.

A few seconds later, I peeked around the corner of the couch, and Jahquez was getting up from the floor. I guess someone had managed to knock the gun from his hand and with a hard right, was able put him down on his back pockets where he needed to be. A few kicks and punches, and they all backed up to allow him room to carry his party-crashing ass on. He was now running down the steps toward the exit

"Y'all done fucked up!" Jahquez yelled as he pushed through the crowd and dashed out before the police came.

Kayla and I scrambled to our feet, and all I could do was glare at her and shake my head.

"That's it, bitch. I ain't never going out with you again if that nigga gon' be acting like that. He just shot up a packed club. The fuck." I shook my head in dismay. Every time she went somewhere, he was tripping. Yet she couldn't say one word if he decided to hang out the entire night.

"I'm dropping you off to yo' mama's house. You can't go home to that nigga acting like that," I argued.

I glanced back at Kayla as we made our way out of the now nearly empty club. She had a worried look on her face. I knew her mind was probably racing with thoughts on how Jahquez was going to act later tonight or tomorrow. To be frank, she looked downright scared. Kayla wouldn't admit it, but I knew he had a hand problem. If he'd snap on her in a crowded club, I could only imagine what he would do to her at home. I asked her a few times if he was beating or banging on her, but of course she would deny it. I didn't need her to confirm what I already knew though. I heard numerous people talk about how they'd seen him wild her out in public.

"Na, I'm gon' go on home. If I don't, he just gon' act worse. Plus, I don't want him going to my mama's house with that drama at this time of night. Whenever he can't find me, that's the first place he goes."

I shook my head in disgust. I couldn't even think of someone disrespecting my mama or her home. Kayla really needed to get it together. I pulled my phone out my back to check the time. It was only eleven thirty. We had barely even been out a full hour.

"Well, you know you can stay with me for the night," I offered.

"Na, girl. Just drop me off."

I sighed and decided to drop it. If she wanted to be a fool, so be it. She couldn't say that I didn't try to help her. Something told me that the situation between BGS and Triple B was going to get uglier. I wasn't sure how, but I could just feel that it was. I just hoped that it didn't affect my relationship with Kayla. I was bound to Quan by Italy, so if I had to choose, the choice had already been made.

❧ 3 ❧

KAYLA

I kicked my heels off by the door and tiptoed as quietly as possible through my apartment after India dropped me off to my home. I already knew it was going to be some smoke after everything that had just occurred at Victory's. Luckily, my son Jaden was with my mom and wouldn't have to witness what was about to go down. I would be lying if I sat up and said I wasn't used to Jahquez's bullshit, because I really was. I was not only used to it, but I was tired of it. It was sad as fuck. Any time Jahquez became emotional or upset, he became violent. I knew he would be especially upset tonight. He had been disrespected and humiliated in front of everyone. Beat up and manhandled in front of everybody. To top it off, he was outnumbered, and it wasn't shit he could do but get up and run out of the club. It was definitely going to be hell to pay. I just hoped that I could at least get to the bathroom and shower before I had to deal with that hell.

"Bitch, you didn't think I heard you come in," Jahquez's deep voice rumbled out of the pitch-black, scaring the shit out of me.

I heard his footsteps rapidly approaching me. Before I could respond, I felt his tough hands grab ahold of my throat and squeeze tight. Out of reflex, I gagged and tried to pry them from around my neck.

"Eckkkkk," I choked.

"Bitch, you thought shit was sweet. You knew motherfuckin' well you were gon' have to deal with me when you brought yo' stinkin' ass in this house. Wanna run around and be a whore," he accused before hurling me across the room. "Got me out here lookin' stupid!"

My body and head hit the hardwood floor with a thud. Luckily, I barely had much furniture, or I probably would have landed against a table or something. I looked up and moaned weakly. Before I could hop up and run, Jahquez had a tight grip on my unraveling bun and was using his other hand to punch me all over.

"I swear I wasn't doing anything. Please stop!" I shrieked at the top of my lungs. Every time he beat me, it felt like I was dying. I would never get used to the pain.

"You should have thought about that when you were running around with yo' hoe ass friend to sit up in them niggas face. Niggas you know none of us fuck with."

He stood over me with a scowl and then drew back and slapped me hard across the face.

"That's what you want to do, huh! Be a whore!" He continued to throw punch after punch into my body. Tears streamed down my face while all I could do was curl up into a ball and do my best to try and shield the rest of my body with my arms.

"Please, Jahquez, I'm sorry! Pleaseeeeeee!" I screamed.

He suddenly stopped hitting me; however, instead of leaving me on the floor, he grabbed me by my feet and dragged me to the bathroom door.

"Don't ever play with me again," he threatened after releasing me. "And I don't want you around India hoe ass or them clown ass Triple B niggas. You understand!" he screamed.

"Y-Y-Yesss," I stammered. I was still in tears. Curled up into a ball again and flinching from every word he said, I prayed he didn't hit me again.

"Good. Now clean yo' self the fuck up. And don't go over there tellin' yo' nosy ass mama our business," he warned. "I'll be back."

I lay still and stiff on the floor for several minutes and then I heard Jahquez walk out the door. I groaned in pain and got up off the floor. I walked slowly into the bathroom and cut the light on. I took a look at myself in the mirror, and I didn't like what I saw. My lip was busted on the side, and I already had an ugly knot forming on the side of my head. Although it was just a small knot, I had no doubt that it would be double that size in the morning, and I would have bruises all over. Bruises that I would have to conceal with layers of makeup.

This was my life and had been my life for the last two out of five years. Jahquez hadn't always been this way. We'd grown up in the same neighborhood, went to the same school, and pretty much knew the same people. He'd won me over with his personality. His charm. He always told jokes, and he always doted on me when I was around. Made me feel special. Jahquez was cute in his own way. He was average height and slender. Had a rough little beard that wouldn't fully grow on the sides and a neat fade with a part. Five years in, and there was no longer shit cute about his ass at all. Somewhere along the line, he changed. And it all started with BGS—Baltimore Gangsta Squad.

Since I'd known him, Jahquez always ran the streets and got money hustling. However, as his little brother Leel began playing around with rhymes and everyone realized that he could rap, that was when things started to change. Everyone knew that to really make it out the hood, you needed to be a drug dealer, athlete, or rapper. Leel chose the latter. Naturally gifted with writing rhymes, Leel quickly became the man in the city and so did the crew that he ran with. Although talented, Leel was tall, obnoxious, and arrogant. He was the star, but in real life, he wasn't really likeable. He was brutally disrespectful in his rhymes, and if he didn't like you, he would flat-out say it and call your name. With his controversial raps and aggressive delivery, no one in the city could touch him. He started booking shows in the surrounding area and started buzzing on social media. Basically, he was getting money, and his name was becoming more recognizable in places other than just Baltimore.

Jahquez, the more charismatic of the two, began sucking up all the attention that came with being his baby brother's right hand. Cars, money, nightlife, it all went quickly to his head. He thrived in it. Unfortunately, it hurt when it all started to fade away. There was a new rising star in town, and his name was Quan. Better looking, cockier, and more lyrical, Quan was flat-out better than Leel. More likeable and not as controversial.

At first, they were friends. However, that didn't last long when Leel was being outshined by the new kid. Before long, Quan named the little crew he rolled with, and the two crews began beefing. Unfortunately for BGS, Quan's talent spoke for itself, and he took off. Literally. Leel was no longer the king of Baltimore. He was being forced to share the crown that he had grown so accustomed to wearing. Quan was reppin' hard for Baltimore, and soon, he was the face you put to the city when you spoke of it.

Before long, Quan was making nearly four times what Leel was making for a show and was traveling all over the country. His growing popularity and success showed. Every time Quan and his crew rolled up, he shut the block down. Everyone was running up to him and trying to get pictures with him. It didn't matter what part of Baltimore it was. It didn't matter what neighborhood. Everyone loved him.

Somewhere along the line, Jahquez changed. All of a sudden, he didn't want me around India, and he started snapping. Getting cursed out and getting my ass whipped soon became the norm. Every time it happened, he apologized. The usual shit. *I'm sorry baby. I won't do it again. I love you so much, and I'm crazy over you. I'm so cared to lose you.* You know, the usual shit an abusive nigga said. Once that grew old, the blame would shift to me. Something I did to make him do it. *If you would just fuckin' listen*, was what he would tell me. Despite the bullshit head games he tried to play, I knew it wasn't all my fault. Yeah, I went out and shook my ass, but I also had my shit together. I took care of my son, paid my bills on time, and worked my ass off as a medical assistant at The University of Baltimore Medical Center. I was twenty-six years old and had the right to live my fuckin' life. Unfortunately, living my life came with a cost. I'd creep out the house and then talk my shit to Jahquez, knowing damn well he was going to act like a whole monster when I walked through the doors of the home we shared.

I knew I needed to leave him. Should've been left. Everyone that knew me well told me so. India. My mother. India, however, didn't know about the beatings. Only my mother did. She'd seen the aggression he displayed firsthand. She'd seen the aftermath of the beatings firsthand. That was shit that I hid from my only friend. Despite his hand problem, I loved him endlessly. Since the hoe from Jamz, he hadn't cheated on me, although I'd cheated on his ass a few times after that. For the most part, when things were good, they were good. Things just had been bad more so lately.

I was trying to stick it out and hang in there. We had a child together. He was just going through some shit. I prayed it got better because, lately, each beating became worse and worse. I didn't know how much more I could take. Besides, I knew that even if I tried to leave, he wasn't going to make that shit easy.

❦ 4 ❦

SHAWN

"I'm getting ready for a flight. I'm going to Baltimore tomorrow to work on an album for a rapper named Quan." I walked out of my living room and headed into the kitchen to make myself a quick breakfast.

"Quan?" She paused for a second. "I've definitely heard of him. He's heavy on social media. He did the song, 'Fly Like Us'. I thought you were going to try and move away from the trap music and more toward pop? Maybe work with Nikki Minaj or Taylor Swift. What changed?"

"Nothing changed. That shit takes time and isn't something that happens overnight. Frankly, I don't really care who I work with as long as the music has potential."

"Well, whatever. Why can't he come here to LA? Produce out of your studio?" my girlfriend, Nisa, asked. "I mean, no offense... Quan is up and coming, and I can't deny that he is hot, but it's the gang activity for me," she admitted. "Do you really want to be affiliated with that?"

I smiled and took a deep breath. Quan wasn't necessarily affiliated with any gangs, but he was definitely always involved in some type of controversy. Most of the time, those controversies were closely followed by blogs thirsty to spin a story. I didn't expect Nisa to understand the life that Quan was trying to move away from, and I had to constantly remind myself that I had to be patient when dealing with her. She was privileged and knew nothing about the culture except for what she saw on social media.

Being born and raised in Houston, Texas, I knew how hard it was getting out of the hood and staying out of the drama once you left. It was always someone that wanted to come for your crown. Come for your spot, despite not having put in an ounce of effort. Clout chasing was at an all-time high.

"Right now. It's just easier. He's doing a lot of shows, and he's paying me extra. Besides, I know if I get Quan over these beats, he's gonna kill it. He spits fire on damn near everything he hops on."

"Yeah, that *is* true. Well, how long you gonna be gone?"

"We agreed on a week. My flight and hotel arrangements are already set."

"Damn. I'm gonna miss you, baby."

I paused. I was hoping she wanted to go with me. I wouldn't have mind the company. It wasn't like she was doing shit anyway. Working at her father's ritzy nightclub allowed her more than just flexibility. She could damn near come and go as she pleased. She also got to party, mix, and mingle amongst wealthy customers and celebrities. That was actually how I had met her.

"You don't want to come?"

"Na. I'm sorry, baby. It's last minute, and besides, I have to help out my dad. He just let the kitchen manager go, and it's been hell finding a new one."

I paused for a minute. That had been her reoccurring excuse the last few days. We didn't live together, but most days she stayed at my crib. Since her dumb ass daddy fired the kitchen manager, she'd been working like crazy and I'd been chilling alone.

"That's cool. I'm only gonna be gone a week anyway."

"Well, you go down there and make some hit records. Then I

get to brag about who my man is. The next Mike Will or Kanye West," She chuckled, giving her best shot at encouragement. To me, it wasn't very encouraging. One minute, she wanted me to lean toward pop, and the next minute, she was pretending she wanted me to be the next Mike Will. It would have been nice if she was happy with who the fuck I was already. I wasn't no broke nigga, and I did quite well for myself. I'd actually done *very* well for myself. I had a slew of hit records under my belt, and the average broke rapper couldn't afford my beats.

"That's cool, babe. Look, I gotta go. I'll hit you tomorrow after I land."

"Why not before you leave?" she asked, her tone suspicious.

"I'm catching a red eye."

Oh, okay then. Well, you travel safe, and I'll talk to you tomorrow. I love you."

"Yeah, you too," I said, before quickly ending the call.

I'd only been dating Nisa for a year, and lately, she was beginning to annoy me. That seemed to be the same situation with every woman I ran into. I'd date them for a while with high hopes and then six months in, I'd lose interest. Trust, it wasn't through any fault of my own. Los Angeles just happened to be full of shallow women that only saw dollar signs. Women of no substance. Women that were only fun to be around when they were on some type of drug or were drunk. The shit was wack. The whole dating scene had me irritated, and frankly, I was growing tired of it. The women I was running into simply weren't the type of women that I was used to. I was used to strong Black women who were really there for you. Not women who were focused solely on how they could come up off you. Being raised by a single Black woman from the hood, it was just something I needed in a woman that I wasn't getting. Maybe I needed the spunk and spice they brought. The strength and love they gave so effortlessly.

My problem with Nisa was her shallow and self-centered personality. Despite being together for over a year, she was still

hard to read. Don't get me wrong, she was extremely affectionate, but at times, it was forced and exaggerated. The average
nigga wouldn't peep it, but I did. It was like she was pretending
to be head over heels for me so I could fall head over heels for
her. Then she could play on my emotions. Maybe I was wrong,
but that was the vibe she gave off. The shit just seemed so fake
to me. She just didn't seem genuine. Despite that, I still
continued to fuck with her. She was young, bad as hell, and kept
me from loneliness while I pursued my career. It also didn't hurt
that she was a freak in the bedroom. Unfortunately, that wasn't
enough to keep her around. Deep down in my heart, I knew she
wasn't Mrs. Right. She was simply Ms. Right Now.

Truth be told, I was the total opposite of what women would
think when they thought of a music producer. I didn't ball hard,
hang with rappers, or parlay with athletes. Sure, I had them as
distant friends; however, for the most part, I was a laidback guy
that just liked making music. No big crazy chains, flashy ass
jewels, or boisterous Instagram accounts. I wasn't really trying to
be seen, I just wanted to be heard. I'd let my work speak for me.
To some, I would be considered corny. I'd been called that a few
times by a few chicks I dated. They were hoes anyway. Chicks
that ran through niggas in the industry trying to find someone to
take care of them or advance their career. Despite being
attracted to those types, the relationships would never work out.
Big butts, big tits, long weaves. While it was all nice to look at
for a while, they weren't necessarily the females that niggas like
myself would consider making a wife. And if we did, we were just
flat-out pussy-whipped or stupid.

I wasn't a bad catch though. Living in LA motivated me to
stay in shape and keep my body in tip-top shape. I looked more
like a personal trainer than a music producer. Brown skin, goofy
grin, and rich black beard that I kept neat and oiled up. I had a
nice ass bank account and enough money to splurge on whoever.
I just needed *that* girl that made me want to.

Shaking my thoughts, I gathered up all the ingredients to

throw me together some breakfast. Luckily, I knew how to cook a little bit. The older I got, the more I began to yearn for someone more meaningful in my life. Someone that I could see a future with. Someone with good intentions who would look out for me and take care of me. As I cracked my eggs on the side of a bowl, I realized that it might not happen anytime soon.

5

ITALY

"**D**ayummm," Quan yelled out like a fool when I walked down the steps of our townhome. He was standing at the bottom looking like fine wine in an all-black tuxedo.

It was my twenty-fifth birthday, and to celebrate, Quan had booked us a dinner at an elite restaurant that I had been dying to try. It was white-linen fancy, so we both went all out to look good for the night. I had on a gold, form-fitting dress that stopped at my ankles. It had a plunging neckline with a split on the side that started almost at my panty line. Breathtaking and jaw dropping was what it was. I looked like a chocolate, Barbie goddess, if there were such a thing.

"Damn, I could bite the fuck out you," Quan growled. He admired me with lustful eyes and then walked up and planted a soft, warm kiss in the nook of my neck.

"I don't know about bite, but you can damn sure eat me." I laughed.

Quan bit down on his bottom lit and playfully looked at his watch. "Shit... We got time."

"No, we don't," I replied.

He was trying to act like he was joking, but I knew if I said come on, he would have snatched that tuxedo off to swallow my pussy whole and dick me down right by the front door. Especially since my mother had stepped out and no one else was home but us.

"Come on Rayquan, our reservation is at eight o' clock. I don't want us to be late. Let me go grab my coat."

I walked over and opened the coat closet and pulled out my maxi dress coat. It wasn't expensive, but it was beautiful and perfect for where we were headed. After throwing it on and hopping in the car, we were off to our destination. Instead of the radio, Quan had his latest song pouring softly threw the speakers. The song was a lot softer than the hood songs he was becoming famous for.

"You like this one?" he asked, referring to the song playing.

"Yeah. It's one of my favorites. I like the whole gangsta love vibe." I flashed him a smile. He knew I liked when he showed his sensitive side.

"Cut it out." He laughed. "Na, on some real shit, niggas fuck with the music heavy." He turned the volume low so I could hear whatever he was about to say. "If I could get the females to fuck with me strong, I'm in there."

"You already in there. You hot. But don't start all that lovey-dovey singing shit. Females like that gangsta shit too. And your music isn't like that come and go shit. One-minute niggas is strictly on gangsta rap, and the next minute it's crunk music, then its trap music made up of mostly mumble rap. What makes you special is you're a chameleon. Your punch lines are sick, and you constantly switch your flow up. Your shit never gets boring. You dope, baby, stop second-guessing yourself."

He paused for a minute and flashed me a smile. "Thanks, babe."

"You're welcome. It's just important to stay true to yourself. Make music that speaks to you. Create art that speaks to you. Don't just do it to grab a certain audience for the time being. That's why so many rappers fall off. You don't gotta do nothing special. Male or female, people know good music." I leaned over and rubbed his leg. "And it doesn't hurt that you fine as hell."

Quan smacked my hand away. "Girl, don't you start nothing in this motherfucker." He let out a toothy laugh.

"You're so extra." I laughed.

After talking about a bunch of random things, we pulled up to the restaurant about thirty minutes after leaving our house. Since we lived in the suburbs, it took us a little time to drive into the city. I noticed that the restaurant looked a little busier than normal. I glanced at the time and saw that we were running slightly behind.

"I hope they let us in. We're late." I couldn't help but worry since I had never been there before. I prayed that we didn't have any issues with our reservation since we both were overdressed for a regular restaurant.

"Babe, stop worrying please. This is your night, and you have nothing to worry about. So put a smile on that pretty face and let's go." Quan hopped out and proceeded to open my door. I took a deep breath and forced myself to believe what he was saying.

"Reservations for Jones," Quan stated to the host once we entered the foyer of the restaurant.

"Jones?" The host opened up his reservation book and scoured through it until he found our name. "Ah, yes. Jones. Follow me." He closed his book and opened the door so we could enter the main part of the restaurant. As Quan and I walked hand in hand through the doors, I was instantly met with familiar faces.

"Surprise!" everyone chanted. My mouth fell open as they clapped, smiled and cheered.

"Surprise, baby! Happy birthday, Italy!" he said. He drew my body into his chest and gave me a kiss. "I love you, baby."

I fought back tears of joy as I admired the celebration that had been put together in my honor. I looked around in awe. The giant room had been beautifully decorated in pink and gold while the ceiling was covered in snow-white balloons. It was beautiful. I glanced over and spotted a buffet-style area with bowtie clad servers standing over stainless steel warmers. Everything about the environment was expensive and elegant. I was so grateful that Quan went out of his way to put all of it together for my birthday.

"How did you do this right under my nose?" I laughed. I looked down and Quan's four-year-old daughter, Kira had dashed over and was now at my leg.

I scooped her into my arms and gave her a kiss. "Hey, Kir-Kir!" I turned to Quan. "Thank you so much, baby." He knew how much I loved his daughter, so having her there to celebrate my birthday was a gift all by itself.

When I met Quan, Kira was nearly a year old, and he and his baby mama, Charlotte, didn't have the best relationship. Charlotte was a mixed girl that had a black daddy but was raised by a white woman *and* acted like the typical, difficult, privileged white person. She wanted things her way and felt entitled to that. When things didn't go the way she wanted them, she would act an entire fool. After several run-ins between her and I, she'd been on a spree of pettiness. Since then, Quan's had nothing but trouble seeing Kira. At times, I felt like it was my fault, although Quan and his mother Jackie assured me it wasn't. Charlotte was just difficult and didn't care for me because I was with the shits. I also wouldn't tolerate the one thing she liked to do the most, and that was be disrespectful. Luckily, Quan now had a lot more money at his disposal, so he had his lawyer involved heavily to ensure that he got to see his daughter. I was thankful because Lord knows I loved me some Kira. She was a beautiful, curly-headed angel. If there were a such thing as perfect, then I was sure she would be it. Both well-mannered and well-behaved, Charlotte had gotten something right.

"I missed you so much," I said to Kira before mashing a kiss into her cheek and putting her down.

As Quan, Kira, and I walked further into the room, everyone

began coming up to me and wishing me a happy birthday while I thanked them for showing up. There were about twenty people there. My family was small so most of the guests that showed up were related to Quan or were people that he knew and we both were close to. His mother was there. A few of his aunts and uncles. His best friends Raul and Loco were also present.

"Why you didn't tell me what this nigga had planned?" I said to India, once everyone had begun sitting down. After handing Kira off to Quan's mother and thanking nearly everyone for showing up, I made my way over to where she and my mother were seated, although my mother had just stepped away from the table.

"Girl, he told me not to. And happy birthday!" she squealed, standing up to give me a brief hug.

"Thank you. Whatchu get me?" I asked.

"Bitch, nothing." She laughed. "What would I get the girl that has everything? Ohhhh, I gotta tell you what happened last night," she said extra hype.

"No, you don't," Quan said, walking up unexpectedly. I watched as he sent an angry glare in India's direction.

"Tell me later," I said to her. She shot me a hesitant smile while Quan sent her a threatening stare like that was going to work. India rolled her eyes and turned her head.

"Always running yo' mouth," I heard Quan mumble.

I laughed it off and took his hand to return to the festivities. Quan led me back to the front of the room.

"Yo! Have the waiter bring me up two glasses of champagne. I want to make a toast!" Quan yelled out, garnering everyone's attention. I blushed deeply. The surprise party was enough, but I hated the spotlight.

A female waitress quickly scurried over and handed us two glasses. I watched everyone grab their phones to begin recording us.

"So if I can have everyone's attention..." Quan began. He fake cleared his throat. In response, everyone turned their attention on us, lights beaming while they hit record and held their phones steady.

"I just want to wish my baby a happy birthday." He turned away from the crowd and looked directly at me with a warm smile. "I know you don't like surprises and I know you don't like all the attention, but I just want to say, you deserve everything that I plan to give you in this lifetime. You're a beautiful person, inside and out. Authentic and selfless. You've stood beside me when I had nothing and loved me with the same intensity. You motivate me and check me anytime I second-guess or doubt myself. The saying is: *a woman's loyalty is tested when her man has nothing. A man's loyalty is tested when he has everything.* I am forever loyal to you, Italy, and I promise I'm going to give you the world. Happy birthday, baby."

I fought back the tears stinging the corner of my eyes while I waved my hand in front of my face to fan myself. "Thank you, baby. You're gonna make me cry," I admitted with the ugliest "trying not to cry" face.

"Save them tears, babe. Before we all sit down to eat, I want to present Italy with her gift. Raul, where you at, my nigga?" Quan called out into the crowd of guests.

Raul threw up his hand from across the room. "Over here!"

"We good?" Quan asked.

"Yep! Loco say he ready."

A smile spread across Quan's face. "I just need everyone to follow us to the front. I promise it's going to be brief and then everyone can eat." He laughed. "I know y'all been waiting and hungry. I promise I'm gon' feed you right. Follow me."

I already knew what Quan was about to do. There was no other reason that he would need Raul and Loco's help to present me with a gift.

"I know the fuck this nigga didn't," I chanted to myself a few times, growing excited.

Everyone gathered outside into a small huddle. Quan and I made our way through the crowd, and just as we got to the sidewalk, a shiny, tar-black Mercedes-Benz A220 pulled in front of us and stopped. Loco was driving. He quickly hopped out, walked up to me, and handed me the keys.

"She's all yours. Happy birthday, Italy." He smiled.

"Ahhhhhhh!" I squealed, jumping up and down like I'd lost my damn mind.

"You like it?" Quan asked.

"Hell yeah!" I dashed over to the driver's seat and hopped in to check out the interior and features. Just as I was taking in the scent of the leather and touch screen, Quan was standing next to the car going live on Instagram.

"What up, y'all! We live with it!" he said to those that were tuned in. "This how we do it. Big bank shit. Y'all see it, 2020 shit." He walked all around the car to show its beauty. "Shout out to my baby, Italy. She turned twenty-five today. Just put her in her first Benz. A little one, but it got hella features. Small shit for real. Especially for someone who deserves the world. I love you, baby."

He turned the camera in my direction, and I let off a shy smile. I didn't really do the social media shit, and I didn't really like being on video. Especially not when I wasn't prepared to be. Besides, the internet was notoriously messy and always had a way of taking a special moment and adding negativity to it.

After admiring all the details of my bomb ass new car, I kissed and thanked Quan and then everyone went back inside to eat and enjoy the rest of the night. I couldn't lie, Quan had made my birthday amazing. It wasn't just about the gifts and lavish gathering. It was the thought and effort he put into everything that moved me. Most women only dreamed of the love we had, and I actually was living it. It didn't get any better than that.

6

QUAN

"Nigga, put that fuckin camera up. You don't gotta go live every five minutes," I argued with one of my closest friends, Loco. Out of all my homies, he got on my nerves the most. Despite that fact, he was loyal as fuck, and I wouldn't trade him for the world.

Loco lowered his phone. "Nigga, yo' ass was just live," he countered as I shot him dirty looks.

"Yeah, not long though. Outside, zoomed in on the *car*. Not showing everybody my entire fuckin' background."

"Facts. All it takes is someone to recognize some shit and run down here tryin' take pictures and shit," Raul co-signed.

"Or to be on our ass about the shit that happened the other night at Victory's," I reminded him as we stood in the corner of Italy's birthday party. "Or over some shit you done said *or* done on social media."

"Whatever. Fuck them motherfuckers. Them pussy ass BGS niggas ain't gangsta for real, and everybody else can catch a bullet," Loco coldly spat, disregarding all the important shit I'd just said. "I'm 'bout to slide out anyway," Loco continued.

He threw his hand out to dap me up and then Raul. I shook

my head as unsaid thoughts swirled through my head. The wealthier we became, the more arrogant Loco became. It should have been opposite. Big Bank Boys were becoming high profile, and we needed to be more careful, especially to protect our loved ones. They were the vulnerable ones. I loved my nigga, and I didn't want to cut him off over something like that, but he had to start listening if we all wanted to stay on top.

"You headed home?" I asked him.

"Naa. I'm headed to this lil' freak bitch I met on Instagram. Shorty mean," he bragged.

I shook my head and laughed. "You need to leave them thirsty, dick-eating bitches alone. I don't care how good they look."

"Whatever, nigga. India ain't trying to give me no play, and I haven't found my princess yet." He paused. "Unlike yo' bitch ass. 'I owe you the world. You deserve everything. I love you, and I'm loyal to you forever, baby.'" Loco burst into laughter, doing his best corny ass imitation of me.

"Yo, I swear you is a corny ass nigga. Fuck you." I grinned. I didn't even really have a fly ass comeback. It was what it was. I loved the shit out of Italy, so his bitch ass could clown all he wanted.

"Na. I'm just fuckin' with you. You know I rock with Italy. That ride was dope, and she definitely deserved it. She definitely got a nigga back. You made a wise choice. But look, I'm out though. I'll hit you in the morning so we can meet up."

"Bet." Loco walked off and headed toward the exit, leaving Raul and I alone to continue talking.

"Aye, isn't the producer nigga coming tomorrow to work on the mixtape?" Raul asked.

"Yeah. This my first time working with him, but I heard good shit about him."

"Yeah, I heard he dope too. He recently produced a song for Drake. That shit was number one for a minute."

"That's exactly what I want to hear. He sent me a couple samples, but I won't make my choices until tomorrow. I anticipate it taking a week, but it could be two. Either way, I want you and Loc to hop on a few tracks so we can get y'all name buzzing. Really put Baltimore on the map."

"Hell yeah. You know I'm coming with heat," Raul promised.

"That's what I'm talking 'bout," I said, glad that he and I both were on the same page.

"Listen, on some real shit though, talk to Loc for me. Everybody gotta start being more careful. I went live earlier to show off Italy's car, not to show everybody where the fuck we were. Niggas walkin' around with racks. We can't be slipping. I'm doing thirty-thousand-dollar shows. We can't have anybody running down on us hoping they gon' come up."

I paused for a minute to make sure it was sinking in. I had no doubt it was. Raul was hood and stayed in drama, but his thinking was closer to mine.

"That shit the other night that happened with that fuck nigga Jahquez—"

"I already know." Raul cut me off. "It's gon' be smoke behind it."

"Right. So we gotta be on point. We can't be dropping our locations and going live and showing the fuckin' address or name of the business," I argued.

"I'll talk to him," Raul promised.

"Good. And thanks, my dude. Look, it's plenty of food. Take some home. I'm about to head out with Italy. She over there buzzed, and Kira knocked out."

I pointed to a corner where my daughter was knocked out, spread across two chairs. Reaching in my pocket, I dug out my keys.

"You rode with Loc, right?"

He nodded.

"Good. Take my shit. Just scoop me in the morning. I'm gon'

drive Italy's car. She been drinking, and she not 'bout to wreck no new shit." I tossed him the keys, and he caught them in his hand.

"Handle yo' business, fam. Let me know if you need anything. You need me to trail you?" he asked.

"Na, I'm good. We not going far."

"Bet. I'll hit you in the morning."

I smiled as Raul walked off. He and Loco were my right-hand niggas. I'd known them since kindergarten, and they'd never crossed me once. Where I was from, that was a blessing. The music industry was just as, if not more, ruthless as the drug game. Jealousy, hate, and opportunists were plentiful. Having a solid circle was imperative. And I was thankful that I had mine.

After arranging for Kira to go home with my mother for the night, Italy and I headed out. Instead of going home, I had made hotel arrangements at The Four Seasons out Harbor East. I figured I'd get her away from the house for the night since she always complained that I never spent time with her.

"Damn, I can't wait to get you back to that hotel room so I can tear that ass up," I admitted, briefly tearing my eyes away from the road so I could steal glances at Italy's fine ass.

She didn't drink much and was tipsy off the couple glasses of wine that she'd thrown back. She was now laid back in her seat relaxed. She had kicked off her shoes and now had my dick throbbing from the sight of her exposed, chocolate thighs and fat toes painted a neon green.

"Or... you can pull over and tear it up on the side of the highway," Italy taunted with a giggle.

If I wasn't doing sixty-five on I-83, I would have taken her up on that offer. However, we weren't too far from the hotel, so I figured I could control my hormones for another ten minutes.

"Please don't tempt me, baby. Our exit right there," I said, moving from the left lane to the right so I wouldn't miss it.

Just as I was switching lanes, I noticed the car directly

behind me switched lanes as well. However, instead of slowing down to avoid tailgating, they sped up, forcing me to increase my speed to eighty so they wouldn't collide with the back of Italy's new car.

"The fuck!" I yelled out. "Dumb ass 'bout to cause a fuckin' accident."

Once I gave the car and its dumb ass driver enough distance so they could get back into the left lane to go around me, they did just that. The driver mashed down on the gas pedal so hard, I almost thought I saw their car jerk forward. They sped up until they were parallel with us.

"The fuck? Is these motherfuckers drunk or something?" I said to Italy, who wasn't paying me the least bit of attention. She was too busy admiring the scenery out the window. She briefly turned her head away from the scene outside and glanced out my window. She frowned once she saw the car driving directly beside us. It was like they were intentionally trying to stay next to us. My gut told me something was up. Apparently, Italy's did as well. She looked nervous as she leaned forward to take glances out the window.

"Italy, sit back," I demanded.

"Why that look like..." Her voice trailed off and then she paused. I had a feeling I knew what she was about to say, but she just didn't say it, because she didn't want to bring it to fruition.

Something told me to mash down on the gas and gun it, but I didn't. However, five seconds later, I wished I had. Instead of passing me or going in front of me, the car next to me steadied their speed to match mine. The next thing I knew, the window rolled down and the passenger of the vehicle opened fire into Italy's car. Sure enough, even in the dead of night, barreling down the interstate, I recognized the face. He definitely rolled with BGS. I'd seen him around on multiple occasions. With no mask, he looked emotionless before aiming out the window.

"Babe, get down!" I screamed out as the windows caved in

and shattered into the car. I didn't have time to speed up. All I could do was brace myself.

"Ahhhhhhhhhhh!" Italy screamed in sheer terror.

With one hand on the wheel, I used my other hand to force Italy's head down into her lap. The next thing I knew, we were spinning, and I saw black.

✤ 7 ✤

ITALY

I awoke to utter chaos. The car alarm blaring. The airbags deployed. Twisted metal and shattered glass all over. I slowly and painfully lifted my head up from where it had landed against the airbag. Small shards of glass falling off my body with every move.

"Quan," I moaned.

I felt a trail of warm, sticky blood flowing from the top of my head all the way down to my chin. I winced in pain as I turned my head to get a look at my man. He was unresponsive and was slumped over against his shattered window. After struggling for a moment, I finally adjusted my eyes and panic set in. Quan was covered from his neck to his chest in blood. I felt my heart pick up speed, but my body wouldn't keep up.

"Rayquan, baby, get up," I groaned with tears now running down my face. With the little strength I could muster up, I reached over and tried to shake him. He still didn't respond; however, I could tell that he was still breathing. His chest rose and fell faintly, his breathing shallow. I looked out the window and saw that several cars had pulled over and had their flashers on for light. A few people had even got out, prepared to assist. I heard the distant sounds of sirens. Someone had called for help.

I was thankful. Now, I just prayed that they got to us quickly. Quan didn't look too good. He didn't look good at all.

"Help us," I called out weakly.

"Ma'am, try to stay still and calm. Help is on the way. I'm on the phone will 911, and they said not to move or touch you guys. Just hold on, okay? We're with you," a Caucasian-sounding lady yelled from outside the car, doing her best to comfort me.

"He's been shot," I sobbed. "He's covered in blood. Please."

"They're getting closer, honey. Just hang tight," she assured me.

I reached up and wiped the blood out of my face. I winced in pain. I could feel the large knot that had formed on the front of my head. I was in pain, but it wasn't pain from a bullet. It was from the impact of the collision. I knew I was hurt. My arm hurt like hell, and I couldn't move it.

As I continued to groan, the events that had just occurred played over and over in my mind like a scene from a movie. Still disoriented, I struggled to keep my eyes open as the siren sounds from the paramedics grew closer and closer. A few minutes later, things became a blur as paramedics, police, and firefighters rushed onto the scene.

❧ 8 ❧

INDIA

"What?" I asked, still half asleep. My heart pounding in my chest.

My phone abruptly ringing in the pitch-black room had startled me. Despite being disoriented, I knew a call coming in the middle of the night couldn't mean good news. I hadn't heard a word my mother had said, and I wasn't sure that I even wanted her to repeat herself. I glanced over to the clock on my nightstand. It was three in the morning, and I was still struggling to fully peel open my eyes.

"Quan was shot!" my mother, Cynthia sobbed on the other line. "Someone shot into Italy's car on the expressway after they left her birthday party. He lost control of the car and they crashed into the rails. Italy's hurt, but she's okay." She paused briefly before choking out. "They don't know if Quan's going to make it." She sniffled.

I knew she was doing her best to hold it together. I could hear the anguish in her voice and knew that she was devastated. I sprang up and flew out of my bed and to my feet. It was so much to my brain at once, I felt dizzy. For a moment, I thought I would pass out.

"Where are you, Mommy?" I asked her, shaking off the feelings of light-headedness. Knowing her, she was probably already headed to the hospital. However, I knew she was in no state to drive.

"I'm still at the house. I just got off the phone with Jackie. They're on their way. The police literally just called her."

I had to get to the hospital. I raced to my closet and snatched down the first thing that I saw—a pair of tights and an old T-shirt.

"Ma, get your stuff on. I'm leaving out right now. I'll come get you, and we'll go up there together."

"Okay." She sniffled before hanging up.

I tore out of the house like a bat out of hell with my heart pounding inside my chest. I prayed that my sister wasn't seriously hurt and that Quan would be okay. Even though Italy was tough, she was also sensitive. If something happened to Quan, I knew it would devastate her. I knew she'd never be the same. We'd lost our father to gun violence only eight years ago when I was eighteen and Italy was seventeen. Our daddy loved to gamble, and one dreadful night, a game of pool ended deadly all because someone accused our daddy of cheating. Although he and my mother weren't together when he was alive, he still came through for us the best he could. He wasn't perfect, but we loved him. Unfortunately, in the hood, it seemed like all the thugs a girl loved wound up dead. That was why I did my best to stay away from them. Music lyrics glorified the trenches when our black men were constantly dying in them.

Italy had gotten lucky when she found Quan. He was rough around the edges, but he was trying to get away from the streets. Unfortunately, his rivals and closest friends kept him bound. Deep in my heart, I knew that if he didn't make some changes, he'd have the same fate that most men tied to the streets did. Hopefully, he would still get a chance to make those changes.

AFTER PICKING MY MOTHER UP, I PUSHED MY CHALLENGER TO the max to get to the hospital. The entire time my mind racing with questions. *What the hell had happened? Is Quan going to be okay? How is Italy?* I needed answers, and I needed them fast.

We arrived at the hospital fifteen minutes after I picked my mother up from where she and Italy lived in the county. Quan's family was already there. His mother, cousins, aunts, and uncles. The grim looks, teary eyes, and gut-wrenching sobs from his mother told me that things were not okay.

"Where's Italy?" my mom demanded to know as soon as we walked into the emergency room and was close enough for someone to hear.

Ms. Jackie turned her head at the sound of my mother's voice. The pain in her aging face broke my heart and scared me at the same time.

"She's in a room. She's asking for you. She's refusing medical treatment until they tell her something. I don't know what to tell her." Ms. Jackie covered her face with her hands and sobbed into them. "I don't know if he's gonna make it. He was shot in the neck. He's in emergency surgery to remove the bullet." She shook her head. "All we can do now is wait and pray."

Ms. Jackie's sister and brother embraced her from both sides to console her and calm her the best way they knew how. They had their work cut out for them. That was a monumental task. How could anyone comfort someone who could possibly be losing their son?

"Jackie, please sit down. God is gonna handle it. Just rest your feet and sit," her sister told her.

"We're gonna go find out what room Italy is in. We'll give her the news," I said to no one in particular.

My mother and I walked off and headed to the information desk to get information on Italy.

"We're here for Italy Cannon. She was brought in here by ambulance not long ago. I'm her sister, India Cannon, and this is her mother, Cynthia Deshields."

The entire time we waited for them to pull up Italy's information, my mother breathed deeply and waited quietly. I knew I would be doing all the talking. I glanced at my mom and shot her a look of reassurance.

"Everything is going to be okay," I said to her. I prayed that I was right. I had no doubt that she was worried and terrified. She loved Quan like a son. Everybody loved Quan. All I could do was pray that he pulled through.

"She's in room 125. I'll have security allow you back."

The nurse led the way to security, and they led us back. After walking down a few longs hallways and making a few turns, we got to room 125. One look at my sister sitting on the bed covered in glass and blood, and my mother and I nearly fell to pieces. Seeing us caused her to also break down.

"Mommy!" she cried. My mother ran to her and threw her arms around her while Italy buried her head into her chest and sobbed.

"How is he?" Italy asked weakly after finally bringing her head back up. "Last time I saw him, he was covered in blood and he wasn't responding to anything I said. I told them he needed help!" she sobbed.

I could tell that she was hurt and angry at the same time.

"I told them that he needed help first. But they pulled me out the car. How is he? Is he okay?" she continued to cry.

Italy's eyes darted from me to my mom in search of answers. Her eyes pleading and begging for good news.

"We don't know, Italy. He was..." I took a deep breath and continued. "He was shot in the neck. He's in surgery... but they don't know if he's going to make it," I admitted.

Italy held my mother tighter and let out a gut-wrenching scream. "Nooooooooooo!" she sobbed. "Please tell me he's going to be okay," she pleaded, her eyes wide like she was in the middle of a horror movie. For her, it probably felt like it.

"All we can do is pray that he will be, Italy. But right now, you gotta get some medical attention. You still have glass all over you, and your arm looks broken," I told her. I pointed to her arm. It was clearly broken. Plus, she was holding it in one spot like it pained her to move it.

"Look, Italy, I know you love Quan more than anything. We all love Quan. But right now, we have to make sure that *you're* okay. Let the doctor come in here and take care of you. Let them give you something for the pain that I know you're in. You've been up all night. You need medical care and rest."

Although reluctant, Italy finally agreed. She got up on the bed, and I called the doctor in to get her seen and cleaned up. Now all we could do was pray that Quan was okay.

❦ 9 ❦

ITALY

"I don't give a fuck what anyone says! He's my son! *Mine*! I pushed him out of my motherfuckin' pussy! So he's staying on life support until I fuckin' decide to take him off! Or until they tell me that he *has* to come off," Ms. Jackie sobbed with her fists balled up and ready to knock the taste out of Quan's daddy's mouth.

We had been in the hospital all night and morning. After asking hundreds of questions and talking to officer after officer, I had finally gotten bandaged, wrapped up, and released. I had a broken arm, a mild concussion, and a few scrapes and bruises, but otherwise, I was okay. Physically anyway. Mentally, I was a nervous wreck.

By the grace of God, Quan had only been shot once; unfortunately, that shot was to the neck, and he was now fighting for his life. During an emergency surgery to remove the bullet, he had slipped out of consciousness, and the doctors didn't know if he was going to ever wake up again. Barely breathing on his own, he was hooked up to all kinds of machines to keep him alive. The doctor had already given Ms. Jackie a choice to remove him from everything. Instead, allowing his body to maintain life on its own. Ms. Jackie, however, refused. She wanted Quan to stay on everything necessary if that would keep him alive longer. She wanted to give him a chance to wake up and grow stronger so he wouldn't need any machines. I agreed, but unfortunately, since I wasn't his wife, his mother had the final say-so on everything.

My heart broke into a million pieces seeing Ms. Jackie so distraught, but it was when she started showing her ass and cursing everyone out that my love for her ran deeper than ever. I was so thankful that she loved Quan with every fiber of her being, just like I did. Lord knows I felt all that shit she was screaming to his daddy and sister. I didn't have an ounce of say-so, but every word she just spoke was exactly how I felt. Quan was staying on life support. Period.

I didn't know what was going to happen next, but if I had to care for him every day for the rest of my life, then that was what the fuck I would do. I wanted him alive, and although many would consider it selfish thinking, I was willing to take him any way that I could, even if it was unconscious. I could only pray that Quan wasn't suffering. I didn't want him to suffer, but I didn't want to suffer either. And suffering was exactly what I would be doing if they took him from me.

I sat in a corner of the waiting room while Ms. Jackie paced back and forth going off on Quan's extended family. His daddy and one of his many half sisters had shown up and were giving their unsolicited advice. Luckily, I didn't have to tell them to fuck off since Ms. Jackie was doing a great job. Quan barely talked to his dad, and he barely knew his fat ass sister who kept glaring at me and rolling her eyes every chance she got. They didn't even really know him. All they knew was Quan, the rising rapper. All they saw was gold and dollar signs. Everyone that hopped their ass on social media and followed Quan could see that he was getting paper. If he died, they knew that he was sure to leave some behind. Money that everybody would want a little piece of. It was a damn shame. If I hadn't been raised with morals and respect, then I would be cursing them out right alongside his mother.

"You need to calm down, Jackie," Quan's father, Darius, demanded.

"You don't tell me what I need to do!" she hollered. "You barely did shit for my son. Now you want to come in here talking about you don't want him to suffer. Like he didn't suffer all his damn life because you weren't around! Did you care then? Hell no, you didn't care, because there was nothing for yo' ugly ass to gain. Quan is strong! Give him a chance to fight!"

"Come on, Daddy, let's just go. I knew she was gon' act stupid before we even got here. Exactly why no one else wanted to come," Quan's sister, Patrice, mumbled impatiently.

"Yeah, go," Ms. Jackie argued, turning her back on them. "I didn't tell you motherfuckers to come up here anyway," she said. "I called you because I felt that you should know your only son had been shot. I thought maybe you'd give a damn like I did, but I was wrong. All you worried about is snatching him off life support so you can try and dig in his bank account."

Darius and Patrice shook their heads in disgust and headed out, not bothering to say goodbye to anyone. After pacing for a few more minutes, Ms. Jackie plopped down into a random waiting room chair and began sobbing uncontrollably.

"Whyyyyyyyy?" she cried. "Why, God?" she asked. "My only baby. *Why?*" She rocked her body back and forth and sobbed into her hands. "Please spare him. Please, God."

Her brother James got up from where he was seated and walked over to comfort her. "It's gon' be alright, Jackie," he assured her while gently rubbing her back.

It had been that way all night. The rest of her family had either gone home to get some rest or was in and out. Quan's daughter, Kira, was with Ms. Jackie's sister, Evelyn. She had watched Kira before, and that was the only one that Quan would have approved of. While he loved his family, they were still the typical family members. Always gossiping, always criticizing, or always with their hand out. As much as I wanted to see Kira and hug her, I knew it was for the best that she not be at the hospital. She didn't need to see everyone so distraught. And even though she probably would have no idea what was going on, she didn't need to hear about it. Besides, I didn't look too hot, and at her age, she was sure to have a ton of questions. My arm was in a temporary cast, I had small cuts and scratches from all the shattered glass that flew in my face, and I had a big, ugly knot on my forehead.

As I watched Ms. Jackie, I rocked back and forth uncomfortably in my own chair. India had taken my mom home but returned to be by my side after she'd cleaned herself up. She was now seated beside me, doing her best to get a little sleep. It had been a hell of a night for everyone. There was no way I could sleep though. Not until I saw Quan. My body was just too anxious. He had been out of surgery for hours and was now waiting in post op until he was taken to a room. With his grave injuries and the type of care that he needed, I knew that he would likely be here for a while.

After sitting idle for a few more hours, fatigue began to override the anxiousness. I decided I'd close my eyes for a few and try to get a little rest. Lord knows I was going to need it. Although I had already spoken to numerous officers, I had no doubt that they would eventually resurface and ask more questions. I also knew that, at some point, someone was going to have to start handling Quan's affairs.

Quan had a deal with a label, but he was still semi-independent. Even though it would soon be public that he had been injured, he still had shows and interviews that were going to need to be formally cancelled. For the most part, Quan handled his own bookings. Being a city boy, he knew far too well that people could get shady during business. He'd asked me to help out, and I declined since I didn't really want to be involved with the business side of his life. Now I wished I had.

I also still had to call the insurance company and report the car being totaled. Since it was brand new, I had to go home and find the paperwork for it. I could only pray it was with the rest of the documents for all the other vehicles. I'd lost my phone during the accident, although I really had no use for it at the moment. My small family and circle were already with me. Everyone that I needed anyway. Most of my mother's family lived in the south, and the ones that stayed in the area, we didn't really rock with. We didn't really know much of my daddy's family, even though he had been born and raised in Baltimore. It had always just been me, my mom, and my sister.

I looked over at India again, and she was still sleeping soundly. I shifted my body around and leaned my head against the side to try and do the same. Of course, that wouldn't last long.

⚜

"WE DON'T HAVE TO ADDRESS THE PUBLIC YET, BUT WE HAVE to tell them something. Otherwise, the media and reporters are really going to start invading your privacy to get answers. It could be his mother, a family member. Or even you," he suggested to me. "But someone has to issue a statement on behalf of the family. It can be a tweet or an Instagram post to his page. Or of course, it can be a verbal statement. But we have to say something," he stressed, looking from me to Ms. Jackie. He had initially come in directing all of his questions at her; however, she quickly informed him that speaking to me was just as good as speaking to her.

I couldn't have been dozed off more than thirty minutes when he came in and begin speaking to Ms. Jackie. The funny-looking white man had been sent from Quan's label, Desert Heat Entertainment, to find out what was going on. Now that they knew, I didn't understand why they couldn't make the statement. It was enough dealing with the reporters looming around. And they were everywhere outside. Luckily, I hadn't had to deal with them yet since I'd never left the hospital. I shook my head and finally addressed his statement. "

"No, I can't. I'm just not in the headspace to keep updating people or speaking to anyone. Neither is his mother."

Ms. Jackie nodded in agreement.

"Why can't you all do it?" I asked. "*You're* his label."

"We will eventually, but I flew in with specific instructions. I need a family member to do it first."

"That's the stupidest shit ever," I snapped, the stress of the events making me impatient. "Don't they know what we're going through? They know he was fuckin' shot. It was all over the news," I argued. "We're in this bitch going through it. Stressed, not eating, barely sleeping, hoping and praying he's gonna make it."

"And so are his fans. They have the right to know."

I glared at him. I knew he was right, but I wasn't trying to hear that shit. What I really wanted to say was, *fuck his fans*. His *real* family and friends needed space and privacy.

"Do we have anyone that wants to formally speak on the family's behalf or as a representative of Quan's?" the label rep asked with a sigh.

"Italy, someone has to do it," India chimed in from beside me with her two cents. "Rumors are circulating, and the last thing we need to do is fuel them with silence. People are going to form their own opinions and create their own false narratives about everything that is going on. Taking sides. It's just going to get worse," she said without saying too much.

I had already told India what I saw when everything went down. She already knew that it was Jahquez and his one of his homies that shot into my car. Although I didn't see a face, I recognized the car from the few times I'd seen Jahquez. He had a gray Camaro with black rims. He had the same car for several years now. Although it was a typical car, it wasn't typical in the neighborhoods he frequented. After briefing me on the shit that went down at Quan's show a few nights back, I had no doubt that it was him. Wasn't nobody pushing that nigga's car but him. Kayla barely drove his car. India and I were both positive that he drove while someone else pulled the trigger from the passenger seat.

"Well, you do it," I said to India. "My sister can do it," I repeated, my attention now focused on the label rep.

I didn't even give her the opportunity to agree. Especially since she had so much to say. Besides, I knew she would mind since, at the end of the day, she was right. She was also heavy on social media and would have no problem communicating *and* shutting down trolls if necessary.

"Okay," she agreed. "I'll get something typed up."

"Please do. *ASAP*," he emphasized. "Does anyone have access to Quan's social media?" he asked, glad that he was finally getting somewhere.

"Yeah, I do," I replied. "I know his passwords. We'll go in, and I'll have my sister make a statement. *One*. That's it. Then we'll update them when he is better."

"Fair enough. I have your number." He turned to Ms. Jackie, who was now sitting quietly. "I'll be in contact with you directly."

"And you, Ms...." He paused so she could introduce herself.

"I'm India. India Cannon."

"Thank you, India. I'm Richard Cross." He handed her a business card. "Once you get that statement written up, please contact me, and you can get it posted to his social media accounts."

"Thanks, India," I told her after Mr. Cross had left. We had left from the hospital waiting room and were now headed back to my house so I could take a shower and head back to the hospital. Even though everyone was telling me I needed rest, I didn't plan on doing any resting until they had Quan comfortable and in a room. I knew I wouldn't be able to sleep unless I knew he was good. Even when they had him in his own room, I knew I wouldn't be doing much sleeping. I mean, how could I? Quan was recovering from a gunshot wound. The doctors didn't know if he was going to make it. That was some real heavy shit, and I was a nervous fuckin' wreck. I was so exhausted, and the skin around my eyes was even tender and raw from constant crying. My heart ached for my man. Ached for me. The thought of losing him was just too much to bear. Despite how I felt, I knew I had to be strong. I didn't know how much longer I was going to hold up before I broke down.

"You're welcome," India replied as we got comfortable and pulled on our seat belts. She exhaled deeply. "It's a whole lot to take in." The look on her face was somber. Not only was she in a tough spot, but I had a feeling that she felt some guilt behind all the events that led up to everything.

India always heard me express how I felt about Raul and Loco keeping him immersed in the drama. However, this time it wasn't their fault. The drama had begun on my end. India always wanted to be at every damn show. Front and center so she could "snag her a baller" as she put it. Dragging Kayla's ghetto ass along for every outing wasn't a good idea. They were best friends, so if anyone knew how Jahquez was going to act, it was India. Now, I wasn't saying that they were to blame for his actions, but I was saying that if she knew that Kayla was attached to drama, then why bring her. Despite how I felt, I didn't speak on it. I didn't want to play the blame game. Everyone was hurting, and the pain was too raw. I just prayed that he pulled through so I wouldn't end up resenting my sister. I loved her, and right now, I needed her.

"Have you spoken to Kayla?" I asked quietly. I gave her a look. What was understood didn't need to be explained. She knew what the look meant.

"Na. I'm going to though. But you already know what it is and how I'm rockin'. You my sister. Nothing comes before that. Quan is family. I mean, what is there to even say? That's Jaden's father."

"Facts. Right or wrong. You know I would rock with Quan," I admitted.

"Right. But Jahquez bitch ass ain't even close to a damn Rayquan."

"Well, you know you gon' have to distance yourself. She not gon' stop fuckin' with the father of her child. Especially because they are still together. But you know this shit doesn't end with Quan. Loco ready to ride. Raul is the more levelheaded one, but he ready to slide too. It's 'bout to get messy. You cannot be around her at all. Anywhere she be, you know Jahquez won't be far."

India nodded.

"I don't want to see people getting hurt, but fuck Jahquez," I spat coldly. "They can box him up as far as I'm concerned." I truly meant that shit. "You know you can stay out in Glenwood with me and Mommy until this shit dies down. Go get whatever you need."

Since the townhome Quan and I shared with my mother was way out of the city, we were safe. Our community was gated with armed security guards. One thing Quan didn't play about was the safety of his immediate family. And he had every reason not to play about it. The one night I decide to carry my ass in the city to celebrate my birthday, we're gunned down on the highway. I had known from the jump that it had something to do with Loco and Raul. Even if it was only a small piece of the puzzle. I hated that the bigger piece hit so close to home with Kayla though.

"Yeah, I might do that," India said softly.

"Seriously, India. I don't want you in the mix of things."

India had an apartment in the city, and although she stayed in a fairly nice complex, she was still *in the city*.

"I'm gonna need some help getting all Quan's shit in order anyway. Obviously, he's not going to be able to perform shows and interviews, but a lot of these people paid deposits. I'm going to have to talk to a lawyer and see if the money needs to be refunded. See who wants to wait." I shook my head and sighed. It was all so overwhelming.

"Don't worry, sis. I'll help you with everything," she assured me.

"Thanks. I know he has a little planner that he keeps all his bookings organized in. We'll have to go through it."

"Cool."

The rest of the drive home was fairly quiet. I stared out the window in thought while constantly wiping away my tears. I prayed that Quan got better. I couldn't imagine life without him.

INDIA

"Did Italy talk to the police?" Kayla's question caught me all the way off guard, and I would be a liar if I said I was even prepared to answer it after the way she'd asked. It was her tone for me, and friend or no friend, she had me fucked up.

"Kayla, hold on for a minute."

I pressed mute and put her on hold while I quietly walked around the large house to make sure there weren't any listening ears. I was still at my sister's house, and I didn't want her getting all worked up from Kayla's phone call. I knew Italy had nothing against her, but things were messy at the moment, and something slight might trigger her. After walking around, I found my mother sleep in her room and Italy in the shower. I unmuted the phone and proceeded to talk to Kayla downstairs.

"Kayla, I swear to God... I love you like a sister, but my *real* sister was nearly murdered last night! Her nigga was gunned down in front of her face! In cold, fuckin' blood, and you gon' call me and ask me did she talk to the police? No how you doing or how you holding up? Is Italy alright? No kiss my ass or nothing! Bitch, you could have at least pretended for one fuckin' minute! But I should have known all you would give a fuck about is whether or not someone gave the police any information implicating your bitch ass baby daddy! I bet his ass sittin' right beside you and got you asking questions for him."

"India, I know you're upset, but it's not even like that. No one forced me to ask shit. And you're right. I should have asked how you and Italy were doing. I already know she's okay because the streets talk and it's all over the blogs and social media. But I still should have asked. For that, I'm sorry. But you and I both know that everybody goin' around saying that Jahquez did it or that Leel had something to do with it. I'm just trying to get some information and clear my nigga's name."

"Fuck his name! My fuckin' *sister* was in that car!" I screamed into the phone to remind her. "Now, I'm not saying it's your fault, Kayla. You know I'm not saying that, but at the end of the day, you know what the fuck is right and what the fuck is wrong. How you just gon' continue to lay up with that nigga after that? Italy should be like family to you."

"So you think he did it to too?" she asked in exasperation.

I paused for a moment. Jahquez had to have been stickin' dick in her brain rather than her twat because she was stupid as hell. It was like her brain wasn't registering the fact that her man could do something like that, or maybe she truly believed the lies that he was kicking to her. It was almost like I didn't know the person I was talking to. This wasn't the same Kayla. She was acting way too dumb to be.

"Kayla, I know he did it!"

"And she told you it was Jahquez?" She continued to probe.

"*Jahquez shot into Italy's car*, Kayla. Now, I don't know whatever lies that nigga feeding you, but he did it. Italy recognized his car when they pulled up beside them on the expressway. Whoever was in the passenger's seat shot into her car. A car that belonged to her, not Quan. So you know what that tells me... That he didn't give a fuck. He didn't care who got hurt or killed in the process. Let's keep it real. Nobody drives Jahquez's lil' cheap ass Camaro. Not even you. He the only nigga that got that car in the hood. How fuckin' coincidental is it that a Camaro follows them, pulls alongside them, and then shoots in their car? Use your head, Kay. Now, I know that fuck nigga sittin' right beside you. But let him know this... I won't speak for any nigga... but you and that nigga already know how Quan people get down. That shit won't go unanswered. You better choose a side, Kayla. And choose wisely," I warned.

"India, you know I love you and I love Italy. I mean, just because it was his car doesn't mean it was him." She paused for a minute, and I didn't say a word. I was just waiting for her to deliver her next line of bullshit. "Jahquez said he didn't do it, but if Italy is saying he did, then you know that puts me in a bad spot. How can I choose a side when that's the father of my son?"

I could hear the emotion in her voice, and I knew that she knew Jahquez did it. I fought back my own tears.

"Kayla." I swallowed hard. "I love you, but you know I'm rockin' with my family on this one. If you fuckin with the opp, then that makes you the opp."

I didn't wait for a response. I hung up the phone in Kayla's ear and exhaled deeply, plopping down on the living room sofa. A few seconds later, the tears that had welled up in my eyes were now cascading down my face. It was all too much. Quan was in the hospital fighting for his life, and I had to cut off my best fuckin' friend. We had to pick sides because of our loyalties. It was bullshit, but it was, what it was.

"India, you down here?" Italy appeared out of nowhere, still damp and wrapped in a towel. I quickly wiped away my tears.

"Yeah. Wassup?" I asked. I inhaled a deep breath and got my shit together.

"I found Quan's planner. He's only booked for a couple shows for the rest of the month. He was about to start working on an album, mixtape—whatever he wants to call it. I'm gonna cancel the shows for this month, but he had a producer fly in today. I'm sure he's already heard about what happened on the news."

"Yeah, I'm sure. That's all everyone's talking about. I've been trying to stay off the social media shit though. It's too easy to get caught up with the back-and-forth. Everybody has their opinion or theory of what happened. I'm just trying to keep from cussing motherfuckers out."

"Facts." Italy took a seat on the chair across from me. "Look, I need you to go meet with the producer. Even though I know he's already heard about what happened, I still want to handle him properly and professionally. Quan put a lot of money down to work with this guy. That's all he's been talking about. That business relationship is important to him. His name is Shawn. He flew all the way in from California, and I don't want him in limbo. Can you go and speak with him? Let him know what's going on. What we expect. Let him know he can change his flight information, and we'll take care of it. If it's extra, we'll cover it. Just do whatever you have to do to keep that business relationship intact for when Quan gets better."

"Okay. I got you."

"Thanks, India. I owe you big time. I can't handle all this shit on my own."

"You know I got you, baby. I'll go talk to him. Just give me his info. A phone number if you have it. I'll take care of it and then make a formal statement."

"Sounds like a plan. I'm gonna catch an Uber back to the hospital."

"Okay. Let me know when you about to leave and let me know when you get to the hospital," I told her.

"Okay. And India... please don't be in the city long. I wouldn't know what to do if something else happened."

She paused for a moment. As if she were hesitant to say what she was about to say. "I just want to let you know that it's okay if you check on Kayla. I know you probably already spoke to her. She can't help the bullshit that Jahquez did. Now, if she on some 'fuck Quan' type time, then you know it's fuck her. But if she isn't, then all you can do is try and be there for her on the side. It's not her fault. And she's gonna need you when this shit is done and over."

"Okay." I didn't need her to elaborate any further. I already knew what that meant. Jahquez was gonna get his, and as usual, the woman that lay next to him was going to feel it the hardest. Italy knew Kayla was solid. She might have been weak in some areas, but she definitely was solid when it came to her character. She couldn't help that her nigga wasn't.

❋ 11 ❋

KAYLA

"Did you try to call her back?" Jahquez asked. He had just walked into the kitchen where I was preparing our four-year-old son, Jaden, something to eat.

"No. She's not going to answer, Jahquez," I replied, exhaling sharply.

"How do you know that if you don't try?" He stood near the entrance of the small kitchen and stared at me while I shuffled around.

"We've been friends for years. I just know... She's not going to answer. Why the fuck do you think she is just going to speak freely to me over the phone after what happened? You the fuckin' opp," I reminded him. "That makes me the opp."

I shook my head and exhaled once again. Just saying the word was a painful reminder that my son and I weren't safe in our own home, because of the fuck shit that Jahquez had done.

"She's not stupid. You my nigga, and they probably told her not to tell me shit," I spat. Jahquez was getting on my fuckin' nerves. "Have you decided what you're gonna do?" I asked abruptly. He was too busy standing in my damn face when he should have been plotting his next move.

While I waited for him to respond, I grabbed a towel and pulled the tray of chicken nuggets from the oven."

"They hot, Mommy?" Jaden asked from the table where he was patiently waiting for his food.

"Yeah, sweetie, they're hot. I'm gonna let them cool down and then you can eat, okay?" I assured him. My son, Jaden always ate right after daycare. Unfortunately, he was eating a tad bit late since I was running off schedule because I was dealing with a bunch of nonsense behind his raggedy ass daddy.

My day started off typical. I'd gone to work at seven in the morning. However, by nine, I'd gotten the news that Quan had been shot. I was in disbelief, and with news spreading like wildfire on social media, I was even more shocked when I learned that Jahquez and his brother Leel were the rumored people responsible. By noon, I was dealing with a big fucking mess. I'd been calling India all day, and she wasn't answering. Jahquez had been calling me nonstop, and I, of course, had to try and get through the workday feeling sick to my stomach with all kinds of crazy thoughts whirling through my head.

By the time I got off work, Jahquez was calling me to pick him up from his homie's house. His car was now parked since he couldn't drive it around as freely anymore. He had no doubt that he would be the target of retaliation. Driving through the hood in that Camaro was an eventual death wish. Quan's homies, Raul and Loco, were sending blatant death threats to Jahquez and whoever was with him when they'd ran down on Quan. From the posts I'd seen on social media, they were basically saying anyone could get it.

After picking him up, I'd asked Jahquez over and over if he had anything to do with Italy's car being shot up, and he vehemently denied it. Deep in my heart, I had a feeling he was lying. By the time I finally talked to India, she confirmed all my suspicions. Of course, my natural reaction was to defend him; however, there was only so much that I could say. The shit was foul, and I had no doubt that it was going to be some major smoke behind it. It was just like Jahquez to do something unpre-dictable and stupid, putting everyone in harm's way.

"What do you mean have I decided what I'm gonna do?" he asked, finally replying to my question.

"What are you gonna do, Jahquez? You claim you didn't have shit to do with it, but you insist I keep calling India to see what they got planned or what they saying. You obviously know it's not safe. So what are you gonna do? They have money, Jahquez. *Lots* of it. You already know that neither Raul nor Loco have to step into that hood to get you touched. They can have someone else do it."

"First of all, get off them niggas' dicks," he demanded. He shot me an angry glare. "They ain't the only ones with money."

I met his gaze and just peered at him. Standing there in a pair of blue jeans and a black Fruit of the Loom hoodie, I was waiting for him to tell me who the fuck else had some because it sure as hell wasn't his ass. The little brick he flipped every month damn sure wasn't nothing to brag about. Leel had a little money, but I knew damn well he wasn't trying to spend it participating in a war he knew he couldn't win. Yeah, BGS was bigger, but Triple B didn't need to be big. Either Quan, Raul, or Loco could send paid shooters to war for them. Leel, Jahquez, and the other niggas they rolled with wouldn't know what hit them.

Growing up on the gritty streets of Baltimore, I'd seen dudes turn the gun and pull the trigger on their brother for the right price. If Triple B offered to pay any one of those broke ass niggas from BGS to shoot Jahquez in his head, they'd likely do it with zero hesitation.

"I'm not on anything," I replied to Jahquez, watching my language in front of my son. "I'm just keeping it a buck. Do you think whoever they send is going to care where you are or who you're with when they start looking for you? If they aren't looking for you already. You could be with me or Jaden. I gotta make sure my son is safe, Jahquez."

"I told you... I didn't have shit to do with that fuck nigga getting shot."

"Okay," I said, exasperated. "You say you didn't, but everyone else seems to think you did. People saying your name on social media. Saying Leel's name. This shit is bad. *If* you did do it, did you ever think how it might affect anyone else? How it would affect your family?"

He could stand there and lie all the fuck he wanted to, but I knew he did it. Italy wasn't going to lie. Who in the hell was he to lie on?

"I suggest you watch how you talking to me, Kay. You goin' off what that hoe ass bitch telling you."

"Whatever. India ain't no hoe, and she ain't telling me shit. She flat-out told me that I'm the opp because you the fuckin' opp. She won't answer my calls. I lost my fuckin' best friend over some shit you did, and now, me and my son aren't even safe in our own home!" I yelled, finally losing my patience. I brought my volume down some when I saw Jaden staring at me with wide eyes.

I wasn't gon' front, I was scared. Italy knew where I lived, and although I wasn't worried that India would give my address up to anyone so they could find Jahquez, I wasn't so sure about Italy. Anybody that knew her knew that Quan was her every-thing. She was fiercely loyal to him. If something happened to him, I had no doubt that her heart would turn cold as ice.

Jahquez didn't even blink or bat a lash as he stared at me following my outburst. If I didn't know any better, I would swear the nigga just flat-out didn't give a fuck. About *anything*. Not me *or* his son.

"I'll stay at my mom's house a couple of days. If you so worried, you and Jaden should do the same. In the meantime, keep calling her and find out whatever you can."

Jahquez didn't even bother waiting for a response. He turned his back to me and headed back down the hall to the room.

"I'm sorry for yelling, sweetie," I said to my son who was now sitting at the table looking worried. He always got quiet whenever his father and I got into it.

As soon as he was done eating, I planned to get the fuck out of there and head straight to my mama's apartment in Gwynn Oak. I had a son to think about. His safety was more important than anything. I knew I needed to leave Jahquez, and this time, I was more serious than I'd ever been before.

❧ 12 ❧

SHAWN

I had just come out of the bathroom when I heard the phone ringing from the nightstand near the bed. I walked briskly to retrieve it.

"Hello?" I asked. I already knew who it was. A woman named India had reached out to me on Quan's behalf, claiming to be his sister. She was coming by to fill me in on what was going on and to see how we would proceed or if we would be able to proceed.

I'd heard the news on social media about Quan being shot. I'd even seen where the lady that I was meeting had made a statement on it. It was so unfortunate, and I prayed he pulled through. He was too talented to have his life end so soon and so tragically. Although my heart went out to him and his family, I was now down in Baltimore for nothing. I wasn't tripping about it, because it wasn't like Quan wanted for this to happen. My issue was that he knew it definitely was a possibility. I saw the guys that Quan hung around. The guys he was posted on social media with and went live with. Anytime someone from the hood started to blow up and make a significant amount of money, they had to decide early on who to leave behind. The saying was true, *everybody can't come with you*.

With him now in ICU and fighting for his life, I had a feeling that his family was going to want some type of refund. Most of the time, when breadwinners like Quan got hurt, locked up, or were tragically killed, it always at some point led to some type of quarrel over money. Who owed the person that was now gone? The family always tried to come and collect. Quan had put down a substantial deposit for production of his album. I was supplying all his beats and had reserved my week specifically for the production of his album. I knew it had to be about that. Clearly, they knew I'd already heard what was going on. They could have left it at that. Since those thoughts were running through my head, I had to admit I was a little irritated about the whole meet up.

"Hi. This is India Cannon. I'm downstairs in the lobby," the woman said to me after I greeted her.

"Cool. You can come up. I'm on the fifth floor in room 514."

"Actually, I was hoping you would come down. I don't mind waiting for you. I'll be at the bar by the water fountain," she advised.

"Cool. Give me five minutes," I told her before hanging up.

I grabbed my things and headed downstairs. After getting off the elevator and walking through the lobby, I entered the small on-site bar. I glanced around for a few seconds but didn't see anyone who looked like they'd be there to meet me. I saw a few white people, one elderly black guy, and finally my eyes landed on a young, brown-skinned female seated at the bar. She had on a Nike sweatsuit and a fitted hat. Just as I was about to tear my eyes away from her, she waved for me to come over.

"How you doin'?" I greeted her, my tall frame towering over her petite one. "India?"

"I am. How are you?" she asked, spinning her barstool around and greeting me with a smile.

I looked in front of her, and it looked like she'd already gotten started. She had what looked like a half-drank Long Island iced tea in front of her. Noticing that I was eyeballing her drink, she spoke.

"Oh. Yeah, I got started without you." She chuckled lightly and then followed it up with a sigh. "It's been a very, very long day," she admitted.

"I can imagine," I assured her.

I took a seat beside her at the bar and studied her. Her baggy eyes looked tired, and her long hair was pulled into a ponytail that hung from the opening of her cap. Despite her tired and basic appearance, she was still very attractive. Smooth brown skin and perfect teeth. She didn't require much. The bartender came up to me and sat down a napkin. I ordered a shot of Hennessy and then proceeded.

"So you're Quan's sister?" I asked.

"No, no. I guess you can say I'm his sister-in-law. He's dating my sister. They've been together for three years. As you can imagine, she and his mother are going through it. It's tough. But look, I don't want to keep you. Basically, I'm acting as a spokesperson for the family. Quan didn't have a publicist, and he really doesn't have too many people he can trust to speak for him, so I'm here to do so. Of course, with permission from his mother and my sister."

I nodded. "Gotcha."

"So they're basically figuring out all of Quan's commitments. Those that he won't be able to honor of course like interviews. He had a little planner that he kept everything written down and organized in. So of course, he had that he was supposed to begin working on an album today with you."

"Right."

"Well, obviously, he won't be able to do so. Honestly, they don't know if he's going to make it. We pray that he does. He's in ICU. I'm sure you know all this from the media. So we just need to know how you want to proceed."

"Well, I'm sure if he pulls through, he's gonna want to still do the album as planned. If he doesn't pull through... of course, there will be no album."

"Right. The main thing is we want to be able to write down

and make verbal agreements on how things will proceed if he does pull through. You're still willing to do the album at a later date with whatever you two have already arranged? I'm assuming you have a contract."

"We did. And I'd definitely be willing to do the album at a later date. He did put down a deposit, and I, of course, don't have a problem applying that to a later date. However long it takes. I understand that this was unplanned. Now, he did pay for my flight and hotel accommodations. If we reschedule, I just ask that he cover them again at a later date."

"Absolutely. Of course," she agreed.

"I'm going to arrange to leave early and go back to LA. If they charge me anything to make those changes, I'll take care of that. That's no big deal," I assured her.

For some reason, I was no longer irritated and was willing to be more accommodating. Maybe it was because they were so understanding about how the tragic incident also affected other people. Or maybe because my heart went out to them and I empathized with them. *Or* maybe because I was surprisingly attracted to the woman in front of me. Whatever it was, I was willing to compromise. I didn't want her to remember me as being difficult.

"That's decent of you, but we'll take care of it. My sister wants to ensure that no one is inconvenienced and that Quan's business relationships are handled with professionalism and care," she said, sounding like she'd been coached to be professional and cover all points.

I couldn't stop the smile that had managed its way to my face. "You don't speak on other people's behalf often, do you?"

She took a sip of her Long Island. "No." She laughed and then paused for a second. "Why? I sound like I'm trying too hard?" She flashed me a bright smile and continued, not giving me a chance to reply. "They told me what to say between my sister and his label. They unfortunately didn't handle any of Quan's shows. He handled all that by himself. They just kept drilling into our heads how terrible it was that he didn't have a publicist or someone to handle his communication when he isn't able to. Honestly, all of this is really hard. Quan worked so hard to get to where he is. A lot of this stems from jealousy. People going at him the very moment they had a reason to do so. No matter how petty it seems. Of course, I can't go into all that."

"Oh, I definitely understand."

"We just don't want this to be a setback for him if he pulls through. He worked too hard for it. My sister is a nervous wreck, and so am I... But somebody's gotta be strong, right? So, for now, I'll be acting as professional I know how."

"Well, you're doing a good job. Let your sister know that I appreciate her being willing to cover everything, but it won't be necessary. And let the family know that I send my condolences and prayers."

"Thank you." India got up from her chair. "It was nice to meet you. Shawn, right?"

"Yep."

"Well, Shawn, I have your number, and I will be in contact with you if anything changes." She tossed back the last swallow of her drink. "We will keep you posted. Gotta get back to my sister."

"Thank you," I said to her, before watching her scurry out the bar.

As she walked off, I couldn't help and think about the sister she spoke of. Although Quan was heavy on social media, his girl-friend didn't appear to be. I'd seen a few pictures he'd posted of what likely was her. Pretty girl that stayed out the limelight. It was nice that he had someone that genuinely cared for him. Instead of hopping on social media and basking in all the attention, she was doing what was most important. She was by his side and being there for him. Concerned with making sure he was okay and that he would be okay in the long run, even in his business dealings. If that wasn't love, then I didn't know what was.

I picked up my phone and dialed Nisa. I didn't want anything, but since I hadn't spoken to her since earlier in the day, I figured I'd check up on her. I wasn't surprised when the phone went directly to voicemail. It usually did when she was busy either at the gym or helping her father out at the restaurant. Despite Nisa not possessing every little thing that I desired in a woman, I had to admit that I admired her spirit. She wasn't a bad catch. College educated, affectionate, beautiful. Although busy, she always seemed to be a team player, helping her father out. For the first time, I was beginning to think that maybe it was I who was the selfish one. Maybe I was the one that was looking at things all wrong.

I finished my drink and headed back to my room. I figured I'd might as well call the airline and change my departure. I prayed Delta had room for me to catch a flight out tomorrow. In the meantime, I was going to check out a little bit of downtown Baltimore before heading back to LA.

❧ 13 ❧

INDIA

"No, I don't care! Why the fuck do I have to find out from a friend—who found out on Instagram—that my baby daddy has been shot and is in ICU!" Charlotte screamed in the middle of the third-floor lobby where we were all waiting to take turns to see Quan.

"You need to calm down," Ms. Jackie demanded.

"I don't need to do shit! Where's my fuckin' daughter? All this happened while y'all have my daughter, and nobody tells me shit! I want my child. Nowwww!" she yelled.

A staff member walked up. I could tell she didn't want to intervene, but since Charlotte had come in their acting like a simpleton, she had no choice.

"Ma'am, I have to ask you to quiet down, or you're gonna have to leave. I know you all have been through a lot, but there's other families waiting in here to see loved ones. There are also sick patients in there. You can't keep screaming and being disruptive."

"Fuck them people!" she spat, glaring around angrily at everyone. "Where the fuck is my daughter!" she demanded to know.

Ms. Jackie walked away from Charlotte and took a few deep breaths. I already knew from Italy that she didn't like her at all.

Since my sister had been with Quan, I'd seen Ms. Jackie argue and go toe to toe with the best of them. I had no doubt it was taking everything inside her to keep from slapping the taste out her mouth.

"She's with Evelyn, my sister," Ms. Jackie did her best to explain. "My brother, James, is calling her now and having her bring her to you." She pointed to the corner of the large lobby area, where James had walked off to make the call. "She can meet you here or wherever you want. We just thought it would be best for Kira not to be around all this." Ms. Jackie did her best to diffuse the situation. I could tell that she didn't like to kiss ass. Her words didn't match the look on her face.

"Well, it doesn't pay to think. You should have called me to pick up my daughter. I don't know your sister. You should have called as soon as it happened." Charlotte's glare turned to my sister. "Italy, you could have called me."

"Charlotte, I wasn't thinking. So much was going on. I was in the car with Quan when all that shit went down. I was brought in here by ambulance just like him—"

"Yeah, I heard," she said, cutting Italy off.

I felt my jaws tighten. The bitch was starting to get on my nerves, and I was only going to allow but so much. Everyone was trying to be cordial with her because they didn't want to ruin their chances of seeing Quan's daughter; however, Charlotte was dragging the nasty ass attitude. She knew that she had the upper hand with Kira while Quan was laying up in ICU. On a regular day, Italy would have put the paws on Charlotte for running her mouth.

"You call any other fuckin' time. Open your mouth any other fuckin' time," she continued to argue while staring at my sister.

Italy just glared at her in response. I knew she didn't even have the energy to argue after seeing her man for the first time since he was brought in hooked to an IV with tubes running through him. Italy broke down when she walked into Quan's room. If my mother and I hadn't been there to catch her on both sides, she probably would have collapsed to the floor. For over an hour, she'd stood over top of him and cried, kissed his face, and held his hand, even while she had a broken arm, cuts, and bruises herself. All Italy wanted was for him to be okay. Her world had been turned upside down in one night, and now, this bitch wanted to come in and be disrespectful.

"It's damn near six at night, and I'm just getting up with y'all. You had enough time to put together a fuckin' statement from 'the family', but you motherfuckers didn't have time to reach out to me and let me know *my* baby daddy had been shot! Or let me know where my child was so I could pick her the fuck up!" she yelled.

"Bitch, my sister is done talking to you, and we through listening to you!" I jumped up out of my seat and advanced toward her aggressively. That was it. I couldn't take it anymore, and I had finally lost my patience. "I suggest you go on, or I'm gon' beat the fuck out you!" I screamed, causing the people in the waiting area to look at me and start whispering.

"Girl, I don't even know you, and my problem isn't with you. Italy knows my number, and so does Ms. Jackie They can call me to run their fuckin' mouth about everything else, so why I gotta find out on social media that Quan has been shot!" she screamed, tears rolling down her face. "Why the fuck do I have to call and call to find out where my daughter is!" For a minute, I almost felt sympathy for her, but then I remembered how disrespectful she had just been.

I couldn't lie, she was right. My sister and Ms. Jackie were definitely wrong for that. Shorty should have definitely been notified; however, her feelings weren't my priority. My sister's declining mental state was. I glanced over at her and watched as she sat still in her chair, lip trembling, looking broken. It was on and off, but of course that was expected. One minute she was good, and the next minute she wasn't. Seeing her man hooked up to machines, weak as fuck, and barely able to breathe on his own was taking its toll on her. Seeing her face and watching her crumble was enough to shatter my heart.

My baby sister was hurting, and there was nothing I could do but pray. It was taking everything in me to hold it together, but I knew I had to. I had to be strong for Italy. Social media, the reporters, Quan's business affairs, and now his baby's mother. It was so much, and I could definitely understand why Italy was shutting down the way she was. It was hard to watch. She'd always been strong. Always been a fighter, but now, it was the other way around. I was my sister's keeper. And I would go to war with anybody who came for her. Despite all that, I tried to put myself in the annoying bitch's shoes for a moment. I took a deep breath and tried to calm myself.

"Charlotte, I know you're upset, and you have every right to be. But now isn't the time." I countered. I took another deep breath and reminded myself that we were all going through it. I couldn't lie though, she was working my nerves, and I was about two point five seconds off her pale ass. "We gotta stick together," I continued. "Quan is fighting for his life, and y'all can't be going back and forth giving motherfuckers online something to run with. You're right. They should have called you, but with everything going on, that got overlooked. It's all still very fresh, and everyone's primary concern is that Quan pulls through. But you were right. And I'm sorry," I choked out.

I hated apologizing for shit, let alone some shit I didn't do. But at the moment, it had to be said. Italy was barely responding, and I knew damn well an "I'm sorry" wasn't coming out Ms. Jackie's slick ass mouth.

Charlotte didn't even bother to respond to me. The look on her face basically spoke volumes. I was irrelevant, and she didn't have to answer to me or acknowledge me. She dismissed my apology and basically gave Italy and me her ass to kiss.

"Ms. Jackie." Charlotte rolled her eyes and turned to address her. "I'll be downstairs by security. Have your sister hurry up with my child."

Charlotte stormed out of the lobby and headed toward the elevator. All I could do was shake my head at her behavior. She didn't even bother to ask how Quan was doing or what the doctors said. I glanced at Italy, who was sitting beside me. She didn't say a word. I noticed that she was no longer rocking back and forth. She was now tapping her foot against the floor. I knew it was nothing but her nerves. I reached over and took her hand into mine. Her lip quivered as she fought back tears. Despite her best attempt to hold them in, they still managed to make their way through and slide down her weary face.

"God, I hope he makes it," she choked out.

"He's strong, Italy. Just be patient. He's fighting," I assured her.

"But what if he..." She couldn't finish the sentence. She couldn't bring herself to utter the words.

"God's got this."

"I'm trying," she cried. "I'm trying to trust Him."

"Let Him work."

I didn't continue, because I really didn't have much to say. We weren't very religious people. My mother didn't make us go to church, nor did she attend. I didn't want to tell Italy it was going to be okay, because I didn't know if it would be. All I knew was that whatever happened was God's will.

❧ 14 ❧

ITALY

Even though I knew I should have been resting, I couldn't stop following all the drama on Instagram. Although I didn't have a page, I had logged in earlier from Quan's laptop so my sister could make the statement his label requested. Once the statement was posted, I knew I should have closed his laptop and logged off, but I didn't. Instead, I kept it open and had been on it ever since.

Raul and Loco were going back and forth with Leel and his squad. Every time I turned around, blogs like The Shade Room were screenshotting and reposting every message aimed at the other. It was nonstop. The situation was getting worse by the minute with each one making death threats. The final straw was when Leel posted, *I hope that bitch ass nigga die*. Finally, unable to take anymore, I closed the laptop.

I didn't understand why they hated Quan and his team so much. Raul and Loco said they were just mad because they were up. It was stupid to me. The whole event that took place at Victory's was stupid as well. I didn't understand why Jahquez would pull a gun out after bum-rushing their VIP section to chase down Kayla. She was cute and all, but she wasn't that damn bad to be going to war over. To me, it seemed that there was a whole lot of hating going on. But then again, it also didn't help that Quan and his team would brag about their money in their raps. But shit, that was what rap was about. That was what everyone did. Quan had done nothing wrong.

Quan's latest song, "Fly Like Us" was soaring on the charts, and apparently the blogs were aware that it was a diss track aimed at Leel. I never understood why the people behind the blogs didn't use better judgment when deciding what was story worthy. They had to have known that they played a significant role in fueling rap beefs. Beefs that sometimes ended with blood spilled because they chose to follow them closely and use them as entertainment. In my opinion, they needed to be held accountable. Rappers were human and had real fucking lives and families. It was often the family that suffered more than anything while people sat their bored, sad asses in front of their phones and provoked bullshit beefs. If Quan died, he would be another rap talent gone and forgotten in six months. Same for Leel. I had no doubt that he knew Raul and Loco were looking for whoever shot up my car and hit Quan. I prayed my baby pulled through. I knew Leel and his bitch ass gang wanted him dead so their poor asses could get some clout. They'd just better hope they made it to see it.

Loco and Raul were two of the first people at the hospital after they brought us in. They were one of the first phone calls that Ms. Jackie made. Although she was a mother, she was also from the streets. Her son had been shot in the neck, and she wanted to see justice served. Raul and Loco had a name. Now all they had to do was put a bullet in that motherfucker's head.

Yawning loudly out of nowhere, I pulled my blanket up to my neck and finally got comfortable. I had been up for over thirty-six hours with maybe thirty minutes of sleep. I needed some serious rest. I glanced at the large wall clock in my room. It was nearly nine at night. I was going back up to the hospital in the morning to sit with Quan. Hopefully something had changed or the doctor had some good news.

THE NEXT MORNING, I WOKE UP BRIGHT AND EARLY. AFTER taking a shower, I headed downstairs to see my mother already in the kitchen cooking breakfast. India was also there, sitting at the table.

"Good morning, y'all. Mommy, how long you been up?" I asked, taking a seat at the table.

"A few hours. Just trying to stay busy. Did some cleaning."

She made me a plate of bacon and eggs and quickly slid it in front of me.

"Did Ms. Jackie call?"

"No. No one has yet. It's only seven."

"When did you come, India?" I asked my big sister.

"Last night around midnight. I fell asleep, woke up, and packed me a bag. Just until shit dies down."

"Yeah. Well, you know you're more than welcome to stay as long as you need," I informed her.

"Yeah, I know." As I ate, she quietly slid me her phone across the table. "Read that."

"Read what?" my mom asked.

"Show it to Ma when you're done."

I picked up the phone and looked at it. It was a post by Charlotte on her Instagram page from last night. I began reading.

Someone please explain to me how the father of my child gets gunned down with his so-called girlfriend, and nobody thinks to pick up the phone and call me? Mind you, he is in custody of my daughter at the time when all this occurs. Why do I have to wake up in the morning and find out from social media that he's in ICU? No phone call, no text message, no email. Nothing! Imagine the panic and devastation I felt as a mother calling Rayquan's mother, Jackie, over and over to get an update on him and my child. Imagine thinking that your child has been hurt or murdered. The whole time, I don't know if our daughter was in the car with him when it was shot up. The news first reported he had a female passenger with him when he was shot. And that she was injured. I'm thinking that passenger was my daughter. I'm disgusted by the ENTIRE family. Fifty calls and nearly ten voicemails I left his mother. Still no response. Only when I take it upon myself to go to the hospital was when I was informed of the location and well-being of my daughter. Thank God she wasn't in the car and was unharmed, but for nearly twelve hours after getting the news, she was nowhere to be found, and I couldn't reach anyone regarding her. Eight in the morning 'til damn near six at night. And when I get there, she isn't even in the care of his mother! Instead, in the care of a family member that I don't even know! Please tell me how this is right! I get to the hospital, and I'm automatically public enemy number one. Made to feel like I'm the bad guy and being disrespectful. Mind you, no one had even called me and told me shit yet. I got that information from social media and calling around. And then Rayquan wondered why they were barely allowed to see her. Since you call yourself acting as and declaring yourself the family spokesperson @indiacannon... BITCH, please address that. You made a public statement, tagging yourself in a post from his page, asking for privacy and naming yourself as the spokesperson, so address this hoe! And if you want to keep it a buck, you bitches are NOT family. Your sister isn't married to him and has no plans to get married because she doesn't even have an engagement ring on her fat ass fingers. Nobody knows EITHER of you hoes. Why, because you're just that. Hoes! Hoes that are too eager for some clout. Tell his mama that HIS BABY MAMA @mixedgirlcharlotte said that!

I felt my blood run boiling hot after reading the post. My heart raced while my lip trembled with fury. Charlotte was so disrespectful. And the bitch even had the nerve to tag my sister. The hoe already knew that I didn't play the disrespect, so I wasn't sure why she had gone left the way she did. It seemed that she was the one that really wanted clout.

"I don't even have the headspace for this shit. I'm so fuckin' sick of her," I admitted angrily. I passed the phone to my mom so she could read the latest nonsense.

"I got time though," India said with the quickness. I could tell she was fuming. "Since this hoe want to tag me. Where she work at? Where she stay? If it ain't far, I can go right to her. Right now. She wants clout. I'll give her all the clout she wants first thing this morning. I'm gon' make sure she in the blogs and on social media just like she wanted."

I rambled off the locations, and my sister took off while my mother yelled for her to stop. But it was too late. India was on a mission to check a social media gangster. What the hoe failed to realize was that we delivered smoke in real life. Disrespect would be addressed. I grabbed my own phone and called Ms. Jackie. I wanted to prepare her for what was about to happen.

🦋 15 🦋

INDIA

Charlotte worked as a front-end manager at an upscale restaurant in downtown Baltimore's Inner Harbor area. Apparently, the fine little establishment was where she met Quan at years back. Too bad, I was about to go in there and fuck it up. I'd already been by her house, but she wasn't there, so now I was headed to the next place I figured she would be—her workplace.

Adrenaline was rushing through me when my GPS stopped, and I pulled in front of the spot. I didn't plan to do any talking. I already had my fitted cap on, and my hair pulled back in a pony-tail. I parked smack-dab in front of the restaurant and hopped out my car. I stuffed my keys deep into the pockets of the sweats I had thrown on when I dashed out of Italy's house.

Although it was still early, the block that the restaurant was located on was busy from the work crowd and tourists. I was glad that the place was even open at that time of morning. Luck-ily, they sold brunch and a whole bunch of other fancy French shit I didn't eat. I really didn't care what they sold anyway. I was just happy that I could dash in and check a shit-talking hoe before she forgot what she did.

I spotted Charlotte as soon as I walked into the restaurant.

She didn't seem to notice me; however, the host by the door did and attempted to stop me. I guess I looked angry and out of place with my gray sweats on and all-white Nikes tied up tight.

"Ma'am, did you have a reservation?"

I couldn't believe that a motherfucker needed a reservation for breakfast. It was unbelievable actually.

"Nope." I kept walking until I was face-to-face with Charlotte's pale-faced ass.

"Remember me, bitch. I'm here to address you, just like you requested."

Charlotte went to say something, but I stopped her when I drove my right fist into her big ass mouth.

"Keep my sister's name out your motherfuckin' mouth!" I screamed as I hit her with a couple hooks, snatched her off her feet, and dragged her ass across the floor.

Being the weak bitch she was, she yelped and hollered but didn't throw one punch. I couldn't believe this was the same broad that stood in the hospital the day before and talked all that shit to my sister and Ms. Jackie. The way her mouth ran, one would have thought she was Mayweather's little sister. That was not the case.

Leaning over top of Charlotte, I held her tightly by a fistful of her hair from the back of her head. Screaming in her teary-eyed, snotty ass face, I told her, "Bitch, the next time you got something to say, call my sister's phone! You know her number. Ain't that what you said! Don't ever disrespect me, my sister, *or* yo' daughter's grandmother on social media ever again in yo' fuckin' life!"

I released Charlotte's now-disheveled hair with an angry thrust and walked off. I hopped back in my car, shoved my keys in the ignition, and took off. As I drove, my anger subsided and reality hit. I could only hope that hoe didn't call the police. I'd just smacked and dragged her ass in a public place that probably had hella cameras. If she did call them, I would charge it to the game. Certain things just couldn't be tolerated.

❧ 16 ❧

KAYLA

Not moving from where I was sleeping, I reached underneath my pillow and grabbed my phone. It was the middle of the afternoon, but I was laying in bed next to my son taking a midday nap. After ripping, running, and being bad all day, I made Jaden's ass lay down. I figured I'd go ahead and lay down with him since I was tired as hell. I was more mentally drained than anything,

I pushed in my code and unlocked my phone. Missed calls. Text messages. Mostly Jahquez. As usual, he had been blowing my phone up all day. It never failed. He always found something to argue about. I groaned and placed my phone back down. I was so stressed. I literally felt sick. I had even taken a few days off from work. I knew for a fact that Jahquez orchestrated the hit on Italy's car, resulting in Quan's injuries, and it was weighing heavily on my conscience. A part of me wanted to apologize to Italy. Take responsibility for everything that had happened at Victory's. I should have answered Jahquez's calls. I shouldn't have left my phone in the car. I should have stayed my ass home like he wanted me to. I knew how he would act. Maybe if I had, one or all of these things, none of this shit would have happened. But, then again, who was I kidding? As usual, after Jahquez did some bullshit, it was me who always felt bad. But that was how it usually worked when dealing with a manipulative, abusive ass nigga.

Another part of me said, *stop apologizing for shit that isn't your fault.* I didn't make Jahquez do anything. I knew that I needed to stop feeling bad for the shit that he did. Stop blaming myself. No matter how much I told myself that my actions could have stopped him from reacting a certain way, I knew that just wasn't the case. Jahquez did fucked-up shit, and that was just what it was.

I'd been calling and texting India since the day she hung up on me, but she still hadn't responded. I'd even tried to hit her on Instagram. I knew she had a lot going on, but I just wanted to speak my peace. Let her know that I loved her and was praying for Quan and Italy. Let her know that I didn't approve of none of the shit that Jahquez did. I just wanted my friend back. I missed India's crazy ass.

I'd been following all the drama on social media, and that was just what it was—drama. The back and forth. If it wasn't Jahquez posting some nonsense, it was Leel. Of course, Leel's posts were more closely followed and monitored because he was the rapper. People were trying to decode his messages. People were saying Leel put a hit out on Quan. That he knew the shooter. That he *was* the shooter. It was crazy how people on the internet came up with shit. The even crazier part was, they had some good ass guesses. The internet knew way more than it should. While some of the shit was outlandish, some wasn't quite so much. It was to the point that Leel had Jahquez questioning me. I'd only been gone from my house a few days, but the longer I stayed gone, the more Jahquez was accusing me of betrayal. Like I was playing both sides of the fence. He'd even gone as far as accusing me of eavesdropping on his conversations. I wasn't even gon' lie, I'd definitely eavesdropped a few times. I needed to know what was really up. And after listening in, I realized, that India was right, and I needed to get away from Jahquez. It wasn't safe.

Just like I suspected, Jahquez was the driver and his homie, Winston, was the shooter. Leel didn't know at first, but he would eventually find out. While he didn't approve of it, what could he do? Although he was the star, he was also the younger brother. Besides, anyone that knew Jahquez knew that he did whatever the hell he wanted. He had already taken matters into his own hand. Leel found out just like everyone else did. Early morning on social media. Once he found out why Jahquez had done what he'd done, he understood. Of course, Jahquez would lie to save face. He'd never admit that it all started because he'd ran up in Quan's VIP section, running behind me. And of course, he would remind me to keep quiet about it, despite the numerous people that saw him in there acting a fool.

I was now at the point where I just needed to figure out how to get the hell away from his ass. I was fed up with my son's father. He was a walking target, and I wanted no parts of it. During all the back-and-forth, I'd seen the threats. It was clear that Raul and Loco knew exactly who was responsible. I had no doubt that Italy had told them. It was only right. She wanted justice for her man. I couldn't blame her. Although she hadn't been terribly injured, she'd still been caught in the crossfire. Her heart was still aching from the thought of losing her man. It was only a matter of time before shit hit the fan.

Feeling the urge to pee, I got up from the warm bed I shared with my son and went to the bathroom. I was thankful that my mother still lived in the same apartment that she had for years and that I still had my old room. I was glad that I could come home whenever I wanted. Unfortunately, I knew I couldn't stay long. Jahquez was eventually going to come looking for me. Banging on the door. Cursing, screaming, yelling. The usual shit he did when he knew I had run to my mama's house to get away from him.

After using the bathroom, I washed my hands and went to lay back down. I watched as my phone lit up and vibrated. I had the volume down because I didn't want my notifications waking

Jaden up from his nap. I swiped and scrolled to the messages. A message from Jahquez popped up.

Bitch, you think I'm playing with you? I promise I'm not.

I didn't even blink. He always sent the same dumb ass threats. My phone lit up again. Another message from Jahquez.

Spring Grove Apartments.

This time I did blink. I actually did more than blink. My heart began racing in my chest. I immediately dialed Jahquez's number.

"What?" he asked on the first ring. The stupid ass nigga was playing games like he didn't know I was going to call him after that bullshit message.

"What the fuck does that mean?" I demanded to know.

"Oh, now you got rap."

I looked down at my son and hopped back out of my bed. "What does that mean, Jahquez? Why did you say Spring Grove Apartments? You know India lives in Spring Grove Apartments. What the fuck does that mean?"

"It means that when bitches can't keep their mouth closed, we pop up for the next best thing."

I hung up on him and called India. The phone rang repeatedly and then finally went to voicemail. I dialed her again. Same thing. I knew she wasn't going to answer, but I still had to try. I paced through the house frantically as I waited for the voicemail to kick in on the third try.

"India, this is Kayla. Look, I know you're upset with me and you have every right to be. But I'm choosing. Right here, right now, I'm choosing you. Fuck Jahquez. I need you to call me. Apparently, BGS is not feeling the fact that Italy is giving the details of what she saw that night. But they can't do shit about that. They know she somewhere tucked like she always has been. They know you're not though. Jahquez threatened me by calling out your apartments. He didn't go into details. He just said that they'll pop up for the next best thing. Be careful, India. Please. Call me back."

I hung up the phone and prayed that India let the bullshit go and believed everything that I said on the voicemail. Her safety was at risk.

"Enough is enough Kayla!" my mother fussed at me. "This shit has been going on too long! You won't leave him, so you've got to go." I knew she was fed up if she was asking me to leave.

"Where I'm gon' go?" I sobbed loudly. "There's nowhere else."

"Anywhere is better than with his ass! How long you gon' let that boy beat the hell out of you?" my mother asked. "Look at you!" she choked. Her voice wavering and on the verge of cracking. "Ya eyes black and nearly swole shut! That boy don't love you!"

I couldn't even respond. All I could do was hold my son tightly and cry.

"Beat you like a dog in front of your child! His child."

My mother walked away, shaking her head in disgust and disappointment. She walked over the kitchen counter and leaned against it. She was right. She'd been telling me to leave him for years. When the beatings started. He of course would tell me that she was jealous of me. *Look at her old ass. Alone with no man. You gon' let a lonely motherfucker dictate your relationship?* Like a damn fool, I listened. All that shit he kicked at the time made sense to me. Now look at me.

"Kayla, that boy is going to kill you. This is the worst I've ever seen you."

"I know, Ma," I assured her.

"No, you don't know! His stupid ass is running scared. Knowing somebody looking for his ass because of that shit he did. His back against the wall. Can barely drive his damn car cuz he knows they after him, and if they see it, they gon' shoot it up.

So he takes it out on you. 'You not loyal. You ain't got his back. You abandoned him'," she mocked.

Those were all the things he said. All the things that I told her he said. I told her everything. I wanted her to know what was going on in case something happened to me. A part of me felt that since Jahquez was under pressure, he was taking it out on me. This particular beating was so severe I should have sought medical attention. From the way he was acting, it would only be a matter of time before I wound up dead from his hands.

"Selfish piece of shit," my mother continued to argue.

It had only been a few hours since Jahquez forced himself in my mama's house and beat the fuck out me in front of my son. Like a fool, I answered the door when he knocked. I knew it was him. I should have let him bang. Called the police. But I didn't. Instead, I cracked the door and proceeded to argue with him. Just like he wanted to. The first opportunity he saw, he pushed through, knocking me to the floor. He showed no mercy as he pounded away on me for what felt like eternity. Fists and feet. The entire time, our son screaming at the top of his lungs for him to stop. That was a couple hours ago.

My mother had just gotten home from work and was pissed. Not only because I was sitting up there looking busted and pathetic but also because Jahquez had torn up her shit in the process. I was severely swollen, battered, and bloody. Sitting there looking like a true domestic violence victim. It even hurt to cry because my eyes were bloodshot and bruised.

My mother walked through her apartment and surveyed the damage. There were holes in the wall. Her coffee table was busted from where Jahquez knocked me into it, and her lamps were shattered from where I knocked them over trying to run and escape Jahquez. I deserved to be put out... But I didn't deserve to be beat like that. My son didn't deserve to see that.

"Kayla. You've got to run, sweetheart. It doesn't matter where you go. He is going to kill you. He did some bullshit, and now he's scared. He's a coward. Cowards kill women."

I swallowed hard and nodded in agreement. She was right. I had to leave. The argument between Jahquez and I had been petty. Even after blatantly threatening to harm India, he wanted me to come out and give him a ride. Of course, that wasn't happening. I didn't want to see him, and I was at the point where I didn't want anything to do with him. To keep the peace while I figured thinigs out, I instead told him I couldn't, because it wasn't safe to be riding around with him in the city. He went off. Actually, he went ballistic. Finally losing my patience, I told him I was leaving him and that of course, infuriated him even more. Thirty-minutes later and he was at my mother's door. Fast-forward and now, here I was—beat all the hell up.

"Give me 'til the end of the night. I'll be out," I promised.

"No. You need to leave now," she said.

My lip trembled, and I broke down into a sob. My son was standing in the corner. He came over and wrapped his two little arms around me. "Don't cry, Mommy," he said, his tiny voice cracking like he was about to cry. I knew it was because he saw that I was crying. My energy was transferring to my baby. It was then and there that I knew what I had to do. I had a few dollars saved up in the bank. I had my car. And I had my son. That was all I needed.

I scooped my son up and left out my mother's house with just him. Nothing else. For a few minutes, I just sat in my car and cried. I wanted to go to my house and get a few of my things, but I knew that Jahquez was still there. He had never left and went to his mother's house like he said he would.

Feeling defeated, I dug my phone out my purse. Turning on the interior light of my car and snapped a few photos of my face. Instead of calling or leaving another voicemail, I sent the photos I'd just taken of myself to India. All I had now was my son. All I needed was my son. However, what I *wanted*, was the support of my friend. I prayed that she showed up for me.

❧ 17 ❧

INDIA

I wasn't gon' lie, Kayla had left me so many voicemails and text messages that I wasn't even going to listen or read any of them. I can admit that I was ignoring her, but just like anyone else, I decided to ignore for good reasons. I would still hear them out through their messages, despite having no intention of responding.

When I finally did go through all of Kayla's messages, I was glad I did because she had just dropped some heavy shit. Jahquez was about to call himself coming for me because Italy didn't keep her mouth shut. What did they expect her to do? The bitch ass nigga had shot in her car and tried to kill her. They were lucky she wasn't talking to the police. But... I guess a nigga like Loco was worse than the police. They didn't call his ass Loco for nothing.

I wasn't gon' front like I wasn't scared, because I was. I was a female. I didn't beef with men. Men handled men beef. But if they knew me... they knew it was one thing my mama had instilled in both me and my sister a long time ago, and that was, *don't play 'bout yo' sister*. And I damn sure didn't play when it came to mine. Yeah, I'd done some dumb shit back in the day, like taking off at the party when she'd met Quan. Out of all the things I'd ever did, that was probably the most fucked up. To some, it wouldn't even be considered that bad.

As I grew older and wiser, I realized family was all we had. I was now fiercely protective of my sister, and I knew she was the same about me. Unfortunately, Italy did have a weakness, and it was her nigga. I didn't understand it, but shit... I really wished I could. I prayed that I would one day know what it felt like to love the fuck out of someone who actually loved the fuck out of me back.

Although Jahquez screamed out the name of my apartment complex, truth was, I hadn't even been there in days. I had been staying with Italy like she'd requested. I had something for Jahquez's ass though. Now that I knew where Kayla was at with it mentally, I planned to give it to him raw just like they planned to give it to me. You see... a lot of niggas didn't realize how much power a bitch possessed. But he was gonna learn. I navigated to my contacts and dug Raul's number up. Luckily, I'd taken and stored it one drunken night.

Instead of texting or calling him, I decided to FaceTime him. He picked up after a few rings.

"Wassup, mama?" He grinned in the camera. I was glad that he seemed to be in good spirits. I damn sure wasn't. After beating Charlotte's ass, going back and forth with disrespectful bitches on social media, and dealing with Kayla and Jahquez, I was close to being a sour bitch.

"Hey, you. How you doing?" I asked, smiling back.

"I'm good. What's going on though? You've had my number for damn near a year and never hit a nigga up."

"I'm glad you asked. I got some information for you."

"What kind of information?"

"Come to the crib, and I'll tell you."

"Quan's?" he asked.

"Yep."

"Alright, India. Give me an hour. This shit better be good. Got me driving all the way the fuck out there."

"Oh, it's better than good, baby. Just get here."

I hung up the phone and crawled out the bed of the guest room I was staying in. I had to get myself together and prepare myself for what I was about to do. It wasn't the moral thing to do, but where I was from, it was kill or be killed.

I hung up the phone with Raul and continued clearing out my call log. After doing that, I began going through my text messages. Most messages were from people Italy and I knew. People from school. People from the old neighborhood. All of them sending condolences and or checking on Italy. They all wanted to see how she was holding up. Of course, I had others from Kayla. I wasn't even going to bother going through any of them. She was probably just saying the same shit that she'd said in her voicemails. I planned to call her after talking to Raul.

I went to clear Kayla's messages but before I could swipe delete, I realized I had picture messages from her. I quickly pulled them up. As soon as my eyes landed on the picture of my best friend, I broke down into tears. Jahquez had beat her so bad she was almost unrecognizable. I immediately called her. She answered right away. I knew she was happy that I had contacted her. Neither of us could barely talk as we sobbed into the phone. I couldn't believe he did that shit to her. My heart ached for my friend. She didn't deserve that.

"I'm not going back, India," she finally spoke through her tears. "I got Jaden in the back seat, and I'm not going back. Fuck that apartment and fuck him. I got to get out of Baltimore. My mama won't even let me stay with her. He tore her fuckin house up. I just can't do it anymore," she broke down.

"Where are you now, Kayla?" I asked, my own tears still falling.

"I'm parked at a McDonald's out Gwynn Oak." She sniffled.

"Okay. Well, drive to Columbia. Find a hotel and check in. Don't worry about money. Just use what you got, and I got you when I get to you. We're gonna help you get through this. I just gotta meet up with someone and then I'm coming to you," I promised.

"Okay," she sobbed. She already knew what that meant. If I had her back, then so did Italy. I didn't have a whole lot of money, but because of my connection to Quan, I had more than the average bitch. Besides, my sister had bank, and I knew that she wouldn't have a problem helping Kayla out. Jahquez was a done deal. I was about to make sure of that.

❦ 18 ❦

SHAWN

I landed at Los Angeles International Airport around five in the evening. I usually took a red eye, but I decided to leave later in the day instead so I could spend the previous day in downtown Baltimore. Although it was nice sightseeing in Baltimore, it was far too to slow for me. And of course, the stores were no comparison to the ones in Los Angeles.

After claiming my baggage, I called Nisa for the fifth time. I didn't understand why she wasn't picking up. I had actually talked to her since yesterday morning. She'd texted me last night, but as usual, I figured she was just busy. I was hoping that she could shoot over and pick me up from the airport. She usually didn't go to work until around seven o'clock. Her father's restaurant was open 'til two in the morning, so she usually went in late and got off around three or four in the morning. Since she wasn't answering, I figured I'd seek alternate arrangements for a ride.

I navigated to my app and arranged for an Uber to pick me up. A half hour later, the driver was pulling up to the front of my home, and I was headed inside. I noticed that Nisa's car was parked in the driveway. I found that odd since she wasn't answering the phone. If she was home, she wasn't busy, and since it was late in the day, I figured she wasn't sleep. Nisa didn't require a ton of sleep. She was fit and active and could easily run off four or five hours. Even though she strolled in the house from work around four or five in the morning, she was still up no later than nine. I punched in my alarm information and then proceeded into the house.

"Nisa!" I called out. When she didn't respond, I called her again. After still not receiving a response, I headed to the bedroom.

I was all smiles when I pushed open my bedroom door, expecting to see my girl, especially after not seeing her for a couple days. I hadn't had any in a while, so I figured I'd pipe her down real quick before she went to work. Unfortunately, all my positive thoughts flew from my mine when I saw Nisa's hoe ass laid up with a nigga in my bed. A white nigga at that. To put it plainly, this bitch had a motherfuckin' white boy in my bed. Nisa was fuckin' a white boy. I had to place emphasis on the fact that he was white. I was being cheated on with a scrawny ass white boy.

Since I was a kid, my mother had always told me to trust my gut. *Always trust your gut, Shawn,* was what she would tell me. I never did, and because of that, I always learned the hard way. My mother never liked Nisa, although she'd never flat-out said it. I just knew my mom, and I could tell. Her demeanor. The warmth that naturally radiated from her was gone whenever I flew in with Nisa by my side. I guess my mom could sense that she was a dog ass hoe.

"Bitch, is you fuckin' crazy?" I muttered aloud, although I knew they couldn't hear me because both of them were knocked out and resting peacefully in my shit. I had to stop and just stare at them for a minute. Nisa never slept in. I guess the white boy gave her a reason to do so. Something told me to look glance down at the floor. When I did, I saw baggies of cocaine and a couple rolled-up dollar bills. Her multiday drug binge was why she was tired. The reason why she wasn't answering the phone or responding to texts. A whole year. I couldn't believe I had overlooked that shit.

I suddenly became furious. Nisa's bullshit was settling in. I had wasted a whole fuckin' year on her. I stormed to the bed, brought my fist back, and punched white boy in his shit. Actually, my fist landed on the side of his jaw, but it was enough to wake his ass up.

"What the fuck!" he yelled, eyes wide with terror. His hand flew to his jaw. He scrambled out the bed and fell to the floor.

"No, nigga, what the fuck is you doing in my motherfuckin' house!" I screamed, advancing quickly toward him like I was about to beat that ass for real.

"I swear I didn't know, bro!" he plead, scrambling to his feet and cowering near the wall in fear. I literally towered over him. I wasn't no small nigga. Seeing me all big and enraged probably had him wanting to piss himself.

"She told you this was her shit?" I asked him. He nodded frantically. "Get ya shit and get the fuck out. I ain't even gon' do you dirty like I want to. It ain't ya fault."

Nisa was now up. Her hair flowing loosely around her face. Despite how barefaced and beautiful she looked just waking up, I looked at her disgust. She was trash. She had some ugly ass ways, and that made her ugly to me.

"Shawn, please, calm down, baby," she began pleading. "I didn't know you would be back this soon."

"Bitch, shut the fuck up and get the fuck out," I said calmly. If she knew what was best for her, she would just leave. I wasn't trying to calm myself intentionally. To keep from hurting her.

"Please, Shawn," she cried. "I can explain."

"Ain't shit to explain. Get whatever you can take and get the fuck out. I'm done with you."

For some reason, the bitch still continued to just sit there. Even after I'd told her to get her stank, coke-doing ass out numerous times.

"Bitch, I said, get the fuck out!" I ran to the bed and

snatched her out of it. The next thing I knew, I had Nisa by a fistful of her hair and was dragging her partly naked body through the house.

"Please don't hurt me," she cried, kicking and flailing as tears poured down the sides of her face.

She knew what was about to come next—the steps that led down and out the door of my home. So far, I'd only dragged her on leveled ground. She wasn't trying to get dragged down those steps.

"Shawn, please!" she cried out again. I looked down at her and stopped. Her sobs made me weak. Only for a moment. I looked past all the beauty she possessed and stared into her scheming, snaky, conniving eyes. It was then I remembered that I was the one who had been wronged. I was the one who had just walked into my own fuckin' house and saw my bitch laid up with another man. A house that I owned all on my own. A house that she was really just a visitor. A roommate that didn't pay shit. A house that she barely cooked or cleaned in.

"I'm not gon' hurt you. You not even fuckin' worth it." I released her hair with a thrust, leaving her laying in the floor. I was raised to never hit a woman, but I definitely wanted to beat her. I was so tempted. I could have spit on her.

"This the last time I'm going to tell you. Get all your shit and get the fuck out. Whatever you don't take now, I'll pack up for you and leave it outside. I'm done with you, bitch. You got five minutes to get out, or I'll be calling ya bitch ass daddy's restaurant so I can brief him on his hoe ass, cocaine-sniffing daughter that thought it was cool to disrespect my house."

I didn't need no explanation. Didn't want to hear no excuses. I'd seen all that I needed to, and she was lucky that I wasn't burying her ass. But... I had seen the signs. It was my fault that I chose to ignore them. I walked off and left Nisa in the middle of the floor. I was tired, and I needed to lay down. I headed to my guest room. I'd be sleeping there until I got some new sheets. I made a quick and silent vow. Moving forward, anyone that I had to question had no place in my life.

ॐ

I SAT IN MY STUDIO AND PLAYED AROUND WITH THE KICK AND snare of a beat I was working on for a rapper in Atlanta. I actually had quite a bit of work lined up. Since I wasn't going to be working with Quan anytime soon, I figured I would go ahead and get some beats made and get them out the way. I figured it wouldn't hurt to be early on the delivery. After going at it for a few hours, I decided to take a little break. I didn't really have a lot of time to watch television, so when I did manage to get a little free time, I would hop on social media.

I grabbed my phone and went to my Instagram. As soon as I opened up the app, I saw nothing but gossip and drama down my timeline. I used my finger to swipe up, figuring I'd stop when I came to something interesting. I slowed down when I saw The Shade Room had posted about Quan. *Baltimore rapper still in critical condition after gunshot wound to the neck.*

I scrolled some more.

Baltimore rapper Quan still in ICU after being shot.

I continued to scroll until something else made me stop abruptly.

Rapper's sister-in-law involved in restaurant brawl with the mother of his child.

I quickly pulled the post up and read through it.

Reliable sources say that Baltimore rapper, Quan's sister-in-law, India Cannon, allegedly put the paws on his baby mama, Charlotte, after she posted a disrespectful message aimed at her sister Italy, Quan's long-time girlfriend, and his mother. Apparently, there's a video of twenty-six-year-old India beating and dragging Charlotte through her workplace first thing in the morning. Chileeee, the drama never seems to end when it comes to this whole fiasco with Quan. Death threats and fistfights. We, here at The Shade Room, have a feeling that the drama isn't done yet.

One thing we do know is Rayquan's folks DO NOT play when it comes to him, so watch ya comments. We're still praying for him and hoping for a speedy recovery. We'll keep you posted as we gather more information about this developing story.

I shook my head at the nonsense. Shit like that was the exact reason that I wasn't into all the exposure or becoming a celebrity. Although I was a producer, I didn't need my face to be recognized wherever I went. I could have easily been a part of it, but having my life under a microscope and constantly scrutinized was just something I wanted no parts of. Good thing. I could only imagine what type of story they would have run on me if they knew I was just boo'd up with a cokehead that was fuckin a white boy behind my back. Embarrassing shit. Of course, I would have looked like a jackass because I had no idea.

After reading that story, I couldn't help but wonder how India was doing. I didn't care that she was trending on social media because of that bullshit. It wasn't like she was clout chasing. After meeting her, I'd gone to her Instagram page. It was private, and she barely had a thousand followers. That right there spoke volumes. Her sister had been with Quan for years, and she wasn't capitalizing off his name in any kind of way. I also couldn't help but admire how hard she went for her sister after Charlotte disrespected her. I hadn't seen the disrespectful post, but I could only imagine what it said. I low-key couldn't wait to see the video of India whippin' her ass. I loved a loyal ass, no-nonsense female.

The more I thought about India, the more I wanted to know about her. I wondered if she was single. I figured there would be no better way to find out then to ask myself. I went to my call log and saw that her number was still there. I had actually saved her in my contacts. I thought about shooting her a text; however, I quickly decided against that. It just seemed a little weak texting her out of the blue. I decided that I was just going to call her. I stared down at my phone and asked myself whether that was a good idea or not. Finally building up my nerve, I picked the phone up and pressed her number.

After ringing twice, she picked up, her sweet sultry voice oozing from the other line. It was now or never. I figured I'd go ahead and shoot my shot.

🐾 19 🐾

INDIA

I had been sitting with Kayla for several hours in her hotel room before she finally dozed off with Jaden. It was getting so late that I contemplated staying the night. I looked over at her. She was sleeping as peacefully as she could. Despite how beat up and swollen her face was, it was probably the best rest that she'd gotten in a long time. For a while after I got there, all we did was hug and cry. Then after that, we just talked about everything that was going on. Of course, I still had to be selective with what information I divulged because there was always a possibility that she was still in communication with her baby daddy.

Deep down, I didn't think that was the case. She was adamant that she wasn't going back to him. Kayla and Jahquez argued, but she never once before said that she was leaving. This time, she'd said it, and I believed her. Now, all she had to do was just figure out where she was going. She didn't feel safe in Baltimore anymore, and I didn't blame her.

After meeting with Raul back at the house, I left to meet up with Kayla. Italy wasn't in the best of spirits after a long day, so I didn't want to bother her by asking for any money. I just went in my own account and got a couple grand out for Kayla. It wasn't a lot, but it would at least put her up in a room for a month if she wasn't able to find a house or apartment. I vowed to help her as best as I could for as long as I could.

I initially thought that Kayla was trying to get away for a little while, but the longer I sat and talked to her, the more I realized that she was actually trying to leave and leave for good. I understood it though. Even when Jahquez got what was coming to him, Kayla still wouldn't feel safe with Leel and other dudes from BGS knowing where she laid her head with her son. It was sad that she was scared of Jahquez's people more than she was scared of Quan's. With her being being too uncomfortable to go back to her house, a permanent move was for the best. Shit, I was considering it too. Baltimore was becoming too toxic for me.

After nearly dozing off in the hotel room recliner, I decided to leave. Only when my phone began to ring did I realize just how late it was. I quickly hit the mute button on the side to cease the loud jingle. I didn't want it to wake up Kayla or Jaden. I looked down at the number. I didn't recognize it. *California?* I thought. I didn't know anyone that lived in California. Realizing that it probably was a call pertaining to Quan, I answered.

"Hello?"

"Hello. Is this India?"

"It is."

"Uhh, hi. It's Shawn."

"Shawn the music producer?" I asked, quickly remembering the name.

Although I was going through a lot, Shawn wasn't a face that I would forget. Although I didn't get to truly admire him when I first met him, I couldn't deny that he was indeed handsome. Not the typical hood nigga that I dated, but honestly, I had gotten to the point that I didn't want or need a nigga that would likely go to jail or get gunned down. The more I thought about it, the more hood niggas were no longer my type.

"Yeah, the producer. How are you? Did I, uh, catch you at a bad time?" he asked.

I glanced back over at Kayla and Jaden. They were still sleeping soundly. I figured I might as well go ahead and leave. I headed out, closing the door softly behind me.

"No, you're fine. Although, it is kinda late," I admitted, as I walked down the hall. I passed the elevator and took the steps instead so I wouldn't lose the call. Stepping out into the night air, I asked, "What's this about?"

It was nearly one in the morning, and I wasn't a fan of late-night calls. They usually always meant something was wrong.

"Ahh, shit. I'm sorry. I'm on this California time. I didn't even think."

"No, you're fine. What's up."

"Actually, I was just calling to check up on you and, uh, your family. How are you all holding up?"

"That was nice of you. We're doing fine actually. Thanks for calling and checking. That means a lot."

"How's Quan doing?"

"He's still in ICU. Still in a coma. Nothing has changed at this point."

"Damn, I'm sorry to hear that." He paused for a moment. Like he was unsure of what to say. "Well, I don't want to keep you. You ran across my mind when I saw you all up in the blogs a little while ago."

I forced out a laugh. "Oh, that." I followed it up with a sigh. "Yeah. I hate that I'm being cast in a negative light," I admitted. "I try to be as peaceful as people allow me to be."

Kayla had already briefed me on the fact that I was now trending on The Shade Room. Of course, I wasn't about to make no statement on Quan's page or my page. Not behind no damn Charlotte. There wasn't really anything to address. She came out her mouth reckless, and I checked her. I wasn't about to explain that to no raggedy ass blog. This was real life, and I was from

Baltimore, Maryland. Where people got punched in they shit if they came out their mouth slick.

"Yeah, I feel you. They doin' too much right now anyway. Especially with everything y'all going through."

"Yeah. It's all for views and likes. It's entertaining to them, but this is our real life. We've been living a nightmare the past few days. And his baby mama just clout chasing. Trying to come up off Quan when he down. I'm just glad she ain't call the police."

"Facts. But at least she learned a lesson."

"They only learn when you teach 'em." I laughed.

"If you don't mind, India, can I ask you a couple personal questions?" he asked unexpectedly.

"Personal like what?" I frowned. I was now sitting in my cold car, letting it warm up.

"Questions about you." I now knew what Shawn wanted. It seemed like he was trying to decide whether or not he wanted to shoot his shot. I didn't mind. He was cute, and I didn't have a man. However, for a quick minute, I almost felt inadequate. Like I didn't have enough going for myself for him to be checking for me. There he was, a music producer. About to produce an album for Quan. I didn't feel good enough. It was weird because I stayed up under Quan at his shows just to catch the eyes of a baller. But now, none of that shit even mattered anymore.

"Yeah, sure. Ask what you want," I half-heartedly agreed.

"I just want to know a little about you. Like do you go to school? You got kids? How old are you? Where you work? Are you single?"

"Oh, okay." I let out a sigh. "Well, that's easy, although that's a lot of damn questions." I laughed. "But I'm, uh, twenty-six. No kids. I don't go to school. I graduated from high school, but I felt college wasn't for me, so I didn't go. I don't technically work, although my sister and I have an online wig store. We don't have a storefront or warehouse or anything, but we make quite a bit of money from it. We pretty much just pay for advertising to get people to the store. They make purchases and then it's drop-shipped from the wholesaler."

"Cool. That sounds dope. Smart."

"Yeah. I'm really into hair. I like all the crazy-colored wigs. Blue, green, pink, purple, and shit," I laughed.

Shawn laughed and then paused again. "You didn't answer that last question though."

I couldn't help but smile. I had intentionally left it unanswered. I just wanted to see if he really wanted to know or not. Obviously, he did.

"I am single," I finally answered.

"Good."

"How about you. Can you answer all those questions about yourself?" I asked.

"Yeah, of course. You already know I'm a producer. I make beats. I work with mostly rappers. No kids, even though I'm twenty-eight. I would like some though. I did go to school briefly out in Houston, Texas where I'm from. Didn't graduate though. And I am single. Actively looking. For someone solid anyway. Genuine. I gotta tell you, coming from Texas and then going to Atlanta and then Los Angeles... you meet people who don't care about anyone or anything. It's crazy to keep running into women like that," he admitted.

"Yeah. I can imagine." For a moment, I thought about myself. I wasn't too much different than the women that he spoke of. Although, I did have a heart. Yeah, at one point I wanted the guy with money; however, I did with the intention of loving them.

"Facts. Well, look, I know you have a lot going on, but I did want to reach out to you and let you know that I'd love to kick it with you. You know... once everything goes back to normal for you. Or you feel comfortable enough."

"You mean kick it in Baltimore?" I asked.

"Unless you trying to get flewed out," he joked.

I couldn't help but laugh. Shawn was down to earth and silly. I liked that. With everything going on, I probably needed it too.

"Maybe in the future."

"Cool. Well, look. You got my number. I have yours. I plan to use yours. A lot. And I hope you use mine a lot. You know... anytime you want to talk. Just say hi. Get flewed out... For breakfast, lunch, or dinner." He laughed. Even though he was laughing, I knew he was serious.

"I'll keep that in mind, Shawn."

"Bet. Well, listen. You get some rest. I'll hit you tomorrow if that's cool with you."

"It is. I'll talk to you then."

I hung up the phone and just stopped and stared out my window at nothing in particular. The call from Shawn had me feeling like I was on some high school shit. All giddy. Little butterflies and shit. His call was so random, and I was so unprepared for it. I was glad it came. Shawn had me seriously contemplating that flight he kept joking about. Who knows? Maybe I needed the change of scenery.

Finally driving out of the parking lot, I eventually slipped back on the expressway and headed out of Columbia and back to my sister's home in Glenwood.

❧ 20 ❧

ITALY

Laying in my bed, I couldn't help but toss and turn. No matter how much I tried to force the negative thoughts out of my head, I couldn't. Every time I closed my eyes, all I saw was Quan. I missed him so much, and despite everyone urging me to be strong, I was finding it harder and harder to do so. Every day that passed stole more and more of the little hope I was hanging to. A nagging voice in my head was constantly telling me that Quan wasn't going to make it. No matter how hard I tried to think positive thoughts. I was exhausted and drained. I could barely eat, and I could barely sleep. Every time I tried to close my eyes and get some rest, all I could hear was him yell before being gunned down. Him pushing my head down so I wouldn't be shot.

It had been days. The doctor had been frank when he came out of surgery. *He probably won't wake up.* They said it, and although I didn't accept it at the time, I was beginning to accept that fate more and more as each day passed. Despite my dwindling faith, I still dropped to my knees on the side of my bed and said a quick prayer to God, asking Him to cover Rayquan. That was all that was left to do. Finally calling it a night, I dozed off only to be awaken in the morning by the sound of my mother's screams.

⚜

"ITALY!" MY MOTHER'S SCREAMS RANG OUT THROUGH THE home. My eyes shot open. I heard the sound of her running through hall toward my room. "Italy!" she screamed again.

I sat up. My heart pounding in my chest. Everything seemed like it was moving in slow motion. My door flew in, and my mother ran into the room. I immediately prepared myself for bad news.

"Italy, get up! He's woke!" she screamed.

I hollered at the top of my lungs. Tears welled up in my eyes and began to run like fucking faucet. "You're lying? Please," I begged. I didn't know if she was playing a cruel joke or whether or not I was dreaming. I wiped away the tears on my face and smacked my own cheeks. I wasn't dreaming. "Mommy, please tell me you're telling the truth."

She choked back tears, and her voice broke. "Quan woke up this morning. Get up and let's go!" she screamed.

I kicked off my covers and screamed again. I grabbed whatever I could find. I threw a little water on my face, did a quick brush of my teeth, and flew down the steps. *My man is woke!* I was so happy I didn't know what to do or say. I was just thankful. My prayers had worked. My man was a fighter. He had survived a gunshot to the neck, and he was awake. I had to see him.

I raced around for the keys to Quan's car. "Ma! Where are the keys!" I screamed, my heart still racing. I was anxious, excited, and racing with adrenaline.

With one shoe on and one off, my mother appeared from around out the hallway. "We're not driving. I called an Uber. That's safer. You're too emotional to drive right now."

I agreed. I was filled with an abundance of emotion. A few

minutes later, our Uber appeared, and we were off. I didn't even bother to wake up India. It was barely six in the morning. I would give her the good news later.

21

INDIA

I wave of relief washed over me when I woke up and finally read my text messages. For the first time in a long time, I was eager to go on social media and read what they were posting. Quan had finally woken up. He'd actually opened his eyes. It was like being in a nightmare that finally ended. I was so relieved.

My sister and mother were already at the hospital. They'd already been up there several hours before I even woke up. I didn't get the news from a phone call. She had left me a voice message crying and hollering that Quan was going to be okay. As always, my emotions got the best of me and then came the tears. This time, I didn't try and fight them back. Nah, this time I let them fall freely. They were tears of joy, and I welcomed them.

I continued to scroll through my phone, checking to see if I had messages from anyone special. Although I had just had my first nonbusiness conversation with Shawn the night before, I was hoping I had a message from him. Anxious almost. Luckily, I did have one. A little paragraph that began with praying hands. I read over it.

I heard the good news. Prayers work. Let Quan know that I'm asking for him way out from the sunshine state. Let me know when you're free, and we gon' celebrate. Definitely a good reason to.

I closed my phone up and got dressed, all the while grinning from ear to ear. I liked Shawn. I actually liked Shawn a lot. It didn't take long. He just made it so easy. He was eager but not quite thirsty. He made it very clear he was interested. Made it clear that he wanted to see me and spend time with me. They way my luck was starting to turn, I was definitely going to take him up on his offer. Maybe even get flewed out. I wasn't giving up no goodies right away, but something was telling me that he was going to be a keeper. After taking a quick shower and pulling my hair back into a ponytail, I finished checking my text messages. I also sent Shawn a response to the message he sent earlier.

Prayers definitely do work. And I will let him know that you've been asking about him. I know he'll appreciate the love. And you're right. Him being given a second chance is definitely a reason to celebrate. Not quite ready to get flewed out, but if you aren't busy, maybe you can fly back. I'd love to hang out with you.

I pushed send on the text message and stuffed my phone into my purse. If he was serious about wanting to spend time with me and getting to know me, he'd take the trip back to Baltimore. I had plenty of time to check out Los Angeles; however, I didn't want to give the wrong impression. Men didn't have problems pursuing what they wanted, and men also made time for what they wanted. I headed out the house, but before I could get into my car, I heard my phone ding. I had a feeling it was Shawn. I dug my phone out my bag and was right. I pulled his name up and read the text.

Booking a flight for later today or early tomorrow. I'll let you know when it lands. Can't wait to see you again.

I guess I was right. Shawn obviously knew what he wanted. With a big grin, I started my car up and headed to the hospital. I couldn't wait to tell Italy my good news after acknowledging hers.

❧ 22 ❧

KAYLA

I was two hours in on a five-hour trip to Raleigh from Baltimore when I decided to stop and get some gas. My son was sleep in the back seat, so the music was off, and the car was quiet. After all the drama he'd endured, I wanted him to rest peacefully anytime he decided to close his little eyes.

I parked at the pump and slid my card. After unhooking the hose and shoving it into my gas tank, I hopped back in the car. I noticed my phone vibrating from my seat. I had been doing my best to stay off social media. I didn't need to hear any negative shit, so I'd been playing on my phone way less. I glanced at the name of the caller. It was my mom. She'd been calling me for the last hour or so. I honestly was still mad at her. I knew that I shouldn't be, but I couldn't help it. She put me out of her house in the winter with my four-year-old son. I knew it was for the best, but it still seemed foul. I guess she was forcing me to get my shit together. Sighing, I reached over and grabbed it.

"Hello?" I glanced at the pump. It was at $14.59. My Hyundai took around thirty dollars, so I had another minute before I had to get back out in the cold and put the pump back.

"Kayla." My mother's voice was solemn. I knew something was up. I knew her.

"What's wrong?"

"Are you sitting down?" she asked. "Where are you?"

"Tell me what's going on first and then I may be able to tell you where I'm at."

"Honey... They found Jahquez this morning."

I froze for a moment. And although I expected tears, none fell. I loved Jahquez, but I guess I wasn't in love with him anymore. I honestly think the last beating he gave me took everything out of me that I had for him. I just couldn't cry. If anything, I felt bad for my son. I knew it was going to happen. I just didn't know it was going to happen this soon.

"He's dead?" I asked for confirmation.

"Yes he is."

"How? Where?" For some reason, I had to know.

"In the driver's seat of his car. He was shot in the head."

I swallowed the hard lump that had formed in my throat. I went to speak, but my mother beat me to it.

"He was leaving your apartment. They found him in the parking lot."

A silence fell over the line.

"I'm glad you left, baby. And I know it sounds harsh, but I'm glad that you're free. I'm glad you're safe. I love you, sweetheart. Let me know when you get to your destination safely."

A tear slipped out of each eye, but they weren't for Jahquez. Damn, I was tired of crying. I was relieved, and I was crying because of the words that my mother had just said. We didn't always have the best relationship, but she loved me, and that was all that mattered.

"Okay, Ma. I love you too."

I hung up the phone and got out to hang up the pump so I could get back on the road. I had a full tank of gas and a heart full of hope. I was about to get that fresh start my son and I so desperately needed.

❦ 23 ❦

QUAN

I was told that I was lucky to be alive. Told that I had been shot in the neck, had ten staples, and a brand-new, nasty-looking six-inch scar near my throat. To say I was lucky was an understatement. I was blessed beyond comprehension. I was in lot of pain, despite being on God knows how much medicine. It had to be lot because I was groggy and higher than a mother-fucker. They said I'd been unconscious for days and that I would probably need to remain in the hospital for a few more weeks. I honestly didn't care about any of that. I just wanted to see my family. I wanted to see Italy.

When I first woke up, I had been calling for her. Well, I couldn't really call for her. I barely could talk. It hurt just to move my neck. When I did try to speak, it came out hoarse, low, and barely audibly. I knew I had a long way to go for recovery. Being on a bunch of pain meds had me in and out. I'd try to fight sleep, but it was hard. I'd get an overwhelming feeling to doze off and then just be out. The first time I woke up, I didn't see anyone but doctors. They were running around all excited, running tests and shit. I guess they had counted a nigga out. Nah, I was built Ford tough. Rayquan Jones was a real nigga.

The second time I woke up from dozing off, my mama was in

front of me. My queen damn near had me in tears. I knew I scared the hell out of her. Seeing her sobbing over a nigga. Kissing all over my face with that bright ass red lipstick she liked to wear. She was happy, and I was more pissed than anything. Pissed that she was even hurting. Any nigga that had my mama shedding tears was a dead nigga. I put that on everything. I knew my niggas Raul and Loco would eventually come through, and I knew that once I was well enough to talk and give them some information that they would handle things for me.

As I dozed in and out, felt my mom stroking my hair. Then I felt her twisting it back out my face. I felt her touch the entire time. I knew she had pulled up a chair or something. She wasn't leaving a nigga's side. But I expected that from her. Coming out of my second nap, I woke to see another crying beauty over top of me. This time it was Italy. She was worse than Ma Dukes. She was directly in a nigga's face. Crying, dropping tears on me. Kissing me on my chapped ass lips. I could feel the love. I fought back tears. They were why I hustled the way I did. I went hard for those that went hard for me. Looking into Italy's face, I knew it had probably been the roughest time she'd ever endured. Her eyes were red. She had little bags under her eyes, and the weave that she had in her head look dry and stiff. She was definitely stressed out. It broke my heart not only to see that she was stressed but that she was also injured.

Although I was thankful that she hadn't been hit by a bullet. I was pissed that she had been hurt at all. She constantly stressed about safety and having security. Only for me to carry her out to the city and have her nearly killed. That shit weighed heavily on my conscience. My baby had a broken arm and was scratched and cut all up. It was flat-out unacceptable, and I wasn't going to let that shit come close to ever happening again.

It only took a few hours before I had family members in and out. Balloons, teddy bears, and cards. I could only have two people in my room at a time, but my mom and Italy refused to budge. They, instead, disregarded the rule and allowed a revolving third person in. India, Ms. Cynthia, my aunt Evelyn, Uncle James. A few cousins. Of course, I was dying to see my daughter, but I already knew Charlotte had probably showed her ass something fierce while I was unconscious. I couldn't talk much, but my mama ran down everything. I wasn't going to stress it too heavy since there wasn't much I could do about it while confined to a hospital bed; however, I definitely planned to fight for some stronger rights in the future.

Time flew by, and before long it was noon. I hadn't seen Raul or Loco yet. Italy told me she had texted the both of them and let them know that I was conscious and doing better. A few minutes later, I heard her phone ding.

"Rayquan, Loco just hit me. He and Raul will be by later to check you out."

I blinked and nodded. I wasn't trying to keep doing too much talking. It hurt way too much.

"Quan," Italy called to me.

I turned my head in her direction and met her gaze.

"Jahquez was found shot in the head this morning."

Nobody noticed the look of satisfaction she shot in my direction. But I saw it. I closed my eyes a few seconds and then held a steady gaze with her for a minute. That was all I needed to hear. I knew Jahquez wasn't the shooter; however, he called the shot. I had faith that my niggas would eventually take down the shooter, but Jahquez was more than enough for now. My mother's tears would never be in vain. For the tears she dropped, a body would fall with it.

❧ 24 ❧

ITALY

For the first time in nearly a week, I felt like I could close my eyes and actually get some rest. Real rest. The last four days had been crazy, nonstop drama, and I was glad that it was all over. I was exhausted, and despite needing lots of sleep, I really wanted to be by Quan's side in the hospital. I had tried to stay the night, but hospital staff forced us to leave once visiting hours were over. He was still in ICU and being closely monitored. Ms. Jackie had gone home, and my mother was laying in her room knocked out snoring.

I'd just taken a shower and crawled in my bed. Before I closed my eyes, I was going to write an official statement from Quan's account.

Rayquan and his family want to issue a personal thank you for everyone that prayed for him and reached out to check on him and his loved ones during this difficult time. He is still in ICU, but he is now awake and expected to make a full recovery. Although it will take some time, he would like to assure his fans that he will be back with new music when he is at 100%. He asks that you respect his privacy and his family while he focuses on recovering.

I read over it several times and then hit post. I had officially relieved India of her spokesperson duties. Don't get me wrong, she'd done an excellent job. I was so proud of and thankful for my sister. I wouldn't have made it through the entire ordeal without her. She really stood up and held it down for me and my man. She was as loyal as they came. I was forever grateful to her. I hated that everything went down the way it did with Jahquez. Especially because it affected Kayla. I knew that if it affected Kayla, then it would also affect India. She was going to be there for a friend. India was just that type of person. She didn't know how to be any other way.

Despite all the drama and fighting she'd gone through for me, India still found time to get dolled up for a date. Apparently, she and Quan's producer had made friends. I was happy for my sister, and I hoped that it went well. I couldn't help but smile seeing her before she left out. Since she'd left all her things at her apartment, she dug through my closet to find something to where. She was all excited. It reminded me of when I had first met Quan.

I lay back and shut my eyes. I was going to call my sister when I got up in the morning and then head on over to see Quan. I was glad I could finally rest. Lord knows I needed it.

25

INDIA

I had gone all out when I scoured through my sister's closet and finally settled on a black lace bustier dress by Dolce and Gabbana. Italy was a tad bit smaller than me, so the dress hugged my chocolate frame just a little tight. Nevertheless, I looked good as fuck stepping out of the Uber that I'd taken to meet Shawn at the restaurant he'd chosen.

Shawn had texted me that he was booking a flight, but I honestly didn't think that he would fly out as fast as he did. I was kind of impressed by it. I loved that he stopped what he was doing and made me a priority, especially for something that I considered important. Quan pulling through was a miracle to us. Although I had never spoke it, I had definitely thought it. The thought of him not making it had run through my mind numerous times. Of course, I had to be strong for Italy, so I suppressed those thoughts and displayed a positive outlook, even when I was preparing myself for the worst. I was just glad it was all over. I had been trying to be there for everybody. Everybody all at once. Italy and Kayla. I was glad that someone had showed up for me. I'd only known Shawn a few days, and I felt like he knew exactly what I needed. Like he was right on time.

My drama, unfortunately, wasn't done yet. Kayla had made it

to Raleigh, and I was going to fly out and help her get settled in. She just needed a friend, and I felt that I owed her one. Especially because I was the one that gave her address to Raul so they could find Jahquez and put a bullet in his head. I didn't wish death on anyone, but Jahquez was no longer fit for this earth. He had to go.

Kayla seemed to be handling it fairly well. That was the only reason I hadn't rushed to her side just yet. However, I knew that grief often came in stages. She could be fine today and feel completely different tomorrow. I had already booked my flight for tomorrow evening. My plan was to enjoy my night, sleep in, and then catch a late flight to Raleigh.

I shook thoughts of everyone else and their problems as I walked into the upscale and dimly lit restaurant. I noticed a few of the men in the room couldn't help but gaze at me as I walked by. I knew I looked good. I sashayed up to the hostess stand and was greeted by a middle-aged lady.

"Are you looking for your party?" she asked.

"Yes I am. It's a table for two. I'm India, and his name is Shawn."

"Oh! Follow me," she said before leading the way. After a quick stroll through the restaurant, I found Shawn sitting in the back. He watched in satisfaction as I approached the table.

"There you are. Your waiter will be right with you," she said before walking off.

"Damn, you look good," he admitted. He stood up for me, gave me a hug, then pulled out my chair. "Glad to see you," he said. He took a seat across from me and just stared at me for a few seconds. "You really are gorgeous. I didn't expect this," he said with a chuckle. "I mean... the first and last time I saw you, you had on sweats and a fitted cap."

"I know how to switch it up." I laughed. I couldn't lie, he was gorgeous too. This time I was able to truly appreciate was a delicious, chocolatey sight he was. God was good all the time.

For the next few hours, he and I talked about our lives.

There wasn't much to him. He'd just gotten out of an ugly relationship with someone who wasn't genuine. Someone who had cheated on him. Meanwhile, I'd never truly had a real deep relationship. Neither he nor I had ever given our full selves in full capacity to anyone.

"Boy, listen…" I laughed. "I would have killed that hoe," I admitted.

"You don't know how bad I wanted to. It wasn't the cheating. It was the disrespect. I didn't love her, so luckily, I wasn't all in my feelings, but it was the disrespect for me."

"Facts."

I was glad that he was able to joke about something that had just happened and was still so fresh. That told me that he was ready to move on and that he truly didn't love her. He had blocked her and planned to have his locks changed just in case. I was glad to hear that because there was about to be a new chick in town. And once I decided to declare Shawn as mine, I wasn't about to play with no hoe.

Shawn wanted a loyal chick. Someone who was genuine and real. Someone like me. I didn't know how to be fake, and a chick like me was as loyal as they came. Yeah, I needed a little work, but I didn't mind putting it in for the right person.

26

SHAWN

"Whatchu lookin' at, punk?" India groaned, turning over on her side to escape my gaze. I glanced at the time on the clock and smiled. It was twelve in the afternoon, and my sleeping beauty was just getting up. I had finally found someone who enjoyed sleeping in just as much as I did. I couldn't lie, I was staring at her. I always did.

I leaned over and kissed the side of her face, her hair flowing at all angles across her pillow. She smiled, her eyes still shut tight.

"Leave me 'lone. I'm still sleep," she moaned.

"Damn, babe. A nigga hungry tho."

India couldn't help but smile before slowly crawling out of bed. "You're always hungry."

She got up wearing my long white T-shirt and stretched her arms out to the ceiling. She was right. I was always hungry, and she was always cooking. India and I had only been together three months, and sometimes I found it hard imagining life without her. Like... where the fuck had she been all these damn years. Sassy, silly, funny, and extremely ghetto most of the time, Italy was like a breath of fresh air that I so desperately needed. Genuine, thoughtful, loyal. It was like I had been dealt a fucked-up hand and then, all of a sudden, a winning one. There was no going back. I had to have her with me.

Although she admitted that coming to Los Angeles to live with me was a big move, I was slowly convincing her. When she wasn't with me in LA, I was flying back and forth to Baltimore to see her. Luckily, I had the the money for it, and I could pretty much work wherever I could get my equipment to. It was probably safe to say that I loved her, although I hadn't told her yet. I guess I was low-key kind of scared. Scared that something would change within her. Although she'd been every inch of what she said she was. And that was funny because she never really made any promises. Never said that she was this or she was that. She basically told me that what I saw was what I'd get. That she was loving and loyal until I tried her or give her a reason not to be. I fucked with her heavy. I had no doubt that we would be together for years to come. I knew she cared about me, just as much as I cared about her.

"What do you want to eat?" she asked. She had walked off into the bathroom to get herself together and had reappeared at the door.

"Something light. Eggs, bacon, and toast."

"Alright, cool." She turned to walk off and then stopped. Turning around she asked, "Are you still coming with me back to Baltimore? I booked your flight, but I know you were saying that you had to reschedule a few things."

"Yeah. I told you I would. I know how important it is."

She smiled and then headed to the kitchen to whip me up something to eat. "Flight leaves at five."

India was eager to get back to Baltimore because Quan was having a party for Italy. It was basically an appreciation party as he put it. For her nursing him back to health and staying glued to his side like the gem she was. I'd heard the term, "queens come out the hood too". People assumed they were rare, but they were actually plentiful. Folks were just too busy searching for their gems in the wrong places. Italy and India were true gems. Feisty and ghetto at times but loyal as fuck. And that there was priceless.

❧ 27 ❧

ITALY

Since being released from the hospital four weeks ago, Quan had been resting, relaxing, and getting his strength up. I enjoyed it since, for the last couple of years while he was moving up in his rap career, he hadn't been home as much. Tonight was our first night having a gathering or get-together. At first, Quan wanted to put together a big, fancy appreciation party for everyone that had been there for him when he took that life-changing shot to the neck. He also wanted to do something nice for everyone who was there for me while I struggled to keep it together mentally. Although it was all great, I didn't want a big shindig at a restaurant. I was happy with just friends and family in our home. I damn sure wasn't going into the city to do anything. I'd had enough of the city.

To make everything work, my mother and I cleared a room out, and Quan hired a party planner that put us something together right in our home. It was elegant and beautifully deco-rated just the way we had pictured. We had lamb, salad, mashed potatoes, and several kinds of desserts. Alcohol, wine, and of course, juice for Kir-Kir, who was finally allowed back into our home after her mother got beat on by my sister. That was a whole 'nother story of course. Let's just say, no charges were filed after we slid her a few bucks and made her sign some documents stating she wouldn't sue or press charges. In the meantime, Quan was working quietly with his lawyer behind the scenes to make sure that he had partial custody of his daughter so she could no longer be used as leverage.

We were all seated at a big, long table covered in white linen and decorated with fancy silverware, dishes, and flowers. Quan, his family, my sister, and her new boyfriend Shawn had even flown in. India was basically back and forth between Baltimore and Los Angeles. It was crazy how so much had changed in three months.

Quan was going to be back performing in another couple of months. Although the beef with Leel would probably never be over, it had settled. Raul and Loco were still around, although not as much. Quan still rocked with them to the fullest. He just decided that they would be more valuable in different roles in his life. He was hiring real security and making safety a priority. Lost in my thoughts, I heard Quan finally yell out to get everyone's attention.

"If I can get everyone's attention," he called, faking a little accent to get a few laughs out of his mama and auntie. "So I basically called everyone here to just thank y'all. Let everyone know I appreciate them. Auntie, Unc." He turned and smiled at his Uncle James and Aunt Evelyn. He had a bunch of others that he was thankful for, but we couldn't have everyone knowing where we lived of course.

"Mama... Cynthia." He looked from his mother to my mother. "Y'all know I love you. Appreciate you both." He looked at everyone at the table, making eye contact to acknowledge all that were there. "You all were there for me in your own way. In some capacity. India... I owe you so much, and I thank you from the bottom of my heart."

My sister smiled from across the table. Shawn gazed at her lovingly and proudly.

"I heard you came all the way through. For your sister. For

me. Acting as my spokesperson. Checking my baby mama for getting out of line." He paused and everyone at the table laughed. They'd definitely heard about it. "And Shawn, I appreciate you too, bro. Nigga went from being my producer to future brother-in-law. *Boyyyy*... Ya priorities."

Everyone laughed again.

"Na. I see you recognized a real broad as soon as you met her and snatched her up quickly. Took another beauty off the market. Fine just like her sister." He looked to me and smiled. Then he looked back at Shawn. "'Treat her right. Don't let no trashy ass side broad steal her light. Put a ring on her finger, make her the star of your life'," he recited lines from a past song he'd done. Shawn nodded and shot Quan a look that verified he planned to honor those words.

"I wrote those lyrics years ago when I met Italy." He turned to me and everyone stopped talking. "I appreciate you most."

He paused again, and I could see his jaws tighten. I knew he was fighting back tears. My baby was sensitive on the low. Staring into his face, I gave him my undivided attention while he continued his speech.

"I love you, baby, and you already know... I'm in this for life. My mama gave her blessing. Your mama gave her blessing. If anything ever happens to a nigga again, you'll be the one calling the shots. You'll be the one making the decisions."

Tears slipped down my face as I looked to his mom, and she nodded in approval. These motherfuckers had got me again. It wasn't just an appreciation party. It was a proposal. A surprise engagement party. Rayquan dug in his pocket and pulled out a box.

"Will you marry a nigga?"

I began sobbing but stopped to briefly look at him and roll my eyes. "Ask right, Rayquan," I demanded, causing everyone to laugh again.

With a giant smile on his face, he asked me again. "Will you marry me, Italy?"

I shook my head vigorously. "Yessss. I will."

Quan opened that black velvet box and that big mother-fucker sparkled arrogantly in my face. He dug it out and slipped it on my finger. I held it up in the air so everyone could see.

"I'm about to be a wife, y'all!" I beamed proudly. Everyone began clapping. Even Kira was clapping her little hands together from her seat. My mother, Ms. Jackie, and India were all crying. They knew damn well I deserved that ring and all the karats that it held.

"I'm not done yet, y'all!" Quan called out. "I got one more thing."

He turned his attention to my sister. "So everyone told me how awesome you did speaking on my behalf when I was down. All professional and shit. Your sister suggested it, and yo' man approved it. So I have a job offer for you. My label says I need to have a publicist. I'll never trust a random person to speak for me. Only the family will do since I need someone genuine and loyal with my best interests at the forefront. And someone who doesn't play and can handle things like a G. You're the most qual-ified. Will you be my publicist and social media manager? We'll draw up the contract, but the label will pay you directly out of their budget set for me."

"You already know," India replied while quickly swiping away her tears.

"Good! Now let's eat," Quan said with a giant smile.

While everyone began digging in and enjoying all the food the caterer had brought and prepared, I sat quietly and admired my ring and family. It was a beautiful sight. We were all happy and well on our way to being healthy. I was about to be a wife, and India had a whole man and was about to embark on a career as a publicist. Anyone that knew me would have never imagined this life for me. I was no sack chaser or scheming chick. I was just a broad from West Baltimore that was loyal and real. Sure, motherfuckers could say that I was just a paid nigga's girl, but it was more to it than that. I believed loyalty was rewarded just like hard work. It paid off me, and it had damn sure paid off for India because, truth be told, she was the most loyal *and* the realest of them all.

❧ 28 ❧

KAYLA

I'd been out of Baltimore for nearly three months, and honestly, I wouldn't go back if someone paid me. Of course, I missed my mother, but I was working on trying to get her to come out and visit.

Jaden and I had settled into Raleigh very nicely. When we first arrived to the beautiful little tree-lined city, I knew that we were in a good place. India came within a day or two and had stayed a week to help us get adjusted. She had been priceless during my transition, and I was thankful that she was even still my friend after my slain ex tried to kill Italy and Quan.

Losing Jahquez was, at times, confusing in my mind. Sometimes I had trouble processing and digesting it. I'd been with him for years, so of course I loved him. There were times where it hurt my heart that he was gone and that my son had no father. Other times I knew it was for the best because of the way he had treated me during our final days together. Despite all that, my son and I were doing just fine. I wasn't ready to date yet, but I was working a good job at one of the hospitals downtown, and Jaden was in a decent school. Raleigh was a far cry from Baltimore.

Life had changed so much. Just six months ago, I was

partying and hanging out with India. Now she was ready to move to LA and eventually build a family with Shawn. He was good for her. A good man. I knew I would eventually find one. I wouldn't rush it. That was probably where I went wrong with Jahquez. It was crazy how the type of man I loved and allowed in my life had such an impact on my existence. The wrong man had the ability to tear a woman down and tear her apart; while the right man had the ability to lift her up and help her glow and thrive.

My advice to all the women out there... be careful and choose wisely. Yo' nigga can distract and destroy or build and complete. On every thug I love.

THE END

ON EVERY THUG I LOVE

North Carolina Edition

KRYSTAL ARMSTEAD

MERCI

"**B**itch, I'm going to need some industrial-strength dick after this bullshit," I huffed, plopping down on a plush stool beside my homegirl, Neeta. It was 9:45 at fuckin' night, and we had been at my bestie, Paris's dress fitting since seven fuckin' fifteen that morning. Paris was getting married in a month, and that bitch was the bride from the deepest part of hell. Do you hear me?

"Look, I said I wanted eggshell, not white!" Paris fussed at the store manager.

"Fa real. Lawd knows that hoe is anything but pure!" Neeta's drunk ass whispered but loud enough for everyone to hear.

Paris rolled her eyes from the nervous store manager over to Neeta. "About as pure as your mama, bitch. Which corner is she working again tonight?"

Before Neeta could stand from the stool, I grabbed her arm. "Okay, ladies, chill. Paris, we've been here all night. I was supposed to finish working that Wilson case tonight, remember? You got us all out here, trying on these ugly ass bridesmaids' dresses that you know none of us are going to wear. Spending all your man's bread on some shit we're going to alter ourselves soon as the shit comes in. This shit should've been done weeks ago. I told you to hire a wedding planner. I'm a detective. I don't know shit about wine or cake tasting. Your ass had all this shit in one day. We are tired, boss."

All ten of our friends nodded and sighed in agreement, all sitting around in our pinned-up lavender dresses. We'd all grown up together in the same small town of Goldsboro, North Carolina. We graduated pre-K, kindergarten, middle school, high school, and college together. Even were part of the same sorority. We were all pretty successful. Among us were lawyers, teachers, therapists, police officers, shit, even strippers who turned into strip club owners. Paris, Neeta, and I were foster sisters for a few years before we were split up, but luckily, we still lived near one another. There was never a dull moment between us. We got along for the most part, had a love-hate thing going on as anyone could see by the way Neeta and Paris went at it.

"Alright." Paris let out a long, exhausted breath. "See y'all next week when the dresses come back in." She watched everyone quickly undress, then scatter to grab their shit and get the fuck up out of there. "Wedding rehearsal is every Friday for the next three weeks, ladies! Make sure you leave my champagne glasses here. I know how you hoes be stealing!"

Neeta and I laughed as we got out of our dresses. I'd been on my feet for days, no rest anywhere in sight. I'd been working a missing child case for weeks. A neighborhood child had been kidnapped for ransom. Gang activity in the county was at an all-time high as gangs went to war over territories and drug distribution. Paris's club was the center of drug activity. She thought I didn't know the shit going down in her spot, but I did. One of her dancers was the one whose child was missing. Her boyfriend owed some pretty heavy drug distributors money. It wasn't easy being a cop in the midst of a drug war between people who I grew up with. My job in the community was to not to only keep the peace but keep my friends out of jail.

We waited until everyone was gone before we started talking amongst ourselves.

"Any word on Tasha's daughter?" Neeta asked me as soon as the last bridesmaid left the room.

"Shit, I was about to ask y'all," I huffed.

"They're not going to give her back until her boyfriend comes up with that money. Nobody has seen her nigga in days." Paris sipped from her champagne glass. "Long as those niggas don't come in the club shooting up my shit, I'm good. I put everything I have into Swollen. Not about to let this turf war fuck up what I have going on." Paris kicked off her heels. "We working out in the morning or nah? I gotta make sure my ass is snatched for this wedding. I'm eight weeks post op, and my body is just getting its shape. I gotta keep this shit up. My man didn't spend ten stacks on this body for nothing."

Neeta and I both rolled our eyes as if we didn't hear enough of how much money her fiancé had.

Neeta looked at her watch. "Well, I need to get going, y'all. I still have papers to grade. Sick of these fuckin' kids. I'm more of a babysitter than a got damn teacher. Shit ain't been the same since this pandemic. All it did was let us know how much parents really don't help their kids with their work. Then this nigga Lorenz—"

"Lorenz and them robbed a bank!" Paris and I laughed in our Cleo from *Set It Off* voice. Every time she brought him up, we recited that line from our favorite movie. We swore up and down we would've done that bank robbery shit right if it were us.

Neeta huffed. "This nigga Lorenz keeps blowing my shit up, talking about why I haven't been callin' him. Cuz, nigga, ya wife is my boss, dafuq? I'm sick of niggas. I'm about to start being gay on the weekends and holidays. Fuck this. If y'all trying to work out in the morning, let me know." Neeta got up from the stool, slipping out of her dress.

"Alright, girl." Paris faked a smile. As soon as Neeta was dressed and out of the dressing room, Paris talked her shit. "Merci, you're the only reason this bitch is even in my wedding. If she eats one more Oreo, she's not going to fit in her dress!"

303

I shook my head. "Neeta is your girl."

"Neeta is *your* girl." Paris rolled her eyes. "She can't afford this dress, let alone coming to Vegas for my bachelorette party."

"Neither you nor I are hurting lending that girl money. You try raising three kids on a teacher salary," I reminded her.

"Teacher's *assistant*," Paris corrected me. "She needs to be asking all three of their daddies for some money. She talks all that shit about her students' parents when she's just like them. Living in public housing, living off the government. If she wasn't on the verge of auditioning for *My 600-lb Life*, I'd let her swing around the pole a few times for some extra money." She snickered.

"The girl is working part time and going to nursing school full time. She's about to graduate and already has a job lined up. You need to work out whatever problems you have with Neeta and stop holding grudges, damn. How many years have we been going through this shit?" I rolled my eyes at her.

We all came from the same house, yet Paris always thought she was better than everyone, myself included. Like I said, my job was to keep the peace. Because of her last foster parents' money, Paris was well connected. Her clients kept me employed, at the same time keeping her club protected. Her club bled purple, the color of The Royals, a dangerous gang who ran the east coast. Same gang I used to run with growing up, the very reason I ended up becoming a cop in the first place.

I undressed from my gown, getting back into my fitted uniform.

"You wear that uniform proudly." Paris scoffed.

"This is the same uniform that keeps you and your nigga out of trouble, ma'am," I reminded her. "When I meet up with you tomorrow morning, at the gym, I'll expect you'll have the bread."

Paris nodded. "Yes, we know the routine. We haven't forgotten you because you haven't forgotten us."

I nodded back. "That's right. Captain has been on my ass about the activity going on at that club. I'm trying to keep y'all out of as much trouble as possible, but I can't hold off the department if you don't keep certain shit from happening at the club."

"We'll have the money for you. Get home safe, Merci." Paris grinned a little.

"You need help cleaning up?" I asked.

"Girl, I'm paying too much for this wedding to lift a finger. The staff here will clean this shit up. Get out of here. I'm good," Paris assured me.

"'CAUSE I GOT YOU SPRUNG OFF IN THE SPRINGTIME. FUCK ALL your free time. You don't need no me time. That's you and me time. We be gettin' so loud. That dick make my soul smile. That dick make me so damn proud..." I sang along with Jhene Aiko that night as I sat in my window, reading over case files. I was going to find Denise Wilson if it killed me.

That little girl was three years old. Gangs don't give a fuck. They would rape and kill a toddler if it meant not getting money owed to them. They could've easily killed Tasha or even her boyfriend Foxx. But instead, they took their child, knowing Tasha would come up with the money if her man didn't. Everyone assumed the sorry ass nigga left her to fend for herself, but I knew Royal better than that.

The doorbell to my three-bedroom house out in the country sounded. I grabbed my Glock 19 and made my way out of my room toward the front door. "Who is it?" I called out.

I heard a man clearing his throat instead of speaking his name, and I already knew it was Hendrix. Hendrix Hughes. There weren't enough words in the English language to define that complicated man. I met him, more like stumbled across him, at the age of thirteen. I witnessed him beating the shit out of his mother's boyfriend. The beating led to the man dying in the hospital. I was called as a witness because a neighbor told the police that I saw the whole thing. Yeah, I saw Hendrix beating the man's head in with a metal baseball bat. I also saw his little sister, Lisa, standing alongside Hendrix as he beat the shit out of the nigga. The nigga who had been beating and sexually abusing Lisa. Lisa told her mother, and she didn't do shit. So she told her big brother, and he did everything her mother should have done. I denied seeing anything. That was the day I knew I'd do anything to protect Hendrix because he would do anything to protect someone he loved.

I exhaled deeply, walking up to my front door. "Don't you have a key?" I started to fuss him out when I saw the blood all over his white T-shirt. I grabbed his arm, pulling him into my house.

"I lost my keys, mama," he told me, eying my ass in my boy shorts before eying the gun in my hands. "Don't shoot." He joked at the wrong time.

"Nigga, what happened? You promised me you wouldn't touch Tasha's boyfriend," I huffed, helping him out of his bloody shirt.

"I ain't touch shit. The bullets from my gun did," Hendrix snarled, watching me eying his chest as I removed his shirt. "Shawty, Foxx stole half a mil from me. What was I supposed to do?"

"Did you hurt Denise?" I watched him shake his head. "Where is she?"

"Safe until Tasha gives us the fuckin' money." Hendrix watched me frown.

"Give her that child back tonight. Tasha shouldn't have to pay for her man's sins," I told Hendrix.

"That's not the way this shit works, and you know it, Merci," Hendrix growled. "Tasha and her nigga snorted my shit and blew through my money. I fronted her nigga, thinking he was good for the money, and the whole time, the nigga was stealing from me. You don't see how high that bitch is when she's on stage? That was *my* shit she got high off of. She's lucky we didn't hand that little girl over to foster care!"

I shook my head. "She's no better off there than with her mother. I'm witness to that. I got taken from my mother and her boyfriend, only to be put with a foster mother with a husband who was ten times worse. If you want half a mil, I'll at least have a hundred fifty thousand for you. I'll give you the money as long as she takes her ass to rehab. I'll make sure of that."

"Why do you give a fuck about Tasha, huh?" Hendrix asked.

"I give a fuck about Denise. That little girl doesn't deserve to be involved. You already killed the girl's father. That shit's honestly payment enough. You made your point to the community—don't fuck with your product or your money. Give her to me tonight. Let me know where to meet whoever has her. I'll be the hero, and you won't go to fuckin' jail." I pushed him in his chest.

Hendrix frowned, temples twitching. He was pissed, but he agreed hesitantly.

"Where's the gun?" I asked.

"My nigga took care of it." Hendrix watched the irritated expression form on my face. "Merci, I trust them niggas with my life. Kace got rid of it for me."

I laughed out loud. "Kace? The same muthafucka in the same department that I work for? That nigga will set you up to save himself."

"The same Kace who helps with distributing my drugs so his kids can go to that private school he can't afford on that police salary? The same Kace who I run a dry cleaner chain and casino with to clean all this dirty money we're making? I've known that white muthafucka all my life. We good," Hendrix told me.

I nodded. "Yeah, until you're not." I walked over to my laundry room to grab my Neutrex detergent. I poured a drop on the shirt and rubbed the shirt together vigorously to pretreat the stains in the shirt. Then I tossed the shirt in my front-loading washing machine, pouring more detergent into the slot marked *liquid detergent*, then pressed start. Oxy cleaners not only visibly get rid of blood stains, but they also make traces of blood unrecognizable to the blood-detecting tests that forensics use. I had to take all precautions. There was always a chance that someone would set me up. It was no secret that I helped cover up everyone's mess the same way they helped cover mine.

"I put some money in your account today." Hendrix walked up to me in the laundry room.

I sighed, feeling his breath on my neck. I tried my best to resist that man. He was so fine and tall, his body sculpted perfectly with a soft, peanut buttery complexion and clean shaven down to his trimmed goatee. He was a hustler, a businessman, a gang leader, and my weakness. Not to mention forbidden fruit, but my heart didn't give a fuck.

"I told you I don't want your money," I told him as he wrapped his hands around my waist, quickly turning me around to face him. I couldn't even look him in his face. I kept turning him down for months. I wanted more than a moment. I wanted a future with him. The more I got of him, the more I wanted.

"You gonna keep running from a nigga?" Hendrix asked, gripping my waistband in his hands.

"You gonna keep chasing me, nigga?" I exhaled deeply as he grabbed a hold of my hips, lifting me on top of the washing machine.

"You already know. I was supposed to love on, fuck on, and kiss on you for the rest of my life. What happened?" Hendrix frowned at me.

"*She* happened." I scoffed.

"It was high school. You never once told me that you had any feelings for me. As far as I knew, you didn't fuck with thug niggas. I never would've started fuckin' with shawty if you would've told me back then that you wanted a nigga and you know it," Hendrix tried telling me, but I knew better.

Hendrix's godfather, Snap Avery, was one of the richest men in North Carolina. He was the reason Hendrix had come into so much money and the reason why he ended up in another woman's arms. There was more to that story, but I'd let her tell it.

"We both know why the two of you ended up together, and it sure as hell ain't got shit to do with anything else but money. You fell into that trap, and now you're stuck." I shook my head at him, actually feeling sorry for him.

"I've been taking care of myself all my life. I'm twenty-five years old and one of the richest niggas out this muthafucka! Yeah, thanks to shawty, but I paid a price, too! I kept my distance from you for the sake of her. But even she doesn't have my back like you do. Who gets rid of evidence for me? Who keeps my crew afloat out here by taking out the competition? Who makes sure my niggas never see the inside of a jail cell? Who makes sure I don't do life for murder? You, not her. You've been down for a nigga since we were thirteen. You've always been more than a friend. Fuck everyone else." Hendrix watched me shake my head.

I pushed him off of me. "You can't keep coming here like this. What if I had a nigga up in here?"

Hendrix laughed out loud. "You almost made me call you out of your name. You know better. Don't fuckin' play with me."

Who was I kidding? No relationship I tried to get in ever lasted. I was a cop and that scared most niggas off. The ones who did try to work it out, I pushed away. Every caseload I had got more horrific. I couldn't talk to muthafuckas about my cases. No one wanted to hear, "Hey, today my precinct found a teenage girl who had a baby cut out of her stomach. Let's go have dinner." Hendrix could relate to me because I could relate to him. We knew each other inside and out. We couldn't be together, because he belonged to *her*. And it ate at me up every time I saw his face. Helping him get away with murder and mayhem seemed to be the only way to be a part of his life.

"I don't want someone else's man!" I let him know. "Leave her and be with me."

Hendrix grabbed and kissed me. He slid his hands around my throat, applying just the right amount of pressure to moisten my panties. "And lose everything I worked hard for? Nah. Don't worry about her. Worry about yourself," he growled in my ear as he snatched my panties and shorts from around my waist, still gripping my throat with the other hand. "Let me find another nigga up in this muthafucka. I'll kill the nigga and make you watch."

I panted as I watched the crazy nigga put my panties to his nose to take a long whiff. I guess the scent my pussy left in my panties must've smelled good to him. I could tell by the way he snatched me from on top of the washing machine and turned my body around. I waited with anticipation, hearing him quickly unbutton, then unzip his pants. I hadn't had sex in almost two months. Not because I didn't want it, but because I wanted it from Hendrix, and I knew better. When we had sex two months earlier for the first time. It was at a park on the hood of my police car the night that he told me that he was about to propose to my best friend.

I let out a passionate squeal as he shoved that big old dick through me. Instantly, my fluids slid down my thighs. Something about doing something so wrong always felt so fuckin' right. There was nothing like "we're not even supposed to be fuckin'" sex. We both weren't shit at that moment and could give zero fucks. I held onto my ruby-red washing machine as Hendrix slow stroked my pussy before speeding up. He gave my ass a smack when he was ready for me to throw that ass back on him. As he grabbed a fist full of my hair, I ground my hips against his pelvis. My body shivered as I felt his balls beating against my pussy lips. The way he churned my insides made my body weak.

"Nah, don't cum yet." Hendrix grabbed my body away from the washing machine. He ran his hands up my tank top and cupped one hand around my left breast and his other hand down to my pussy. He rubbed my clit in a circular motion. He turned our bodies toward the entryway of the laundry room. With his dick still inside of me, hard as a missile, he walked me out of the laundry room. As soon as we got to the sofa in my living room, he bent me over the arm and took my soul to pound town.

I cried out as he slid his dick in and out of me, round and round, as I threw my ass at him in a full circle. I stood on my tippy-toes before climbing up on the couch, resting my knees on the soft arm of the chair. Hendrix grabbed me by the ankles, digging as far into me as he could go. If he hadn't been holding me by the ankles, my ass would have run from the dick. But I couldn't run. He was tired of me running from him. And I was tired of running, too. I took all ten thick, throbbing inches of that nigga that late night on my couch. Hendrix growled as he bust inside of me, still going strong, stroking the pussy until he got brick hard again, fuckin' me like he was never gonna get my pussy again. I loved him with everything in me when I wasn't supposed to. He gave me no choice but to love him, every piece of him.

He pulled out of my pussy, watching me look back at him as he started stroking his dick. I sighed at the sight of the veins throbbing on that thang. I spread my ass cheeks wide enough for him to see my waxed pussy and ass clearly. I could feel his juices sliding out of me. I licked my lips, watching him bite down on his lip. He gripped my waist with one hand and gripped his dick with the other hand. I sighed, looking back at him as his hand moved up and down his shaft.

"Touch her for me," Hendrix commanded.

I sighed, sliding my hand between my thighs, fingers rubbing my clit in a circular motion. I applied pressure, mouth falling open as I felt my body open up.

Hendrix's dick was sliding through my anus with ease. "Don't stop," he snarled as he felt my body jerk. "Rub that pussy. Relax that ass around this dick. Yeah, like that. Rub that pussy faster." Once he got his dick a few inches inside my ass, he let go of his dick and grabbed my waist.

I pressed my face against the sofa, nearly biting a huge chunk out of the couch. Wasn't no way I was going to be able to take all that dick without some help. I reached under the cushion and grabbed Monica, my pink wand massager.

Hendrix chuckled. "Yo, you keep your vibrator under your couch cushion, mama?"

"Hey, man, mind your business. This is my house, shit. Don't nobody live here but me and Monica," I snapped at him, powering the bitch on.

"Do what you gotta do to take this dick. Because a nigga is about to have no mercy on this ass, Merci," Hendrix let me know as he started to stroke, watching me place the wand over my clit.

Monica vibrated on my clit, sending intense sensations through my pussy as Hendrix's dick slid in and out of my ass. The combination of the two set my soul in flames. The pressure built up in my pussy, and I squirted all over his thighs. I felt a spreading wave of pleasure. As soon as Hendrix felt my body relaxing, he went to digging in my ass like a power drill. He growled as I howled, screaming at the top of my lungs in pleasure. I felt a surge of energy in the nerves surrounding my anus as the tension that built up was released throughout my body. Hendrix's dick throbbed inside of me, the friction causing him to release deep inside me. He gripped my waist as he released, groaning and moaning until the very last drop. I panted as he pulled out of me. He massaged my booty cheeks together, watching as his nut slid down the crack of my ass.

I let out a long sigh as he helped me up from the couch, my body falling up against his. He gently kissed me, sucking my lips in between his. "Let's shower, get cleaned up. I wanna eat that pussy while Netflix watches us tonight."

I looked up into his face, shaking my head. "I meant what I said about Denise."

"I got you." Hendrix frowned. "You gonna let a nigga stay the night or nah? I wanna hold my baby. Not just trying to fuck and dip."

I couldn't. "I'm supposed to be meeting up with ya girl tomorrow at the gym. You're going to get us in trouble. Go home to her."

Hendrix huffed. "Did she find her dress yet?"

I shook my head. "Not yet. You know Paris. Everything has to be perfect. Did you find your tux?"

Hendrix nodded. "Yeah. Me and my niggas straight. Shit getting altered this weekend. Nigga cleans up nice." Hendrix peeped the hurt expression on my face. "We're not wrong for this. You're just fuckin' with who makes you happy. And if that's your friend's man, oh muthafuckin' well."

"My foster sister's man, Hendrix?" I exhaled deeply, watching him look into my face like he couldn't care less. "I might have something you can change into. You can shower here, but you can't stay."

"Nah, I'm good. I have a shirt and jacket in the car. You already know if I shower, I'm climbing into bed with you." Hendrix looked down into my face, licking his lips.

"See you Friday at wedding rehearsal, Hendrix," I told him.

Hendrix grinned, shaking his head to himself. "See you at the church, shawty."

2

PARIS

Another cold December night in bed alone. There we were, the month of our wedding, and I'd never felt so distant from Hendrix. He tried sneaking into the house around 3:30 that morning. To top it off, before getting into bed, his ass took a long, hot shower. Afterward, he didn't even bother coming to bed. He went into his game room, shut the door, and probably went to sleep on his couch. I was used to nights like that, but something felt off. Hendrix was all about that street life. There was a war going on that he'd never tell me about. My dancers kept their ears to the streets, telling me what was going down. Hendrix never confided in me. We didn't have that kind of relationship. Our relationship was based mainly on business, at least from his standpoint.

I met Hendrix in middle school. At the time, I lived with my fourth foster family—Sheelah and Greg Avery. They were a very rich family, mostly old money. Snap Avery was Greg's brother, not to mention Hendrix's godfather. When Hendrix's father died, Snap was supposed to look out for him. Snap introduced Hendrix to the drug game. While in school, Hendrix played every sport there was. I tried out for the cheerleading team just to be around him. That was how I really got introduced to Snap. My foster parents never took me around their family. Greg was too busy raping me while his wife tried to cover the shit up. Neeta was my foster sister at the time. Greg made her watch. She was basically the lookout. Even paid the bitch so she wouldn't tell. And she didn't. I went to the nurse's office one day with abdominal pain, only to find out that I was pregnant. I went home to tell Sheelah that I was having her husband's baby. The bitch beat me before having her maid staff tie me to the bed. Sheelah sexually assaulted me with a rusty wire hanger. Needless to say, I ended up in the hospital only to find out I would never be able to have children.

I was too afraid to tell what happened to me. I lied to the hospital staff, telling them that I was trying to make myself have a miscarriage. That I punctured my own cervix. The Averys were questioned, and that was how word got back to Snap. He visited me in the hospital, and I told him that his brother was raping me every night. That his wife killed my baby and any future baby that I might have. To save his family name, the nigga bribed me. He told me that if I kept my mouth shut, he'd put me in his family's will. That when I was old enough, I'd own half of his family's casino. That I'd own his father's night club. That I could have anything I wanted as long as I didn't tell what Greg and his wife did to me. I was young and scared at the time. The only one who came to see me at the hospital other than the Averys was Hendrix. He was a popular kid with a rough upbringing. He had his own problems at home to worry about, let alone worry about some shy girl who was being sexually abused at home. I appreciated the fact that he showed me he cared about me. When Snap came back to pick me up from the hospital, I told him that the only things I wanted were to be taken from the Averys house and that club when I turned eighteen. I told him to give the casino to his godson, Hendrix. Hendrix never knew I was the reason he got that casino from Snap until we were in high school. On his eighteenth birthday, I told Hendrix that though I inherited the casino, I gave it to him. And we'd been together ever since.

I just knew we were in love. I was too young and naïve to realize the boy was just grateful that I'd given him something no one else but his godfather had. A chance to do something big with his life. Though Hendrix was about to be the youngest black rich nigga in our county, he wouldn't leave the street life alone. The casino only gave him more access to more niggas with more drug connections. It wasn't long before Hendrix found out the real reason why Snap gave me that casino. It was out of guilt for what his family did to me. Once I told Hendrix what Greg and Sheelah did to me, their days were numbered. He never let his godfather know that he knew what they did to me, but I was sure Snap knew his brother's murder revolved around me. Their house was mysteriously set on fire one night. The two were found burned alive in their beds. Forensics proved that they were shot in the head while being burned alive. The house had been broken into, but nothing was stolen. Snap never questioned us, but I was sure he knew. We were safe for the time being, but I knew there would be a time I'd have to face Snap for opening my mouth.

❧

"HOW LONG WE GOTTA DO THIS SHIT, BITCH?" NEETA WHINED the next morning, barely moving her fat ass on the treadmill at Planet Fitness.

"Maybe if you didn't eat half a dozen donuts from fuckin' Krispy Kreme this morning, you wouldn't be so fuckin' tired," I huffed, running effortlessly on the treadmill alongside hers.

"I eat when I'm stressed, shit. I don't get my grades back until Monday. I graduate next week, and I'm trying to make sure I passed. I got the job at the hospital pending my degree," Neeta panted, turning off the treadmill. "I'm tired of substitute teaching them bad ass kids. I have kids of my own at home, shit, that I barely want to deal with."

I gave her the side-eye. "Then why did you have kids if you didn't want them?"

Neeta eyed me, watching my booty bounce as I ran on the treadmill. "That's not what I meant. Parents get tired. We all need a break."

"At least you can have kids, Neeta," I reminded her.

"Are you still blaming me for what Greg and Sheelah did to you? How many years ago was that shit? Eleven years ago?" Neeta hopped down off of the treadmill.

"It feels like yesterday to a person who's still in pain, Neeta," I snapped at her.

"You weren't the only one abused. What about Merci?" Neeta reminded me. "Our first foster mother used to trade her pussy for heroin and liquor! She was six! She didn't get a break until we were placed in that second foster home."

"Yeah, the white people who wouldn't touch Merci because she was just as white as them. Or you because your period started at eight. I was the dark-skinned girl with the fluffy hair who her husband jacked off to while watching in the shower. You might be over that shit, but I'm not. I spend hours in therapy because I'm not over it!" I told her, turning off the treadmill, walking along with it until it slowed down enough for me to hop off.

Neeta put her hands on her thick hips. "Who said I was over that shit? I just moved on with my life so my kids wouldn't have to feel my pain. You can't treat everyone like shit because of your pain. Yes, I blocked that shit out because it was easier. Yes, I watched you get raped and accepted money from that crazy family we stayed with. That money paid my way through college! That shit they put you through got you a successful business and a man who loves you! You turned a bland ass gentleman's club until a strip club that celebrities travel from all over the world to go to! You are about to marry a man who moves heaven and earth for you whenever you ask. Some of us wish they had it like you! You out here looking like a black Barbie while some of us look like a fuckin' refrigerator. You always had a great shape, but look at you now, snatched as fuck. I'd kill for your life. Hendrix kills for you! Stop living in the past before that shit haunts all of us." Neeta grabbed her gym bag and walked toward the door, bumping into Merci on her way out.

Merci was excited to see Neeta until she realized Neeta was leaving. Merci frowned in confusion at me before she went over and checked in at the front desk. Merci was late as usual. Her job kept her occupied. She became a cop to help us, her friends, out of the jams we always seemed to put ourselves in. She wasn't dirty, but she wasn't exactly clean either. I wasn't going to fuss her out for being late. I knew she was searching hard for my dancer's missing baby. Hendrix's team was holding her daughter hostage until she paid the money her man owed to them. Hendrix tried keeping me out of his business, but I was all up in it. Most of his clientele frequented my club. Most of my dancers carried drugs into the club in their pussies. I helped Hendrix in ways he didn't even realize.

"Well, look who finally decided to show up." I rolled my eyes at Merci as she strolled up to me looking cute in her Pink crop top with matching biker shorts. Her naturally curly jet-black hair sat on top of her head in a full curly ponytail.

Merci rolled her eyes back. "Girl, I was up late last night."

"Ooh, finally someone had a date." I nudged her.

Merci shot me a quick glance before taking a long gulp of water from her water bottle. "No, but I did get Denise back."

I looked at her. Hendrix didn't mention to me anything about letting the baby go. "She's back with Tasha?"

Merci shook her head. "No, she's back at the precinct. They're trying to place her now. She doesn't need to be anywhere near Tasha. Tasha would let that baby stay home by herself some nights. I don't want her in foster care. I'm thinking of letting her stay with me."

"With you?" I asked.

Merci looked at me. "They killed her father in front of her. She saw their faces. She knows their voices. I got her to calm down enough to sit with my secretary for a little while. If that little girl talks, it's over. Everything about this war has your fiancé's name all over it. I don't know how much longer I can keep saving y'all two from yourselves."

I rolled my eyes at Merci before she set her gym bag down and climbed into the treadmill, changing the settings to fit her stride.

Before I could speak out against her statement, she said, "And why did Neeta go storming out of here? Dafuq did you say to that girl?"

"The truth, which she never wants to hear." I rolled my eyes, grabbing my towel. "The bitch keeps rubbing it in my face about the fact that I inherited money from the Avery family."

"But you did. She was raised by that family, too. She didn't get half the shit you did when they were killed." Merci scoffed.

I looked at Merci as she started to jog. "You think I inherited money from them muthafuckas because they died? Do you have any idea what the fuck I went through with that fuckin' family?"

Merci glanced at me before looking straight ahead, holding her head high. "I know you survived."

I exhaled deeply. We never exactly discussed what I went through with that family. And I see Neeta felt too guilty to tell her. The only reason Neeta knew the truth behind what Sheelah did to me that night was because she overheard the maids gossiping amongst each other. I didn't feel telling Merci would make any difference. She was battling her own demons.

"All the money in the world can't put my heart back together. I thought marrying Hendrix would do the trick, but he's been preoccupied these days." I hopped back on the treadmill.

"Oh really?" Merci pretended to sound interested, the same way she always did when I brought up anything concerning my relationship. She didn't like Hendrix or anything he represented.

To her, he was just some thug using me for a come up. She didn't know that he saved my life, putting an end to the family who took something from me that I'd never get back—the ability to create a family of my own.

"The casino, the dry cleaner, the crew, the money. He hasn't helped with anything concerning this wedding. We haven't so much as had a ten-minute conversation in the past few weeks. I don't even connect with him in bed. I disassociate myself from sex. I've learned to separate my mind from my body. It's a defense mechanism I acquired over the years. It's not his fault what I've gone through, but try telling my mind that. We haven't had sex in weeks. And honestly, I haven't even wanted to. All I want..." I sighed, "is a baby..."

Merci looked at me.

I turned on the treadmill again, previous settings in place. The treadmill slowly went into motion as I walked along with the belt. "My body's been through a lot of trauma. I was told I couldn't have children when I was younger. Haven't found a doctor yet who could reverse the damage. I'm just going to have to spend money on a surrogate. Would you consider being my surrogate?"

Merci looked at me like I was crazy. "Like carrying your and Hendrix's baby? In my line of work?" Merci laughed in disgust. "You must be out of your mind."

I shook my head, laughing to myself, laughing off the pain. I had to tell her what I'd been through. "The Averys did this to me, Merci. The reason I can't have any babies is because Greg raped me, got me pregnant, and his wife killed my baby! She had her maids hold me down on the bed. One poured Everclear down my throat, damn near drowning me! Others held my hands and feet. I watched as that bitch shoved a fuckin' wire hanger into my vagina until I felt a pop, a gush of fluid, and pelvic cramping that the words can't even describe!"

Merci gasped, jumped down off the treadmill while it was going. She rushed over to me, turning off my machine as she watched me slow my stride and gradually stop. "Paris..." Her whisper was drenched in remorse.

I looked at Merci, watching her eyes water. "They found a liter of blood in my abdomen when one of the maids so gratuitously took me to the hospital. I almost bled to death. The Averys threatened to kill me. Once Snap found out the truth, he bribed me with his money and family businesses. Since his godson Hendrix was the only one around who gave a fuck to come visit me at the hospital, I asked Snap to leave the casino to him. Once I came around to telling Hendrix the truth about the Averys, he put an end to those muthafuckas. That's why I fuck with Hendrix so heavy. That's why I give that nigga everything I got!" I yelled out in pain, a few people stopping to stare for a moment.

Merci's eyes filled with tears. "I didn't know."

"You never asked." I shrugged.

"What do you need me to do?" Merci asked.

"The damage has already been done, Merci. Just when the time comes, have my baby, okay? You're the only one I trust." I watched Merci let out a loud cry.

Merci rushed over and grabbed her things.

"Where you going? You just got here?" I asked her, watching her get her stuff together.

"I need to get back to the station, check on Denise." Merci looked at me one last time before leaving me at the gym alone.

❦

"IT'S SLOW OUT HERE TONIGHT, BOSS LADY." MY DANCER, Tweet, sat down at the bar of my club that night.

I sighed, cleaning off the bar while my bartender cleaned the machines behind the counter. "The night is still young. It's only 10:30. You know it's not lit in here until twelve."

Tweet looked at me, watching me clean off the bar vigorously.

"You must really got some shit on your mind. I never seen your boujee ass clean shit."

I rolled my eyes. "You need to mind the business that pays you."

Tweet laughed out loud, adjusting her G-string, pulling it out of her ass just for it to get sucked right the fuck back in. "Bitch, you *are* the business that pays me!"

"Corny." I chuckled a little.

"But for real though. You trippin' over what Tasha said to you earlier?" Tweet hesitated to ask.

Tasha and I had words as soon as I drove into the parking lot of my club that night. She didn't appreciate me "letting" Merci take her child as if I had control over what that girl did. Tasha never had a sober day in her life. Merci only let the girl stay with her to avoid putting the child in the system, somewhere we knew from experience that she didn't need to be. Tasha let me know that she hadn't seen or heard from her boyfriend in days, that she knew Hendrix's crew killed him. Said she couldn't prove it, but when she did, we were all dead.

"Nobody's trippin' off that shit that crackhead is talkin'. She needs to take her ass to rehab, or she's never getting that little girl back. Tasha represents every foster kids' mother that I know. The reason why some of us were put in the system at infancy." I scrubbed the bar top as hard as I could. "She better be glad them niggas let her daughter go."

"Yeah, I was surprised about that. These niggas around here are ruthless. The shit is too close to home, boss lady. I told you that you don't need this shit at the club. Hendrix is going to get you caught up." Tweet got up from the bar stool, making her way out onto the floor.

I exhaled deeply. She had one thing for certain: Hendrix was going soft. I played stupid, but I knew Hendrix stayed getting revenge for any agony that anyone brought to him. I wasn't saying he would have hurt that baby, but Tasha would've never gotten her back. Not after all the money her nigga owed. He got the money from somewhere.

I was so deep in thought that I didn't even realize that anyone was sitting directly in front of me until he cleared his throat loudly. I rolled my eyes at the sight of Hendrix's homeboy, not to mention Merci's partner, Kace. Kace Gwinnett. What could I say about him other than the fact that he looked like a white version of Chris Brown? I promise you haven't seen a white boy smoother than Kace. Smooth talking, smooth dressing, smooth dancing. Merci worked with him but didn't really trust him. He might have been Hendrix's day one, but he and Hendrix were night and day. Heaven and hell was what I called them. Kace was the voice of reason, where Hendrix was the definition of didn't give a fuck. Kace thought things through before he did anything, whereas Hendrix never looked before he leaped. Kace kept the peace, whereas Hendrix was always ready for war. It was funny that my DJ threw on "Heat" by Chris Brown when he noticed Kace sitting at the bar.

"You the only one I'm tryna make love to, pickin' and choosin'. They ain't really love you, runnin' games, usin'. All your stupid exes they gonna call again. Tell 'em that a real gangsta's steppin' in," Kace sang over the music, laughing out loud because he knew I'd slap his ass if he said the word nigga. "Like how I did that, huh, boss lady?"

I rolled my eyes. "White Breezy, you lucky because you almost got slapped." I peeped the display on his iPhone 12 Pro Max as he set it down on the counter. "Jewelry? What you looking at jewelry for? Trying to get Karen back?" I smirked.

Kace frowned up at me. His ex-wife left him three years ago. Left him with their two kids and never looked back. "Always got jokes about that bitch. Ain't seen her kids in three years and haven't tried to. What woman would leave a baby six months after they were born? Our son doesn't even remember her, while our six-year-old daughter can't seem to forget. How do you look your daughter in her eyes and tell her mommy's never coming back?"

I gave him a remorseful look. He really looked hurt. The bitch broke his heart though he'd never admit it. "Breezy, I'll watch the kids for you so you can get a break. I'm off tomorrow. I got my homegirl running the club for me tomorrow while I sit home getting this wedding together, making a few calls. Go out, have fun, and I'll watch the kids."

Kace shook his head to himself, looking back at his phone.

"What?" I asked.

"You asked what I was doing. Your dude has me picking out jewelry." Kace barely got the words out when I snatched the phone from him.

I peeped the pearl necklace and matching earrings before Kace snatched the phone back from me. "Pearls? If that nigga shoppin' for me, he definitely doesn't know my taste. When have you ever seen me wear pearls?"

Kace shrugged. "He said he was trying to find some jewelry to match this sexy white dress that I saw him pick out. You'll like it. It'll hug all them hips and dips you got, that's for sure." Kace looked me over a little before signaling my bartender to fix him his usual drink, Hen and Coke.

I looked him over as Felecia slid him his drink. He was dressed in gray hoodie, white T-shirt, gray joggers, and gray Jordans. He could make a simple outfit look runway ready. He could've been a model, yet he chose a dangerous career like becoming a cop. He grew up with us, the only white kid in our crew. His parents weren't rich, but they gave their kids their all. I never saw Kace in anything that wasn't name brand. He came from the kind of parents who would go broke to make sure their kids had it all. Kace was supposed to go to college, then on to medical school. Instead, he stayed behind to become a cop, to protect his friend, kind of like Merci did for us. His parents weren't too happy about his line of work, especially since they knew he only took the job to watch over his friend who kept him in trouble. Fuckin' with Hendrix paid his son's medical bills and his daughter's private school tuition. But I could see Kace wasn't happy. He hated the street life, but I think he hated to see his friend living on the edge even more.

"You're off tonight?" I asked.

Kace nodded. "Yeah. Your boy is over at the casino, making moves as usual. He said I could go home and chill. My son is driving me crazy. Had to get out of the house. My neighbor has him. I'm in the process of getting him tested for autism. Something just seems off, you know? The babysitter thinks he's a typical three-year-old, but nah. He's behind on things his sister was doing at that age. He spends most of the day screaming and having meltdowns." Kace signaled Felecia to make him two shots.

"You need a woman." I sighed.

Kace shook his head, picking up the two shots that Felecia slid him. He threw one back behind the other. "I got this," he assured me. "Women never caused ya boy anything but pain. I just need some peace, which I'm never gonna get in this life. Between kids and your dude, my life is always on edge. I keep track of all the money flowing in. Today he dropped a hundred fifty thousand on me. Says it was from Tasha."

I looked at him. I knew for a fact Tasha didn't give him shit. Said she wasn't giving him shit until she got her daughter and her boyfriend back. "Y'all seen her boyfriend?"

Kace scoffed. "You know better than to ask that."

"And you know better than to think Tasha had that kind of money to give. Her nigga stole the money. Hid that shit somewhere." I looked at Kace. "And I'm hoping y'all hid whatever gun you used to get that nigga with, too."

"I put it somewhere no one would ever look," Kace spoke softly as I leaned forward to hear him. "In evidence. I'm the one who handles inventory. No one will look in that muthafucka, trust me. I put it in a case file that's at least six years old. He's good, y'all good, we're good."

I watched Kace exhale deeply. He was sick of all of our shit, I could tell. "What time you bringing the kids over tomorrow?" I hesitated to ask.

"What would your man say about that?" Kace scoffed.

"That we at least owe you that much. Come by the crib tomorrow morning. I got you," I assured him.

Kace got up from the barstool. "He doesn't deserve you," he mumbled, but I heard him loud and clear.

Still, I asked him to repeat himself. "Say what? I didn't hear y—"

"I said..." He cut me off. "He's my boy, but you deserve more than this." He looked around the club before looking me back in the face. "Someone is gonna help you escape one day."

I watched him walk away from me, all the strippers in the club stopping for a second to get a glimpse of that smooth muthafucka.

3

MERCI

"He's got you watching his kids?" I shook my head at Paris as I sat down at a bistro table with her at Starbucks the day before the wedding rehearsal.

Paris shook her head at me, pushing the loose strands of her dark hair behind her ear. "I volunteered. Them kids are driving Kace crazy. It's the least I can do for him. He needs a break. Works too hard. He needs a girlfriend. I'ma hook him up with one of them white girls who works at that casino."

"You never babysit a muthafuckin' thing in your life." I laughed a little before taking a sip of my hot white chocolate mocha.

Paris rolled her eyes at me. "I might as well get my practice in for when you pop out two of my babies." She watched me damn near spit out my drink.

"We haven't even agreed on me having one, much less two." I looked at her like she was crazy. Right then, my phone chimed. I looked at the display. Another private number calling me. It was the thirtieth time a private number had called me. I knew it was Hendrix. I hadn't spoken to him in a week, since the night he showed up in a bloody shirt at my doorstep, the same day his

327

dick went in dry and came out soggy. I blocked his calls. I felt guilty as fuck after finding out the truth behind how he and Paris ended up together. Their shit was deeper than love. He killed his godfather's brother because of what he did to Paris. A part of me knew Hendrix was protecting her because she was my sister. He'd do anything for me, and she thought it was all about her.

"Someone's been blowing your shit up all day." Paris laughed a little before looking over her shoulder. Her eyes widened a little.

Before I could even look back over my shoulder to see who was coming, he was already at our table. Speak of the devil. Snap Avery was standing at our table tall, brown, and handsome. He was a Marine veteran with that poetic military demeanor. Dressed in his Armani suit, causing everyone around us to do a double take before just staring altogether. I was surprised to see him standing before us. He almost never came out of hiding. I peeped over my shoulder, watching his driver park a shiny chrome Bentley alongside the curb.

"Good morning, Paris. You seem to not know how to answer your phone, even though it's planted in her hand." Snap pointed out the fact that I wasn't the only one not answering calls.

Paris rolled her eyes nervously. "I've been busy with the wedding. Nothing personal."

"It's always personal when it involves my money," Snap let her know. "Can we talk in private?"

Paris shook her head. "Anything you can say to me, you can say in front of my homegirl, *Officer* Banks."

Snap could give two fucks about me or the fact that I was a cop. "When I gave my godson that casino, I didn't expect him to bring his street clientele there. That casino might be his, but I gave it to him hoping he'd still keep my family's casino clean. He needs to keep the streets in the streets. The two shouldn't mix. He's playing too close to home. And that club you own belongs to my brother."

"*Belonged*, Snap, as in past tense," Paris reminded him.

"Remember, I earned that club, and Hendrix more than earned that casino, not to mention the dry cleaner you gave him to run. You didn't *give* us anything. It was the very least you could do. You could've put your brother in jail instead of sweeping what he did to me and other foster children under the rug like the shit never happened. Money doesn't change shit."

"They never found my brother's and his wife's killer, but trust me, they will," Snap growled.

Paris smacked her lips. "Well, if you ask me, whoever did the shit took care of a problem that should've been handled way before then. *You* should've handled it when I told you what the bitch did with that hanger! Nobody misses them muthafuckas but you. Your own mother and father didn't even show up to that funeral, which ought to tell you something."

Snap looked at Paris like he wanted to smack her off that stool that she was sitting on. I didn't know what made her think she had an "S" on her chest that day, but she was really feeling herself.

"You turned a gentlemen's club where men who just finished playing golf went to unwind, into a strip club where bitches suck dick in the bathroom to make payout!" Snap snarled. "My brother told me not to give the club to you or the casino to Hendrix. He told me to let you go to the police. He said they'd never believe that a slut was ever raped."

Paris eyed me place my hand over her gun before looking back at Snap.

"Tell your nigga to choose one life over the other before I choose it for him," Snap warned before walking away. He stormed out of the dining area, door slamming behind him.

"How the fuck did he even know we were here?" I asked, before eying her fire-engine-red Mercedes with black and red rims and shook her head to herself. "Oh, yeah. Kind of hard to hide in a car like that, boo." I looked back at Paris, watching her shake her leg anxiously. "What's wrong? Fuck what he said."

Paris shook her head. "Nah, he's been coming around lately

threatening to have my club shut down or the casino shut down if Hendrix doesn't chill out. He wasn't going to talk all his shit around you. Snap said Hendrix's crew is cutting into his business, fuckin' up his profits. His crews have been taking over territories that Snap's crews were supposed to work. People trust Hendrix's boys. They don't fuck with Snap like they fuck with us. And Snap is tired of it. He's still trying to prove that Hendrix did what I told you, but without evidence, he has nothing. I still don't think it's safe for you to keep Denise. Muthafuckas in the streets are talking. Tasha's nigga, Foxx, has niggas who don't really care for Hendrix. Yeah, they deal for him, but everyone wants to be Hendrix. You need to find out more about Foxx. There's more to this nigga than we know. I have a strange feeling whatever Hendrix did, he fucked up. So anyway..." Paris exhaled deeply, changing the subject. "So everyone is wearing white for the wedding rehearsal dinner tomorrow, boo."

৩৯৩

"WE'RE SUPPOSED TO BE AT THE CHURCH IN AN HOUR, SHAWTY. You already missed Neeta's graduation this morning," Kace reminded me, sneaking up behind me at my desk back at the precinct.

I exhaled deeply, eyes glued to my computer screen. "Yeah, I know. I have so much going on. Neeta will be alright. Her graduation party is this weekend. Captain had me looking over Foxx's case. Who is this muthafucka? I can't find anything out about his family, where he's from, nothing."

"I'll look into it," Kace let me know.

I exhaled deeply. "Did you know Tasha put in a missing person's report? She is determined to find out what happened to him. Captain put me on his case, knowing this shit is too close to home."

Kace hesitated before approaching me. He set a package down on my desk.

I looked at the package and then back up at him. "What's this?"

Kace frowned a little before sitting on my desk, facing me. "I came by your crib the other night to drop off some paperwork. And I saw Hendrix's car parked outside," he whispered.

I shrugged. "Okay, so?"

"Okay, *so* isn't he someone else's man? A man that you're not even supposed to be associating with, not only because of his gang affiliation, but because he's engaged to your sister." Kace frowned at me, disappointment saturated all over his face.

I scoffed. "Says the muthafucka who runs businesses with the muthafucka, both legal and illegal. Let's see how the captain feels about what's cooking up in your basement as we speak."

Kace looked at me like he could wring my neck in the office in front of everyone who was there that night, and no one would give a fuck. "I pulled up just as Hendrix was leaving your crib. He grabbed and kissed you in the doorway before he left. You're gonna really tell me that I didn't see what I know I saw? I didn't see my homeboy kissing his fiancée's sister?"

"*Foster* sister, Kace," I reminded him.

Kace chuckled. "You really think you're about to suck and fuck the love he has for that girl out of his dick, don't you?"

"Keep playin' with me, Kace. Who do you think you are?" I snapped at him. "And don't come to my house without calling first, muthafucka."

Kace shook his head at me like I was fuckin' pathetic. "Hendrix's heart may be yours, but remember his loyalty is with Paris. You could fuck with any dude in the world. Why would you chose a muthafucka your sister would move heaven and earth for?"

I shook my head. "I have no idea what you're talking about."

Kace laughed off his anger. "This muthafucka hasn't helped his fiancée so much as pick out a flower arrangement or even a design for his wedding invitation. Shit, he had *me* help him pick out his tux for his own wedding. He hasn't contributed anything but money toward this wedding. He hasn't done anything to let Paris know that he's really all in. Did you know that Paris's legal last name is Avery?"

I wasn't aware of that. "No," I answered.

"Snap told Hendrix that even though he agreed to give Hendrix the casino, legally the family could take it back. The only way he could keep it was to—"

"Marry an Avery." I finished his sentence.

Kace nodded. "You know he doesn't want to do this. *I* know he doesn't want to do this. And I'm sure Paris knows he doesn't want to do this shit. I'm not saying he doesn't love her, but something is holding him back. And I see what it is now, or should I say *who* it is? Here I am thinking this muthafucka had me picking out a gift for his wife to be. But then I thought, wait a minute, whose birthstone is a pearl? Paris is born in April. Merci is born in June. It seems like you just keep digging yourself deeper and deeper into this shit with Hendrix. Stay the fuck away from him, partner. She's my homie, my best friend. Shit, I thought she was yours, too, but I guess I was wrong. Play with me if you want to, Merci. I promise, I'll risk it all to protect her."

I sighed heavily looking at the package.

"See you at wedding rehearsal." Kace shook his head at me, getting up from the desk.

I stared at the box a few minutes before opening it. Inside the box was a sexy silk white mini dress, matching stilettos, and a pearl necklace that had tiny diamonds between each pearl. The outfit was a replica of what I was supposed to wear to prom but never made it because I was sick. Hendrix and Paris showed up in their white stretch Navigator to pick me up that night, and I got sick to my stomach while we stood outside taking pictures in front of the limo. I stood there in my little white dress, watching them kissing on one another, looking like something out of a hood Disney movie. Paris in her long-flowing sea-foam-blue dress, and Hendrix in his all-white tux. I threw up all over my dress as soon as Paris wrapped her arm around my waist to take a picture with me. I didn't have a date to the prom anyway. Not because I wasn't asked but because I didn't want to go with any of the muthafuckas who asked me. Not to mention I knew Hendrix and Paris were going to be prom king and queen, and I definitely didn't want to see that shit. And there I was again, six years later, about to be front row and center of something I didn't want to attend.

I got dressed in the locker room that afternoon. Slipping into my dress, all I could think about was everything I'd gone through in my life. From growing up in foster care, to cleaning up the messes that my friends made. Hendrix and Paris deserved one another. Both were hardheaded and never listened to reason. Hendrix watched the both of us growing up in the foster system. He took care of his little sister, trying to protect her from his mother's addiction. His mother would do anything for the crack, including selling her own daughter. Hendrix hated all the side effects of the drug, except for the side effects of making money from it.

Paris went from foster home to foster home, witnessing the side effects of drugs as well, yet the steady stream of income it brought her pulled her further into the game. Taking on the job of hiding evidence and taking out their competition was destroying my life.

That silk dress felt so damn good against my skin. The shoes fit snugly on my feet. The string of pearls felt cold against my collarbone. I couldn't get what Paris told me about her past out of my head. How could I be her maid of honor knowing I'd slept with her fiancé? After all she'd gone through? After all he'd done for her? Sure, he loved me, but she needed him. Kace was right—Hendrix's loyalty was with Paris. He'd do anything for her because she'd do the same for him. I should've spoken up in middle school. We'd all met each other around the same time. Hendrix knew Paris from sports, whereas, I knew him through the neighborhood. She was a part of his team from the start. The only reason he even noticed me then was because I was a witness to his court case. He always said I saved his life. I never knew he saved Paris's.

I walked into the church that night looking like a million bucks, feeling less than trash. I had to sit there and watch Hendrix and Paris pretend to be a happy couple. They held hands while all of our friends gave speeches. I watched the way Paris looked up at Hendrix admirably. She respected him, loved him more than anything, would do anything to keep him in her life. The first time Hendrix got me to make love to him outside in the rain on my squad car, he told me that Paris wouldn't ever touch him like I did. Said it was like she was absent from her body when he was inside of her. And after hearing her story about what the Averys did to her, I understood why. Yeah, we'd all been victims of sexual abuse, but not like her. Hendrix was her hero. There was no way after hearing her side of the story could I continue to deal with him. She needed him. I wanted him.

I didn't even give them a chance to try to pass the mic to me, her maid of honor, or should I say *dishonor?* I made up some excuse about my throat hurting as soon as the mic came to me. Paris looked hurt that I couldn't even give her two words of encouragement that night. The food from the church's kitchen smelled that it was seasoned just right. I couldn't even wait for the caterers to start serving us. I got up from my table and tried sneaking out into the church's lobby.

"Leaving so soon?" I heard Hendrix's voice over my shoulder.

I stopped in my tracks, tightening the belt of my Burberry trench coat around my waist.

"You couldn't even say a few words to congratulate your sister in there?" Hendrix growled in my ear as I turned around to face him. He frowned down at me as I reluctantly looked him in the face. "The fuck are you going to so soon?"

"I have to get home to meet up with the baby sister. Tessa said that she knows a woman who's a great foster mother. I need to meet up with her, speak with her before I just hand Denise over to her," I stuttered a little, looking into his face. He looked so handsome, standing there in all white—a white crisp button-up shirt and white pants, hanging off his hips a little. He smelled so good. The warm fragrance of his cologne danced under my nose.

"You look fine as a muthafucka tonight. I love this dress." Hendrix grabbed me closer to him by my dress.

I pushed him in his chest. "You should like it. You picked it out. Thanks, by the way."

Hendrix looked at me like he didn't know what I was talking about. "It's funny because I had it saved in my phone. The necklace, too. When I saw it, I thought of how you looked the day of prom. I didn't order this though. Who gave it to you?"

I didn't have time to play games with him. "Look, Hendrix, whatever this is, I can't do it anymore. I blocked your calls, blocked you on social media, totally distanced myself from you. Why didn't you ever tell me what you went through with Paris? Neither of you let me know what they did to her! You mean more to that girl than you'll let yourself realize. She chose you because you took out the muthafuckas who hurt her. She loves you with everything she has left in her."

Hendrix looked at me. "What about you? You love me, too."

"Yeah?" I laughed a little. "Well, I'm not the one with a ring on her finger." I started to walk away, but he grabbed my wrist.

"Don't walk away from me, Merci. I'm done with you yet," Hendrix warned me.

"If you really want me in your life, you'll just have to settle for being friends," I told him.

"There's no way we can just be friends. Not after I felt your heartbeat from the inside," Hendrix whispered to me. He was really making it hard for me to resist him. I loved him with everything in me, but I'd settle for being his friend to keep him in my life in some way.

"Merci!" Heels pranced against the church lobby floor as Paris made her way towards us. "Where are you going, Merci?" She glanced at the hurt look on Hendrix's face before she looked back at me. "What are y'all two out here talking about?"

"Paris, I have something to tell you," I hesitated to say.

Paris laughed nervously. "What could you possibly have to tell me that you couldn't tell me after dinner? Food is being served. Come on, let's eat."

I shook my head. "Paris, I can't be your maid of honor."

Paris looked at me like she didn't hear me. "You can't do what?"

"I have so much going on with work and Denise." I had to think fast before I tried taking my words back. "I'm not around enough to be able to help you with the wedding. I missed so much in your life that I'm just finding out. I really don't deserve this spot. I haven't had your back like I should. I think it's best if I step down."

Paris was probably about to go off on me when the photographer stepped up to us, camera flashing in our face.

"Step aside, Hendrix, and let me get a picture of the bride and her maid of honor." The photographer shooed Hendrix away.

Hendrix glanced at me before grabbing Paris's hand, pressing it to his lips. "See you at the table, baby."

"Okay, boo." Paris grinned at Hendrix before her smile faded as she looked back at me.

"Okay, say 'cheese!'" The photographer focused his lens, looking at the both of us standing side to side. "Merci, take off that coat so we can see your dress."

I hesitated as his assistant helped me out of my coat, taking it from my arms.

Paris did a double take, looking at me in that outfit, eyes

glued to the necklace around my neck. "Pearls," she whispered herself before looking back into my face.

"Now, everyone say 'cheese!'" The camera flashed, catching us off guard.

⊗⊗

"HOT DOG, HOT DOG, HOT DIGGITY DOG..."

I swear that child watched *Mickey Mouse Clubhouse* that entire night on YouTube. Denise was the prettiest little girl I'd ever seen. Perfect chocolate-coated skin. Full head of wooly dark hair. Cute chubby cheeks accented with deep dimples even when she wasn't smiling. All she did was watch television and color. I'd have to check in on her because she barely made a peep. I told my captain that she could stay with me a few days until we placed her. I didn't want that sweet baby in foster care, but I couldn't send her back with her mom who'd yet to even look for a rehab center, though the court ordered her to. The night Hendrix's crew met me to give Denise back, I took her to the station. Tasha showed up high as hell, causing a scene. She swung at me, and I pressed charges on her so I could get her in court. The judge ordered her to check herself into a rehab clinic in order to get her daughter back. A whole week had gone by, and the only thing I saw Tasha do was quit working at Swollen only to end up at some hole-in-the-ground strip club that looked more like a trap house.

The girl I hired as my babysitter was short notice. She was the girl everyone at Paris's club used to watch their kids. The woman who was supposed to take Denise in was supposed to call me that night to meet, and I had yet to hear from her. Tessa offered to take Denise off my hands for a few hours so I could get some work in, but I refused. I had too much on my mind to work. All I wanted to do was meet the woman who was supposed to take Denise in. After meeting her, I was supposed to put Denise to sleep and drink me a whole bottle of wine. After the night I had, I needed a drink.

"Do you want a fruit snack, baby?" I asked Denise as I got up from the couch.

Denise sat on the carpet in front of the television. She looked back at me like I was interrupting her show.

I laughed out loud, throwing my hands up offensively. "My bad. Don't want to interrupt Mickey and them." I walked toward the kitchen. Just when I walked toward the cabinet alongside my refrigerator, I heard footsteps outside of the door to the kitchen. I quickly grabbed my Glock from on top of my refrigerator. I glanced over at Denise, whose eyes were still glued to the television. It was funny that even though things happened so quickly, they seemed to play out slowly in your mind. Before I could even make my way to my window to peep outside, bullets started flying through my windows from all angles.

My first instinct was to make my way back over to Denise. Denise ducked down by one of my bookshelves. I ducked behind my sofa, firing toward my kitchen window where I could see someone firing at us. Denise saw her teddy bear lying on the floor near the television. She got up to go get him before I could scream at her to stay back. Before the poor baby could even scream out, she'd been shot in her shoulder as another bullet went straight between her eyes. I screamed, going over to grab her. I grabbed her in my arms, getting into a corner, away from the bullets flying through my house. The bullet went straight through her shoulder. Blood oozed from her forehead. I placed my hands over her wounds, screaming out in agony. I was so busy trying to stop her bleeding that it didn't register to me that I'd been shot in my side. I let go of Denise for a few seconds to grab my phone from my pocket to voice dial 911. I felt myself growing weak as blood gushed from my side.

"911. What's your emergency?"

"This is officer M-Merci Banks. I've been shot... We've been shot! They just shot a little girl!" I spoke over shots still firing through my house. "Muthafuckas are shooting at my house!" I ducked down in the corner, slouching down as low as I could get, with that little girl in my arms. I just zoned out, watching the bullets fly through my house. Glass splattered everywhere. Feathers from my couch floated gracefully through the air. I didn't know when the firing ceased. All I knew was I felt that little girl's heart stop before I blacked out.

I woke up to the sound of a heart monitor beeping. As my eyes began to focus, I felt a shooting pain in my side. I groaned, trying to sit up in my hospital bed.

"Man, my first week on the job, and I gotta take care of this bitch," I heard Neeta's voice approaching my side. She adjusted my bed, sitting me up so I wouldn't have to.

I looked at my sis before lifting my blanket and gown to look at the bandage in my side. "What day is it?"

"December sixteenth. You've been here about five days. Missed my graduation, bitch." Neeta grinned a little, watching the confused look on my face.

I looked up at her, trying to remember what happened. A flash of Denise's blood all over my hands flashed through my mind. I tried getting up from the bed in a panic. Neeta pushed me back down my shoulders. "Denise!" I screamed. "Where is Denise? Is she okay?"

Neeta looked me in my face. "Baby, there's no more Denise."

"What?" I cried out.

"They're saying some muthafuckas from Kinston who used to roll with Tasha's nigga shot your place up. You know Hendrix is out there looking for them. Tasha has been at your precinct all week, talking about suing for her daughter's death. Says there's no way her daughter should've been staying with you based on who your foster sister is. I told y'all." Neeta shook her head as she fluffed my pillows. "They're saying the bullet that killed Denise was from your gun. A bullet from your gun ricocheted off of the wall or something and hit her in her head."

"Oh no!" I cried out.

Neeta nodded. "I'm sorry, Pooh."

There was a light tapping at the door before the doctor stepped into the room. Never in my life had I seen a doctor that damn fine. The doctor was tall, at least six feet two. He was of Asian descent, with a deep-almond complexion, and though he was wearing a white coat with a collared shirt underneath, I could see that he was covering neck tattoos.

"Good evening, Miss—" He looked at his chart, "Excuse me, *Officer* Merci Banks." He looked into my face as he pulled up a stool and sat down on it at my side. "How are you feeling?"

I rubbed my head anxiously. "Confused. Last thing I remember was calling 911."

"You were shot. If the ambulance didn't get there when they did, you wouldn't have made it." The doctor pulled up my gown, eying my bandaged wound. "We'll change this for you. I'm Doctor Gio Chang. Nice to meet you. I wish it was under different circumstances, but nice to meet you." He grinned, giving a small glimpse of those perfect white teeth.

I eyed his smile before looking into his face. "Shots ricocheted off of every surface in my house. Those muthafuckas were trying to make sure whoever was in that house with me was dead!"

Doctor Chang exhaled deeply. "I shouldn't even speak on this, but... pieces of Foxx Hill's body were found floating near the Cliffs of the Neuse. I overheard cops from your department discussing it yesterday. They mentioned that the little girl you were staying with mentioned to your captain that she saw who killed her father."

I looked at the doctor. Whoever shot up my house was trying to shut that little girl up. I wasn't sure whose face she saw the night of her father's murder. I prayed it wasn't my partner's, who would do anything for Hendrix. I hadn't been answering Hendrix's calls either. He might have been trying to warn me to get that little girl out of there. But then, Tessa was trying to get Denise out of my house, too, that night, and I wouldn't let her.

My mind was spinning in circles at that moment. If I hadn't been laying down, I would have passed the fuck out.

"You lost a lot of blood, but the baby is fine." Doctor Chang threw more fuel on the fire.

I looked at Neeta. "I thought you said Denise was dead?"

"He's not talking about that baby, shug." Neeta smiled nervously.

I looked back at the doctor. My heart pounded in my chest. "What baby? Who's having a baby?"

"We had to do an ultrasound to make sure the bullet hadn't caused too much internal bleeding. Everything looks good. The bullet went straight through, not hitting any major organs. The ultrasound confirmed pregnancy, at least six or eight weeks give or take." The doctor watched the horrified look on my face.

I didn't have periods because I was on the Depo shot. I didn't have any morning sickness, and I hadn't gained any weight. Pregnant? I hadn't been fuckin' anyone those past two months except for Hendrix.

"Even after you're released, you will most likely be visiting us every week. Though the bullet went through, we still had to perform surgery to repair a few blood vessels and tissue that were torn when you were shot. If everything goes well these next few days, you will be able to go home in a few days." Doctor Chang stood from the stool, eying me sitting there in shock. "Do you have any questions?"

"What am I supposed to do?" I asked myself out loud. "My life, my career, my everything is at stake right now! A baby? I can't bring a baby into this shit!"

"She'll be fine, Doctor. The staff will take care of her needs," Neeta assured the doctor.

Doctor Chang gave me a sympathetic smile before leaving the room.

"Baby, you need to get yourself together." Neeta exhaled deeply. "You hate this job anyway. You only took it to watch out for Paris. Let her handle her own shit. Looking out for her caused you to get shot the fuck up. Now you're caught up because that baby died while in your care. Now you have your own baby to worry about!"

"This stays between me and you, Neeta. I mean that shit," I told Neeta. "This is the last thing I need right now. Paris has been asking me to be her fuckin' surrogate."

Neeta rolled her eyes. "Don't nobody wanna give birth to her and Hendrix's trap baby."

I sat there, breathing heavily.

Neeta looked at me. "Who's the father?"

I looked back at her, shaking my head. "You don't want to know. Let's just say he's someone I have no business fuckin' with."

"You fuckin' with your partner? Oooohhhh!" Neeta teased.

"What I look like doing some shit like that? I work with him." I rolled my eyes.

"Shit, what you lookin' like fuckin' with someone who's off limits? Who else is off limits? Do I know him?" Neeta thought for a few seconds until it finally hit her. Neeta's eyes widened. "Don't tell me that it's Hendrix's baby. You're fuckin' on Hendrix? Paris is going to beat your muthafuckin' ass!"

"It only happened twice." I exhaled deeply.

"Does anyone know about this? That y'all fuckin' around?" Neeta shook her head to herself, folding her arms.

I hesitated. I didn't want to tell her that my partner suspected something. She'd go to Kace and ask him what he knew. Neeta was nosy as fuck, and I probably shouldn't have mentioned it to her. As much as she loved Paris, she hated her just the same. She'd keep my secret just to spite Paris.

"Just you," I hesitated to say. "I'm not keeping this baby."

Neeta looked at me. "When she comes to you again about being a surrogate, and she *will* come to you again, tell her you'll do it."

I looked at her. "What?"

"Just trust me. We'll take care of this. You don't need that girl as your enemy right now. You have enough problems, like trying to figure out where you're going to live until all this shit is over. They're going to have to transfer you out of this county, if they don't decide to make you go on leave until shit dies down. Someone wants you dead, and at this point, there's no telling who," Neeta assured me.

✤ 4 ✤

PARIS

I watched Hendrix pace the floors of our three-story home for five days since the night Merci's house got shot up. The death of Denise stirred up some shit in the streets. The fact that her baby was killed by Merci's bullet took the pressure off of Hendrix, who was suspected of having something to do with Foxx's death. Hendrix couldn't care less if the heat was on him. The fact that Merci was in the hospital was killing him. He had no idea who shot her house up, but he was going to shake some shit up in the process of finding out.

"Them niggas from Kinston tried to kill Merci, man. I'ma get them niggas back, believe that!" Hendrix snarled, drunk as fuck, waving his gun around.

"Yo, Hendrix, chill." Kace tried calming him down. They stood in the foyer, Kace trying to stop Hendrix from leaving the house. "You don't know it was them. Rumors spread like a wildfire around this muthafucka. It could have been Tasha's people for all we know. They probably didn't know the little girl was in the house. These muthafuckas are trying to say that the little girl saw who killed her father. Sounds like they're trying to say we had some shit to do with this if you ask me. I say you lay low. And get your wife out of here for a few weeks."

344

Hendrix looked over his shoulder at me, who was standing alongside our six-foot white Christmas tree as I held a glass of Japanese plum wine in my hands. Hendrix looked back at his friend. "I'm about to get some more Henny, bruh. I'm not drunk enough." He pushed past his friend to make his way toward the kitchen.

Kace exhaled deeply, running his hands across his close-cut hair. He turned around, walking back toward me. "I know you want to go see your girl in the hospital, but it's not safe right now."

I cleared my throat, lowering my glass. "So I just wanna know one thing: why was Merci wearing the same string of pearls that you said Hendrix was supposed to be getting for me?"

Kace frowned at me in confusion. "Say what? What are you talking about?"

"The night of my wedding rehearsal dinner, Merci showed up in this sexy ass white dress and the exact same necklace that *you* said Hendrix was going to buy for *me*." I watched the *oh shit* expression form on Kace's face. "You knew they were fuckin', didn't you?"

Kace laughed a little, shaking his head at me. "You're worried about those two fuckin' when your best friend, your *sister*, is in the hospital?"

"She's not my sister or my friend if she's fuckin' my fiancé!" I pushed him in his chest.

"Well, he's not your fiancé if he's fuckin' your sister, I'm just sayin'." Kace shrugged. "Whoever did this shit to Merci is probably after you, too. So you'll need to skip town for a few weeks, mama."

I exhaled deeply, taking a long sip from my glass. "No they're not."

Kace was reluctant to ask me. "How could you be so sure?"

"That little girl wasn't supposed to be there that night." I barely got the words out when Kace started going the fuck off on me.

"Paris, that shit was *you*? Over *him*? A muthafucka who doesn't even care enough about you to know your sister is off limits?" His peach skin turned red.

The night of my rehearsal dinner, I tried to hold it together after seeing that necklace wrapped around Merci's neck. It didn't take me two seconds to put two and two together. That outfit was similar to what Merci was supposed to wear prom night. Only Hendrix would think of some sentimental shit like that. He was good at buying gifts to show his emotions. Merci put that shit on to let me know that she was fuckin' my man. Then the bitch had the nerve to come to my shit, giving some lame excuse for why she couldn't be my maid of honor. Damn right, I paid some muthafuckas who hated the police to go shoot up her shit. I told Tessa to get that little girl out of that house that night. Not only did I put the pressure on Merci, but I took it off of Hendrix for a while. But of course, Kace wouldn't see it that way.

"Hendrix is my boy, but he's not worth all of this," Kace told me. "You don't know they're fuckin'. All you know is he gave her a dress and a necklace. You jumped to conclusions for what? To cause more problems? Why not just question the muthafucka?"

"So he could lie to me? Nah, I'm not going out like that. She's my best friend. I knew her all my fucked-up life! She's supposed to love me enough not to take gifts from my man, fuckin' or not!" I cried out.

"You jumped too soon, mama. Now you got some heat on you. You're gonna have to act as normal as possible. I know you wanna cut your friend off, but you're going to have to play the part for a few months. Act like you don't know shit. If Hendrix finds out about this shit, you're as good as dead."

I looked at Kace, heart at a standstill.

"If Hendrix knew what?" Hendrix asked, coming into the living room.

Kace glanced at me before looking at Hendrix. "How much she spent on the food for the wedding. You don't even wanna know, bruh, trust me. New Years is in just two weeks. That's a big day for a wedding. Y'all are supposed to be planning the rest of your lives instead of a war on whoever did this shit to Merci."

Hendrix wasn't listening. "Man, fuck that. Merci is your partner. You're supposed to be investigating this shit! You're supposed to be looking into this shit so I can take these muthafuckas out! If you got shot, Merci would be all in, helping a nigga track muthafuckas down. She'd help muthafuckas search for the bodies, the whole time having the bodies in her trunk! That's the kind of partner that you have, nigga!"

Kace looked at his friend. "Did you know that Foxx was Snap's little brother?"

I gasped, looking at Kace before looking at Hendrix. Hendrix was already under fire for what Snap knew he did to my foster parents. The streets talked. The fact that he killed another one of Snap's family members wasn't going to play right with Snap. Not only that, but if Foxx was his brother, that meant Denise was his granddaughter.

"Snap put his little brother with your crew so the muthafucka could spy on you. Foxx was stealing from you and giving it back to Snap. This entire situation was a setup. Whoever did this shit took the pressure off you for a little while. Let them think muthafuckas in Kinston shot up shawty's crib, trying to get to Denise. You don't need any more heat on you. In the meantime, while I clean shit up, Paris needs to get out of here. She can plan her wedding from my parents' house in Maryland," Kace suggested.

Hendrix didn't object, but I did.

"I'm not leaving him here in this shit." I refused.

"Tasha's been telling muthafuckas that she's going to kill Merci. I gotta take the bitch out," Hendrix snarled.

"Hendrix, are you not listening to me? Fuck Merci right now!" Kace exclaimed.

Hendrix looked at Kace like he would've shot the muthafucka in his face if he had his gun on him for saying some shit like that. "Nigga, what?"

"Merci will be fine. I will have details outside of her room and outside of the hospital. In the meantime, pack your shit, Paris. You're coming with me." Kace turned and walked away from me, toward the front door. "I'll be in the car. You have twenty minutes. Kiss ya fiancé goodbye, homie."

Hendrix drank straight from his Hennessy Black bottle, watching his friend leave out the door. Hendrix turned to me. "You alright, bae?" he asked me, watching me drink my drink down to the last drop.

I shook my head. "My best friend is in the hospital, Hendrix. No, I'm not alright." *I guess I'll play along*, I thought to myself.

"I'll get the muthafuckas who got her, baby, believe that," Hendrix assured me.

My heart skipped a beat. "Kace is right though. We need to lay low, baby. We have a wedding to worry about, boo. Let's concentrate on that."

Hendrix scratched his head.

"Are you having second thoughts? Is there someone else?" I questioned.

Hendrix looked at me. "Nah, baby, don't nobody want my ass but you. Trust me."

I looked into his face and all I could see was pain. I wanted to ask what happened between them. Why her? Why couldn't he love me, flaws and all? Maybe he resented me because he felt obligated to me because I helped him come up. If he wanted her, he should've just told me from the jump instead of letting me put my all into him.

"Do you love me?" I asked him.

"Baby," he kissed my lips, "more than anything."

"But—" I started to question his loyalty to Merci, but he cut me off.

"Kace is right though, baby. You need to leave town for a few days. Pack you a little bag. Your girls can cover you at the club while you're gone." Hendrix looked into my face.

"But the wedding..." I whispered.

"We need to set it off for a little while. At least for a few months." Hendrix watched me already about to catch an attitude. "Baby, this isn't the time for this. You said yourself you wanted to plan things out better. Maybe get a wedding planner. Let's set it off until April fifteenth."

I looked at him, my temper settling a little. "My birthday?"

Hendrix nodded. "I'll pay to have all the invitations reprinted. I'll pay for everything to be rescheduled. I'll make sure everyone can change the flight information on their plane tickets, for the ones who were coming in from out of town."

It was the first time he'd ever offered to do anything concerning the wedding.

I nodded. "Let me go pack my things. Are you going to be okay?"

"Ain't I always okay?" Hendrix grinned, kissing my lips.

❧

"I'MA SMOKE THIS JOINT, THEN I'MA BREAK YOU OFF. I'D BE lying if I said you ain't the one. All these tattoos in my skin, they turn you on. Lotta smoking, drinking, that's the shit I'm on..." Kace sang along with the song playing through his chrome Mercedes E-class's speakers.

I peeped over my shoulder at his kids, Amber and Eliott, bobbing their heads to whatever they were listening to through their AirPods while watching on their iPads. I looked back at Kace. "You didn't have to do this for me," I told him. "I created some mess that you should've left me to clean up."

Kace frowned at me a little before looking back out at the road. "Do you like the way I flick my tongue or nah? You can ride my face until you're drippin' cum. Can you lick the tip, then throat the dick or nah? Can you let me stretch that pussy out or nah?" He continued to sing along with Ty Dolla $ign and The Weeknd.

The sound of his voice resonating through my eardrums

caused my pussy to have a pulse. "Ummm, I'm glad your kids have their AirPods in, sir."

"My parents will be happy to see you." Kace changed the subject. "Did you know my mom wanted to adopt you when she found out your birth mother gave you up while we were in pre-K?"

I looked at Kace. "She did?"

"Yeah, but my dad wasn't feeling it. He already had five mouths to feed. You know me and my brothers can *eat*, eat." Kace watched me sink back in my seat, trying not to think about my past.

"You sure they'll be okay with me staying with them for a few days?" I asked.

Kace nodded. "It'll be an early Christmas present." Kace glanced at me, winking his eye. Little did Kace know, they had a surprise for him.

After six and a half hours on the road, we were in Glen Burnie, Maryland. When we were in the tenth grade, Kace's father moved his family to Maryland in hopes of changing his family's surroundings. He'd finished law school and gotten a job at a pretty big law firm. Kace didn't want to leave Goldsboro and stayed with his aunt. Kace and his father never really got along. The youngest of five boys, Kace was under pressure to follow in their footsteps. All his brothers had high-paying jobs. Kace's father thought his line of work was dangerous and low paying. He worked hard so his children wouldn't have to. Kace knew early in life that he wasn't anything like the rest of his family.

"Kacen!" Mrs. Gwinnett grabbed her son in her arms as soon as she saw him at the door. She hugged and kissed him before hugging and kissing her grandkids. She screamed with excitement as soon as she saw and recognized my face. "Oh my goodness, Paris? Is that you?"

I smiled nervously as Mrs. Gwinnett grabbed onto me, smothering me between her breasts. "H-Hey, Mrs. Gwinnett."

"Kacen, I didn't expect to see you for another week, *if* you decided to show up then!" Mrs. Gwinnett pushed her son in his chest, still looking at me in awe. "Wow, you grew up to be so beautiful. Come in, come in! We were just about to eat!"

Amber and Eliott giggled, running past their grandmother into the house.

Kace looked back over his shoulder at the white Lexus sitting in his driveway. He looked back at his mother. "Whose car is that in the driveway?"

"Well," Mrs. Gwinnett cleared her throat, "I should've set the table for eleven. Let me add four more plates. We have more than enough to eat. I had help..."

Kace frowned at me in confusion as we followed his mother into the house. We stopped in our footsteps as we stepped into the dining room and saw Karen, his ex-wife, sitting at the table with his family. Karen was sitting next to his brother, Carter. She stood from the table when she saw Kace standing next to me. Karen was pregnant as fuck. You should have seen the look on little Amber's face when she saw her mother after not seeing her for years. She ran over to Karen, throwing her face into her stomach, crying and laughing at the same time. Eliott ran back over to his father, hiding behind him.

Mr. Gwinnett, Brad, Bently, Shane, Carter, and Karen were at the table while Mrs. Gwinnett added four more place settings in front of four empty chairs. Food was laid out on the table like it was Thanksgiving. Everything smelled and looked so good. The family looked like they were actually enjoying themselves until we walked in. Judging by the way that Karen sat there with his family, she must've visited often. Karen sat too close to his brother and was too comfortable being there with his family for her to have been a guest they hadn't seen in a while. And if my guess was correct, Carter was her baby's daddy.

Kace looked like he wished he would've brought his gun in the house. I was sure he would've blown his oldest brother Carter's head right off of his shoulders. Amber hugged on her mother, even though her mother barely touched her back. Karen patted her head like she was a fuckin' puppy before shooing her away. Amber went back over to her father. We kind of stood there for a few minutes before sitting down at the table.

Mrs. Gwinnett was so happy to see her family back together that she didn't notice Kace giving his father and brothers the death stare while she was serving the food. Karen stared at me the same way, as if she was wondering what I was doing with her ex-husband. I rolled my eyes before eying the food that Mrs. Gwinnett slapped on my plate.

Three-year-old Eliott burst out singing. "Pour up the whole damn seal, I'ma get lazy. I got the mojo deals, we been trappin' like the '80s. She sucked a nigga soul, gotta Cash App! Told 'em wipe a nigga nose, say slatt, slatt! I won't never sell my soul, and I can back that! And I really wanna know, where you at, at?" That little boy loved some Roddy Ricch.

Kace's parents looked at Eliott before looking at Kace.

"Wow, really, Kacen?" Bradley shook his head.

"Shit, at least he's talking," Kace responded.

"That little boy loves some music, boy." I laughed it off. Eliott was autistic. Music was his therapy. You never saw him without seeing either his AirPods or his Beats headphones over his ears.

"Where do babies come from?" Eliott struggled to say.

Kace looked at his son. That was the first time I'd ever heard Eliott ask a question, and I was pretty sure that was the first time Kace heard his son talking, too. And so clearly. The sad part about it was that he was staring at his mother's belly. The mother who had yet to acknowledge him.

"Well..." Amber smacked her lips, about to bite into a big piece of baked chicken. "The man puts his dick in the pussy..."

Kace's parents gasped. His brothers tried their hardest not to laugh. I nearly bit my tongue off. Karen scoffed. Kace sat there slouched in his chair, nonchalant look on his face.

"I see what you've been teaching our children." Karen shook her head at Kace.

"Shit, isn't that how babies are made though?" Kace growled, his glare switching from Karen over to Carter. "Hmmm, Carter? You gonna tell your niece that her uncle Carter has been fuckin' her mom? That whatever spawn is growing inside of her is either her sister or brother *and* fuckin' cousin?"

"Calm down, Kacen," Mr. Gwinnett huffed.

"Pops, Carter's been fuckin' my ex-wife, and you're going to tell *me* to calm down? She hasn't seen our kids in three years! She left them! She hasn't even said hi to her son or hugged her daughter who cries for her every fuckin' night! Y'all knew—"

"Breezy, there's really no point in talking about this. Not around the kids. They've been through enough," I whispered to Kace.

"Who the hell is Breezy?" Bently asked.

I laughed to myself. Kace was so different than his preppy, stick-up-the-ass brothers. They were like Carlton, and he was like The Fresh Prince. Too much sauce. They were always jealous that he blended in with the Black and Hispanic kids at school. Kace was so cool that when you saw him, you forgot about his color. His brothers couldn't fit in if they tried. Their slick racist comments used to piss me the fuck off. I knew it wouldn't be long before they started fuckin' with me.

"It's my nickname for him. Been calling him that since we were kids. It's our thing. Mind your business, Carlton." I rolled my eyes over from Bently to his mom. "Mrs. Gwinnett, these rolls smell great."

"I made them," Karen boasted. "They're a little too *dark* if you ask me."

I dropped the roll back down on the plate. "Never mind. They're a little dry and chalky, kind of like Karen's skin."

"So how have you been, Kace?" Mr. Gwinnett drew the attention back to his son. "We haven't seen you for the holidays since Karen was pregnant with Eliott."

"Dick in the pussy," Eliott muttered to himself.

"I work seventy hours a week some weeks. This is the first

vacation I've taken in three years." Kace watched his mother put salad on a plate for him.

"And you thought it was okay to just pop up here unannounced?" Mr. Gwinnett frowned.

"I didn't think I needed an invitation to see my own family." Kace dug into his food.

"That's a nice ride outside, bro," Brad teased. "I didn't think a cop could afford a ride like that."

"He runs a casino and a few dry cleaners with my fiancé," I snapped.

"Fiancé?" Mrs. Gwinnett questioned.

"Hendrix, ma'am. Yeah, we're engaged." I exhaled deeply. "We're getting married on the Outer Banks in April. We've been rehearsing at a church in Goldsboro for the time being. We have to reprint the invitations. I still get my bridal party into their gowns. Soon as we get the invitations reprinted, Mrs. Gwinnett, yours will be the first one I send out. Hendrix will be glad you see you."

"You're marrying that troublemaker, who's the reason why my straight-A son couldn't manage not to skip class almost every day? That little black boy from the neighborhood who used to sell crack to old ladies?" Mr. Gwinnett scoffed. "You still associate with that drug dealer? He's still on the streets and not in jail? You're a cop, Kacen. What does that say about you? I wouldn't be surprised if you're helping him distribute the drugs throughout the community with Kelly Roland here."

"She's not Kelly. She's Beyoncé, Pop-Pop." Amber rolled her big hazel eyes.

"Well, Beyoncé..." Mrs. Gwinnett laughed. "You were a straight-A student growing up. What is it that you do now?"

I glanced at Karen who was eager to know what I was doing as well. "I inherited a strip club from the Avery family."

"A strip club?" Karen laughed a little.

I glared at Karen. "A small strip club might average about seven thousand dollars a week. My club is dead in the outskirts of Goldsboro, North Carolina. We have a population of about thirty-four thousand people. My club averages fifty thousand dollars a week. That's a few thousand less than what a club in a *metropolitan* city would make. Celebrities come from around the country to my club. If I could have kids, they'd be set for life. My club is called Swollen, just like my bank account. So yes, I own a little strip club."

Karen slouched back in her chair.

"Is that your little white car out there? It's cute. I bought a few of my dancers that car for their birthdays." I dug into my plate.

"The Avery family passed that club down to you?" Mr. Gwinnett questioned. "That family who died in a fire a few years back?"

I glanced at Mr. Gwinnett. "Yeah..."

"News articles about your family—"

I cut Carter off real quick. "They were *not* my family."

"The article about your foster parents said that you killed your own baby with a coat hanger. Said you did that so you'd be removed from their custody. Why would you kill your own baby?" Carter questioned.

Everyone looked at me for an answer, all except for Kace, who didn't appreciate them questioning me.

I stopped Kace from defending me. "I didn't kill my own baby. My foster mother killed my baby. To shut me up, my foster father's brother promised his family's assets to me once I turned eighteen. That family got away with rape for years before they were killed in that fire."

"What's rape?" Amber asked, her bright eyes glistening.

"Something that can't happen to a slut," Karen snapped.

"That's enough!" Mrs. Gwinnett banged her fists on the table like a gavel.

"Y'all better get Karen before I drag her face across this table and make her snort these mashed potatoes." I cracked my knuckles.

"I haven't seen my son and his friend for years!" Mrs. Gwinnett exclaimed. "This is my second time meeting my grandson! Yes, Kace, your brother has been sleeping with your ex-wife the past three years! Yes, your father is still mad at you for not going to an ivy-league school like your brothers! Yes, you could have gotten a better job, yet you chose to be a cop! Yes, you had to settle with being friends with the girl who got away!"

I looked at Kace. "The girl who got away?"

"Yes, she just told us she's engaged," Shane muttered between his perfectly white teeth.

I stared at Kace's profile, watching him eat.

"We are going to sit here and have a nice family meal like a normal fuckin' family! I didn't make this mac and cheese from scratch and bake all these got damn pies for them to go to waste!"

"Mom, you bought these pies from Walmart." Shane laughed.

"Shut up, Shane!" Mrs. Gwinnett shut his ass up. "Are you here to stay for a while, Kacen?" she asked.

"Just for a few days. Until things die down back at home. I'm all the family Paris has. She needs this break, if you don't mind, Mom." Kace looked from his mom, over to his father. "Pops?"

Mr. Gwinnett sat there eating, mumbling to himself.

Mrs. Gwinnett looked at me. "Some mail came for you a few days ago."

"For me?" I questioned.

Mrs. Gwinnett got up and went into the kitchen. After a few seconds, she came back with a card-sized envelope and handed it over to me.

"I'll fix up the guest room as soon as we're done eating." Mrs. Gwinnett smiled, despite the fact that everyone else at the table was frustrated as fuck. "So about this wedding... Did you want me to make you some pies?"

I SAT ON THE PORCH THAT NIGHT, CARD IN MY HANDS, TEARS sliding down my cheeks. It had been at least twenty years since I'd heard from the person who sent the card. The person who decided to finally reach out to me was my egg donor. Nakia Perry. I hadn't seen her since I was four years old, in preschool. The last time I saw her, she was getting high in a gas station bathroom with some truck driver she'd just met. She overdosed in the bathroom, passed out in her own piss when one of the cashiers found me. Last thing I remember was the police taking me to the station. Up until I got that card with a picture inside of it, I didn't even remember the bitch's face. I held the picture in my hands, laughing out loud at the sight of that woman smiling in the picture with about five teenage girls around her. She looked happy and sober. Rich chocolate glowing skin, long thick hair, dimples. All her girls were about my complexion, melanin poppin', hair for days. This woman hadn't reached out to find me in over two decades. She went and had five other children. Didn't even look for me. I started to rip up the picture and the cheap ass Christmas card before footsteps approached behind me.

"Don't do that, Paris." Kace sat down beside me, taking the card and picture from my hands. "She went through a lot to find you, mama. I guess she figured you'd swing by my parents' house eventually. Probably found their address in a phone book or some shit."

"Why now?" I laughed to myself.

"Maybe you need her now." Kace shrugged, looking the picture over. "You look like her. Chocolate-dimpled muthafucka." He nudged me in my side, watching me roll my eyes.

"Between the ages of four to eighteen, I lived in eight foster homes. Did you know that?" I looked at Kace. "I've been beaten, raped, starved. I've eaten kitty litter, tree bark, dog food. The Averys pimped me out, allowing their rich friends to sleep with me. If I didn't want to do it, they'd beat me or starve me for weeks. I've run away too many times to count, only to be caught and returned right back to my abusers. All I've ever wanted is to be treated like somebody, a fuckin' human being. I went through hell and back, and this woman wants to send me a cheap ass fuckin' Christmas card with children she replaced me with? Rip that shit up, Kace."

"Do you remember that song our pre-K teacher used to sing to us?" Kace redirected my attention. "That song from the *Space Jam* soundtrack? 'For You I Will' by Monica. How does it go?"

I shook my head, drying the tears on my face. "I'm not in the mood for this, Breezy."

"When you're feeling lost in the night. When you feel your world just ain't right. Call on me, I will be waiting. Count on me, I will be there," Kace sang in my ear.

I burst out crying, laying my head on his shoulder.

"Anytime the times get too tough." Kace continued singing, "Anytime your best ain't enough. I'll be the one to make it better. I'll be there to protect you, see you through. I'll be there, and there is nothing, I won't do." Kace kissed my forehead before putting the card and picture in his jacket pocket. "You gotta learn how to put the past behind you, mama," he advised. "I know it's hard. But you can't move on if you keep looking back. Your mama looks clean. I think that's what she wanted you to see. She doesn't want your last memory to be of her in that bathroom. She wanted you to see that she moved on. She gave you her address, leaving it up to you whether or not you want her in your life. She wouldn't be the first muthafucka in your life who really doesn't deserve to be there, but you let them stay anyway. Shit."

I lifted my head from his shoulder, watching him frowning. "Has Hendrix called?" I sniffled, tears sliding across the bridge of my nose.

"Nah. He's probably doing the exact opposite of what I told his ass to do," Kace huffed. "Swear I can't get through to him or to you. I can't even get my life together, worrying about y'all two.

That's definitely something that me and my partner have in common."

I rolled my eyes, drying my face with my fingertips. "Please don't talk about that girl."

"He only went to that girl because she was probably giving him something that you weren't," Kace didn't hesitate to say.

"So you condone niggas cheating?" I snapped.

Kace shook his head. "Nah, I never said that. But I know Hendrix. He's a fighter. Doesn't normally give in or up. This shit with him and old girl has to be recent. Something must've happened."

I exhaled deeply. "Well, the doctors have been telling me for eleven years that I couldn't get pregnant. By some miracle, a few months ago, I got pregnant. It was an ectopic pregnancy, but it was a pregnancy. I think he got his hopes up until I had to go to the hospital for yet another operation. Our sex life is nonexistent. Not because of him but because of me. He wants a family. I can't carry his baby. I look real stupid asking Merci to have my baby."

"You deserve that much out of this. I'd still ask her to do it. I told you to play this shit out. A baby won't fix whatever problems you have with Hendrix, but hey, you'll be able to pass down your assets to the child should something happen to either one of you. Don't let Snap get that shit back. His brothers are dead. He didn't have any proof of who killed his brother, but I bet he does now. Hendrix needs to chill, lay low before some shit pops the fuck off. Merci's too stubborn to quit her job, but I'll make sure she's put on desk duty." Kace exhaled sharply.

"I didn't mean for Tasha's daughter to get killed. I know Merci is blaming herself for that." I honestly felt bad. Not about Merci getting shot—fuck her—but about that little girl losing her life because of me. "I tried getting that little girl out of there. I paid some of my strippers from the club to have their niggas shoot up her spot. I'm sure I'm going to be blackmailed for life from them bitches. You're right, though. I'm going to have to play along like you said. There's no telling what'll happen if Hendrix finds out that shit went down because of me. He's out there now trying to find out who did that shit to Merci. I'm sure once he sobers up, he'll assume it was Snap's people. They'd hurt her to hurt us."

"I'll handle it," Kace assured me.

I rolled my eyes. "How you gonna handle it?"

Kace made a face. "Like I handle everything else. Dafuq?"

I exhaled, eyes searching his profile. "Dinner was great."

Kace shook his head. "No, it wasn't."

I laughed a little, feeling his pain. "Yeah, it wasn't."

"Listening to Dad brag about all the bread my brothers are making because of their jobs and side hustles. I make twice the amount of money them muthafuckas make, but did you hear him bragging about me? He called my money 'dirty money'. Talking about it's got to be dirty if I'm in business with Hendrix. Talkin' about I need to go into business with one of my brothers to clean my money. Man, Pops was about to get smoked at the dinner table. I started to tell the muthafucka 'clean deez nuts'," Kace growled.

"At least you have parents. I'd give anything to have a healthy argument with a dad or a mom," I reminded him.

"Man." Kace got up off of the porch. "Enough of this depressing ass shit. I'm on vacation. First vacation since I became a cop. My kids are asleep. Our bags are in the crib. We're in Maryland. Clubs just opened back up after this COVID shit. I'm trying to get drunk, forget what we did. Come on, get changed. Let's pop out."

Leave it to Kace to go out to a club when we had a plateful. But he was right. No use dwelling on anything that we couldn't change. The damage had already been done. I had to clean up my own mess. I had to get my emotions in check. A dress didn't mean they were fuckin', but the thought that Hendrix put into that gift hurt. He had yet to really talk to me about what I had gone through. Never talked me through the pain. I needed love, and all he knew how to give was protection. We all had issues from being neglected at a young age. I just wanted someone to care enough about me to see where my pain came from. I knew it hurt Kace to see that his brother ended up with his ex-wife, yet Kace was calmer than most. But I knew enough about Kace to know there was always a storm coming.

"I did some wrong, but I'm always right. Said I know how to shoot, and I know how to fight. If I tell you once, won't tell you twice. I'm real discreet, like a thief in the night..." The sounds of Pop Smoke flooded through the club speakers that night. It might have been cold outside, but the heat was blasting in that club. The club wasn't too packed, probably right at capacity, everyone in masks that matched their outfits. I wore a chocolate, off-the-shoulder sweater and brown leggings. Chocolate-nude red bottoms on my feet. My thick hair was pulled up into a princess bun, edges laid. Luckily, I'd just had my chick Crystal, owner of Baddie Blinks, fill in my lash extensions, so there was no need for a face full of makeup.

"Did you want something to drink?" Kace leaned over, speaking over the music.

I looked him over, eying him in all white from his head to his feet. White hoodie, white T-shirt underneath, white joggers, white Jordans. His warm tatted hands held on to me. He glowed under the flashing black lights. All eyes were on him as soon as we stepped through the doors of Club Fix. I nodded as he took my hand, leading me over to the crowded bar. I didn't even have to tell him what I was drinking. He knew I always started off with a Long Island iced tea.

You'd think by the amount of people at the bar that it would've taken us about thirty minutes to get a drink, but nope. That lil' skinny, bowlegged bitch bartender took one look at him and was right in his face. We had back-to-back drinks for a good hour. After two Long Islands, two shots of Henny, and a liquid marijuana, I was lit. He had about five or six shots of Hennessy, two rum and Cokes, and a Heineken but didn't seem the least bit fazed. We sat at the bar, vibing to the music playing, just happy to be out of Goldsboro and away from life for a while. Lord knows I needed it, and I knew he did, too.

The bartender slid Kace another shot of Henny before fixing me a margarita.

Kace held up his shot glass. "To no looking back."

I held up my glass, clinging it against his. "Big facts." I took a few sips from my drink, watching Kace throw his shot back. "Breezy, it's time for you to move on. It's been three years."

Kace shook his head in disagreement. "Shit, it's been longer than that. I never loved Karen. She knew it, too. I was just tired of Pops always raggin' on me, telling me I wasn't shit and nobody wanted a cop making forty-eight stacks a year when they could have a doctor or a lawyer or anyone other than ya boy, who makes a good hundred to two hundred fifty stacks a year."

I rolled my eyes. "Little does he know, you run businesses that bring you in more money than they'll ever see in a lifetime. Fuck him. Fuck your brothers. And *definitely* fuck Karen with a sick dick. You did good with those kids. I know they're a handful, but they love their daddy. They need a mommy though."

Kace frowned at me as the DJ threw on some old-school jams. When they threw on '90s music, I can't help but sing along. I swayed in my seat as my favorite song by Erykah Badu flowed through the speakers.

"First time that I saw you, boy, it was a warm and sunny day..." I vibed with Erykah.

Kace laughed to himself.

"What?" I asked, drunk as fuck, feeling like I was floating.

"This song is a whole vibe." Kace shook his head to himself.

"What you know about this song?" I joked.

"I know I'll probably see you next lifetime..." Kace signaled the bartender to fix him another shot.

"Boy, bye. You ain't thinkin' about my black ass." I rolled my eyes, sipping from my glass. "Your energy feels so damn good to me..." I sang to myself.

"Oh, I've definitely thought about your ass. Thighs, titties, pussy, lips, all that," Kace told me, catching the shot glass that was slid to him.

My lips trembled as I kept on drinking. And I wasn't talking about the lips on my face either.

"You've been through a lot. Your mind, body, and soul went through trauma. As a black woman, people expected you to just get up and keep going. I think what happened to you not only scared you but scared your dude, too. He's reduced you to your past. Yet and still, he doesn't notice your triggers. He doesn't notice the fact that you hate to be approached from behind. If your assault was manual, I'm sure you don't like a lot of digital foreplay either, and I'm sure he doesn't notice that either." Kace threw his shot back. "I'm sure if you start feeling sexually stimulated, you start feeling guilty. I'm sure he didn't even ask you if it was okay to kiss or touch you when you first let him inside. You probably cried, and he probably didn't even notice."

My heart pounded in my chest. "In my sexual assault support group, a woman said her husband waited six years to have sex with her. Hendrix would never wait for me."

"I would have. Shit, I waited twenty-five years. You didn't want me though. Too stuck on a popular basketball player than a muthafucka in marching band. You know I only tried out for the drum line so I could watch you cheer at every game? Muhfuckas dissed me every day, swore a white boy didn't have any skills. But I showed them what having skillz really meant. I showed up to every practice, on time, just to watch you on the field. I remember how that ass looked in those little shorts y'all used to wear to practice. When I used to see those thighs, those hips, those perky breasts, even the way you wore your hair in a messy bun, I used to lose it. Dick stayed on hard in practice watching you." Kace shook his head at himself, probably thinking he sounded pathetic. I thought it was cute.

"That's cute." I laughed to myself.

Kace looked at me like I had him fucked up. "You wanna

hear some 'cute shit'? A'ight, bet. There's some shit you don't know about the night of the fire at the Avery house. Merci was in on it, and she didn't even know."

I lowered my glass. "W-What do you mean?" I asked reluctantly.

Kace frowned, probably upset that he even had to bring up that night of graduation. "I told Merci to make sure she made you go with her to that graduation party at Neeta's place. Had y'all thinking that the crew and I were out celebrating me leaving the next morning to go off to the police academy in Durham. I took a few of my crew members and broke into their house while they were asleep. My crew got their waitstaff out of the house. When my gun cocked, Greg woke up first. The muthafucka begged and pleaded for his life. I wasn't trying to play God, but I brought their lives to an end. Soon as I shot him in his shoulder, his wife woke up. Since Sheelah wanted to assault you with that hanger, I made Greg assault her with a gun. Made him shove the gun inside of her and pull the trigger.

"Soon as she screamed out in agony, I shot the bitch in her head before I shot her husband in his. Hendrix had no idea what I did until I called him that night. He's the one who burned down their crib. He's the one who got rid of the gun. I never knew what happened to you until we were graduating high school. The day Hendrix showed me the casino he'd inherited is when he told me what happened to you. I would've done that shit in middle school when it happened if I knew about that shit. But it was best it happened when it did. I was going away to the police academy the next morning. Eighteen years old and had committed murder. You think I gave a fuck? I considered you blood, and it didn't come any thicker."

My heart was thumping in my chest watching Kace talk about committing murder. A murder that I just knew Hendrix committed. Hendrix never really said he did it, but he never said that he didn't either. We never talked about it. He just came home that night and told me that I never had to worry about that couple ever bothering me again.

"Hen-Hendrix saved me." I shook my head.

Kace shook his head back. "Nah, *I* saved you. Hendrix told me he'd handle everything. I never knew that he had you thinking that he was the one who did that shit until I saw how serious that you two were getting. You were supposed to be mine, and he used that night to get closer to you, knowing I was the one who risked it all to put an end to the people who hurt you."

I got up from the bar, drinking my drink to the last drop before grabbing my chocolate-brown sequined mask from off the bar top.

Kace grabbed my arm before I could walk away from him. "Falling in love with you was the first choice I never had. The second was when I got the muthafuckas who hurt you. I didn't have a choice. A muthafucka can't hurt who I know in my heart is mine and get away with it."

I sighed heavily, looking up into his face. "You're my best friend. Shit, you're *Hendrix's* best friend! He thought he could trust you around me!"

Kace scoffed. "Shit, he *thought*. He's lucky I waited this long to say anything. You were everything to me. You were made for me, and Hendrix took you from me. My mom always knew how I felt. She told me to get you to fall for me, all I had to do was make you laugh. But the thing is, every time you laugh, every time I see you smile, *I'm* the one who falls in love."

"He'll kill you," I warned him.

"Does it look like I'm scared?" Kace let me know I had him fucked up. "Can I borrow a kiss? I promise I'll give it back to you."

I shook my head. "I'm getting married, Kace." I looked down at my heavy engagement ring. Just as I looked him back in his face, he grabbed my chin, pulling my face to his. I grabbed on to his hoodie to brace my soul for impact. My soul was snatched as soon as he sucked my bottom lip into his mouth. If you ever wanted to stop time, kiss someone who'd waited all their life to finally kiss you. I felt relief in that kiss. I'd known that boy all my life, but in that kiss, I felt like we'd spent years apart. I would have never known that the best kiss I'd ever have was the one that I never had. He grabbed onto my waist, warm hands grabbing onto my skin as he slid his hands up my sweater enough to feel my skin against his. When the kiss was over, I think we both realized things were just beginning.

I wanted to dance with him, but I knew I was too drunk. And the way he was looking at me, the last thing he was thinking about doing was dancing with me. Kace looked at me before digging into his pocket for his wallet. He removed a hundred-dollar bill from his pocket, placing it down on the counter, telling the bartender to keep the change. Kace grabbed my hand, leading me through the crowd, on the way out of the club.

"Breezy, we just got here!" I squealed over the music.

"You're right. We should've been here years ago," Kace spoke over the music.

The cold air hit us as soon as we stepped outside of the club. We rushed off to his car that sat on the far end of the parking lot. Kace pressed the remote start button on his keychain. The car started, the heat already blowing at a comfortable temperature. We got into the car, getting into the back seat where we had a bottle of Crown Peach waiting on us.

"Kace, I'm drunk, but I came to the club to dance," I told him.

"We can dance in here." Kace took a sip from the bottle before reaching for my feet to take off my heels. "Shit, you can dance on this dick."

I sighed as he rubbed both of my feet in his warm, strong hands. "We can't do th—"

"Can I take your clothes off?" Kace asked, removing his hoodie, throwing it in the front seat before grabbing my legs from behind my knees, pulling my body into his.

I sighed as he kissed my lips. I felt as if he had me under a spell. The events that happened next were out of my control. No one had ever talked me through sex before. It was a type of intimacy only a friend who cared for me could give. I sighed in his mouth as he grabbed onto the waistband of my pants, pulling them down and off.

Kace looked at my pussy print in my sheer Savage Fenty cheekies. "I knew that pussy was going to be phat. Can I see her?" And just when he started to remove my panties, my cell phone rang.

I looked at Kace.

He looked at me, shaking his head. "This shit is way past due. We have a lot of making up to do. I'm telling you, don't answer that shit."

I looked at the display. It was Hendrix. I had to answer it. "Hello?" I answered.

Kace huffed, pulling my panties off, damn near ripping them.

"Baby, you still up?" Hendrix asked.

I gasped as Kace scooted back, pulling me to him by my legs so fast that it caused me to fall back against the door. I watched as Kace looked my pussy over.

"Hello, kitty, nice to finally meet you," Kace whispered. He licked his lips as he spread my pussy lips wide, exposing my clit from hiding behind the hood.

"Y-Yes, I'm up." I glanced at the bulge in Kace's pants. I noticed Kace's dick years ago, when we were in high school. That thang always swung back and forth in gym class when he was on the court playing basketball. I knew that muthafucka was about to fuck me like I was his enemy.

"What you doin'?" Hendrix asked.

I braced myself as Kace leaned over and kissed the insides of my thighs. "I'm..." I exhaled sharply. "I'm drunk..." I laughed nervously.

"Oh, you're drinking with Mrs. Gwinnett?" Hendrix questioned.

"Oh my God..." I sighed under my breath, gripping the seat in my hands.

Kace kissed and sucked his way from my thighs to my clit. He kissed her like he was kissing the lips on my face a few times before sucking her into his mouth. I swear I felt every nerve in my body tingle.

"You good?" Hendrix questioned.

"Y-Yes, I'm good. I gotta go, baby." My lips trembled as I tried getting off the phone with Hendrix.

"Baby, I'm about to FaceTime you..." Hendrix sounded as if he knew something was up.

I gasped, watching *Bae FaceTime video* flash across my phone.

While still sucking on my clit, Kace snatched the phone from my hands, putting it on vibrate, tossing it up front. I couldn't even argue with him. I was too busy shaking and moaning at that point to put up a fight. I'd never had my pussy eaten. Ever. The way he kissed my pussy set my soul on fire. His fingers felt so good against my wet skin as he spread my lips and ass apart. He ate that pussy like he loved me. Like he'd been starving and had to eat everything on his plate. He did clockwise circles around the glans of my clit. He moved that tongue side to side, up and down, round and round, He pushed my hips into his face, helping me brace myself as my pelvic floor tightened. I screamed out in ecstasy as I experienced my very first orgasm. He still wouldn't let up. He held my hips in place, taking me through a second orgasm. He ate the pussy so good that I forgot the nigga came with dick, too.

I could barely breathe as Kace came up for air and reached for his phone to reconnect his phone to his car. I sat up, entire body tingling as the sounds of my favorite artist, Jhene Aiko, flowed through his speakers. My pussy juice glistened on his pink lips. I couldn't even tell him how good that shit just felt. I was speechless, looking into his face as he pulled me back to him by my sweater before lifting it up and off of my body. He unhooked my bra, eying my titties as they popped out of the lace.

"Perfect," he moaned, before pulling his shirt over his head, muscles, triceps, biceps, and tattoos everywhere.

I watched as he pulled his sweatpants and boxers from his body. His thick, long, engorged pink dick popped out of his pants, curved like a ripe banana, standing up, waiting for me to touch it. My eyes damn near rolled to the back of my head as Kace grabbed my hands and placed both hands on his dick. Yes, I needed two hands to hold that thick muthafucka. Whoever said white men didn't have a dick worth talking about lied to y'all like a muthafucka.

I looked into his face, watching his lips separate as I began to stroke his dick. "He's beautiful," I told him, drunken gaze fixated on the cum my pussy left on his lips. "Can I taste him? I wanna choke on him."

"You ever sucked dick before?" Kace asked, watching me shake my head.

"I'm gonna learn today..." I told him, bending over, taking him in my mouth. Sure to place my lips over my teeth, I went up and down on it a few times before my jaw relaxed a little. The liquor in me was definitely acting as my courage that night. Sober me wouldn't have sucked dick, let alone a dick that was sure to touch the dangly thing in the back of my throat.

By the way Kace moaned as soon as he felt my lips on the head of his dick, I knew he wanted to grab me by my neck and press down, causing me to gag on it. But he didn't. He let me lick and suck and stroke and learn. I could taste the sweet precum in my mouth, and I swirled my tongue around his dick.

"Fuckkkkk..." Kace sunk back in his seat. "Baby, I wanna fuck you. That's what I want from you. I can get this later. I've been waiting on that pussy too long. Save some. This, shit, this feels so good." He pulled me off of him by my bun, gripping it in his hands as I pulled my lips from his dick, saliva dripping from the side of my lips.

I got onto his lap, straddling his hips. I cried out in ecstasy as he sucked a nipple into his mouth. "Do you have a condom?" I was drunk, but I knew better.

"I wanna feel your insides. Fuck all that. Ride this dick like its stolen," Kace growled, gripping my hip with one hand and gliding his dick to the opening of my pussy with the other.

I looked into his face as Kace eased his way inside of me.

"Am I hurting you?" Kace asked.

I nodded, tears sliding down my face.

Kace exhaled deeply, kissing my tears. "I don't want to hurt you."

"It's a good hurt, Breezy," I told him. "You feel so good inside of me."

"It feels so good inside of you, baby," he whispered to me, wrapping his arms around me as I started to grind on him. "Shit... got damn..."

I wound my hips and slid up and down on that dick. I squealed as he smacked my ass, gripping it in his hands. He gripped my booty, slipping a finger in my asshole. The stimulation to my anus combined with his dick thumping against my cervix sent a surge of energy throughout my spirit that I'd never felt before. It was the first time I'd connected through sex and it was with someone I had no busy fuckin'. Not fuckin' but making love. Sweet love.

Though I was on top, that boy was throwing dick at me like he was hitting it from the back. He dug so deep it was as if he was placing a coffin. Our bodies were rhythmically in sync. When I got too tired to ride him, when my knees felt like they were on fire from rubbing against his heated leather seats, Kace held on to me and laid me down on the seat. And he went to work, stroking deep in my guts until the friction caused me to cum on his dick.

"Baby, I'm cummin'," I moaned in his ear.

"Yeah, cum on this dick. This is my pussy. I don't give a fuck about that ring," Kace told me. "You're mine, and we belong together. Do you fuckin' hear me? He's not supposed to have you. He doesn't deserve you."

I cried out, holding on to him as he ground his pelvic bone against mine. My pussy gripped his dick like a glove. She did not want to let him go. "Just shut up and get this pussy. She's been waiting for this. Nothing has ever felt like this. Give me that dick, Breezy! Throw that muthafucka at me!"

Kace quickly pulled out of me, pulling my body from the seat to turn me around so that I was face down, ass up. I arched my back and gripped the seat, and he eased his way back into me and did exactly what I asked him to do. He threw that dick at me like he was trying to knock my uterus loose. The intensity caused me to reach back and press against his abdomen to release some of the pressure.

Kace pushed my hand away. "Move your fuckin' hand. You need this, remember? Relax that pussy, baby. Breathe. I got you." He slowed his stroke and didn't pick up the pace again until he felt my body relax. He gripped my waist in his hands and gave me the dick like I asked.

"That dick is so big, daddy!" I whined.

"Oh, I'm daddy now? Okay, bet." Kace loved the sound of that. He knocked on my cervix like he was trying to get in. We moaned together for a good twenty minutes after that. I threw my ass back, and he tried to pull out and switch positions, but I wouldn't let him.

"Nah, don't run now." I looked back at him as I twerked on him, booty cheeks clapping against his dick. He was trying not to bust, but I wanted to feel that gooey shit inside of me. "I wanna feel you bust in me. Bust in this pussy." I threw my pussy at him as he threw his dick back at me.

"Shit, mama," he moaned, panting, breathing heavily. "I'm about nut in this pussy. Fuckkkkk." He grabbed my hand, that was gripping the seat. Our fingers intertwined.

I screamed out as I felt his dick throbbing inside of me, nut spurting out against my cervix. My pussy walls throbbed, trying to pull him back in as he pulled out of me. I gasped for air as I watched him reach up front and go into his armrest for a pack of wipes. I sighed, chills taking over my body as he wiped his cum that dripped from inside of me. I sat down on his leather seats as soon as he finished. I watched him grip his dick, eying my cum that glistened on it. He used another wipe to wipe my juices from his skin. We were drunk and exhausted. And the windows were fogged all the way the fuck up.

Kace grabbed the bottle of Crown, unscrewing the top. He watched me sitting there, chest heaving in and out as I struggled to catch my breath. "I needed this, Paris. I hope what happened doesn't push you away from me."

"You-You..." I stuttered. "You held my hand while you pounded my shit."

Kace laughed a little. "Of course. I'm a gentleman." He eyed my phone on the front seat. He frowned a little before asking, "You gonna call the muthafucka back?"

I shook my head. "Let's get dressed. You still owe me a dance."

❧ 5 ❧

MERCI

"**M**a'am, you have a visitor," a nurse told me before opening the door and letting Hendrix in. I really wasn't trying to face Hendrix, but after three days of being awake in the hospital with nothing to eat but beef broth, I needed him to bring me some food I could sink my teeth into.

I sighed, inhaling the fumes of my tray from Mission BBQ. "Oh my goodness. I smell them damn baked beans. Bring it here, bring it here!" I reached out for my plate.

Hendrix chuckled. "Glad to see you're making progress, lil' mama."

"Umm-hmmm. Give me my plate." I watched as he handed me my food. And I didn't hesitate to dig in. "Oh my goodness. Thank you. I'm about to fuck this upppppp!"

Hendrix pulled up a chair to the head of my bed, facing me. "How you feeling?"

I glanced at him as I dug into my food. "I've been better." I watched him frown. "You good?"

Hendrix nodded. "Yeah. Shawty's been gone three days. She's in Maryland, with Kace's people. Need her to lay low until we find out who did this to you. One of my niggas tells me he heard some niggas around here bragging about shooting up some cop's

373

crib. Maybe it was some niggas from the Westhaven set trippin' because they're not making any money. My casino in Raleigh is boomin', and the club out here has been rackin' in that bread, too. Paris doesn't think I know, but her dancers have been helping get my product recognition. That's probably bringing some heat our way, too."

"Haters gon' hate," I said, smacking on my juicy BBQ sandwich.

"My crew handled that Tasha problem." Hendrix watched me immediately stop eating, closing my tray.

"Is that the way you handle everything?" I whispered loudly. "A bullet is not always the fuckin' answer!"

Hendrix shook his head at me. "But how else was this shit gonna stop?"

I shook my head back. "Snap is not going to rest until he finds out who keeps taking his family out! If he gets rid of both you and Paris, what happens to all this money? Y'all don't have any children. I'm sure that's what that family will say!"

Hendrix knew I was right, but he wouldn't admit it.

"Paris got the fuck out of town for a few days. You should've taken your ass, too," I told him.

"You think I'm going to start running from muthafuckas now after not running for twenty-five years? Yeah, okay," Hendrix huffed. "Got me fucked up."

"You're in a grumpy mood today." I scoffed. "You miss 'shawty'?"

Hendrix looked at me. "I miss *you*. What you doing for Christmas?"

I laughed out loud. "Not spending it with you. Call your wife, tell her you're coming to Maryland."

"She's not talking to me right now. Not really sure what I did, but she's not answering my calls." Hendrix frowned, more like pouted. Never knew it was in him to actually miss someone until I saw the look on his face when he mentioned Paris ignoring his calls.

"Niggas never miss a good thing until it's gone, huh?" I laughed off my hurt feelings. "She's probably upset about the wedding being set off. Neeta says you moved it until April, said she got a text from Paris about it a few days ago. Why did you put it off?"

"Just in case muthafuckas decided to get even at the altar," Hendrix snarled. "I was trying to protect her, but she wouldn't see that."

"That girl wants to see that you care about her. She thinks you're always leaving her out of shit. Include her in something besides what only benefits you." I sat up a little more in the bed. "If you want to fix things with Paris, you're going to have to try harder. She wants a baby. I think I want to help y'all have one."

Hendrix looked at me. "You'd do that for me?"

I rolled my eyes. "I'm doing it for *her.* Call it guilt or whatever you want. But after all the damage I've caused, she deserves that much. Text her, tell her that. I'm sure she'd text you right back."

Hendrix thought to himself for a moment before taking his phone out of his pocket to text her. He exhaled deeply before pressing send. Sure enough, seconds later, his phone chimed. His eyes lit up, but he didn't smile.

"What did she say?" I really didn't want to know but asked anyway.

Hendrix grinned a little. "I texted her that I'm ready to give surrogacy a try. She texted back, *When?* First time shawty texted a nigga back in three days."

I faked a smile. "See? What did I tell you?"

Hendrix looked at me. "We'll start whatever it is we need to start. We'll find the right doctors. We'll start as soon as shawty comes back. Send me your bills when they come in. All costs on us. We'll pay you for this." He watched me shake my head.

"No, no, this one's on me. Consider it a wedding gift." I laughed nervously. Now all I had to find was a doctor willing to forge paperwork for me. I had to figure out a way to hide the fact that I was already having his baby.

IT WAS CHRISTMAS EVE WHEN I WAS FINALLY RELEASED FROM the hospital. I had to call Neeta to come and get me. She thought it was best that I stay with her, given the circumstances. Though I was in pain, I was pretty antsy. I needed to stop by Starbucks and get some of that white chocolate mocha crack they served. We went inside and sat down at our usual chair in the corner. That Starbucks was the only one I'd been in with a black manager who played '90s and early 2000s music. My girls and I were lit every time we went in that muthafucka.

"And if you want it, we can do it in the Black 500 with the top down. In overdrive when we ride, 'cuz I'm hot now. You got me goin', I don't think I wanna stop now. Z feenin' like a criminal on lockdown. So let's get a way the ghetto way. You gettin' hot, baby, please don't melt away. I got a crib on the beach Palmetto-way. And here's your personal key to see me every day. 112," I rapped Lil Zane's verse on 112's "Anywhere" track.

"Aye! She lit!" Neeta hyped me up as usual.

I laughed out loud, holding my side, a few people around us trying to hype me up, too. "Y'all wild!"

"You and that partner of yours always rappin' or singing. Y'all need to do some TikTok or YouTube videos." Neeta watched me roll my eyes.

I smacked my lips. "Girl, Zac cannot stand my black ass. He'd never get in the studio with me. Paris been trying to get us to perform together at the club for years. We've been frienemies since we were kids. Kind of like you and Paris."

Neeta rolled her big pretty eyes at the thought of her relationship with Paris. "Would've never thought we grew up together or lived in the same household by the way we go at it. And by the looks of things, *ex*-maid of honor, you don't seem like you like the hoe too much either, shit."

I looked at her, taking a long gulp from my hot white chocolate mocha. "I didn't mean for things to go the way they did with Hendrix. Shit, he kept pushing me."

Neeta looked at her double crunch chocolate brownie. "It's almost like these got damn brownies. I know I don't need these bitches, but shit! They keep callin' my name!"

I giggled a little. "These muthafuckas are good though."

"But I know better. I'm supposed to be trying to lose weight so I can fit in this fuckin' wedding dress. Luckily, she moved the wedding until April. That's enough time to lose weight. By the time I slim down, you're ass gonna fluff the fuck up." Neeta chuckled mischievously to herself.

I glared at her, watching her giggling with that damn grin on her face like the Grinch had when we just knew he was about to fuck up Christmas. "I don't see shit funny." That made her laugh even harder.

"Paris is going to blow that police station up looking for you if she finds out about this! You better figure out a way to fake this surrogacy." Neeta looked over my shoulder. "Oh, there goes Doctor G."

I looked back over my shoulder to see that fine Asian doctor walk into Starbucks looking like a fashion model, dressed in everything Givenchy. Gray from his jacket to his dress shoes. Dark shades covered his eyes as he came into the building removing his scarf.

"It's not even that cold for no damn scarf." Neeta rolled her eyes, chomping on her brownie.

"I'm going to go over and say hi..." I let her know. As soon as the cashier handed Gio his coffee and he headed over to a high-top bistro table to sit down, I made my way over to him.

"Hello, Doctor." I cleared my throat when I approached him.

The doctor grinned a little as he took out his laptop from his laptop case and placed it on the table. "Miss Banks? How are you feeling?" He frowned at me in confusion as he removed his shades. "I thought I told you to get some rest for a few days? I specifically said bed rest for the next three days and not to return to work until Monday."

"I know, but I have some last-minute Christmas shopping to do." I cleared my throat again nervously. I stood there getting my thoughts together.

Gio looked up at me, waiting for me to speak up and say what I'd walked over to say. "Have a seat." He signaled for me to sit down in the seat across from him. "I'm sitting here trying to help my mom order these products for her nail shop and spa. She's opening up a shop on New Year's Day over there on Berkeley. She's naming it Gio's, after her handsome son."

I looked at Gio, watching a grin form on his face. He was trying to make me feel comfortable, and I appreciated that. I needed to just come out and say what I wanted. "I don't want this baby."

Gio nodded. "Okay, you have plenty of options. Terminate the pregnancy or adoption. These days, you don't even have to bring the baby home from the hospital."

"Damn," I said out loud at his insensitivity.

Gio shook his head, realizing I took his statement as cold. "I mean, you have choices, and you shouldn't feel guilty about them."

"My best friend is getting married in a few months. She's having trouble conceiving because of a sexual assault at a young age. She really wants a baby," I told him, watching him nod his head.

"Okay. You want to let her adopt your baby?" He thought he understood.

I hesitated. "I want to be her surrogate."

Gio frowned in confusion. "Wait, what? But you're preg—" It dawned on him. "You want me to help you commit fraud?"

"Well, when you say it like that..." I scoffed.

"What else would you call it?" Gio sipped from his coffee.

"Helping myself by helping my friend," I told him. "I'm pregnant by someone who has enough going on. He won't be able to be in my baby's life. The baby deserves a two-parent household. My friend can give him or her that and more. I'm a cop. When will I get to spend time with this fatherless baby? I don't want her to adopt the baby. I want the baby to be hers."

The doctor looked into my face, thinking to himself for a second. "What if something goes wrong? What if the baby needs a blood transfusion later on in the future and she finds out she or the baby's father isn't a match?"

Shit, the father will be a match, I thought, wanting to say it out loud, but I caught myself.

"We will cross that bridge when we get there," I told him, watching him laughing to himself.

"*We?*" he scoffed. "I speak Korean, not French. What makes you think I would do something that could cause me to lose my license if they find out I helped you forge paperwork or fake a procedure? Your friend will have to go through extensive fertility treatments for nothing. Have you ever had a baby before, or is this your first rodeo?"

I hesitated. "Well, I had a stillborn when I was sixteen."

Gio looked at me. "We will have to put your friend through expensive and extensive treatments for nothing to retrieve multiple eggs for nothing, Officer Banks," he repeated to me. "The male has the easy part as long as his semen contains sperm."

"You sound like you've done this personally." I watched the frustrated wrinkle in his forehead.

"My mother is Doctor Sun Toa-Chang, founder of UNC Fertility. I used to work at her clinic." Gio watched my eyes light up. He shook his head. "This is unethical."

"They raped her with a rusty hanger." I had to let him know Paris's story. "She's lucky she still has her uterus and one of her ovaries. She has scarring in her uterus and scar tissue lining her fallopian tubes. I just want her to have my baby... please."

Gio looked at me sternly as soon as I mentioned the rape. "What did you say your friend's name was?"

"I didn't say. Paris Avery," I told him.

"The foster child who lost her foster parents in a fire about six year back?" Gio stated, watching me nod. He frowned for a minute, leaning back in his seat. "You have to be really desperate to fake a surrogacy," he finally said after a few seconds.

I sighed heavily. "I am..."

"Okay," Gio agreed.

My heart thumped in my chest. "*Okay* as in you'll help me?"

Gio nodded. "Yes, I'll help you." He reached in his coat pocket to pull out a business card. "Have your friend contact me for a consultation so we can get started."

"All the money that she pays for her invitro needs to be billed to *me*, not her, please," I asked of him.

Gio nodded.

I looked at him, a weird feeling taking over me. "Wait, why the change of heart?"

"Your child deserves a good home, no matter the circumstances. This will cost you though," Gio let me know.

"Yeah, I know, I just told you to bill me not her." I looked his face over.

"You're asking me to forge billing, fake an egg transfer, take up time at my mother's clinic that she could use for her own honest patients, risk my career all because of something you're not telling me. You're already three months pregnant, which means not only am I lying about the fact that you're already pregnant, but I'll have to lie to the woman and her husband-to-be about how far along you are. I'll have to sit the three of you down to have a consultation to discuss the procedure. I'm risking everything for you, a woman I only met a little over a week ago." Gio took a few long sips from his coffee.

"I'm risking my life and my career as well, Doctor. I will pay you whatever I have to. Name your price," I told him.

"Let me take you out to dinner," Gio said randomly.

I laughed out loud. "What?"

"You're making demands; why can't I make some, too?" Gio scoffed.

I looked at his hands, noticing he wasn't wearing a ring. "Why would I go out with you?"

"I need to know more about you. The shit you're asking me to do is something I'd only do for someone who I could trust not to blackmail me in the end if things don't go the way you want." Gio was straight up with me. "I need to make sure you're trustworthy, so I need to get to know more about you. What better way than over dinner? Tonight at eight?"

"I thought you said I needed to be on bed rest?" I hesitated.

"We'll be meeting at your place. I'll cook for you." Gio grinned. "So it's a date then?"

I didn't even know how to respond, except to say, "My house was shot up, remember?"

Gio exhaled rigidly, sorry that he forgot that quick how that bullet got in my side. "Yes, I forgot. Well, check into a room at TownePlace Suites." Gio reached into his pocket, pulling out his leather wallet. He took out three crisp hundred bills and placed them on the table.

I looked down at the money before looking back at him.

Gio's cell phone rang. He picked his phone up from off of the table, looking at the display. He looked back up at me, watching the stuck expression on my face. "You have my cell number on that card I just gave you, Officer. Text me the room number. I'll bring some food. I'll be there at eight. Get some rest." He grabbed his things and winked at me before walking out of the building.

Neeta hurried over to the table where I sat. "Girl, what did Doctor Fine as Fuck say? Did you really just ask the nigga to fake a surrogacy for you?"

I looked at her, still in shock. "He's coming over tonight for dinner."

"Aye!" Neeta twerked a little. "Wrap your legs round that

nigga. Make him give your ass a child!" she said in her Cardi B voice.

I rolled my eyes. "There you go. Thinking about fuckin' in a time like this."

Neeta shrugged. "He's got something up his sleeve. Better watch him. There's a reason he agreed to do this."

I'd find out soon enough. We all would. But in the meantime...

🕮

"WHATEVER YOU WANT FROM ME, I'M GIVING YOU everything. I'm your baby tonight. You've given me ecstasy. You are my fantasy. I'm your baby tonight," I sang along with Whitney playing over my Bluetooth speakers that night at the hotel. I had to distract myself with music. I was nervous out of my mind. I never went on dates, as you could see, and my situation was obviously different than most. What did the doctor want with me? He wanted something. Sure, he was right about the trust situation. I was sure he wanted the dirt on me because I was about to have dirt on him. And I couldn't even blame him.

I stood by the window, watching the police cars that sat outside of the hotel. Shit was crazy out in the streets for months but had gotten worse over the past few weeks because of the shit that was going on with Hendrix's crew and Snap. Snap was seeking revenge on his family members, but I could tell he was being smart about it. Looked as though he was sitting back watching everyone kill each other.

Paris finally texted me that night to wish me happy Christmas Eve. As kids, we would stay up really late to see if we saw Santa's fat ass come down that chimney. He never came, and he damn sure never brought us anything. When we graduated high school and made a name for ourselves, we made sure our Christmas trees were surrounded by presents. Most of the presents under my tree were for her, and most of the presents under her tree were for me. Somewhere along the way, our friendship changed. I found myself pulling away from her, not even realizing that she needed me. I never took the time to go to any of her support group meetings with her, even when she asked me to. I let my jealousy of her relationship with Hendrix stop me from being there for her. I never stopped to see how troubled their relationship was, even after the first time I had sex with Hendrix. All he told me was that she didn't touch him the way I did, but he never explained why. How could he be so selfish? Shit, how could *I* be so selfish?

My heart rumbled in my chest as I heard the doorknob to the room click before slowly turning. I sat up on my couch as Gio walked into the room, holding a bag of groceries. He was dressed in a black toboggan, black Nike sweatshirt, black sweats, and black and gray Air Maxes. I knew he had tattoos. His neck was tatted. I could tell his arms were tatted at least up his forearms because the bag he was holding in his arms lifted his shirt sleeve enough for me to get a glimpse of his forearms. I stood from the couch in my gray tank top and matching gray joggers.

Gio grinned at me before walking over to the kitchenette to place the bags on the bar countertop. "This is nice." He admired the room, placing his keys alongside the bag. "How are you? Did you get some rest today?"

I hesitated to nod before shaking my head. "Somewhat," I admitted. "Called the station to let them know I'm coming back Monday. I already know they're about to place me on desk duty. I don't think Paris is coming back in town until after New Year. When are we going to start IVF treatments? And once treatments are started, I know we have to wait a few weeks before telling her that you implanted the embryos. I think I want to get this done the first week in January. That way I'll be pregnant before Valentine's Day. My unit will know that I'm pregnant by then, and I can get out of that fuckin' Valentine's Day dance at work. Shit's corny as hell watching Captain think he's cool because he's playing hip-hop songs from the '90s. That muthafucka just started listening to Tupac. I can't tell you how many times a day he plays 'California Love' down at the station. Okay, so I know that you're going to have to fake implanting the embryo inside of me. I know Paris enough to know that she'll want to go with me. Will it hurt really—"

"Whoa!" Gio laughed out loud. "Someone's nervous to be in my presence. Relax. Take a few breaths. Regroup. It's cool."

I exhaled deeply watching him unpack the bag. "I *am* nervous. I don't know you. How do I know you're not sick? You could be some deranged lunatic."

"Come on, toots. My name is the Prince. Besides would a lunatic have a Porsche like this?" Gio continued the lyrics to Will Smith's "Parents Just Don't Understand".

"Okay, Doctor." I grinned a little. "What you know about that '90s shit?"

"Apparently just as much as you." Gio scoffed. "We're about the same age. That song is before your time, too."

"Nineties music is where it's at," I told him.

Gio nodded. "Facts."

Gio seemed a lot more laidback that he was earlier. He wasn't a doctor at that point. He was just trying to relax. Forget whatever he was going through for a while.

"I must admit, I'm not a fan of cops. Haven't met one who isn't dirty," Gio remarked. "They always have a motive, yet they have the nerve to interrogate criminals. Gangs on the streets have nothing on the boys in blue. Girls, too, may I add."

"Are you here to judge me?" I walked over to where he stood in the kitchen.

Gio nodded. "A little. When I pulled out my wallet earlier and you saw all those hundreds—don't act like you didn't see them—what were you thinking? Most women would be like, 'ooohhh, this man has money!' You were probably thinking, 'if I wasn't a cop, I'd rob this muthafucka.' Now am I right?"

I rolled my eyes, resenting the fact that he was right. "What's your point?"

Gio grinned a little. "I just want to understand why you're trying to play someone you're saying is your friend. You're doing this for you, not her. Honesty will get you everywhere with me. It's going to be a long night if you think you're going to beat around the bush with me."

I watched him remove food from the bags. I expected him to have food already prepared that he bought from a restaurant, but no, he had fresh meat, fresh vegetables, rice, noodles, fresh fruit, spices, oil, even a wok to cook everything in. I couldn't get over his total transformation from his work environment to the street environment. I watched as he walked over to the sink with the food, rolled up his sleeves, and started washing the food off.

"I made a mistake," I admitted.

"Mmm-hmm..." Gio commented, washing the vegetables before grabbing a bowl from one of the cabinets to put them in.

"Paris's fiancé... is my baby's father," I admitted.

Gio paused for a minute before moving on to wash the vegetables. "That explains everything. It all makes sense now. Do you love him?"

"Not enough to fuck up a friendship with my foster sister." I watched Gio chuckle to himself.

"Your sister? This situation is the very reason my mother said trust no one." Gio shook his head to himself. "You might think this will fix things, but I assure you that little breadcrumbs are going to lead your friend—I'm sorry, I mean your sister—straight to you and her husband."

"Are you going to help me or not?" I asked him.

"Yes, under one condition: you help me find my mother's birth parents." Gio started washing the fruit.

I nodded walking over to him. "Well, I'll be on desk duty these next nine months, so why not, right? What does she know about them?"

Gio shrugged. "Only that her birth mother left her on a doorstep forty years ago. I figured that you're familiar with the foster care system. As a cop, you have more avenues of finding out information than the average person."

"I'll help in any way that I can. I admire people brave enough to find out who their parents are after their parents abandoned them. I haven't seen my birth mother since I was around four or five, don't remember her face and don't want to remember her either. What kind of mother leaves her daughter?" I asked.

Gio looked at me, tossing the fruit in a clean bowl before pulling out a pack of rib eye steak. "The kind of mother who might have had no other choice. My mother's parents were probably poor immigrants, probably running from immigration. Maybe before her mother was caught, she might have had no choice but to leave her. They probably would've been separated anyway. You know immigration doesn't give a fuck about families. My mom just wants closure. She's Korean and knows absolutely no Korean. You should see how her own people look at her. I had to curse out a few of her employees from her shop who were talking about her.

"My mother put me in classes to learn Korean from birth so I could translate for her. She made sacrifices in her life so I wouldn't have to. She worked three jobs to put me in private school, staying on my ass so I made straight A's. She worked three jobs and went to school full time and then onto medical school. She's a successful doctor, despite her painful past. She taught me that if you come from less, you're gonna have to do more. She's a cervical cancer survivor, which was her motivation for the IVF hospital she founded. She wanted more children but couldn't have them. She wanted to help other women have children by any means."

I watched Gio gently clean the steak before grabbing a cutting board from the drawer. "Do you know who your father is?"

Gio frowned a little. "If that's what you want to call him. I met him when I was about thirteen. That was the first and last time that I saw him. I stay in touch with my uncle from time to time. You're going to love this food, I promise you."

I looked back at the ingredients on the countertop. I noticed there was baking soda sitting on the countertop. "Baking soda? We cookin' crack, my dude?"

Gio chuckled. "The baking soda is going to aid in tenderizing the meat. It's going to melt in your mouth, I promise you. I'm making Korean beef stir fry. I brought the steak, onions, carrots, green onions, sesame seeds, baking soda, cornstarch, gochujang, which is like Korean barbeque sauce, sesame oil, vegetable oil, soy sauce, and beef broth. I left out oyster sauce and garlic, might not be good for the baby."

"Well, I'm sure it'll be good. No one's ever cooked for me before." I sighed. "Even though this is a bribe, I appreciate it."

"A bribe?" He resented that statement. "I'm helping you and you're helping me. I don't see nothing shady about that. I work eighty hours a week at the hospital. I have to leave my phone on all day, every day. I'm always on call, like they don't have three hundred doctors working at that fuckin' hospital. Speaking of hospital, go grab a blanket or something. Prop your feet up and relax on the couch while I make dinner. You're on bed rest, remember?"

I wasn't going to lie, I damn near ate every drop of food he made, down to the soy sauce that covered the plate. After eating that stir fry, he served me sweet Korean watermelon punch. If he hadn't have been there, I would've licked the plate it was so good. "Damn, Gio, I swear you just made love to my mouth with that food." I sighed, looking at my empty plate, then over on the countertop at the Tupperware that contained the food.

"Do you want another plate?" Gio started to get up from the couch, but I grabbed his arm.

I shook my head. "No, I'll save some for tomorrow. Thank you. I'm sure you have to get home to your girlfriend or wife. I won't keep you long."

Gio made a face. "I don't have either of those, Officer. I had a fiancée once."

"Yeah? What happened?" I asked.

"She was fuckin' my best man." Gio laughed to himself.

I exhaled deeply, feeling real low at that point. "Wow."

"Again, I work eighty hours a week, sometimes more. I don't have the time for a relationship, even though I'd like one. It would take someone whose work ethic is like mine to handle me. Now I don't know what made you deal with your sister's husband to be or what made him deal with you, but time, commitment, communication, loyalty, all that plays a part. She said I was married to my job, and she was right. What made you do what you did?" Gio wanted to know.

I sunk back in the sofa. "Just needed some love I guess."

"Love that belonged to someone else?" Gio questioned, holding his plate.

I rolled my eyes at Gio. "Well, obviously, if he's coming to me for affection, he can't love her too much."

Gio shook his head. "You just said why he came to you—for affection. Affection is hard for someone to give who's been through what you said your friend went through. Instead of taking the time to talk her through her pain, he took the easy way out and had sex with you. Shit, she's not getting from him what she needs either—understanding and compassion. I wouldn't be surprised if she's looking for what she can't get out of him from someone else, too."

I laughed out loud. "That girl loves that boy. She won't even look at anyone else."

"Everyone has their breaking point eventually. Just like her fiancé broke, she's going to break, too." Gio took my empty plate from the couch, then got up to go over to the sink to wash the dishes.

I'd never had someone I could talk to that spoke wisdom into me. He wasn't being judgmental, just truthful. It hurt a little bit, but I needed to hear it. "So," I got up from the couch, "what do you like to do for fun? I mean other than work eighty hours a week." I got up from the sofa and walked over to him at the sink.

Gio glanced at me before continuing to wash the dishes. "If I'm not at work, I'm either at the gym or at Raw."

"That sports bar?" I questioned, watching him nod.

"Yeah, I go there to play pool with some of my college mates. You should join me sometime, Officer. You know, once you get yourself situated." Gio finished up washing the dishes, drying each dish and utensil off before sitting them in the dryer rack. His phone chimed in his pocket. Gio exhaled in frustration. "See what I mean? What these bitches want from a Blasian?"

I giggled a little, watching him grab his phone out of his pocket to peep the display.

Gio looked at me as he put his phone back in his pocket. "Well, you have enough for lunch and dinner tomorrow."

I walked Gio to the door, grabbing his arm as he pulled the door open. He turned to me, and I gave him a hug. He hesitated to hug me back, looking at me like he didn't hug very often.

"Thanks for the food, Doctor. I have your card. I'll be calling you soon as Paris comes back in town." I barely got the last few words out when I spotted Hendrix walking past my room.

Hendrix did a double take, stopping in his tracks at the sight of Gio coming out of my room door. "Dafuq?" He didn't even bother to think to himself. He said that shit loud and clear in Gio's face.

Gio had to be a few inches shorter than Hendrix, yet he was looking down at Hendrix like he was beneath him. I quickly stood in between the two, pressing against Hendrix's chest to create space between the two.

"Hendrix, meet Gio Chang, the doctor who is going to be performing the IVF treatments on Paris. Doctor Gio Chang, this is Hendrix, Paris's fiancé." I tried to shine some light on the situation.

Hendrix wasn't trying to hear it. "What kind of doctor meets his patients at a hotel room?"

"The kind who has to clean up your mess," Gio let him know.

"What was that, my nigga?" Hendrix snarled.

"He said that he's the kind who makes house calls when his patient is on bedrest. I know you see the police outside. I can't go anywhere without an escort," I reminded Hendrix.

"When your sister gets back in town, Officer Banks, you know where to find me." Gio gave Hendrix a dirty look before walking away from the both of us.

Hendrix stared in the direction Gio was walking until he was out of our sight. "I know that nigga from somewhere."

I rolled my eyes. "From the hospital. He was my doctor."

Hendrix shook his head. "Nah, I never forget a face."

"Well, he didn't go to school with us. He went to private school," I told Hendrix.

Hendrix turned to me. "Dafuq was he doing to you in that room?"

"The same thing you're about to do to me—absolutely nothing." I shook my head at Hendrix. "What the fuck are *you* doing here?"

"Meeting up with the lawyer for a potential third partner for the casino. Snap is trying to get his hands back on that casino, and I'm not going for it. He thinks he's going to shut us down. I'm partnering up with a partner whose brother is head of the planning and development department in Raleigh." Hendrix looked my face over.

"Planning and development department? Hold up. These muthafuckas sound like Kace's relatives." I shook my head. "Have you talked to Kace about this?"

"Man, if Kace wants to stay in business, this is our best option." Hendrix watched the skeptical expression form on my face.

"Which brother do you have working with Kace?" I hesitated to ask.

"Carter." Hendrix watched me throw my hands up in frustration.

"Kace can't stand that muthafucka! You're supposed to know that. You're his homeboy, nigga. If you ask me, I think the muthafucka was sleeping with Karen. You're crazy for doing this to him," I told Hendrix's stubborn ass.

"Snap won't fuck with that family as long as those two are involved. Mr. Gwinnett fucks with those two heavy." Hendrix frowned. "We gotta make some changes to stay afloat, including cutting some shipments. I'm about to meet with a new supplier in a few. Snap got niggas stealing from me and shit. Why the fuck would I continue to use the supplier who supplies him, too?"

"A new supplier would mean you'd be working with muthafuckas who work for that new supplier. Working that new supplier's territories. Hendrix, what are you doing and why? You act like you don't fuck with Kace anymore." I looked up into his face, trying to read his facial expressions.

"One of our crew members got arrested. Turns out, the gun he had on him was connected to three murders that happened three years ago. Murders that *I* committed." Hendrix frowned.

I shrugged. "So?"

"So?" Hendrix tensed up a little bit like he wanted to push me, but he didn't. "So... Kace is the one who gets rid of our guns, nigga, after there's bodies on them! He's doing shady, sloppy shit. There's no telling what type of other fuck shit this nigga is doing. If he got rid of the gun, then how did my nigga end up with it?"

I sighed heavily. "Evidently, you must've gave Kace the wrong gun to get rid of. Who supplies your crew with weapons?"

"Kace has a supplier, so he says," Hendrix snarled.

"Y'all need to talk this out before you go doing some stupid shit," I tried telling him.

"I tried calling him, but he won't answer or text a nigga back. His shit on DND. If I'm stuck here to handle business by myself, then I'm going to make business decisions on my own. Including business with you. First line of business, get rid of that doctor. Something doesn't sit right with me about that nigga either." Hendrix looking me over.

I huffed, folding my arms. "We are getting a great deal on this IVF treatment. Whatever you got going on at home is affecting how you're starting to handle shit in the streets. Me and Kace have had y'all's backs from day one. Kace wouldn't do anything to hurt either of you."

Hendrix wasn't trying to hear me as normal. I was sure he was off to do some fuck shit as soon as he left my room. He stood there, looking at me like he wanted to ask me something but knew I was about to curse him out for asking.

"What, Hendrix?" I huffed.

"I found out through one of my homeboys that Paris called him asking him to do her a favor the night that you were shot." Hendrix let me know.

I looked at him. "A favor?"

"What did you say to her the night of our rehearsal dinner?" Hendrix questioned me.

"Only that I was stepping down from being her maid of honor. She looked upset, then looked my outfit over like she'd seen it before," I told him.

"Where did you say you got the outfit from again?" Hendrix asked.

"You, fool." I rolled my eyes. "You left it for me at the police station that night."

Hendrix made a face like he didn't get me shit. "You think I'd get you a present to wear to my rehearsal dinner? Shawty stays going through my phone, man. She probably saw the outfit saved in one of my shopping carts. I'm sure she thought it was for her and was surprised to see *your* ass in the outfit."

I laughed in denial. "You think Paris tried to have niggas shoot my house up over a dress? A little girl is dead over a fuckin' dress? Who else had access to your phone? Who did you tell you were thinking of getting this dress? Who does your shopping for you or helps you buy gifts for your girl?"

Hendrix's nostrils flared. "Kace. See? Fuck shit."

I grabbed his hand before he went to do something completely irrational. "Come on, Hendrix. Kace isn't the only muthafucka who can hack into someone's shit. The types of muthafuckas who come to that casino could've got your ass. They can walk by you and scan all your account information off of your phone."

"You always look for the good in people where there is no good, sweetheart," Hendrix remarked.

"They're our friends," I reminded him.

"Yeah, until they're not." Hendrix scoffed. "It's Christmas Eve. I was going to check on moms and stop by my sister's, but that shit is depressing."

"I'm sure your little sis needs her brother," I reminded him.

"I sent her money for her rent, lights, and car note. She's good. I'd rather be with you. I don't want to be alone." Hendrix tried reaching for my hand, but I pushed it away.

"Hendrix, we talked about this. You think your wife-to-be had niggas shoot my shit up, yet you're still willing to risk my life?" I laughed out loud. "Who's the one who's really not my friend?"

Hendrix was about to clean up his statement.

"Go," I demanded."

"Merci, baby—"

"Go!" I yelled, shoving him in his chest before slamming the door on him.

I leaned back against the door, covering my face, side aching. Everyone knew I was crazy over Hendrix. If she thought he bought me that shit, yes, she'd lose her mind. I was bold to wear that shit to her rehearsal. Yeah, that was really on me. But what was up with Kace? Why the fuck would he want me and Paris to think Hendrix bought me an outfit?

I SPENT MY CHRISTMAS WITH NEETA AND HER BAD ASS KIDS.
Watched them running around and Neeta struggling not to pull
her hair out was pretty amusing. Her last foster mother, Miss
Baker, was really good to Neeta and loved her, despite the rebel-
lious side she was introduced to when she first took Neeta in.
Miss Baker came by with her kids to help bring in the holidays.
She even helped change the dressing on my wound. Love on the
holidays was what we all wanted and rarely ever received. That
was why Neeta had all those kids. She was looking for love, and
she knew her babies would love her no matter what.

I stayed with Neeta until New Year's Eve while the holes in my
house were being prepared. I didn't want to go back home until I
got to the bottom of what happened to me. I wasn't going to believe
Paris would try to take me out until I heard it from her mouth. In
the meantime, I was preparing my heart and mind for our consultation with Gio. Paris came in from Maryland that morning, bright
and early. She hugged Neeta and I like she hadn't seen us in months.
I'd never seen Paris's stuck-up ass so happy and bubbly. Neeta and I
were confused as fuck. That night, the whole crew went to Paris's
club to celebrate. She often closed her club the night of New Year's
Eve because her club almost always got *too* lit. So we got used to celebrating the new year on New Year's night. Hendrix, Paris, Neeta,
and the bridal party were all in attention. The only one not present
who was expected to be with us was Kace. He never missed a night
out. I tried calling my partner, but it went straight to voicemail.

The following Monday was the day of reckoning. We met up
at Gio's mother's clinic. Hendrix, Paris, and I sat nervously on a
sofa across from Gio's desk. Honestly, they looked more anxious
than nervous. I was the one nervous. Gio played it cool, putting
on his professional persona, the way he did me when he first
met. He explained the procedure to us while Hendrix sat looking
at Gio like he was an enemy who he needed to study. Gio asked

questions about family history. Of course, Hendrix knew more of his health history background than either myself or Paris did. All we knew was the obvious. We were Black and in pretty good health. Gio mentioned the fact that my abdominal area needed to heal before we started the procedure, but I insisted that the show go on.

"A technique known as 'in vitro fertilization', or IVF for short, makes it possible to gather eggs from the mother, fertilize them with sperm from the father, and place the embryo into the uterus of the surrogate," Gio explained, nodding toward me when he referenced surrogate. "Officer Banks will carry the baby until birth. She and the baby don't have any genetic ties because neither her egg nor eggs were the ones that were used. Though Officer Banks is called the birth mother because she is the one who is giving birth, Ms. Avery is the biological mother because it was her eggs that were fertilized. Gestational surrogacy is legally less complex in the US because both intended parents have genetic ties to the baby." Gio glanced at me, then back at Paris and Hendrix.

Hendrix frowned a little, thinking to himself before saying, "Yo, Paris already started signing her name as Hughes. How the fuck did you know her last name was Avery?"

Gio tried to remain professional, though I could tell by the way that he clenched his fists that Hendrix had one more time. Gio shifted through the paperwork on his desk before looking back up at Hendrix. "We do extensive background checks on our clients. As soon as Paris called me Saturday evening and gave me the information to proceed, I conducted the background check on every party involved. Ms. *Hughes* emailed me shot records for the two of you, and I was already given permission to go into Officer Banks's shot records. So, as I was saying, we need to sign the legal documents to proceed. The documents are basically saying that Officer Banks is only carrying a child that genetically belongs to the two of you, and once giving birth, the child is handed over to the two of you. Any questions before the documents are signed?"

Paris raised her hand to speak. "Ummm... my body has been through a lot. Will this hurt?"

Gio glanced at me, then shook his head at Paris. "The procedure is rather painless for the both of you. You will be given medication so that you'll develop more eggs. We will retrieve the eggs. The eggs are then fertilized with your husband's sperm in a lab, where it'll take about three to five days to develop into an embryo. That special culture medium will then be placed inside of Officer Banks, who will also start fertility treatments that she will continue to get throughout her pregnancy. It'll take about six weeks to confirm pregnancy after the implantation. At that point, a heartbeat will confirm pregnancy."

I watched Paris look up at Hendrix hopefully.

Paris looked back at the doctor, tears in her eyes. "How soon can we start? My period started today."

"Perfect. I can clear my schedule for the rest of the day, get my patients to reschedule, and we can start the treatments this afternoon." Gio smiled at Paris.

Hendrix looked like he was trying to be happy, but I knew he didn't trust Gio. I wasn't sure if it was because he thought something was going on between us or if it was just his instincts about knowing Gio from somewhere. Regardless of his feelings about Gio, he allowed his wife to go through the process.

After a few weeks of fertility treatments, Paris's eggs were extracted. Gio and I pretty much avoided one another throughout the process in order not to leave a string of contact between us. I had questions, but he seemed to have everything handled, down to the way that he was going to play off the implantation.

"Is Paris okay?" I asked that day of January twenty-seventh, a few days after the eggs were fertilized in a lab. Gio perfectly calculated everything to make sure he played off our situation perfectly. I was laid back on a hospital bed, legs cocked in the air, feet in stirrups. A window behind my head allowed Paris, Hendrix and a nurse to watch the procedure.

"Paris is fine. She's cramping a little from the procedure we did last week, but she's fine. Hopefully Hendrix is comforting her. The muthafucka came into the clinic the day of her extraction with a cup we gave him the night before, talking about he had to jack himself off because Paris wouldn't help him." Gio scoffed, throwing a blanket over my legs before pulling up a stool, grabbing a table, which had the supplies similar to a pap smear, other than the long thin catheter, which had a syringe containing the embryos attached to the end of it.

I exhaled deeply, watching Gio grab the speculum. "Are they watching?"

"Yup," Gio answered. "But they can't see what I'm doing under this blanket. How have you been feeling? The tests I did on you prove you're about eleven weeks pregnant. Almost at your end trimester. Have you been taking the prenatal vitamins I prescribed you?" Gio asked.

I nodded. "Yessir."

"Good..." I felt his fingers spreading my pussy lips apart as he pretended to insert the speculum.

"Can I be unprofessional now?" Gio asked.

"Yes..." I hesitated to say.

"You get Brazilian waxes, don't you?" Gio asked.

"Yes... The girl who does them is amazing. She even does scrubs and steams. I love it," I answered.

"She looks nice..." Gio told me.

"She?" I laughed nervously, pussy starting to throb.

"The pussy," he told me. "If they weren't standing behind that window, I'd eat this juicy muthafucka." The sound of him removing one of his gloves underneath the blanket damn near caused me to stop breathing.

Oh my goodness. He about made me pee on his ass. I wasn't ready for that to come out of his mouth, but what I really wasn't prepared for was his fingers to slip inside of my pussy. He started with one. When he noticed that I was biting my lip, he inserted the other. I gasped. "Doctor..." I moaned.

"That's the speculum going in you, Officer." Gio tried convincing me that I didn't know the difference between plastic and someone's fingers. "I'm about to insert the catheter. Relax and look at the ceiling," Gio demanded, grabbing the catheter with the syringe from the table. "You will be coming to me and only me for your pelvic exams and checkups, do you hear me? We are going to have to play with the delivery date. Maybe around your real due date, tell them you need to deliver early because of complications. Agree?"

I gripped the bed, legs trembling as he started to dig his fingers inside of me seductively.

As Gio pretended to insert the catheter inside of me, he started to massage my clit. "Breathe in, Merci," he growled. "Breathe out..." His fingers make a *come here, girl* motion inside of me. I loved how he started off slowly and didn't dig into the pussy like he was trying to unclog her.

I inhaled as much air as my hormones would allow me to before exhaling. The air rattled through my lungs as I tried my best not to moan and scream out loud in ecstasy. "Doctor, what are you doing?" I whispered through my attempts not to moan.

"Feeling your insides, wondering what it was that made this muthafucka do Paris so wrong after what she's been through." Gio dug his fingers a little deeper. "Your pussy smells and feels like a wet peach. Do you know how busy my work schedule keeps me? I haven't felt any pussy in months. This is what I'm missing out on? I hope you don't mind while I feel my way around, get familiar with you. You've been avoiding me."

"Y-You've been avoiding me, too." I gripped the sheets as my pussy gripped his fingers.

"I asked you to go out to dinner with me several times. I know you're out and about. Your wound is healing faster than expected. As long as you're not heavy lifting and are confined to your desk at work, you should be fine. If you were my woman, you'd be at home resting. If you were really Hendrix's side piece, he'd take care of you like he's supposed to. He hasn't noticed your eating habits? He hasn't noticed the way your beige skin has been glowing or even the fact that your dark curly hair has grown over just this past month?" Gio talked to me as if he wasn't about to bring me to orgasm.

"I try staying away from the muthafucka... shitttt..." I hissed, legs jerking a little as I bit my lip.

"Good, stay the fuck away from him." Gio's circular motion around my clit sped up. "He needs to spend time with his wife who's waiting for his baby. In the meantime, you can spend time with me, get to know me."

"This isn't professional. You're about to make me cum on your fingers..." My mouth gaped open a little, saliva dripping down my chin.

"I asked your permission to be unprofessional. We're almost done here." He let me know, his fingers encouraging the blood to flow through my vagina. My clit engorged as that man rubbed her. I could feel my fluids saturating my thighs as he brought me to the edge or orgasm. With his other hand, his fingers rubbed my perineum.

"I'm having his baby... You don't want to know me, Gio," I told him.

"No, you're having his and *Paris's* baby," Gio growled. "Now cum for me." His fingers swirled inside of me, caressing the spongy tissue inside of me, moving rhythmically in and out of me. At that point, he could hear how wet I was, similar to the sound of macaroni being stirred in a pot. Gio chuckled a little. "Macaroni in a pot, this some wet as pussy."

My breathing intensified, growing faster and heavier.

"I feel your pussy tightening around my fingers. I wish it was my dick, Officer. I bet you can ride dick like a fuckin' soldier, can't you?" Gio felt my pussy tightening around his fingers.

Most men had to learn my body to make me cum by digital foreplay, but not Gio. He brought me to orgasm perfectly. I moaned softly to hide the fact that I was screaming like '90s Mariah Carey on the inside.

After I came, Gio slid his hand from inside of me. I heard him placing on his gloves before standing from his stool so they could him behind the glass. He gave them a thumbs-up before helping me sit up from the bed, then remove my feet from the stirrups.

I panted, looking up into his face, mind still processing what my body just went through.

"I'll see you in about fourteen days. Get dressed, Officer. We have a long journey ahead of us. It's only the beginning," Gio warned me.

⚝

"Turn us loose, set us free from all the chains that bind me. Let us run in our own direction. Let us go, set us free from all this propaganda and lies that your people try to teach us..." I sang along with the powerful woman on the 1995 *Panther* soundtrack. Never had I heard a song more powerful than that song. And the women they picked for that song all stood for something, blending generational gaps. That song is over twenty-five years old and still holds truth.

I needed those words to bring me back down to reality. I was floating on a cloud, daydreaming about Gio ever since he finger fucked me on that damn hospital bed. I had to focus on the case files and inventory that was stacked in my new apartment. The boxes were all mixed up. Evidence wasn't marked. Guns, murder weapons, clothes, nothing was marked. I had to put everything that wasn't marked in a separate box, then label and enter everything else into our system. I had my work cut out for me. If I wasn't pregnant, I would have had myself a bottle of wine to go with my stress.

There was a knock at my front door. Immediately, I grabbed my gun from my desk. I purposely didn't give anyone my address, not even my unit. I finally got rid of top-flight security, sick of having to live my life under surveillance. I inched my way toward my front door. "Who the fuck is it?"

"Picka color and wash your hands, please. You want eyebrow and pedicure?" Gio mocked his people, laughing to himself outside of my door.

I rolled my eyes, lowering my gun to my side as I walked toward the front door. I opened it, looking Gio in his face. That smile was to die for, I swear. "Not cool to make fun of your own people," I told him.

"Mama always said you need to learn to laugh at yourself so it won't hurt when others laugh at you." Gio watched me roll my eyes at him before turning around to walk back through my house. "Whoa, do you need help unpacking?"

I sighed, setting my gun on the coffee table before plopping down on the couch. "No, but I do need help putting a few of these boxes back in my car."

"Boxes of what?" Gio looked around at the boxes stacked ceiling high in my apartment.

"Stuff from inventory. Murder evidence, rape victims' clothing, stuff like that. Since I'm on desk duty, I'm stuck organizing shit that other muthafuckas are too lazy to do. You see I'm vibing in here, trying to sing and rap my way through all this shit." I exhaled deeply. "If I wasn't pregnant, that wine would be going down my throat right about now." I watched Gio remove his gray hoodie before sitting on the sofa beside me. Why did he have to be wearing gray sweats? That devil stayed fuckin' with me. "Just make yourself comfortable. Sure. Go ahead."

Gio grinned, kicking off his white and gray Nikes. "Don't mind if I do."

"What happened to seeing me in fourteen days?" I asked him.

"I just came by to check on you," Gio responded.

"How the fuck did you know where I stay?" I asked him.

"I just followed the smell of peaches." Gio grinned a little, that one dimple piercing his cheek.

"You had some nerve, that shit you pulled at the clinic with everyone watching! What if the blanket fell and they saw you finger fucking me? What happened to keeping this about business?" I asked him.

"I don't have much time for pleasure, so I thought why not mix the two?" Gio answered.

"In case you haven't noticed, I'm pregnant by another muthafucka. Fuckin' around with muthafuckas I'm not supposed to is what got me in this mess! I could've done like a few other bitches I know who would have thrown their baby in the trash can like Brenda did and kept it moving. But no, I'm carrying this baby and giving it a good home. I have too much on my plate with these cases and trying to play off this pregnancy. You're going to get us caught if you keep this seductive shit up. What exactly do you call yourself doing?" I asked him.

"Distracting you from worrying about something that you can't change. The damage has already been done. Like I said, everyone has a story. However you ended up here doesn't even matter. You're making moves toward correcting your mistakes," Gio tried convincing me.

I shook my head. "I've made more mistakes than you'll ever know, and most of them center around Hendrix. I think that's how this shit between me and him happened. Cleaning up after him. Helping him get away with murder, literally. I remember a time when some broke in my car a few years ago. Hendrix found out who it was. He caught up with the muthafucka, made me watch him kill him in front of me. The muthafucka only stole a few dollars from the armrest and my license plate. Hendrix burned the muthafucka alive in my car. I learned then not to tell the muthafucka if anyone crossed me. Then there's Paris. I never thought for a second that she'd literally shoot me over a nigga, but when I think about it, both of them muthafuckas are crazy. All they know how to resort to is violence because that's all they've been exposed to all of their lives."

"Can you blame Paris though?" Gio shrugged. "Someone is always crossing her. No parents, no lover, no friends. All she feels she has is herself, so that's who she's looking out for. You lived to see another day."

I looked at Gio, watching him slouch back in my chair.

"I bet being shot gave you a whole different perspective about how easily life can be taken away. I bet you won't touch anyone else's man again." Gio scoffed.

"You've never thought about fuckin' anyone else's woman before?" I questioned his ethics.

"What do I want with another man's pussy?" Gio made a face. "I don't get off from a woman fuckin' me, then going home to fuck him, too. Too many diseases out here to be fuckin' behind someone."

"So why fuck with me? I just fucked a muthafucka back in December who belonged to someone else!" I reminded him.

"I'm your doctor. I performed your STD screenings, remember?" Gio reminded me, too. "You're good to go."

I shook my head. "I'm not joking, Gio."

"Neither am I," Gio let me know. "I'm straightforward. You know that by now. I'm never going to hesitate to tell you about yourself. Right now, all we got is us," Gio let me know.

"It's not like you're doing this shit for free. Hendrix and Paris are paying you, even though I told you to send their bill to me. I've yet to see a bill," I huffed.

Gio frowned. "Let the muthafucka pay for the shit he caused. It's the least he can do."

"He wasn't in this shit alone." I had to take some blame for the situation.

"But you acknowledged your wrong. I'm sure he's still hitting you up, trying to fuck. Don't tell me he's not. I've felt your pussy. I know he misses her." Gio started playing with my hormones again.

I shook it off for the moment. "If I think I'm lonely now, I can only imagine what's going to happen after I drop this baby off with the Hughes. I can do bad all by myself. Last thing I need is muthafucka in my life who doesn't plan on staying."

"Who said I was going anywhere? I already got paid for my services. Shit, if I planned on leaving you alone, I would have been gone as soon as their check cleared and let you see someone else for your prenatal visits." Gio looked my face over.

"I have work to do. I don't have time to be playing with you, Gio." I got up from my couch.

Gio grabbed my wrist, pulling me down into his lap. He wrapped his arms around me, pulling me to him so that I was sitting right on his dick. "You feel that?" Gio growled in my ear.

My eyes damn near crossed as I felt that thing jump up and tap me between the legs like he was saying "let me in".

"You want some? Shit, do you want *all*?" Gio asked me, sliding his hands into my thighs, gripping my boy shorts.

"Maybe just a little... I have a lot of work to do." I creamed as Gio started kissing on my neck.

A little turned into a lot. A lot turned into allowing myself to fall asleep in his arms. I thought I knew better than to mix business with pleasure. I found myself in a hole, and my dumb ass just kept on digging. I had to get out before I got stuck. But how could you put down the shovel when someone like Gio helped do the digging? Keep on digging, right?

6

PARIS

"There's some holes in this house..." Amber sang loudly, jumping on my got damn couch before Neeta told her to get off my couch.

"What you know about some WAP? Get off her couch like that! And it's *hoes*, not holes!" Neeta rolled her eyes over from Amber to me. Then she huffed, pointing over at Elliott by the staircase. "And would you look at this shit?"

I burst out laughing. That little boy had his sisters Barbies wrapped around the stair rails, flicking ones at them like they were sliding down a pole.

"This some bullshit." Neeta rolled her eyes at me laughing at my god kids. "Paris, why the fuck are you watching Kace's Bébé's kids on Valentine's Day?"

"Girl, his babysitter dropped them off about an hour ago," I told her. "Kace's mom is in town. She's on the way to pick them up in a few. I don't have to be in the club tonight until ten, so chill." My cell phone chimed on my coffee table. I couldn't get to my phone fast enough. I was waiting for Doctor Chang to hit me up. And there he was calling my phone.

"Please tell me you have good news!" I crossed my fingers, clenching my eyes shut.

"Good afternoon to you, too, Mrs. Hughes." Doctor Chang laughed on the other end.

"Sorry." I exhaled shakily. "I'm just anxious."

"Well, we brought Officer Banks in to confirm pregnant, and... we heard a heartbeat." Doctor Chang barely got the words out when I was jumping up and down with joy.

"Oh my goodness! I'm having a baby!" I squealed, and cried, and laughed, and had to sit down on the couch to catch my breath. "Okay, so what's next?"

"Well, this works just like a normal pregnancy the next few months. November first is your due date, Mrs. Hughes. Congratulations and happy Valentine's Day," Doctor Chang told me before hanging up.

"Good news?" Neeta pretended to not be ear hustling.

"That was the doctor. We're in business! Baby Merci or baby Hendrix are on the way!" I squealed.

"Merci?" Neeta's eyes glistened over.

I nodded. "Yeah, she's doing this for me when she really doesn't have to. Why wouldn't I name my baby after her?"

Neeta stood from the couch, sighing. "Last thing we need is another Merci in this world. Shit, another Hendrix either to be honest. Name that baby after someone who values your friendship enough not to step down from being your maid of honor. It's Valentine's Day. Where is Hendrix?"

"Making sure my baby's club is packed tonight." Hendrix walked down our winding staircase and into the living room. "Your friend needs to get some business and stay out of yours."

"I would tell you what you should stay out of, but I wouldn't want to ruin Valentine's Day for the happy couple." Neeta rolled her eyes and her neck. "Merci is pregnant, nigga."

I huffed. "Thank you, Neeta. Thanks for ruining it for me." I held my arms open as Hendrix walked into them. "But yes, baby, we're pregnant."

Neeta smacked her lips. "I'll see y'all at the club." Just as she walked toward the door, there was a knock at the door. She barely turned the knob when the door flew open. And in stormed Kace, brushing past her. She started to go off until she noticed the angry expression on his face. He was so mad that his peach skin was damn near fire-engine red. Neeta slipped out the door as Kace went off on Hendrix. I hadn't seen Kace since we got back from Maryland, almost a month and half earlier. Our last conversation wasn't a pretty one. I was sure his anger had something to do with that.

"What's up, homie?" Hendrix turned to his friend as I unwrapped my arms from around him. "You're just in time for the news. We're pregnant, nigga."

Kace looked me over then back at his friend. "What?"

"Merci is having my baby. The doctor just called," I hesitated to say.

Kace clicked his teeth at me before glaring back at Hendrix. "Why am I just finding out that you cancelled my shipment? The boys got to the warehouse today, and there was nothing waiting for them! Snap called me, telling me that you're working with his competition. Why the fuck would you do that when this mutha-fucka suspects you of killing his brothers? You're making yourself look suspect!"

"No, I'm making myself look like I have some fuckin' sense. Why work with nigga who planted his family member on my team to steal from me and give right back to him? Our new suppliers aren't in as deep as we are. My supplier is a senator's son. More ways for us to stay clean if we ever get caught up. You're getting too sloppy, man," Hendrix told our friend in his face. "Your fuckup got our boy some jail time. All he has to do is get a sweet deal, and it's over for us. Well, it was over for us until I found a third partner for the casino whose father is a lawyer."

"Who?" Kace sounded as if he hated to ask.

"Carter." Hendrix barely got the words out when Kace attempted to swing on him before I jumped between the two.

"Carter? Of all muthafuckas, Carter?" Kace yelled.

"The muthafucka knows the ins and outs of business marketing. We can expand with his help before Snap tries to shut us down. Get your feelings out of this. This is business. It's nothing personal," Hendrix told his friend in his face.

"Hendrix," I turned to him, "Carter is fuckin' around with Karen. The bitch is pregnant!"

Hendrix looked down into my face like I had some nerve getting in their business. I wasn't sure when the muthafucka decided to do business with Hendrix, but I was sure it was when Kace and I were in Maryland. Karen caught Kace kissing me good night on the porch steps a few days before Christmas. I had to put the shit up in the air to calm Kace down so he'd think before doing anything crazy. Carter was coming through to blackmail us.

"Paris, I told you about getting in our business. This shit has nothing to do with you!" Hendrix shoved me a little.

"Aye, homie, I'm only going to tell you once not to put your fuckin' hands on her like that again," Kace told his friend, moving me out of the way so that he was face-to-face with his friend.

"Dafuq? Now are *you* in *our* business?" Hendrix snarled.

"Muthafucka, y'all ain't married yet," Kace reminded him.

Hendrix laughed that crazy laugh of his. "You're in your feelings because your brother fucked your wife. I get it. I'd be pissed, too. But don't come in my shit questioning me and decisions I'm making to expand *my* fuckin' casino. You are my silent partner. Muthafuckas don't even know you fuck with a nigga's club."

"Silent partner doesn't mean I don't have a fuckin' say-so, muthafucka! Am I your silent partner in the fuckin' streets, too?" Kace asked.

"Yes, nigga, you are, Officer Gwinnett," Hendrix reminded his boy of his place.

"It's because of me that your club is still running the way that it is! I run that muthafucka while you run the fuckin' streets! You wanna blame me for your crew member getting arrested? The cops are on you because muthafuckas keep coming up missing! They don't want the little fish; they want the fuckin' shark! He's a distraction while I help clean up *your* shit! If it wasn't for me, your ass would've been in jail fuckin' years ago!" Kace shoved Hendrix, reminding him of *his* place. "I am a muthafuckin' police officer. I could easily use that shit to my advantage!"

"Is that a threat, nigga?" Hendrix held his hand over the gun at his waist.

Kace looked at Hendrix like Hendrix had him fucked up, as if he didn't have guns, too. "It's a reminder of who I am and who you are. I could kill you right now, and you'd just be another black drug dealer dead, and nobody will give a fuck. I have the advantage, and I never use that shit against you! Yet as soon as you could turn on me, you took the chance. My brother, man? If he turned on me, what the fuck do you think he'd do to you?"

Hendrix's temples twitched. "You coming with me to meet the new supplier or nah, nigga?"

"I'm not your fuckin' 'yes man'! I'm not one of your employees or crew members! This power has gone to your head, homie, and you don't even see it. You can have all this shit because I don't want it. Let's see how well you do without me, muthafucka." Kace turned away and stormed out of the house.

I started to go after him, feeling like he was walking out of my life at that point as well.

Hendrix grabbed my wrist, pulling me back to him. "Where the fuck are you going?"

I pulled from him. "After your fuckin' friend that you've known all your life!"

Hendrix shook his head. "You can't lick his wounds all the time, Paris. Let him go."

"*Let him go?*" I scoffed. "That man knows every combination to every safe you own! He knows where every warehouse is where you store and manufacture your drugs! He knows your account numbers! He knows all of your dirt! He could get half of your crew to turn on you if he wanted to! He has the power to lock you away and throw away the fuckin' key!"

"I have just as much dirt on him as he has on me," Hendrix growled.

"Yeah, well, he's the one wearing the fuckin' badge! Who are they going to believe, huh?" I shoved Hendrix in his chest. "Go talk to him!"

Hendrix huffed, knowing I was right. "I'll let him cool off. He'll come around."

❦

I HAD OTHER SHIT TO WORRY ABOUT. I NEVER EXPECTED A romantic evening on Valentine's Day with Hendrix. He always did the usual—flowers, candy, a credit card to max out. Nothing too thoughtful. At first, hell yeah, I loved the way he let me spend the way I wanted to. But then after a while, I realized it was just his way of getting me out of his face so he could come and go as he pleased.

"Boss lady, we're almost out of Cristal, and them ballers in VIP are asking for more!" my bartender shouted over the music at my club that night.

I stood at the bar in my chocolate-nude maxi dress. "Girl, break out a bottle of Louis Roederer Brut Premier. Them drunk muthafuckas will never know the difference."

"That's a little unethical, don't you think?"

Imagine my surprise when I look to my right to see Doctor Chang sitting down at the bar. He was dressed in all black from his long sleeve Gucci shirt to his Gucci leather dress shoes.

"Okay, Gucci, I see you." I tugged on his shirt a little. "I didn't think this was your scene."

"It's not," the doctor let me know, "but I thought I'd check it out since it's what everyone's talking about. Can you get your bartender to fix me a cup of hot tea?"

I laughed out loud until I saw that he was serious. "White, green, or black?" I cleared my throat.

"You pick." The doctor looked at me through his glasses.

I told the bartender to fix the doctor some tea.

"So how are you?" he asked me.

I nodded. "Good."

"Officer Banks is doing good as well. I'm glad she's resting for the night and not out here wildin' with you and your crew." The doctor looked around before looking back at me. "Have you told your in-laws about the baby?"

"What in-laws?" I scoffed. "Hendrix's mama is on that shit, and his sister only calls when she needs something."

"What about your parents?" he questioned.

"What parents? The last foster family I stayed with only calls when they need help with a bill or two," I let him know.

"And your birth mother? Has she reached out to you?" the doctor inquired.

"No," I lied. "Last I saw of her, she OD'd after sucking dick at a truck stop to pay for our dinner because she didn't have enough money to pay for our food."

The doctor gave me a sympathetic look. "You're out here working when you should be at home, laid up with your husband. And your friend is at home, pregnant, healing from a gunshot wound."

I looked at the doctor. "She's a soldier. A bullet ain't stoppin' that bitch."

"It stopped the little girl who was in the house with her," the doctor just had to remind me. "She didn't deserve to die over a business between adults. So much can be avoided if people just communicate. That beef was too personal to be gang affiliated. I'm a doctor, but I know when someone is targeted over personal shit."

"You're really opinionated tonight, sir." I folded my arms.

"All I'm saying is you deserve a life that doesn't put you in danger. You're supposed to be at home with your man on Valentine's Day. What kind of man lets his woman work on a special day like this? The same man who would let you think he killed your foster parents to avenge you, huh?"

"Hendrix isn't the romantic type. He—" I stopped talking, realizing the last thing that Gio just said. "Wait, what? How did you—"

"Contact your birth mother," the doctor said before getting up from the stool and walking away.

"Where is he going? I got his tea!" The bartender hurried over to me.

I looked in the direction that the doctor walked through the club. He dapped a few of Kace's crew members who lined the wall that night. How he knew the muthafuckas, I had no idea. But I had a weird feeling about him the moment he mentioned my foster parents' murder and the fact that he knew Hendrix didn't do kill them. Nobody knew about that other than muthafuckas who were there that night. Up until Kace told me, I didn't know shit. I spent the last six years of my life thinking that Hendrix was the one who buried my past. And the whole time, it was Kace.

"Boss lady." One of my strippers, Nicki, ran to me, titties bouncing in her tiny crop top. "Tammy is supposed to be on the stage next, and she's in the dressing room throwing up!"

I huffed. The DJ already had his playlist set for the night. Every stripper had already rehearsed their performance for the night. They were nervous enough about their part, so they weren't about to take on Tammy's part, too.

"Dimi, get out there," I told the bartender on duty that night.

She shook her head frantically. "Hell nah. Them thirsty, horny, lonely, wife-just-left-them niggas ain't gonna be grabbin' on me tonight. You go, boss lady."

I bit my lip. If Hendrix came in the club, he would trip. He always said I was too friendly with my employees. Unlike him, I didn't let my power go to my head. My dancers were loyal to me.

They didn't hesitate to get their niggas to take care of things for me the night of my rehearsal dinner.

"You owe us," Nicki had to remind me.

I rolled my eyes at her. "I guess she wants me to give her the tips I make tonight from this dance tonight, too?"

"You already know." Nicki grinned.

I shook my head, signaling the bartender to give me a double shot of tequila. I took the drink to the head before making my way to the stage.

"Oh, shit, boss lady stepping down off her throne to give us a show!" DJ Loops put the pressure on me as he started to engage the crowd.

I rolled my eyes nervously. "Now," I stepped up the stage steps, "usually I don't do this, but uhhhh..."

The strippers in the audience hyped me up as the music transitioned to the song Tammy was supposed to dance to that night. Just when I started to slip out of my dress, I spotted Kace coming in the club. He looked surprised, angry, yet curious when he saw me on stage.

"Ugh, oh, 5-o in the building!" DJ Loops teased, silencing the track.

Kace threw up a middle finger. One of the dancers grabbed a mic from the DJ booth and brought it over to Kace. He shook his head, not in the mood to sing or rap.

"Come on, Officer," YoYo begged him, speaking over the microphone. "For boss lady? Please. It's Valentine's Day. You sing to her. She dances for you." Yoyo winked at me, knowing I was going to curse her out later on that night.

Kace took the mic from her, holding the mic to his lips, walking in my direction. "I left my girl back home. I don't love her no more. And she'll never fucking know that. These fucking eyes that I'm staring at. Let me see that ass... Look at all this cash..." Kace sang over The Weeknd, and the crowd went wild.

And I felt more comfortable that he shared some of the pressure with me. He came on the stage, sitting on the throne that sat alongside the pole. We often allowed VIP members to come sit in that chair to get an up close and personal view of ass. I undressed down to my chocolate lace Fenty unlined bra and G-string. That was the closest my club would ever get to see me naked. The lace blended with my skin, giving the appearance of no clothes.

Kace slid back in the chair, microphone in his hands. "Bring your love, baby, I could bring my shame. Bring the drugs, baby, I could bring my pain. I got my heart right here. I got my scars right here..." Kace sang to me, eyes glued on the sway in my hips before I grabbed onto the pole.

I often took classes with a few of my girls. I commended them after taking those classes. That shit is work. Takes stamina and upper body strength to swing around that pole. I held onto the pole, swinging around it, legs spread wide as I came down the pole into a full split. I didn't know what it was about Kace, yet being in his presence gave me more confidence than I'd ever had. I was about to give some lame little dance on stage to engage the crowd a little until Tammy got herself together. That was until Kace walked into the club and agreed to sing, something he never did, because he didn't like drawing attention to himself because of his job. The last thing he wanted was for word to get back to his unit that he was at a strip club known for helping with drug distribution. I was probably the only female in the club who didn't have a pussy or asshole full of drugs.

I danced all around Kace, did everything but touched him. He looked my body over, watching me dance around him in my lingerie and stilettos. He reached out to me, grabbing on to me, pulling me down into his lap. I really wasn't trying to sit on it. I'd done enough of that in Maryland. I laughed out loud, playing off the situation, signaling the DJ to stop the music.

Money floated in the air, falling on stage as the crowd booed.

"Oh, shut up." I rolled my eyes, getting up off of Kace's lap. "I'm giving the stage back to my dancers. Enjoy the show tonight. Ladies, rack this shit up."

I grabbed my dress and made my way off of stage. I headed in the back of the club, down the hallway to my office. Just as I was about to breathe normally and shut my door behind me, Kace made his way into my office.

"Oh, Lord," I huffed, watching him close the door behind him.

Kace frowned at me, looking me over. "Dafuq were you doing on stage, mama?"

"Last time I checked, this was *my* shit," I snapped.

"Hendrix wouldn't want you doing that shit, and you know it. I started to cause a scene, but like you said, this is your shit. I call no shots. Just like your man said earlier tonight. He let me know where my place is." Kace watched me roll my eyes before going over to my desk to sit on top of it.

I sighed. "No, that's not what I meant."

"Yes it is." Kace wouldn't let me take it back. "You think I give a fuck if Karen saw me kiss you? I could give a fuck if she saw me fuck you! She doesn't run shit. She talked my brother into going into business with Hendrix. Carter will threaten Hendrix's business if I don't back out of the shit. He'll threaten to tell your man his wife or whatever the fuck she is to him saw us kissing. And if I don't give him my portion of the casino, he'll expose me. If I back out on Hendrix, what else leverage does my brother have?"

"But backing out on Hendrix will cause more beef between y'all," I told him.

"Let me deal with that." Kace stood between my legs. "I see Merci is giving you the family you always wanted. It's the least she could do."

"Kace, you shouldn't be here in my office. I'm sure someone saw you walk in here." I sighed as he started running his fingers through my hair.

"You really thought you could just avoid me, Paris? You already know you fucked up when you gave me some pussy."

Kace gripped my hair in his hands. "Have you fucked that muthafucka since you've been home?"

"Nigga, that's my fiancé." I rolled my eyes, playing off the fact that he was turning me on. His cologne lingered around me, causing my pussy muscles to jump to the bass of the music playing outside of my office door.

"You heard what the fuck I asked. Did he touch my fuckin' pussy?" Kace snarled, gripping my hair.

Those two shots of tequila started kicking in a little, joining forces with Kace to play with my hormones. I shook my head. "I could barely look at him this past month and a half, let alone let him touch me."

"That's a good girl." Kace grinned, digging into his pocket. "Close your eyes."

I closed my eyes, exhaled as Kace held my hands to put something cold in my hands. The way it fell into my hands, I knew it was a necklace. I opened my eyes to see a gold necklace with a gold heart locket hanging from it. I cried out loud as I opened the locket to see a picture of myself as a three-year-old girl and a picture of my fourteen-year-old mother. I hadn't seen that necklace since pre-K when I thought I lost it in the sandbox.

"I swear, you pay close attention to detail." I dried my tears, holding the necklace in my hands. "Where did you get this?"

"You know my mom was friends with our pre-K teacher. Turns out she's been holding onto it all the years," Kace answered.

"You're so thoughtful." And then it dawned on me. "Wait... it was your idea to get Merci that fuckin' dress? You're the one who told the nigga to buy it for her?"

Kace shook his head. "Nah, I'm the one who bought it for her."

I laughed out loud, getting up from my desk. "*You* bought it for her? You wanted me to think Hendrix bought it for her? Because of you, my best friend was nearly killed!"

"Nah, because of me, your best friend is feeling guilty enough to have your baby for you and the man she was fuckin' behind your back!" Kace told me, grabbing me back to him.

"You did all this shit so that you could get me away from Hendrix so you could fuck me. Is that it?" I shoved him.

"Did it work though?" Kace grinned.

"You're crazy!" I shoved him.

"About you. I've always wanted you, Paris. I've always hated how he treated you. You don't even know your worth. So I had to show you." Kace took a long velvet box out of his pants pocket. He opened the box, revealing a sexy, sleek diamond tennis bracelet.

My eyes widened as Kace removed the bracelet from the box. I watched him slide the box back into his pocket before grabbing my wrist to wrap the bracelet around my wrist. Soon as he clasped the bracelet around my wrist, the tears started flowing. "First my mother's necklace, and now this? I can't wear this around him. He'll know you got it for me."

"So? Let him know. It'll make him step his game up. He'll work overtime to keep you away from me. That's what you want, isn't it? After the week we had in Maryland, you still want to marry that muthafucka, right?" Kace laughed to himself, laughing off his pain.

"You could snap my neck right here in my club, in my office, and the police wouldn't even give a fuck. Your power scares Hendrix. It scares me, too. Because the moment I don't do what you want, you could get rid of me," I told him.

Kace made a face. "You think I'd hurt you? Everything I've done, everything I didn't do is because of you! I could've been a doctor, went off to med school in New York. I got accepted to five ivy league schools! Yet I stayed here to look out for you! Shit, you know a brutha can sing, rap, dance, you name it! I could've had a record deal. Record execs hit me up every week on IG and TikTok after seeing some of my posts. I got skills, mama. I turn shit down every fuckin' week because I can't leave you with him!"

I cried, listening to him pour out his feelings to me. "He's stuck by me through my difficult times. I'm not easy to deal with, and he puts up with me every day."

"Nah, he puts up with the money you bring in every day." Kace wasn't trying to hear me. "I love you. I want you. I've always wanted and loved you. You can't run from this."

"We can't keep doing this. I'm trying to pull away from you, and you keep pushing your way back in!" I shoved him. "We are friends, Kace! Friends! That's it! I've been through some shit. You might not wanna love me, Kace."

"We're supposed to be Foxxy Brown and Kace, remember?" Kace spoke to my heart, calling me the nickname he had for me when we were in school. Kace pulled my body to his by the clasp in my bra. Soon as he did that, my bra popped open. Kace looked my body over before looking into his face. "You really think I'm just going to let Hendrix make it to that altar? I'll bust up in that muthafucka like Dwayne did Whitley and Byron on *A Different World*. Remember, you showed me that shit when we were younger?"

I blushed as Kace removed my bra straps from my arms. "For a second, I thought you meant taking Hendrix out."

"I did," Kace growled.

My heart skipped several beats. "Kace, just leave him alone. I know you're upset with him over your brother and your ex and doing business behind your back, but—"

"He's always doing shit behind my back!" Kace cut me off. "I'm done with your boy. He's on his own. I can't help him now."

"What do you mean?" I barely got my statement out when Kace grabbed behind my knees, pulling my body into his. He planted his lips on mine. As he slid his tongue through my lips, I sucked it into my mouth. And clothes started coming off right there on my desk.

"Two eyes, one nose, one mouth, one head." Dr. Chang laughed while running a probe across Merci's swollen abdomen while conducting an ultrasound at his office.

I watched the monitor as Merci lay on the bed, peeping at the monitor, too.

"She's fourteen weeks today," Dr. Chang told us that nineth day of April, just six days away from my wedding.

"She looks like she's a little over twenty weeks if you ask me, fat ass." I laughed watching Merci roll her eyes.

"She also has gestational diabetes, which will make her baby bigger than the average baby. We are closely monitoring Officer Banks to ensure a safe delivery of a healthy baby. I know I said she wouldn't be able to know the sex of the baby for another two weeks, but do you want to give it a try now?" Dr. Chang asked the two of us.

Merci hesitated to nod, watching me smiling in anticipation.

After a few seconds, Dr. Chang's concentrating gaze turned into one of full of enthusiasm. "It's a girl, ladies."

I placed my hand over my heart, sighing, trying to hold in my excitement. Merci, on the other hand, looked a little hurt. I looked at the doctor. "Yes! Oh my goodness! I can't wait to tell Hendrix!" I clapped my hands together with excitement. "I already have the baby's name picked out. Mercedes Selena Hughes."

Merci looked at me, her eyes glazing over after hearing that I was giving my baby both her first and middle name. "Doc, can you give us a minute?"

Dr. Chang nodded, cleaning off Merci's stomach before getting up from his seat and then leaving the room.

I helped Merci sit up on the bed.

Merci sat up, gripping the bed, looking down at her feet.

"You okay?" I asked her.

"Yeah." Merci looked up into my face. "Remember that baby I lost when I was sixteen?"

I nodded. "Yeah?"

"I was going to name her Selena, too. I had her whole name picked out. Selena Paris Banks. No way I was giving her that nigga's last name on the football team. I didn't even tell the nigga I was having his baby." Merci laughed a little, drying the tears that dripped across her nose. "Who knew that I would be twenty-four having a baby for my sister?" She looked up into my face.

I grinned a little. "Yeah, who knew?"

"You know your hubby is still looking for the muthafuckas who shot up my house." Merci let me know. "It's crazy how I get shot the same day that I stepped down from being your maid of honor."

I looked at her. "You think I had something to do with that shit? Over you deciding not to be there next to me on my big day? I'd shoot a bitch over that?"

"No, but you'd shoot a bitch over thinking I was fuckin' your man," Merci let me know she wasn't the least bit stupid.

"Now why would I think that?" I asked her.

"Because you thought that dress I was wearing that night was from Hendrix when it was from Kace." Merci looked into my face. She was interrogating me the same way she did the mutha-fuckas at the precinct. She was trying to read me.

"Why would Kace buy you a dress?" I laughed it off.

"I don't know. You tell me. Kace is full of surprises these days." Merci scoffed. "The muthafucka made sure Captain stacked my desk with files from evidence. Those files haven't been organized in weeks. I had so much shit. Kace has the shit stacked at my house for me to go through. Shit is going to take months to organize. It's like the muthafucka put me on desk duty to distract me or to keep me busy. I wouldn't be doing this shit if none of this would have happened. Denise was killed. I'd hate to think you had anything to do with it."

I looked at the hoe like she lost her mind. "Merci, if I wanted to kill you, you'd be dead."

"Well, maybe the bullet that poor little girl took was meant for me. Maybe your crew missed their mark." Merci still continued to push the issue.

"My shooters don't miss," I assured her.

Merci pointed to the wound on her side. "They sure don't." She looked back up at me. "Your dancers aren't that loyal, Paris. It doesn't take much to bribe dancers with addictions and debt. A few of your dancers need their tuition paid or even immunity from crimes that they committed. A dancer of yours told me that you contacted her the night of your rehearsal dinner and told her to tell her nigga and his boys to mount up. Said you told her that you'd give her nigga and his crew twenty-five percent of the club's profits and twenty-five percent of the money made from selling Hendrix's product out of the club. Not only that, but you'd make sure they'd get extra bricks when the shipment came in on the house. Does Hendrix know about all this money of his that you're giving away?"

Wow, shawty totally flipped the script on me. She really thought she had me scared. She should've known by then that life didn't raise no pussy bitch.

I laughed at her nerve. "The only person who would go snooping into my personal business is a person who was guilty of something. For you to even think I would try and kill you over Hendrix, you must've been fuckin' around with him. I would look really fuckin' stupid asking a bitch who was fuckin' my husband to carry our baby. Just like you'd look real stupid asking a stripper who's committed multiply felonies to tell you exactly what you wanted to hear for immunity. Which one was it? Tammy? That girl's committed so many felonies with her man that her ass should be under the prison. She spent her whole life in and out of jail. She'd give me up to save herself, stupid enough to believe that a cop can give her immunity. You ain't no district attorney or anyone who has the authority to cover up anything she's done. She's stupid to believe you, and you're even more stupid for coming at me like this."

Merci looked into my face as if she were still trying to read me. Made me think that the shit she was saying was all made up just to see what my response would be. I didn't want to sound too defensive, because then the bitch would think I was lying. And I didn't want to sound like I was angry, because that would make it sound like yeah, I got my niggas to shoot you and if you do that shit again, I promise they won't miss.

"Well, you know how our investigations go. We have to ask everyone that I came in contact with that night. It's procedure." Merci's hormones had her not knowing when to turn her fuckin' badge the fuck off.

"Bitch, is it procedure to grill me at the doctor's office? And this doctor must really like your ass. Usually, the ultrasound technicians are the ones doing this. Doctor's don't do small shit like this. Why is he so personally vested in you?" I had to ask her.

That shut her ass up really quickly. "Huh?" Her beige cheeks instantly burned red.

"Oh," I laughed out loud. "You ain't talkin' that 'who shotcha' shit now, huh? How did you get hooked up with the Blasian?"

Merci let out a long sigh. "We met at the hospital the day I woke up after a week of being in the hospital. During my follow-up appointment, I mentioned to him that I was interested in being a surrogate. He mentioned that his mother is the founder of this hospital. His mother was Sun Toa-Chang. Have you heard of her?" Merci pointed over to the picture on the wall.

I walked over to get a closer woman of the pretty woman in her white coat, stethoscope around her neck. She couldn't have been older than forty. I knew her face from somewhere. I grabbed my phone, googling her. Her bio on Google was barely a few sentences. Nothing about where she was born. Nothing about her birthplace. Nothing about her parents. Just that she was brilliant and made her mark in history.

"There's not much history on her," I told Merci while googling Dr. Chang as well. "Shit, even less about her son."

"You're right..." Merci thought to herself before getting up from the bed. "Well, I have to get to work on that pile of shit at my new apartment."

Merci decided to fix her house up and sell it after what happened. She couldn't bring herself to sleep in that house after what happened, and I couldn't even blame her. Every time I heard Kace's daughter sing "there's some holes in this house" in an attempt to sing "WAP", I thought about Merci.

"You tell them niggas they better have better aim next time." Merci joked with all seriousness.

And I did the same. "Well, next time you fuck with my husband, I promise *I* won't miss. I won't send some else to do my job next time."

❧ 7 ❧

MERCI

T hat talk at the clinic really had me thinking about Gio. He'd already asked me to look up his mother's family history. Whoever adopted her went through great lengths to make sure no one knew who she was. The only thing I could find on her was her ex-husband's information. Dr. Lee Chang. His office was located in Greenville. He was a psychologist. I had to book an appointment just to get to speak with him. I didn't have time to go back and forth with Paris. I couldn't tell if she was telling the truth or not. The old Paris was a little easier to read. She'd changed over the past few months. She became a little more calculating. She didn't want me to know she lost her cool for a moment and did something that cost a little girl her life. Paris was one of those people who hated to let the next person know they got to her heart.

The wedding and the planning for the baby to arrive kept Paris busy for the moment. She posted pictures of her baby's nursery all over social media. The baby's room was beautiful beyond words. Everything was lavender and white from the wall trimmings to the curtains to the embroiled blanket in the baby's expensive crib. I tried my best to avoid social media, but the bitch kept tagging me. I started feeling guilty, like I should just come clean. But my relationship with Gio had gotten a lot more complicated. He was at my place every day when he got off work. He would work long shifts at the hospital, then come home to help me organize case files. He'd message my feet. He'd help wash the hard-to-reach places in the shower. He'd cook for me and help me clean, even unpack all my stuff. He'd help me pick out furniture. He'd wipe my tears when I cried, looking at the pictures Paris posted of all the stuff she bought for the baby. Instead of going to Vegas for her bachelorette party, she wanted to throw me a baby shower. She was playing with my emotions, as if she knew it would fuck with me. She knew something went on with me and Hendrix, whether she knew if we fucked or not. She wanted to rub in the fact that I was carrying their baby.

I managed to avoid Gio up until the day before Paris's wedding, making my way to his stepfather's clinic to get some answers. I assumed it was his stepfather by the way Gio referred to himself as Blasian and Chang obviously was an Asian last name. After waiting in the lobby for a few minutes, I was called into Dr. Chang's office. He was a friendly looking middle-aged Asian man of small stature. He welcomed me into his office with a warm smile.

"Oh!" He noticed the roundness of my belly as I sat down in the sofa across from his desk. "Congratulations! What are you having?" He definitely sounded more happy about it than I was.

"A girl. She's not mine." I let him know.

The doctor made a face. "Excuse me?"

"I mean I'm a surrogate. The baby is my best friend's." I watched the doctor nod when he understood what I meant.

"Oh, okay. Still, congratulations. It's a blessing to help warm someone's heart and household with a baby." The doctor's eyes smiled as his lips formed into a grin. The doctor opened his file, looking over my chart and the questionnaire that I filled out while waiting in his office. "Miss—excuse me, *Officer* Mercedes Banks."

"I go by Merci— Mercedes was my mother's name. And I

don't feel like an officer. I was reduced to desk duty after being shot a few months ago," I let the doctor know.

The doctor nodded. "How does that make you feel?"

"Relieved sometimes because I don't have to spend my time arresting old schoolmates or getting asked to cover for some of them." I rolled my eyes to myself.

The doctor looked at me over his glasses. "How does getting asked to be included in crimes of your friends make you feel? Do you feel that people who really cared for you would allow you to take the fall for their crimes? Do you feel that they're worried about your well-being? The streets are for officers to protect. How can you protect the streets if the streets are asking you to come out and play?"

I looked at him, never taking the time to think things through the way he'd put them. "I took the job to protect my friend."

"How are your friends protecting *you?*" the doctor questioned.

I exhaled deeply.

"You have to look out for you because, in the end, your 'friends' are only going to look out for themselves. What does your friend whose baby you're carrying do to look out for you during your pregnancy?" the doctor asked as he faced his desktop computer to start typing in some notes.

"She still has me working out at the gym with her to keep in shape. As long as I remember, this girl has had the perfect body. She went and enhanced her body, making her look even more like a chocolate-covered Barbie doll. Everyone loves her, admires her, hates her, wants to be her. She has the world at her fingertips. The only thing she doesn't have is a baby, which is why I decided to help her," I told the doctor. "We used Dr. Sun Toa-Chang's clinic to perform the surrogacy."

The doctor looked at me as soon as I mentioned his ex-wife.

"I was looking into her history when I was doing some research on clinics and couldn't find anything on her. I'm a police officer, have access to so many databases, yet I couldn't find her anywhere. No adoption agency had any record of a Sun Toa." I watched the doctor remove his glasses.

"That's because her name was changed." The doctor exhaled, rubbing his eyes in frustration. "Eunji Gwan was her birth name."

"Why change her name to Toa?" I asked him.

The doctor shook his head. "She was left on a porch step when she was a baby. To make sure her birth parents could never find her, her adoptive name was changed several times. They homeschooled her all her life. Changing her first name about five times whenever they would think her parents would try to find her. Changed her last name about ten times from birth until the age of thirteen."

"Why did they stop changing her name then?" I hesitated to ask.

"She'd run away only to find out that she was pregnant. She lived on the streets for up until she went into labor. She delivered her baby in the bathroom at a Target. One of the employees heard her screaming and called 911. After leaving the hospital, she ended up in a shelter, lying about her age and stealing someone's ID to be able to lie about her age. Thirteen and alone until she ran into the employee who helped her, my mother," the doctor explained.

I shook my head, sympathy taking over me as I found out about Gio's mother.

"My parents cleaned her up, got her in school. We started dating in high school. Got married when we were in college. Two kids getting married." Dr. Chang laughed to himself. "Had no business getting married. We divorced when we were about twenty-five. Not because we didn't love each other, but because we weren't ready for marriage. We had separate goals, separate lives. She never got over what happened to her as a child. We were never intimate, which caused me to stray."

"What happened to her as a child?" I asked, though I shouldn't have.

Dr. Chang looked at me before laughing to himself. "I'm supposed to be talking you through your struggles, yet here I am, telling you about someone else's."

"No, it's okay. Knowing her struggles will help me through mine," I told him.

"The son of her adoptive parents was raping her every night from the age of ten until the day she ran away. He had to be about seventeen or eighteen then. Let's just say the ones who hurt her can't do it anymore. The man and his wife were killed in a house fire a few years ago." Dr. Chang watched me sit up in my chair.

"A-A fire?" I asked him, remembering the night the Averys house was burned to the ground.

Dr. Chang nodded. "Greg Avery and his wife were burned alive a few years—" The doctor watched me grab my jacket and keys. "What's wrong? Where are you going?"

"I have to go. I just remembered I have to check in with the Captain at five." I couldn't get out of that office fast enough.

🐙

"HEY, BABY," GIO CALLED FROM THE KITCHEN.

I walked into my apartment, the sweet yet tangy smell of sweet and sour chicken hitting me in the face. I cried to myself the entire ride home, trying to figure out the right way to tell Gio that his father was Greg Avery, the same muthafucka who abused God knows how many people. That his mother was their adopted child, and the reason we had such a hard time finding out about her was because the Averys hid her identity so that they could prevent her parents from finding her and her finding them.

I'd really gotten attached to Gio. We'd spent long nights together damn near every night. He genuinely seemed to care for me. He definitely spared no expense on my feelings. He definitely knew how to put me in my place. It wasn't just about sex. He was the first person who actually tried to connect with me on a personal level. I was really falling for him. I hated to ruin things between us by telling him about his mother. If he was an Avery, that meant he was entitled to an inheritance like the rest of the Avery children.

I tossed my keys on the coffee table as I made my way over to Gio. He looked so sexy in front of my stove, nothing on but tattoos and a pair of gym socks. He turned to me, pearly white teeth shining through his grin. He held a spoon up to my mouth for me to taste the sauce.

I faked a smile, licking my lips. "You got off early tonight?" I asked him, looking around the room at everything that he'd straightened up for me, including the files on my desk.

"Yes. I was going to take you out to eat, but I'd figured you'd be too tired to go out after being on your feet all day." Gio watched me licking the sauce from my lips before he kissed me, taking my bottom lip into his mouth.

"You didn't have to cook. Tonight is my baby shower, remember? We're supposed to be doing it big for Paris's big day," I reminded Gio.

"They're probably just going to have finger foods anyway. I wanted to feed my baby before she went out with her girls. I feel like I haven't seen a lot of you these past few days. You've been working those files hard. How was work?" Gio asked, tasting the sauce for himself.

"I didn't go to work. I went to visit a psychiatrist," I hesitated to tell him.

"You okay?" Gio was concerned. He put the spoon down on a clean dish towel before turning to me and pulling my body up against his.

"I needed to find some things out about... your mother." I looked up into Gio's face as he loosened the grip he had on my coat.

"Who did you go see?" The light dimmed in his eyes as he looked down into my face.

"Dr. Chang. Your stepfather." I watched Gio exhale deeply. "I couldn't find your mother's information in the system, and I found out why. Because her name was changed numerous times growing up. I found out that she was a runaway from the Averys. That Greg raped her when he was about seventeen, and she didn't know she was pregnant until she gave birth in a bathroom. Gio, Greg Avery is your father."

Though Gio let go of me, temples twitching, frown on his handsome face, he didn't look the least bit surprised at the information that I'd just given him.

"I'm telling you all of this, and you're looking at me like you already knew this." I looked up into his face.

"Snap is my uncle. He's the one who funds my mother's hospital. I didn't want a damn thing from that family except to help my mother live her dreams. I guess that's why I have a soft spot for your friend, Paris. She didn't deserve any of this." Gio sounded as if he hated to tell me.

"You knew this already, yet you sent me on a goose chase? Why?"

"To give myself some time." Gio turned the stove top off, before leaning back against the countertop.

"Time for what? I don't understand," I told him.

"I'm a private criminal investigator. I work with police departments statewide to bring investigate big-time criminals, armed robberies, homicides. The night you were shot, your captain called me." Gio watched me laugh out loud in disbelief. "They wanted me to tail you, get to know you, because they suspect you of helping Hendrix get away with crimes. I used to roll with Kace when I was in high school. I was skinny back then, looked a lot different, which is why Hendrix doesn't remember me. You know Snap wants to bring him down to get back the streets and his money-making casino. Your boy helped in killing members of that man's family."

"You mean *your* family?" I walked away from him, over to my files to make sure everything was in place. "I confided in you! I criminalized myself telling you the things I did for that mutha-fucka! I had you helping me fake a surrogacy! Kace is my partner, but he's Hendrix's right-hand man, or at least he used to be. Is he being investigated, too?"

Gio shook his head. "I had another supplier contact Hendrix, and I contacted Kace's brother to go into business with Hendrix. I didn't want him around when shit went down whether it was from the police department or from Snap himself. They wanted him, and I got him."

My heart slammed against my chest. "How did you get him?"

Gio looked at me, hating to tell me. "You helped me."

I looked around the room, realizing that Gio helped me label and sort through all the weapons that were in those boxes. Hendrix mentioned that Kace claimed he got his guns from a supplier. Kace spent a lot of time in the evidence room. That had to be where he hid guns. And the fact that I was put on desk duty, helping to sort through inventory would make it look like I was helping set muthafuckas up.

"You took some of the weapons I had in the boxes, didn't you? Who did you give them to?" I asked him, sifting through the files on my desk. "If any of those weapons were used by Hendrix or his crew to kill Foxx or Tasha, he's going to think I set him the fuck up!"

"You need to worry about yourself, Merci," Gio tried telling me.

"You set me up!" I yelled at him. "You got to know me because it was a job for you? I should've known that you were too good to be true!"

"Stay out of this. They'll be after him. Forensics is confirming fingerprints on the guns. They will bust him as soon as they can get hard evidence. Snap will probably get to him before they do."

"When does Snap plan on making a move?" I cried.

"At the casino, the night of his bachelor's party, April fourteenth," Gio let me know, walking toward me.

I grabbed my gun from my desk, aiming it at him. "Stay the fuck away from me!"

Gio held up his hands offensively. "Don't get involved with this."

"*Don't* tell me what not to do!" I screamed. "I'm already involved! You used me!"

"You weren't supposed to find out like this." Gio still continued to walk toward me.

"Oh, when was I supposed to find out? While Hendrix was in prison and sent one of his hittas to kill me for setting him up?" I cocked my gun back.

"Put the gun down, Merci. I'm telling you, don't do this," Gio warned me.

I wasn't listening. What shattered heart listened to reasoning? All it wanted to do was inflict pain because, at the time, that was all it knew. "You made me fall for you!" I responded, turning gun sideways.

Gio nodded. "I fell, too, Merci. I'm sorry."

"I'm sorry, too." I placed my hand over the trigger, about to squeeze that muthafucka when I heard a branch snap outside of my living room window.

Instead of taking the chance to grab the gun from me, Gio tried to rush over to me to push me out of the way. It all happened so fast. Glass shattered as a bullet went straight through my window, into Gio's head. He took the first bullet that was meant for me. And before I could even fire in the direction of where the first shot was fired, I met my fate. I screamed out in agony as the second shot was fired. My shirt was completely saturated in blood. I grabbed my stomach where I'd been shot. I felt a burning, blistering sensation that radiated out from where the bullet hit me. I fell to the floor, fading in and out of consciousness as my door burst open and in came members of my squad. My captain ran over to me, calling for an ambulance over the PDA.

❀ 8 ❀

PARIS

"I got a feeling that you might be high. Do I turn you on? You can tell me if I'm wrong. Girl, I think you might be high. And she don't even smoke, but she swear I got that dope dick. Love it when I fuck her and I'm high..." DJ Nasty flowed through my club the night of Merci's baby shower.

Leave it to Neeta to get with my strippers and plan a baby shower. They decorated my club in purple and pink balloons. Cookie—my top moneymaker—made Merci vanilla cupcakes with buttercream icing. Each cupcake had purple baby booties on top. Presents were stacked to the ceiling for my baby, as if she didn't have enough stuff at home.

I should've felt like I was on top of the world. Hendrix thought it was best that we went ahead and got our marriage license that day instead of waiting until after the wedding ceremony, so I was officially Mrs. Hendrix Hughes. It was a bittersweet moment to kiss him before the magistrate in the courthouse. Our witnesses were Neeta and my bartender, Lee, when our witnesses should have been Merci and Kace. Merci couldn't make it, and since Hendrix and Kace weren't speaking, Kace wasn't coming to that bullshit. As soon as Kace got the memo, he texted me, *It's just a piece of paper. You're still mine. You want a love that he doesn't even believe in. I'm going to be the reason you divorce him. I bet my life on that.*

I sat at the bar, sipping champagne, drinking enough for me and Merci when I realized that Merci had yet to show up to her own party. Just when I was about to call her, I realized that I didn't have my phone on me.

Neeta came twerking by me, plate of meatballs and chicken in her hand, just smacking away. "Girl, who made these mutha-fuckin' meatballs? This shit takes good as fuck! Girl, you've drank enough tonight. Damn near drank that entire bottle on the shelf. Y'all don't give her anything else to drink. She's getting married tomorrow! Save some room for the honeymoon. Drunk sex is the best sex. Hendrix's dick is gonna taste so good in your mouth while you're drunk, girl. Gonna have your ass like, 'Damn, this dick tastes good, bae! Did you barbecue this muthafucka?' Gonna taste just as good as these meatballs!"

I shook my head at her goofy ass. "Neeta, have you seen Merci?"

Neeta shook her head. "Has she called you?"

"I don't know where I left my phone," I told her.

"I think we left our phones in your office earlier. Some lady's waiting for you over in VIP though. That's why I came over here. She's with about five other girls who look about our age or maybe younger," Neeta told me, nodding toward the lounge area in VIP. "She rolled up on me in a Jaguar when I went outside to my car to get more plasticware. I told her that we were closed for business tonight, but she said she only needed a few minutes."

I looked over in the direction the woman was sitting. And there she was, Nakia Perry, my birth mother. My brain was screaming, *fuck her. Neeta should've told her ass to go the fuck back to where she came from.* But my heart led my feet right over to where she was sitting with five other young women who were just as beautiful as she was.

I stood at the foot of the stairs that led up to VIP. Nakia stood from the sofa when she saw me. She was dressed very classy, like a businesswoman. Blazer, knee-length skirt, high heels, hair pulled up into a bun, string of pearls around her neck. She opened her mouth to speak, but a tear fell down her cheek instead.

I cleared my throat. "May I help you?"

"I—" she choked out. "There are no words to explain to you the things I put you through as a child. But you have to understand I was a child, too. Twelve years old with a baby. Your father was my rapist. I didn't know how to face myself, let alone face you. I grew up in the system. It was all I knew. I didn't want you there, but that's where they put you, only for you to end up back from where I ran away from. Another girl talked me into leaving that night. He was raping her, too. He raped that sweet Asian girl in front of his wife, and she stood there and watched every night."

I glanced at the five young women with her before looking back into my mother's face. "Why are you telling me this?"

"I cleaned up my life after years of drug abuse. I got married to a very wealthy doctor. I went to med school to become a doctor myself. While attending med school, I ran into that sweet little Asian girl again. Well, she was a grown woman by then." Nakia laughed a little, drying her tears. "She'd changed her name over the years. When we were little, I knew her as Khiya Lang. When I met her in med school again, her name was Sun Toa-Chang."

"The founder of the clinic in Raleigh?" I questioned.

Nakia nodded. "You've met?"

I nodded. "Yes. Her son performs the fertility treatments on me and my foster sister. She's having my baby."

"So you've already met your brother?" Nakia asked.

"My—Wait, what?" I was confused. "Gio Chang? What do you mean I met my brother?"

"Greg Avery's parents adopted me. They had a whole foster

scheme going on. Taking in poor kids, allowing their son to have sex with the foster girls, impregnating us, then selling our kids off to other families." Nakia watched the look of disbelief on my face. "Greg raped at least two of us per night until we got pregnant."

I shook my head. "You mean to tell me that... Greg Avery was my father?"

Nakia nodded.

I laughed out loud. "Did you know I ended up back at that place? Did you know that Greg raped me? Did you know his wife killed my baby with a rusty fuckin' coat hanger?" At that point, I was yelling over the music. "And you're telling me that nigga was my father? You left me with my father, the same man who was raping you? Then you have the audacity to come here and tell me that you cleaned up your life? What about *my* fuckin' life? That bitch fucked me up to the point where I can't have any kids! They ruined my fuckin' life! *You* ruined my fuckin' life!"

"Dr. Chang can fix you. Her fertility treatments have been known to heal scar tissue, clear Fallopian tubes, regenerate cervix, and—"

I cut Nakia off, hand in her face. "There is no fuckin' fixing me! Can she erase the memories that I carry? Can she erase the past? Can she erase what they did to me? Can she change history?"

"I know I shouldn't have left you," Nakia cried.

"Can she undo that for you?" I laughed off my pain. "I see she must've given you a new family. Let you start over and forget all about me, the life you left behind at that truck stop. That's my last memory of you. What's your last memory of me?"

"Watching you cheer at a basketball game your senior year," Nakia told me.

I shook my head at her. "Get out of my club and don't come the fuck back."

"Paris, please, I—"

"I *said* what the fuck I said." My nostrils flared.

Neeta came scurrying up to the stairs of VIP. "Paris, we gotta go *now*! Kace has been blowing your phone up! He's at the hospital! They shot Merci!"

⚜

"How could this happen?" I cried to Neeta in the lobby of Wayne Memorial Hospital.

Neeta patted my back, trying to console me. They would only let Neeta come with me into the lobby being as though it was packed with police officers who wanted to interrogate me instead of explaining to me how Merci was in critical condition, Gio was dead, and Hendrix was in police custody. Snap's crew thought they were going to run up on Hendrix, only to be gunned down by Hendrix and his crew that night. Neighboring businesses heard the gunshots that went off in his casino and called the police. That was how Hendrix ended up in police custody. Turns out, forensics recovered guns that connected Hendrix and his crew to several homicides. I knew it wouldn't be long before one of his crew members snitched and gave up the locations of our Hendrix drug warehouses. We were married but had yet to combine our assets, but I knew it wouldn't be long before they tried to take everything I had, claiming I paid for everything with his drug money.

"Ma'am, we have to take you in for questioning." One of the officers was about to cuff me.

"Hold up, don't do that shit." Kace's voice came around the lobby corner before he did. "Whatever Hendrix had going on had nothing to do with Paris. She runs a legit club, legit laundromat, legit hair salon. Whatever Hendrix did is of his own doing. Y'all already proved that Merci is the one who helped him cover up murders. Nothing you discovered ties Paris to any illegal activity, so you have no probable cause to arrest her. You might can seize everything in his name, including that casino, but you can't take any of her assets that are in her maiden name."

"You can't tell me that she didn't know her husband committed all those murders. We are going to dig up every piece of dirt we have on Mr. and Mrs. Hughes," the officer snarled in Kace's face.

"Well, Officer Dover, until you have probable cause for arrest, I suggest you leave Paris the fuck alone," Kace snarled back. "Her friend is fighting for her life right now! Let the girl deal with that instead of throwing more shit at her. Y'all got the muthafucka you want!"

The officer frowned at me before making his way back over to the other group of cops.

"Gio's gone, too," I whispered. "I just found out today that he's my brother!"

Kace grabbed me from Neeta, surrounding me in his arms. "Baby, I'm sorry."

"What happened? You have to tell us something," Neeta questioned Kace.

Kace rubbed my back before letting me go. "Gio was working for the captain under investigation. He uncovered come weapons that had Hendrix's fingerprints on them."

I looked up into Kace's face, my heart on full speed, my mind flashing back to the night at the club when Kace told me about putting the gun that shot Foxx in old case files in their evidence inventory room. "Where did they find the weapons?"

"Inventory." Kace looked down into my face.

"Inventory?" Neeta made a face, watching the way that I was looking at Kace. She saw the doctors standing over by the nurse's station. "I'm going to go see what's going on with Merci."

I looked into Kace's face as Neeta hurried off to see about Merci's condition. "You set him up."

Kace shook his head. "They wanted him. I gave him what they wanted. I told you that there was no way I'd let you walk down the aisle with that muthafucka."

I was about to go the fuck off when Neeta called me over to where the doctors were. I glared at Kace before going over to hear Merci's circumstances.

"Ms. Banks is in very critical condition," Doctor Frank let me know. "She's going to need blood in the event she loses too much blood during her emergency surgery."

I nodded frantically. "Well, I'm a universal donor. I can give blood right now! Whatever you need to save Merci and my baby. She's my surrogate."

The doctor nodded. "Well, we'll have to confirm that you are in fact O-negative. The gunshot wound went through her uterus, causing fetal distress. They are performing an emergency C-section as we speak."

I cried out loud. "But can a baby survive that was only in the womb for fifteen weeks?"

The doctor looked confused. "The ultrasound results prove that Ms. Banks was about twenty-two weeks pregnant."

I shook my head. "That's impossible. We just started fertility treatments in January. We were told that on Valentine's Day that she was six weeks pregnant, okay? This doesn't make any fuckin' sense!"

"Paris!" Neeta grabbed my arms to calm me down. "They played you, okay? They faked the treatments. Merci was found out she was pregnant the day she was shot back in December."

I looked at Neeta. "And how do you know this?" I felt weak.

"Because I was there when Gio told her." Neeta sounded as if she hated to tell me.

"And who is child's father, huh? I need to know!" I shoved Neeta.

"Hendrix," Neeta whispered.

That was when my world went black. The next thing I know, I woke up laying in a hospital bed, ice pack on my head. I looked to my right to see Kace was the one holding the bag over my head. Though my head was banging, I used all the energy I had to roll my eyes at him.

"I know you're angry at me. I'm sorry. I didn't want things to be like this," Kace whispered to me, removing the bag from my head.

"I guess you want to say I told you so." I looked at him.

Kace shook his head. "Nah. I was cool with Gio, but he never told me any of this. My boss hired him to investigate drug and murder crimes at the unit. The only reason why he didn't investigate me is because of our history. And he made sure to do what he had to do to protect you because you were his little sister. He was trying to look out for you, which is probably why he faked the surrogacy, to drag this interrogation out until he got what he needed. I just had to call his mother and tell him the news. She knew about the surrogacy situation, said Gio has your money orders sitting in a folder in his office. He had you pay him in money orders for a reason. He kept it to the side just in case some shit goes down and they try to tie up your money."

I cried, laying there on that hospital bed, wondering how my life turned upside down in one night. Truth of the matter was, my life was turned upside down, inside out from the day I was born.

"Do you think Hendrix knows she's pregnant?" I asked.

Kace shrugged. "If he did, he never said anything to me. That's something you need to ask the muthafucka at visitation."

There was a light tapping at the door before Doctor Price stuck her head in. "You hit your head pretty hard on that floor, huh?" She joked a little, making her way in.

I wasn't amused by her dry humor, and she peeped my angry expression really quick. "What's going on with Merci?"

The doctor cleared her throat. "The C-section went well. The baby is in NICU at the moment. She's in critical condition but stable."

"And Merci?" I hesitated to ask.

"She died on the table." The doctor hated to tell me. "I'm sorry."

I laughed and cried at the same time. "Oh my goodness. I lost a brother and sister all in the same night? This can't be real!"

"We did draw some blood from you, and we did confirm that you were an O-negative. The blood test also confirms that you're pregnant..." the doctor told me.

I quickly sat up in bed, watching Kace sit up from slouching in his chair while the doctor spoke. Nakia was right. The fertility shots that Gio was giving me during the treatments cleared the scar tissue that lined my uterus.

I shook my head. "No, I can't be."

"We can do an ultrasound to confirm if you'd like," the doctor told me.

"Can we get a few minutes, please?" Kace asked the doctor.

The doctor slipped out of the room as Kace pulled his chair closer to the bed.

"I'm supposed to be walking down the aisle tomorrow," I told him.

Kace grabbed my face in his hands, drying my tears. "Foxxy Brown, I know this is painful, but you deserve this baby."

I looked into Kace's face. "I haven't been with anyone else but you since that first night we touched in Maryland."

Kace nodded. "Baby, I know."

"Hendrix is going to kill us," I cried. "He did me wrong, too, but I promise you he'll get someone to get us."

Kace grinned. "Does it look like I'm scared? I have something worth fighting for. I'm ready whenever he is. The question is are *you* ready?"

Pain was a feeling that was all too familiar for me. It was the byproduct of my life. I learned to face pain head-on. Without facing my pain, I wouldn't have gotten to experience the laughter, the joy, the love, the Kace. My pain would pass, but the laughter, the joy, the love, the understanding I had in Kace was worth fighting for. Worth dying for. So much was lost that night. A little girl was fighting for her life. I couldn't let her live without a mother. There were documents, fraudulent or not, that said she was *my* baby. So she *was* my baby. With Kace at my side, I'd fight for her. I'd been through worse than having to tell my husband that the man who he once considered his best friend was possibly going to father the child that I never even knew I could have. All my battles had been won, but the war was just beginning.

END OF BOXSET QUESTIONS

QUESTIONS FOR THE ATLANTA EDITION:

1. In the Atlanta edition, who was detained by the police for questioning after the incident at the pizzeria?
    2. How did Melinda and Dominic meet?

QUESTIONS FOR THE BALTIMORE EDITION:

1. Who orchestrated Jahquez's karma?
    2. What two major gifts did Quan gift Italy in the story?

QUESTIONS FOR THE NORTH CAROLINA EDITION :

1) Where did Kace hide murder weapon?
    2) Who murdered Greg and Sheila Avery? And why?

Made in the USA
Columbia, SC
24 January 2021